HEAVEN HAS NO GROUND

HANA ANDRONIKOVA

TRANSLATED FROM CZECH BY ROMAN KOSTOVSKI

Plamen Press
Where Words Ignite

Washington, DC

Plamen Press

9039 Sligo Creek Pkwy, suite 1114, Silver Spring, Maryland 20901

http://plamenpress.org

Published by Plamen Press, 2023

Printed in the United States of America

10 9 8 7 6 5 4 3 2 1

Publisher's cataloging-in-publication data

Names: Andronikova, Hana, author. Kostovski, Roman, translator.
Title: Heaven Has No Ground / Hana Andronikova;
Description: Silver Spring, Md: Plamen Press, 2023
LCCN: 2023945741

Identifiers: ISBN 978-1-951508-03-6 (paperback)
ISBN 978-1-951508-30-2 (pdf) | ISBN 978-1-951508-11-1 (epub)
ISBN: 978-1-951508-37-1 (hardback)

Subjects:
LCSH: Czech literature—Translations into English.
Czech literature--21th century. | Eastern European literature.
BISAC: Fiction / European / General
Fiction/Russian & Former Soviet Union

Edited by Rachel Miranda
Edited by Klára Kolínská
Cover art: Franišek Přikryl © 2010

The translation and publication of this novel was completedthanks to a generous grant from:

NATIONAL ENDOWMENT for the ARTS arts.gov

MINISTRY OF CULTURE CZECH REPUBLIC

I dedicate this book to all mothers who ever were, are, and will be

Foreword

When Czech writer and playwright Hana Andronikova lost her battle with breast cancer, she was only 44 years old. The news of her death was overshadowed by the passing of another Czech literary icon, Vaclav Havel, who had died two days before her. But her passing was no less devastating to the literary community of her country; in fact, it was felt throughout the world. She left behind two novels, several short stories, and a few plays, achieving critical acclaim both at home and abroad. Her first novel, *The Sound of the Sundial* (Odeon 2001 in Czech; Plamen Press 2015 in English), won her the 2001 Magnesia Litera prize, Czechia's highest literary award, in the New Discovery category. Radio Prague declared it one of the most important books written after the Velvet Revolution. And its reach has endured: just last year, the UK's Calvert Journal named it one of the "seven contemporary Czech novels everyone should read."

Andronikova's second and final novel, *Heaven Has No Ground*, earned her another Magnesia Litera award in 2011, just weeks before she died. Unlike the historical theme of her first novel, in *Heaven Has No Ground*, Andronikova offers an intimate and very personal story with a deeply philosophical narrative. Although the author never identified it as such, the novel follows Hana's life story so closely that it can be viewed as a form of autofiction—a cross between fiction and autobiography in which the protagonist is understood to be the author, and uses the devices of fiction to explore her own lived experience. Using striking metaphors, sentence fragments, intensely emotional language, and associative imagery that borders on surrealism, Andronikova tells the story of Ama, a protagonist, who, like herself, is in the process of coming to terms with the death of her father when she receives her own cancer diagnosis.

Thematically, *Heaven Has No Ground* deals with the very human fear of facing a deadly disease, and the battle to come to grips with the idea of death. It is also about the struggle between rational thought and intuition, as, contrary to the wishes of family and friends, Ama (like Hana) at first decides to seek alternative treatments rather than undergoing conventional chemotherapy and radiation. She travels to Peru to consult a shaman healer, and there, experiences life with the Amazon natives who are guided by the laws of the vast jungle. As the reader might guess, Ama does not find a cure, either there or in the American desert where she spends some time in a stronghold of Christian faith. However, she returns changed, with a new understanding and the will to face conventional treatment, whatever the outcome.

As publishers, literary translators, and editors, *Heaven Has No Ground* presented a knotty and memorable challenge. It was hard enough rendering Andronikova's unique and innovative style, filled with witty metaphors and lyrical conjunctions, in English for the first time—but *Heaven Has No Ground* goes far beyond the conventions of an ordinary novel. In embracing the auto-fiction concept in form if not in name, Andronikova chose to render much of the story as a sort of personal travel journal—with all the inconsistencies you might expect in such a document (whether or not it was, in fact, based on Hana's own diaries, of which we have no explicit evidence)—and to embrace, as well, the novelties of communicating in the information age, often using Skype, chats, and emails to advance the narrative. In its format, the novel is devoid of the conventions of direct speech, such as line breaks and quotation marks; the paragraph breaks and section headings are scattered and inconsistent; and while punctuation is certainly present, the book contains no capitalization. Written with a sense of urgency, this text conveys the chaos of being a traveler in an unknown land, as if cut and pasted from leaflets of paper scribbled on top of a log, a bench, a cafe counter, a thigh. At the same time, it is a deeply personal account, conveying the protagonist's disturbing, profound, and transformational experiences as she seeks to become reconciled with her fate through her very presence in the world around her:

inside is outside and above is below, and everywhere is heaven. it's fluttering above my head, splashing under my feet. wherever i look, i see it—a heaven that has no ground.

Andronikova was adamant about preserving the book's format; she turned down several publishers who wanted to bring *Heaven Has No Ground* into a more conventional shape. At Plamen Press, we too, were inclined to make such alterations, once we had wrestled our way through the translation, reasoning that it would make the story far more accessible to readers of English, who are, after all, not accustomed to the tense-switching that characterizes the Czech language, or the surrealism that pervades Czech literature—and who already have their work cut out for them in making their way through the maze of this story. But Andronikova is no longer with us, and we had no means to seek her approval for our choices. In the end, we decided to lean in favor of the original published text; to preserve Andronikova's urgency to tell her story straight, in a raw and unfiltered form, coming from the hand of the writer directly to the eye of the reader.

You know how Hana's story ends—but as for the novel, she completed it during a period of optimism, when she believed, however briefly, that she had beaten the cancer. We will leave you to discover the narrative choices she made as you go on this strange, whimsical, and wondrous journey with her.

Roman Kostovski
Publisher, Plamen Press
Translator, *Heaven Has No Ground*

Rachel Miranda
Managing Editor, Plamen Press
Lead Editor, *Heaven Has No Ground*

HEAVEN HAS NO GROUND

1

the most important question facing humanity:
“is this universe a friendly place?”

—albert einstein

glen gould • the art of silence • ruby blues

she stares at the blue flickering of the monitor. her fingers start beating on the keyboard like a downpour. gaps in time. in each language, we hide ourselves behind the layers of unique sound. the rain echoes back and forth like a loop, like a road home. it's as if she is uncovering whatever lies between the lines of this language that could never be called her mother tongue. she dives in deeper and holds obsessively onto that image as it begins to fade out. the sound dissipates. the sun shines behind the window—no trace of rain.

i am sitting in your study and thinking of you, glenn gould, the art of the fugue, and bach's fourteenth counterpoint. at the end of the 239th measure comes a jolt. gould's hand shoots up into the air and then suddenly freezes.

i'm sitting in the hospital and staring at a man who looks so much like you. he is unapproachable, motionless—his body full of cables, cannulas, and tubes. he is eloquent without saying a word. not a peep. only the beeping of monitors and the rigid rhythm of a machine that fills your lungs with air. i can't find you in this silence of needles, dripping funnels, and bags of blood that shine like gelatin.

so i'm talking, talking to the silhouette on the hospital bed. talking to what's left of you. i remember when i last heard your voice. that day, i was writing about the river styx, and i couldn't recall the name of the ferryman who carried the dead to the other bank. and so, i called you because you always know everything. i heard you chuckle softly, your amused voice saying, it's charon, charon of course. but remember, you will need an obol to pay him a toll.

and if i don't pay him?
then you will wander aimlessly along the dark river for a hundred years

two days later mom calls me. her voice is unbearable, carving wrinkles in my forehead. her breath is murky, her reins are pulled tight. she's setting words in the air, laying them down like bricks. her words are molded, weighted, and fired. words, words, and more words. they're rushing through the receiver, oozing along the walls, falling from the ceiling, shuffling on the floor. but they're nothing more than words. i am catching them like envelopes, looking inside. seeing nothing. i know that they mean something in another dimension, in another land. there are so many of them. i'm standing in a circle, in a chimney stack of words. they grow and ricochet from side to side. heart attack...ambulance... emergency room. they clench at my throat. resuscitation...nine electric shocks...coma.

i hang up and wave my hand to swat the words away.

when it all comes clear, i toss out my calendar and drive three hundred miles to be with you, to break into you and stop you. day after day, i visit. apparently, they saved your life. another empty envelope. if they saved you, then why don't you thank them? why aren't you skipping, rejoicing? they may call it that, nodding their heads, those diligent medical lackeys: coma vigil. i call it torture. they've trapped you. they can't save you, but they won't let you die.

six week later, i've aged five years. and six weeks after that, i feel sick from the stench of bed sores and disinfectant, from the glass walls, the hospital doors, the faces, from my own nightmares. i'm sick of your silence and my monologues. sick of those shapeless answers. the silence. the unspoken words that lie between me and the wreckage of you. bridges that you will never build. you pressure me with your silence, nudge me like you always do. and i am standing up to you, resisting, like i always do. and so, we carry on like this, and you push me, step by step. you force me to pray, which i detest. you take it too far. i resist the gesture of letting you go, but you keep pushing me. there is nowhere to go. well then, get on with it! go ahead and die! i've been praying all night, pleading for your death.

the phone rings, stirring up the morning. i know what i will hear on the other end. that icy shower. your checkmate. the keys of your piano become rubies and dragonflies—they fly out the window. and then it comes. the flip of a switch. the proverbial click. something snaps inside me. i want to explode. break open and fly away. i need to scream, throw things, break them. i roll the pen between my fingers until i bleed. my watch band tattoos a dark gray grill on my wrist. i want to tear apart my clothes, my skin, my veins. the white walls. your paintings, books that you lent me to read. your favorite excerpts. i want to crush them all like paper cups—objects, emotions, memories—and throw them in the trash.

but we're still hanging by a thread, each of us on one end, pulling in the opposite direction. you towards death, me towards life. my life, your first gift to me. i see it, my life, standing at the end of the street. when i come closer, it beckons me, smiling, asking for a dance.

* * *

medical record
10.2.2002

today at 16:10, after finishing a cigarette, patient felt pain in his chest at rest, ambulance was called, loss of consciousness during transport to hospital, clonic seizures, monitor showed ventricular fibrillation, cpr administered, defibrillation 3x300 joules, patient delivered to the er, admitted, resuscitation continued approximately 45 minutes, circulation restored, in-house consultation requested.

at 19:00, patient transferred to cardiology to receive coronary angiography. procedure completed with no complications. patient was transferred to the icu.

note: endogenous depression in the anamnesis
i call cardiology at the hospital in motol. could you put me in touch with the department head, dr. alan? what the hell is cpr and what does this

all mean? david's voice begins to calm me. he puts me back on my feet with the naked truth.

cpr is cardiopulmonary resuscitation. in other words, resurrection. i called the icu in zlín, i spoke to the department head's assistant. she said that their response was first rate. they did what they could, but the prognosis is not promising.

the odds were bad? everything seems like it's going downhill way too fast. my divorce just a month ago, and now this shit. i'm clutching the table to keep from collapsing. ok, david, but what does it all mean?

when resuscitation takes too long, a patient often doesn't come to. he remains unconscious. it's called a conscious coma or apallic syndrome. it means that some functions of the body reactivate but the brain is too damaged to function normally. it depends on how long your brain was without oxygen. in his case, it was a long time.

so, either he will die or he will become a living corpse.
he could come to. but chances are slim.

* * *

i inherited your art. the art of black magic. the skill of being and not being somewhere at the same time. to listen but not to hear, to drown the world in books as if you could live off their scent. as if the words anger, happiness, love, and resistance meant anger, happiness, love, and resistance. i would read myself into a state of unconsciousness. into an educated delirium. i don't know how to walk this earth. i see inside my head, there are two parts, and between them a bridge, just a thin stream of light. i'm scared that it will burst, that it will break apart. that's how it's going at the moment.

i see inside my head. i see how this is going to go down. when the light bursts, there will be two heads, two brains. there's a treatment for that. a few months in the loony bin, problem solved, and a lifelong

prescription to keep your head spotless. venus in the morning, medusa at night.
but isn't it crazy to build bridges out of pills?
mellaril, moditen, fluanxol will build a bridge, plant roses, and your head will bloom again. everything will seem greener. those miraculous pills. a modern day *unio mystica*. night turns into day, and light is built out of darkness. a pile of shit becomes a brain. and that brain will suddenly be filled with universal truths, and everything will be clear, splendid, and fragrant. happiness on a stick. i know what the pills did to you. fevarin, deprex, vivilan.
it was black magic.

the nurses at the zlín icu are angels. they tell me we should bring music, talk to you, because no one can know for sure whether you are registering anything or not. so, i bring you your glenn and oratories and requiems and masses, and i play them in your headphones. so that after hearing them you will rappel down to get back to your body. i sit by your bed all day, every day, bending your ear about whatever comes to mind. not too long ago, i saw almodóvar's newest film, talk to her. there were two women in a coma. one would come to, the other would die. and so, i am hoping that you will not end here. that you will return to the flesh.
i'm reading you excerpts from kahn, silence and light. it sounds like poetry. i'm reading karafiat's *bugs*, the book you used to read to me so long ago. before the kitty lays an egg. everything will heal. sometimes i realize how far away you are, nowhere in sight. and then suddenly, i spot you walking by. you smile and put your hand on my shoulder.
a coma is a straight line that replaces the curves of the brainwaves splashing around inside your head. when the monitor shows a straight line, then there's nothing splashing. i once read that in such moments, we experience the power of silence. you would like that.

i'm running out the sands of my sleepless nights. your piano, record player, and rows of lps, cds, your collection of gould's recordings. i was in high school when you played him for me for the first time. gould, and beethoven—sonata seventeen. as if it were yesterday, the feeling of fear, that someone was stealing our family silver or destroying antique furniture.

who is this? it sounds like a practical joke.
glenn gould was a bit of a musical prankster.
more like an alien.
he thunders with such ease, then he rises up as if he were laughing in the eye of the storm. his voice sounding above the stairwells. the keys on the piano can't keep up with him. his fingers forge new frets, and he sings into it. he lets out a wail like errol garner, and it smells like jazz.
i wanted to hold on to my old favorites, but he tore me away and took me with him. he turned every bone in my body. such rigorous heresy could only be irresistible.

i'm sitting in your studio, beneath your bogged-down calendar, in a river of paper and thoughts. i'm sitting in your chair, and i picture you leaning over plans, over rolls of tracing paper. searching for order and form. your sense for the character of space, for curves of light and shape. your sense of flow. your aversion to the ubiquity of patchwork. models of your designs, administration buildings, hospitals, factories. you once told me that architecture allows movement and flow, and architecture can also stop this movement and flow. i know you wanted me to learn your trade even if you would never admit it. if i ever were an architect, i would build viaducts, overpasses, and bridges.
there is a chacmol on the table. i have a feeling that it is observing me, and for an instant, it has your face. it is a statue that i brought you a good many years ago. chacmool, the altar of the ancient mayans. the reclining figure of a man with folded knees holding a tray on his belly. during ritual sacrifice, the mayans would stretch out a human over it and cut open his chest to remove his heart.

i'm still searching for you, catching your shadow in a net. so talk to me, for crying out loud! i know that you can see all my questions. they're trembling, hovering like crows over a plowed field. each question pulling me in a different direction, tearing me to pieces. luring you into a trap.

finally! i knew you were still here. i'm holding on to you, because you have wings. when i'm hanging onto your neck, i'm flying. i can't let go, i would fall.

do you remember how you learned how to swim?

sure, somewhere in baška voda. i am a water lover just like you. and you always swam so far from the bank, and i wanted to go with you. mom was on the edge, and we were playing around. the waves came in, and you laughed at me catching my breath. i could see you even through my salty tears. i laughed as well, because i knew that nothing would happen to me when i was with you. you swam farther, breaking the waves. i was glued to your back like a koala bear. a wave came, larger than i thought. it pulled me in and flushed me down, then spit me back out. i'm catching my breath, gurgling, i'm looking for you. here i am, you wave. i plunge after you. three strokes. i'm swimming! i know how to swim.
you're grinning like a fish.
you already knew how to swim. you just needed to let go.
you start spilling out of a dam. back to your fish-like form. you flow beyond time. you are on the other side, the midnight sun. i'm searching for dead water. you have to die first before you're reborn, and so i run to the river. the fisherman's voice is deep: whoever is standing near me is standing near fire. i'm reading books about death to be closer to you. i'm lying there with you, burning, the machines are waving their arms, screaming falsetto, frightening away your dreams. i'm dreaming inside your head. we've been like this for a week now. you are still lingering in a no-man's land between life and death.

the doctor standing over your bed shines a tiny light into your eyes. your pupils are as straight as a guard on duty. motionless. just like you. she eruditely tightens her lip and shakes her head.
it's *coma vigil*. what did you expect?
it might be coma vigil to you, you fucking bitch, but to me, he's my dad.

i can hear my thoughts, my teeth grinding. she is already at the door. i can feel you behind my back, your hand on my shoulders, my anger is wilting, drying out. all that is left is my fear, your silence.

suddenly, i hear commotion behind the glass wall next door. they have brought in another patient. the staff is hustling. flat-irons on his chest, then massage, then flat-irons, massage, again and again. back and forth. one more time. could he be...? he comes to, just for a moment, and then no response again. silence. just the sound of rapid motion and the breathing of the doctor and nurses. they don't want to give up. they don't want to let go of this man who is turning blue in their arms. ten minutes, fifteen, twenty. note down t.o.d.
that was quick. like cutting your finger. i have to leave. i want to go home, even if i don't know where home actually is. but i still go. i will leave you here among the machines, and the bodies with their souls nowhere in sight.
the waiting room in the icu is always empty. no one sits there, no one cries there. but suddenly it's packed. wailing and whining all over the place. it's barging in, bouncing off the walls. there's no getting away. the space is cramped with only one person. she could be about twenty years old, possibly less. she is torn up, trailing pieces of cotton and gauze. the girl is climbing the walls. i thought such a thing could never be possible but i see it with my own eyes. behind the door she cannot enter, a part of her story unravels. a parallel universe. her husband, father, brother. and she is screaming, crawling up the white wall. she is being absorbed into it. they haven't told her yet, but she already knows.
i take off the hospital scrubs, throw my mask into the trash. one last time, i look back at the girl who became a wall, and then i close the door behind me.

at night you tell me that death is a gift. that you can only choose what to do with it. a gift that you accept is priceless. a gift you don't take is worthless.
suddenly i know that you won't return.

you're right. death is a gift. dying is too, and this experience here at the icu. if you ever thought that god is a cold-hearted, boring old fart, you should visit the icu for a day. you'll realize how much god can let loose. sometimes it's so much fun here that you can't possibly bear it. for example, take your medical record. maybe you don't even know your diagnosis. heart failure with a successful resuscitation. sure they write it down, even though i understand that you don't believe me. it sounds just like that old joke: the surgery went well. the patient died. but you're a lot worse off, because you ended up where there's a whole pile of fun. today you underwent a procedure in which they cut a hole in your neck so that you could merge with the machine that will breathe for you. tracheostomy, they call it. if you happen to come to, don't get scared. you would be without a voice, though most likely you would not mind that at all. one male and three female nurses came by to prepare you for the surgery which turned out to be quite an ordeal. they messed with you for about thirty minutes, detaching tubes and attaching them elsewhere so that they could take you to the doctor on the hospital bed. i watched them work, and i felt like i was on a tv show, "e.r.," or whatever they call it. they were in sync, professional, pleasant, even funny. and when they were all done, another nurse ran up to them and told them that the doctor had gone out for lunch. those four nurses who worked on you for half an hour suddenly burst out laughing. and so, they took you apart again. it's a real hoot over here. you've got to believe me.

coma vigil. it's called that because sometimes you open your eyes. it sometimes seems as if you've awakened. they say that there is nothing more they can do. i ask them if they could really do nothing.
that jolts them to attention. they almost cross themselves. what do i really mean by "do nothing"? there are laws against it. we are sorry, that's not an option.
and so, there you have it, my dear. you have to earn your own death. it's like that folk song. "when i served for the seventh year." they've caught you and stuck you on a pike so you won't run away. they conduct a few more useless experiments on you to clear their consciences, to stick to the heartless letter of the law.
i'm leaving the icu, i'm looking at the window behind which your body lies. the window has a light. i see the white coats surrounding your

bed. so i fly a few meters and land on a parapet. with my face stuck to the glass, i see how they are turning you on your right side. and next door, behind the glass wall, that little boy whose soul is also fluttering, nowhere in sight. his parents visit him every day. they quietly sit next to the empty bed for hours. i say to myself that you probably know whether their wait is in vain or not.

i thought that i was different. different from you or mom. still, i never doubted the fact that you were my parents. what brilliant reasoning. it would be a waste to look for any logic in it. how could i be different when i am you plus her? two in one. a pure cocktail. no additives. you knew this. you would look at me and see the resemblance. my stomach was on strike, and so they stuck a tube into me to see what was inside. then i called, reporting that they didn't find any helicobacter pylori. i heard you translating my words to mom. she doesn't have any bacteria in her stomach, but she has them on her brain. i could tell you a thing or two about that.
you raised me in a house of a thousand books. i'm sorting out your drawers, crayons, morals. less is more. he who is silent will learn the most. your photos, prints, rolls of music scores.
your pills, depression, alcohol. i saw you live in this strange fear. it was internal. it would hide from you, that darkness the fates bathed you in. it nourished you like breast milk that didn't come from your mother. neurol, deprex, rohypnol.
how did you escape it? how did you finally settle into your own skin? your late-in-life happiness. your bible, quran, kabbalah.

you're my father, and at the same time, you're not mine. i'm lying next to your feet, and i'm wishing for your death.

i wanted the luna. i wanted you to shoot the moon out of the sky so i could take a look at it. you laughed and said that would be a piece of cake, and i believed you. i could lean on your sentences. there were so few of them available. you woke me up one night and took me into your arms. i was half asleep, and you carried me into the garden. the

darkness of summer was above our heads. look, you said you wanted the moon, here you go.
i'm squinting at a barrel of rainwater.
can you see it there?
i'm leaning over the barrel and staring at the full moon floating in the water.

sometimes i have the feeling that i only dreamed you that night.

* * *

an epic crisis

despite all therapy and care, patient died suddenly at 06:00 on 11.12.2002. given the prognosis, resuscitation was not attempted. autopsy was suggested, but patient's family refused. in view of the clinically indisputable diagnosis, we respected the family's wishes.

louis i. kahn says it is hard to talk about a literary work when it is finished. you can still feel its incompleteness.

i'm reading your life story from the remnants of your ashes, still hot, they stick to my fingers. i know that you would buy her rubies, but instead of a wedding, we're celebrating a funeral. on the anniversary of your wedding, your bride will lay you in your grave instead. and i will put a copy of *heart on a hook* in your coffin. it smells good and rustles with the sound of freshly cut paper. you'll never know that it's for you.
i was quite surprised by the number of people who came. you mattered to so many people who felt obliged to come all the way to the cemetery in this cold weather. your guild did not forget you. folks could barely fit into the room. i have a feeling that it snowed, but i could be mistaken. maybe the blood in my veins flowed more slowly, my platelets hardened into little white crystals.

silence has a linear character. words and noise can hide anything. i believe in silence, it's naked and concise. i'm squeezing it in the palm of my hand like a handkerchief. your legacy. my inheritance.

life is not a perfect work of art, a masterfully done movie from which you can edit passages that somehow don't fit. scenes that are missing something or have too much of something. you know that all too well. you won't chide me for a few dingy truths that are, no less true because they're dingier than others. instead, their dinginess gives a bit of luster to times long gone and to those ancient tragedies. a tragedy is like the song of a goat. i must listen to it. i don't even know how a goat sings. maybe that's why i'm missing something.
i never heard you play in broad daylight. music always came with the dark. bach's partitas—pure equations. the hands of your glenn run down my vertebrae, and they bring you back to me.

you're more present now than when you were here.

true living runs its course in absolute silence, in the reliable pattern of the tide swelling and receding. like fruit that quietly ripens to a point when it lets go of the mother tree, when it breaks away by its own weight.

2

“i envy the dead. once i even hated them, because they were in the majority.”

—thomas bernhard

gloria de jujuy • santuario huishtin • all the saints

03.14.2008

to peru? i didn't know you spoke spanish.
there is no way you could have known, because i don't speak it.
for a moment, i can hear the buzzing of the receiver, the mumble of static between prague and tasmania before loreen can catch a breath.
ok, but someone has to come with you. at least for a few days.

a friend from argentina has offered. gloria.

skype chat:
i've booked my tickets. the flights are mostly filled, but i'll arrive on tuesday.
gloria, you would have to wait two days in lima, that's not a reasonable solution.
look who's talking. so how do you expect your friends to be reasonable?
okay. if it's meant to be, it'll work out.
it'll work. so stop pissing me off! i'm going with you. on monday, i fly to bolivia. i'll be in lima on tuesday.
bolivia?! that reminds me of butch cassidy and sundance kid. they both traveled to bolivia for vacation.

and they never came back.

i receive my last rites at radka's place. radka is the only one who really knows where i am traveling to. what should i take? organic shampoo in a box. it looks like soap and lasts for a long time. more important instructions: look out for snakes. two kinds are deadly. shushupe, a mute rattlesnake. triangular head, neurotoxic, you asphyxiate. and the jergon, poisonous, yellowish green. mostly moves on the ground but can also climb trees and swim. hemotoxic. a quick death. next on the list: scorpions, both black and white. lastly: poisonous frogs.

03.16 palm sunday

massive anxiety, cloudy weather, a draft out of nowhere. a list of things to do. what the hell are you scared of? i have a mess everywhere, two days' worth of unwashed dishes. all that's left to deal with is the bank. what the hell are you still afraid of?
she wishes it would all disappear, or maybe that she could disappear.

skype chat:
gloria: tell me, are you still crazy enough to do this? do we need to bring towels and a sleeping bag? will we be able to wash ourselves/take a bath there?
ama: take the towel, forget the sleeping bag. it's hot down there. they'll give you a blanket. as for the bathing...
gloria: *pirañas*?
ama: no *pirañas*. the river is about 85 degrees celsius. nothing can survive at that temperature.
gloria: there is no way i'm going to bathe in that. i'm not a crawfish. why is the water so hot? *¿volcano?*
ama: the entire amazon jungle sits on oil. the locals wash themselves by scooping up the water into tubs, and then they let it cool down.
gloria: great! i can imagine what type of roads we're going to travel on – lots of curvas.[1]
ama: yes. a whore on every corner, and they will be riddled with holes.
gloria: let's just hope that the bus can handle it all.
ama: i'll pray, and you can hope, since you're a pagan.
gloria: i don't believe in god, but i believe in mechanics.
ama: that'll be really useful to you in the jungle. are you packed?
gloria: almost. i'll call you tomorrow.

in the evening, ama is prancing around her luggage. should she take a comb? medication? fuck that! you're going to the tropics. just pure alcohol. every scratch must be disinfected immediately, said the globetrotter. there's a knot in her stomach. she's completely out of

---

[1] *Translator's note*: The Spanish term "curva" means curve; the phonetic equivalent in Czech ,"kurva," means whore.

shape. packing triggers a mixed reaction. at times, she just wants to go hang herself.

the doorbell pulls her out of her thoughts about how many pairs of socks she should pack and what color they should be. she stumbles over piles of her things to get to the door.
hey, jára. come on in.
they sit together in the messy living room and drink tea. he insists that the whole universe has come together so that she can go.
i've never seen anything like it: everything has been going so smoothly. all the people around you, how they all got on board, what they are all doing for you. do you realize how lucky you are to have such support?
no, i don't think i realize a thing.

03.17.08 holy monday
elsa has brought me a raincoat, aa batteries, and a stack of bandages. this is exciting for me too, you know. watching all this—it's like a thriller. i love it!
ama believes her. she, too, would rather watch all this from a distance on tv.
do you have a rope?
what for? to hang myself?
for a bunch of things. to hang your laundry, to tie your horse, to hunt a crocodile. my god! it's good to have a rope.
ok. another trip to hudy sports. the fourth one today. the salesperson grins every time he sees her at the door.
what's it going to be this time? a rope.
how thick?
he lowers his voice noticeably.
how long would you like it to be?

at night, she's tying up loose strings, the world is spread out on her table in interconnecting hemispheres. prague, toronto, tasmania, new york. argentina. an email, one for everyone she knows, about how her life has been turned upside down and about her decision to take control of it once again.

my dear friends, this is not a joke. in january, i was told that i have cancer. but i believe that the soul has to fall ill first in order for the body to do the same. so i am traveling to the rainforest to cure my soul. something is guiding me, and if i had to ask myself whether this journey has a heart, i would say yes. and so i am going.

she has to pat herself on the back for a job well done. words suited for the spartakiad.[2] an enthusiastic crowd and hope for a better future. forward, march! she has written it very well. ain't that the truth? it sure is. what a strange word: "truth." the dictionary claims that truth is all that is genuine, correct, and that has actually happened. but every truth is true only in a certain moment, at a certain point, and then it shatters and breaks. the truth is like the leaves on trees. they turn yellow, fall, and decompose in order to regrow. truth is barley just sowed into the ground and isn't ale yet, but soon could be.
so, must everything be exposed to its core, in order to be the truth? or can it just be sketched—a few lines jotted down—and everyone will assume the rest? for some reason she can't write everything down! when she tries, the sentences begin to resist. words become treacherous. surely she won't write down that she doesn't have the slightest idea why she's going on this trip. maybe she's running away from those close to her, but also those distant from her. away from their dilemmas, their imploring stares pushing her to the wall. choking her with their sleazy love.
what does an unsifted truth taste like at this moment in time? she will have to add a few doses of cyanide. they say she's going to look for the meaning of her desiccated life.

---

[2] *Translator's Note*: The Spartakiad was a mass gymnastics event organized by Czechoslovakia's communist party every five years to commemorate the Soviet Union's liberation of the country in 1945.

03.19.08

lima. a soft landing. scenes of the ocean and desert. and then the andes suddenly appear. they stick out from the water like crocodiles' teeth. an over-cooled taxi. a neon cross hovering above the city. and its smell. every place has its distinctive smell. sometimes she imagines that she's traveling blindfolded. best western embajadores, and in front of it stands gloria and her laughter. she smothers ama with motherly care and a touch of hysteria.

it seems unbelievable that you're here.

same here. it's all crazy. i absolutely can't understand what you're doing. could you fill me in a bit? rei told me that you see ghosts.

gloria, i know how this sounds, and i totally understand your reservations. i know that you don't believe in such things, so i'd rather not talk about it.

what's wrong with you, i want to know?

ama thinks about this a bit and finally realizes how strange her situation must seem from the outside. but she doesn't know yet how to speak about these worlds that are untouchable. they are impossible to describe.

shortly after i received my diagnosis, the spirit of a raven visited me. i've been seeing him ever since, and i think he's guiding me somewhere. i still don't have it all straightened out in my head. do you understand?

i do. the raven's spirit is guiding you into the jungle. is he with us right now?

yes, he is. sometimes more so and sometimes less. that's all i can say about it for now.

he's not threatening you, is he? this raven ghost.

no, he's not threatening me, he just whacks me on the head from time to time. otherwise, he's friendly to the core. does that make sense?

the room is hot. ama opens the window, allowing lima to enter. her body smells like a wet dog. it reminds her of new york in the summer, when raindrops fall on the hot concrete, and the steam mingles with the stench of garbage.

03.20.08

melons, papaya, anise tea, and two zombies at breakfast. then the airport. the airplane is bursting with tension and noise. the little boy across the aisle won't shut up, simply won't shut up. i don't want to ride on a plane, mommy, i don't want to ride on a plane, do you hear me mommy? i don't want to ride on a plane. well you're shit out of luck, little brat. we're 5000 meters up, and under our butts are the andes. i don't want to ride on a plane! he cranks the volume up, i don't want to ride on a plane! gloria rolls her eyes. so get the fuck off the plane, you little shit. i don't want to ride on a plane. my first spanish sentence: "i don't want to ride on a plane." after repeating it so many times, even a dodo bird would be able to remember it. mostly the words *no quiero*, he stresses them in such a high-pitched voice, like barry gibb, "ah ah ah ah stayin' alive." i don't want to ride on a plane. my god how many times can he repeat it? halfway into our flight, gloria's smile fades. do you have any valium? how long is our flight?
why? is this bothering you? you don't like children.
three of my own is more than enough.
after two hours of turbulence and the repetitive wailing of *no quiero viajar en avion*, we're soaring over pucallpa. a feeling that it will never end. we're drawing circles around and around. the clouds below, a few pockets of fog, and then a rainstorm. down on solid ground, nothing is solid. everything merges into one swamp. dear god, where did you send me? this looks like the biblical flood. don't blame it on god, you were sent here by jára, that idiot. he's never been farther than france, and there all he saw were army barracks. the legionnaires must have messed with his head. and you're an even bigger idiot because you listened to his advice. you must be a colossal dumbass. ok, breathe, don't forget to breathe, everything will be all right. of course it'll be all right, this is a great place to kick the bucket. in a few thousand years you'll turn to coal.
gloria presses her face to the window.

do you see that?
it'll be alright, gloria, it'll dry out . . . at some point.

i've got a feeling that we're going to need to dry out first. everything is underwater.
don't exaggerate. once in a while, something sticks out. yeah! i see.
what did you expect? it's a rainforest.
i live in a rainforest, but i've never seen anything like it. is this the rainy season?
yeah, just a bit. i didn't mention that?

finally, we land. we walk from the airplane through chains of water. the airport lobby is a 20 x 20 room exploding with people. our luggage is a few kilos heavier, soaked with rain. outside the lobby, crowds of people waiting. do you know what he looks like?
nope.
do you have a photo or something?
nope.
so how are you going to recognize each other?
i don't know. somehow i'll recognize him as soon as i see him.
that sounds logical.
trust me.
i trust you. i trust you, but there's a forest of people here.
over there!
when our eyes meet, he nods slightly. he has a strong grip. eyes that don't waver. he takes my backpack and then gloria's, and leads the way to the go-karts. it reminds me of the tuk tuks in bangkok. it is a happy ride. the man behind the wheel is covered in a plastic sheet that protects him from the rain. only his head is sticking out, catching all the splatter from the ground and from the wind. the market and port. murky water in the wide river ucayali that merges into the amazon a few hundred kilometers downstream. the muddy roads of pucallpa. gloria with her bursts of laughter. boats and piles of merchandise. cattle, mango, bananas. monkeys, and black vultures.

the last dinner in civilization and then another lecture on spanish. this time it's about health: how to say pain, fever, diarrhea, constipation. gloria? what's the matter?

unbelievable, i dreamed about this. *estrenimento*. i had a dream that...
what is *estrenimento*?
constipation.
you dreamed about constipation?
about a month ago, i dreamed that we were sitting in a restaurant, and i was teaching you how to say *constipation*. it was exactly like this. it seemed really hilarious and absurd at the same time.
great. it looks like we're in the right dream.

we change rooms so many times that in the end, it feels like the father who left home with a cow and came back with a rusty old safety pin. the air conditioning functions more as a sound barrier to the noise outside than for cooling. the go-karts rumble deep into the night on the streets of my brain. the city's pulse: turmoil and unbreathable air. in the middle of the night, a flash and then a dizzy spell. i have no idea where i am. somebody has opened the door to our room and turned on the light. sorry, my mistake. the darkness comes back. unconsciousness till morning.
i need to ask for directions. how do i get to the sixth dimension? they must have an elevator here. the alarm clock says 5:30. gloria is in her pajamas on the bed next to mine, in a fetal position. it's still dark outside. in front of a bank, there's a policeman stretched out on a bench. he's sleeping.

03.21.2008

holy trinity, great friday, a full moon, and the first day of spring

an old beat-up toyota with the front windshield taped all over. the driver must have x-ray vision, he's jerking the steering wheel like he knows what he's doing. the car is bouncing up and down the slushy road like a yoyo. gloria is freaking out and possibly even praying that she'll manage to get back in two days. behind the muddy window, we see farms, horses, cows, and a few brave souls riding go-karts. after three hours of bone rattling, during which, unbelievably, enrique nods off, the driver stops. welcome to honoria. rio pachitea is flooded here.

its watery sludge reeks of mud, the boatmen refuse to set out on the water.
hey tigre! will you cross over? enrique shouts.
the old tiger is not afraid. he nods. he will ferry enrique and the two ladies across. he is gaunt and toothless. he carries the cargo onto the deck, places it carefully to balance both sides of the boat. then he summons a handful of natives to get on board as well. tigre pushes the boat off the bank. the boat splashes, riding low in the water because of all the provisions on board. enrique exudes calm. the lady sitting next to gloria smiles and shows a mouthful of gold. long gray hair. and on each leg, a huge blister that stretches up to her knees. gloria stares, then asks. i was crossing the boiling river, you know, jumping from stone to stone, but i didn't have my glasses. one stone that i stepped on wasn't actually a stone but froth from the river. well, the demon of fire had his way with me. i almost lost my legs.

rio pachitea is cold and wild. a river the color of the indians. driftwood and branches float by like deer antlers. ama jots down the description of the landscape: lonely shacks, human faces in the boat, white water rapids they are leaving behind. she likes that feeling, not knowing where she is, that strange sensation that occurs when you don't know where your next step will lead you. what scene waits around the next corner, beyond the mountains, beyond the other bank of the river? she knows she's wandering aimlessly to find what she used to have. she knows that it is somewhere inside of her. in some parts of the world, there are people who find what they need by sitting on an old, withered couch. she admires them. but she has to stay restless, constantly wandering, until something in her snaps back into place.
we're getting off here.
the entrance to the jungle. it's time to put on rubber boots. enrique takes her large backpack. she can manage the small one on her own. gloria is uncompromising. she throws her pack on her back. she insists on carrying it herself. she has the strength to do it. on the first steep hill, gloria starts wheezing. she is roasting. it's not going her way. she slips. aaah! eenriqueee! she slides down on her stomach, no traction in

the mud. she is trying to grab onto something with her hands, crawling on all fours and losing stamina. a vicious thorn trenches a bloody gash across the palm of her hand.

it's nothing. it'll heal. enrique is now carrying two backpacks as well as his own bag, and he's climbing as if his legs have wings. i'm not sure he's even sweating. behind him the duo of *gringa & gringa* are huffing and puffing and crawling up the hill. gloria, do you see the beauty? no. i'm sweating like a pig, and i'm being eaten alive, though i practically took a bath in bug spray. those fuckers can get through anything, even my shirt and my pants.

ama looks at her as if she can't believe what she is seeing. they have known each other for a short time, not even a year. ama knows that her greatest advantage is her friends. she should write greek odes to her greatest treasure. where would she be without her friends? sometimes she wonders how she got so lucky to have found them. the world feels small when it's held together by a network of voices, faces, bodies. the network supports her. it doesn't let her fall through.

gloria, i think that we met in iowa so that you could come with me to this jungle.

that occurred to me, too. i would never think of doing something like this myself.

a little rest to catch their breath. on the last hill, the view spans all the way down, and tempts ama to fly. the horizon is like something out of a movie, or some other place she had seen before.

enrique, wait!

gloria and enrique have the same conversation for the fifth time.

how far are we?

just a little bit further, just a little bit more.

no, that's not good enough. how far are we? how many more minutes, twenty, thirty?

fifteen max.

what did he say, gloria?

fifteen more minutes.

you see? we'll manage that.

yeah, but that's what he said fifteen minutes ago.

does it matter? we still have to get there. then you can take a cold shower and lie down in a bed.
yeah, a cold shower. you're just a bag full of jokes today.
just around a bend the shaman's brothers and his apprentices appear. they relieve him of his load, shake hands, greet us.
now, it's just a little ways from here.
a view suddenly opens up and reveals multiple roofs covered in palm leaves, supported by pillars that go down into the hot water. the dining space, a kitchen in clouds of steam and noise. no walls. only the hot breath of the river.
gloria loses it on the bank. i can't cross this! i really can't. i'll fall, i'll boil up like a snail. leave me here. one of the men helps her cross. hold onto me and take this pole with your other hand. you can lean on it. bursts of uncontrolled laughter spiral above the water. reina is waiting for us on the other bank of the river with fresh *chapo*. welcome to santuario.

santuario huishtin. in the shipibo language, *huishtin* means star. more precisely, morning star.

the kitchen layout is a long table, benches on both sides, a partition wall that looks like a cabinet from a distance. everything is made of rough wood. and an open fire pit.
gloria, you're a hero. i never would have pictured you in a place like this.
neither would i.
during our introduction, some strange names are dropped: manu, belisario, hegner, franko, ginder, and then there are diego and carlos, both full-blooded indians. the others are half-breeds, *mestizos*. each one of them is all skin and muscle, flexible and light on his feet when carrying bags of rice and potatoes across the river.

santuario huishtin. i saw this place in my dreams, and i knew i had to find it. god brought me here, then he told me: you shall live here.
i get it, enrique. it seems as if even gloria—who only believes in mechanics—doesn't doubt his words. she translates his introductory speech, her eyes getting teary, her voice stuttering, the beads of sweat dripping down her face into the crevice below her neck.

in order to heal, you must have positive thoughts, peace in your soul and love for all things. nature will help you, but it first has to get used to you. the trees, plants, and water will accept you as soon as they get to know you better. when you become one with mother nature, she will give you strength. the spirits told me that you have the ability. i will teach you all i know, if you want.
she would love that. she came here precisely for that reason. she wants to become one with nature. even hemingway constantly tried to come back to mother nature. he lived with her. he drew strength from her, inspiration. he merged with her. and in the end, he shot himself.

an evening ritual, songs to summon the spirits. sacrifices and incantations. the candles flicker out by themselves when the spirits appear. they float through the night. they unlock the gate with the rain, their shadows released from the underworld. spiders gleaming in patterns. the spirits are laughing inside of her, she can't make it stop. her body is convulsing, a bundle of spasms, a thorny crown. my god, why? mosquitoes and chants continue to crisscross through the darkness. three days and three centuries have just passed through her body. but outside, there is that same night. she's begging: could we possibly skip this ritual? could we make it shorter? the raven's laughter bounces off the ceiling, he's hanging upside down, swinging inside her from left to right. she'd like to rise from the dead without having to die. she feels the light of the *luna* in her stomach, flashes of the world revolving, clicking loudly, and falling with the turn of a key.

maloca • the orange goddess • the fire river

22.03.08

breakfast by the river. tiny flies are biting, and the men are serving the food. reina is still sleeping. after the ritual, she needs her sleep. *ayahuasca fuerte*. the men explain that here in the jungle, men and women are equal, but it seems as if they are convincing themselves rather than us. they begin to ask questions, to inquire. where do you know each other from? how long does it take to fly from europe? and what about ama, is she married? gloria begins to chatter. she takes on the role of the boatman, ferrying phrases back and forth. none of the locals have ever flown on a plane or seen the ocean. the concept of a thirteen-hour flight is like a trip to the moon. gloria keeps trying. she explains the time difference. the remarkable fact that it is morning in europe when it's midnight for them. some of them shake their heads, amused by the notion that they have darkness while we enjoy daybreak. ama doesn't realize what is happening here. all she notices is that a few of the men's faces ignite strangely.

i told them that you were divorced, so they're asking if you have a boyfriend or if you live alone.

of course, she has a boyfriend. he's a big guy, a professor of literature at a university.

remember what you tell them. i'll write it down, in case it ever comes up again.

sí, sí. now they're asking if he's coming to visit you, this professor of yours. of course, he's coming to visit. as soon as the semester ends. he'll get on a plane, and before you know it, he'll be here.

ama is amused by this game. but gloria seems to have lost her sense of humor. i really don't think that i should leave you here alone. aren't you even a little afraid?

afraid of who? men? they're more afraid of me. i'm just nervous about the snakes.

in the afternoon, they're chomping on plantains, papayas, bananas, and unripe yucca along the trail. then they hit the jungle and their first *tambo*, a hut in the middle of the forest with a roof made of palm leaves, a floor of hard-packed clay, and boards for sleeping. the door is always open because there is none. gloria begins to look for a handkerchief in her pockets, as well as words to express herself. this looks like a wildlife feeder. enrique? are there any wild animals here?
just monkeys, capybaras. jaguars and pumas will catch your scent like sulfur and keep their distance. it is very difficult to see them.
ama, please tell me that you don't want to sleep here. not right now. after i get used to it.
to a jaguar?
he just told you that they keep their distance.
careful here. it's slippery. there's an incline, a basin in the creek. the water is murky from the rain.
enrique laughs under a dome of languages, both loud and green, blending above his head. *aqua fria*. a magical and beautiful bathhouse.

in the evening, under the mosquito net in one bed, whispering and giggling. the local air feels like a face lift, did you notice? if nothing else, at least that's worth it.
thank you gloria, you were wonderful.
i thought i was more of a burden. i'm not the sort of companion you'd take into a jungle.
all the more respect i have for you now.

in the morning, it's time to say goodbye.
your friend is leaving, but you won't be here alone. don't worry. mama reina will take good care of you. she will cook for you and do your laundry. she will sing to you.
gloria in a tropical hat, her eyes shaded and swimming underwater.
do you really want to stay here? are you sure you don't want to leave with me? argentina also has a few...
no, i don't. i came a long way, and i'm not packing it up because of a few bruises and bug bites. this is the place, there is nowhere else to go. and besides, it's really lovely here, don't you think?

you're right, she nods. if there ever was a paradise on earth, this is the place.
it's obvious that gloria is glad to get the hell out of this paradise.
just remember that you can leave any time. you have a home with me in jujuy or even in buenos aires.
i know. have a safe trip, gloria.
the sky is falling on her shoulders. she can't move. somewhere in the back of her mind is that strange feeling: the fear of never seeing her again.
you are a rare beauty, my friend.

her white shirt flashes through the rainforest and past the river. it pierces the eye like a grain of salt. she doesn't understand ama's path and doesn't understand her quest. still, she travels by her side. somehow that sounds like the definition of unconditional support.
ruby red dragonflies sift through the clusters of steam. a never-ending hum going back and forth. hundreds of clocks begin to tick inside her head.

franco, her new spanish teacher, wears rubber boots that come all the way up to his butt. he must have stolen them from one of the local men. this is my mango and that there's my *gallina*, he says as he points towards a chicken. a house, *la casa*, lizards, centipedes. a ground survey. he walks barefoot for a while. ama carries his rubber boots as she watches his dark little feet squishing mud between his toes, the leaves, branches, and maggots. he's about four or five. they both climb over stumps and fallen trees. franco suddenly lets out a hissing noise. he covers his eye with his hand. he lifts his lower eyelid. get it out, dona, dammit, some sort of bug or something. how is she going to get it out? she's completely useless. all the schools she attended just amounted to a big pile of "sh..." franco reads her mind. he points toward his shirt. she begin fishing out the fly wings with the corner of the dirty cloth. he bravely holds still.
done. she gives him a hug. *bien? sí.* ama can't tell who is more relieved, her or franco. he grabs her sunglasses and puts them on backwards. he

starts looking at the sun. he tries to reach for it. *sol* he says. *sol grande*, big sun. great. they're already covering adjectives. *gallina bianco* – white chicken. yeah, this might actually work.

evening. a lesson of rainforest phonetics. a bird sounding like a plonk in the water. plonk. plonk. another bird just rattling its beak. *drrrrrrzzzzhhh drrrrrzzzzhhhh*. then there is a whistler. *whoo wheee. whoo wheee.* letters become scribbles. *whoo wheee. whoo wheee!* she can't keep up with transcribing the birds' languages. *krzeeeeeeeet krzeeeeeeeeet.* how is anyone supposed to put that down on paper? how can a person transcribe sound carried by the wind as it slips through the branches, the smack of a bat's lips as it munches on a piece of noni? how can a person write down the breathing of a leaf as it falls, the short gasp it lets out as it lands flat on the surface? how can she write about the air interleaved with green sheets, landscapes inside a river? noni after the rain? fruit that smells like vomit?

comer – to eat, *arros* – rice, *papa* – potato, *pareja* – partner. she tries to put together a simple sentence but there is too much noise. no one can concentrate in that ruckus. she is lying down and looking up at the ceiling, more noise, a bustle and a swarm. cells in the body. every little piece flickers and is restless. grasshoppers, spiders and their webs. here, you are never alone. you can see outside through the roof. when it rains, the water falls from the palm leaves, and yet the floor never feels a drop.

03.24

easter monday. she watches how to make light. she puts on half-soaked pants with a layer of mud that reaches all the way to the hem. a few nervous thoughts in the morning twilight. she bangs her head into a clump of bananas. it begins to sway back and forth. *trrrrrzzzzz, trrrrrzzzzz*. is it a bird or an insect? *dzhumm chooooo dooooo dooo doooooooom*. red ants have come charging in like the spanish inquisition. they have gone through her things, forming a barrier with their tiny

trails as they headed for her tote bag, where they've discovered the rest of her almonds.
first, she gets scared that she has contracted measles, but then she calms down and starts looking at all her insect bites, mostly on her arms. she notices how they're planted symmetrically, the same distance apart, the accuracy is unbelievable—a jungle acupuncture. with each sting, every jungle insect has selflessly stimulated the healing points on the intruder's body.
she's sitting in the dining area, the steam from the river sliding down her back. the men are at a table in the kitchen. sometimes, they will suggestively sit beside her with a glance. the jungle and the harsh daily work, and with the exception of reina, no women in sight. everything done by hand, the fields, the dwellings, the furniture. each one of them is a cabinetmaker, carpenter, woodcarver, and homemaker. *camina* – a stroll.
amita, come take a stroll with us. franco is wearing a wifebeater. reina holds a machete and a cigarillo. you bathed in this, do you remember? *ajo saja*. a viney bush with leaves that smell like garlic. it's used for a cleansing bath prior to a ritual, and it protects you from evil spirits. and this tree here is medicinal, it's a strong laxative. the camera captures the rugged terrain. up and down the forest path. a native woman and boy on a stroll. with them, a puffy blond from the city, white as salt, with a pocket dictionary in her hand.
halt! franco takes her by the hand. a tarantula. dark brown. hairy. should i kill it? no, reina, please don't. the tarantula wisely clears out of the path and the stroll continues. and there's a tree that looks like a porcupine, the trunk is covered in spikes. a concoction from its bark is good for ulcers. the bark from medicinal trees is often macerated in liquor made from sugar cane. a rosette of ferns and bromeliads above her head, the sharp shrieks of birds. ama manages to imitate one of them. franco is startled and turns around.
a brisk tempo up the hill. the path turns into a swamp. boots in the mud. every step is squelching. good workout. the hill is behind them, but the mud is not. there is a brook to cross the river and above it—butterflies, a frog as colorful as a circus. and suddenly a tiny plantation appears:

bananas, coconuts, papayas. *la casa*. luis is not at home. only chickens and an unfinished kitchen, a palm leaf roof held by pillars, a wooden floor supported by a frame. most of the structures here are standing on stilts because of the rain. a short rest on the bench. reina tries to spark a conversation. franco takes off his muddy boots and puts on luis's tennis shoes that are several sizes larger. he's swimming in them. he walks like a puppet drowning in a pair of seven-league boots.
click. she has seen this before. the same scene, just a different movie. years ago, in the park, a sloe-eyed kid walking like a slow robot. his feet in large shoes. he was holding a key in his hand. strange how some images come back and force themselves on us. they keep imposing until they finally change us.
the atmosphere changes—a suspicious tranquility, a strange unease before a deep exhale. the siesta is over. *vamos?* off they go. the wind is tossing its arms about, fiddling around. they pick up their pace. a rhythm in the distance. a stampede of hooves. a herd of mustangs. it's coming closer, rushing ten miles with every step. dusk is arriving, almost dark. noise and then the cracking of branches. dolby stereo. one wave after another. they are falling on the road. a crash and then squealing. franco starts to whimper, and reina barks at him to be a man. ama takes him by one hand and clamps the dictionary in the other. ideal for an expedition to the jungle. yep, if it was my own, i would have tossed it into the ferns, but it's not. besides, it can still be useful. once in a while, she runs up front when a tree cracks and falls apart, ripping the branches off other trees before it hits the ground. it's amazing how fast this storm comes rushing over them.

when she was a little child, she would walk outside during a storm. she would sit in the garden under a tall, thick silver spruce. it hid her in its arms. not a drop would fall through its branches. she would watch the strings of rain, the arrows from the archer in the sky, and listen to the thunder as she followed the shadows in the gusts of wind. her father would discover her and scurry her home. that is the dumbest idea a person could have, to sit under a tree during a storm. if it got hit by lightning, you would be roasted to the bone.

we're running. franco is panting heavily. once in a while, i pull him out of the mud. his hand has grown into my palm. a sweetish smell of the swamp and the awakened spirits of the plants, the path is a suction cup. mud above the knees. finally, the rain comes like a curtain, and then in gusts, and at last, as if it has been released from a cage. someone is laughing on the inside. baba yaga in her magical cauldron. she sits in it, and off she goes. this is her moment.
franco begins to ask when we will get home and if we we're going to stay overnight in the jungle. at moments it looks that way. we're sliding over the fallen trees. reina makes fun of him. i would tell you not to be afraid, franco, but i don't have any time to look it up in the dictionary. and so, i am just holding you tight and pulling you behind me. we're almost there. the downpour is chasing us with a whip. a thousand arms. for the final tens of meters, a sprint. franco's joy, *la casa! la casa!* yes, we're home. the *gringa* barbie looks like she was just scraped off the potter's wheel: wet, sweaty, puffy, happy. she changes from her dirty wet clothes into dirty dry clothes. that's what you call an upgrade.

the cellphone—the only thing telling time—gives up. the battery has gotten wet and died. she can donate the solar charger to all the beetles so they can use it as a slip-and-slide. will she have to resort to carving lines into wood?
laughter. what good is time for you anyway?

what exactly is time? she looks around, but not a single encyclopedia or academic dictionary is anywhere in sight.

so let your memory do all the work. time as a value in physics defines a period when an action takes place. great, but then you have to define an interval, space-time continuum, distance, coordinates, and the direction time moves in. we start cutting off pieces from this fictitious line as if it were slices of bread, and we complain that there's never enough time to go around.
jeff once explained to her that einstein's theory of curved space-time unequivocally demonstrated that no one should expect time to be linear. the concept of time as a linear continuum is a product of human

imagination. so there. perhaps all we need to know is that no single and clear definition of time exists.

within two drops of rain, darkness falls. everything is screaming and piercing. the river is boiling into the night. ama hears elephants trumpeting. she's afraid that they will trample her, but there are no elephants in this jungle. surely, she's having nightmares.

* * *

once in new york, a snake bit her. it was green and camouflaged in central park. it struck her three times. she could feel the fangs on her right leg. her calf took the brunt of its bites. she had an antidote in her pocket in a rose-colored ampule. she held it in her hand but was hesitant to use it.

doing the laundry in the tropics means a half-day of sheer joy. ama is drenched even before she manages to pour water into the tub. the hardened mud doesn't come off so easily. the insect bites are stinging, and her pale back hurts. bird voices are all around. electric singing like the yodeling of a trolley. a group of shipibo indians emerges from the noon jungle. a man, two women, and three children in traditional attire. their faces shy and hungry. the children are munching on sugar cane. from a distance, it looks like they're chewing on a tree branch. they have come for food. when they leave, the adults carry bundles on their heads as they all quietly disappear into the jungle.

those flies that look like a grain of dust, like a period after a sentence, grind meat into sausages like a butcher. sometimes she feels that she will lose it because of the insects.
uno, dos, tres, cuatro – one, two, three, four. she is shit out of luck. she has reached the highest point of dimwittedness, and she has the linguistic capability of a jellyfish. your brain has melted into mush, amazon warrioress.
camisa – a shirt. *tengo hambre* – i'm hungry.
someone is coming, pushing a piece of furniture in front of him.

biblioteka—library. tadaaaaa! hegner has the expression of a scientist who has just put together a lunar module. shelves that look like they came straight out of a moravian village. on the bottom shelf, there's a short pole sticking out. and what is this for? asks ama, as she points at the pole that sticks out like a sore thumb. that is for toilet paper. ahah! she would not have guessed that. a bookshelf with a holder for ass-wipe. *muchas graci*as. she offers him a smile that would do justice to a princess in a palace.

she starts contemplating what she should put on those shelves. for the first time in her life, she is without books. for the first time in her life, she has nothing to read. she is only carrying a small spanish conversation book and a dictionary. the only real book she thought to bring, in case she ended up on a deserted island, was goswami's *self-aware universe,* a book that jeff sent her, but she left it on her flight from amsterdam to lima. when she realized it in lima, she got so angry, it gave her the hiccups.

she's writing by candlelight, covered in mosquito netting. the thin net chases away fear. when the flame dies out, autopilot will turn on the usual overplayed repertoire: doubts, questions, conversations with spirits. no, she couldn't have done otherwise. she's in the right place at the right time.

bullshit! you know that you could have done this differently. no one forced you to come here, did they?

no, but the messages were clear.

do you mean messages from the kingdom of arabela?[3] from delphi? put a wet cloth on your head. the voice in the darkness is near.

ama? come to the ritual. it's time.

manu is in his ceremonial garb, with his very dark skin and white smile. he is definitely the sexiest of all the locals. he doesn't usually speak to ama. he always seems to be at arm's length.

maloca, the candle on the altar, is blazing. hegner sits down and then briskly jumps back up. with a quick swing, he whacks something and

[3] *Translator's note*: Princess Arabela is a character in the popular children's TV series, *Arabela*, that aired in Czechoslovakia from 1979 to 1981.

then throws the dead creature outside. just great. ama doesn't know what it was, but she is praying that when the candles burn out, nothing similar lands on her head.

just calm down. forget about it. what do you have to lose? the worst that can happen is that you'll croak. isn't that what you came for? a quick death?

if something crawls on her in the dark during the ceremony, she won't know what it is, or even whether it exists in the first place.

ayahuasca. a bitter taste with a bucket full of doubts. where else would you want to be? the raven brought you here.

says who? the raven is a delusion, and you are a lunatic if you listen to the words of a bird that appears in your sleep or when you are feverish. *mareado*? enrique's voice startles her

poco.

he laughs.

do you want more?

sí quiero mas. yes, i want some more.

a few minutes later, she sheds her body and flies through the crown of her head. the shipibo indians are playing their flutes made from cane that fell from the heavens so that they could reach the stars.

granny? i see you. pale shadows are swarming, swirling in droves. i see you. you're lying in bed.

the awareness that all she needs is a thought carries her through. she succumbs to it. enrique is talking to her. she doesn't realize how long it takes her to open up shop, to lean over and say her words and link them into a sentence. *mareado*?

yes, bottoms up!

the body that is no longer hers, and muddled laughter in the darkness. perhaps it's manu's. the moon is watching through the mist as he throws his rocks toward the stars.

in the morning, enrique insists that during the ritual, she was speaking spanish fluently.

you were complaining that the mosquitoes were biting you and that your head was spinning. you got angry that i poured you too much drink and that you shouldn't have asked for more.

strangely, she remembers how he was showing her stones and telling her about the plants and the power of trees, animals, the secrets of the jaguar. the jaguar is a guardian. it guides the shaman through the space between the earth and the realm of the dead. it growls and shows its teeth when evil spirits dare to come close. there's a plant that grows here, i will show it to you. it's called the soga. if you consume it, you will turn into a jaguar. but you have to earn this plant's respect. you have to bring it gifts and sacrifices. it has to give you permission to change. if it takes a liking to you, you will cut down the plant and carve an image of a jaguar in it. then you will have to boil it and drink the broth.
how could she possibly understand everything he said? she doesn't know what to think of his story. but do you really have to think all the time? do you always have to have a logical explanation?
she couldn't give a shit about logic. she hopes that logic is that lump she vomited up the night before.
the bathhouse topography: a floor made of boards above the river. planks that are rough and about an inch apart from each other. the walls are up to the shoulders of an average european, but they will cover a local completely. there are scrubbing brushes for laundry and basins on a bench. bath with fresh herbs in one of the basins. on the floor a tub, and next to it, a bowl to pour water over her. there are hangers on the wall, but rubber boots have to be left outside. the bathhouse does not have a roof. when it rains hard, you don't have to pour water over yourself.
the bathhouse doubles as a steam room. ama can see from it to the other side of the river. she can see a magical tree that speaks to her. she takes off her clothes, the terra cotta bark lightly peels off like sunburned skin. all she has to do is imagine the tree and something happens inside her. a knot in her stomach, the clinking of ice cubes.

the cleaning of dirty rubber boots in the river is a daily ritual. just like the mandatory shake every time you put them on. the locals have this down pat. they turn the rubber boot upside down and hit the heel against something hard, either a tree or the edge of a table so that a potential impostor who made himself at home in the tip of the boot would fly away or fall out.

everyone in the jungle wears rubber boots purely for practical reasons. most of them are either black or green. rubber boots can be worn for other, non-pragmatic purposes. ama has rubber boots with a silverfish seam, made from waterproof fabric, that can be tightened with a shoestring. they are very chic. when she cleans them, she feels as if she is in new york.
manhattan, 2007. the biggest fashion fad is rubber boots. women on fifth avenue in multi-colored boots with skirts, pants, in all kinds of weather. that is the pure truth. no hallucinations. the locals here have no idea how hip they are.
ama realizes that she can look at everything in different ways. her situation can be defined in a simple manner, clearly and concisely.
subjectively: a feeling of peace and belonging.
objectively: a desperate white girl is getting emotional about every stupid little thing after a week in the jungle and continues to convince herself that she's in paradise.
she knows that her current experience can be tagged with all kinds of labels or psychoanalytical terminology. there is medication for such conditions. sedatives. she could determine a diagnosis for herself: psychosis with delusions. permanent anxiety and mental disorientation, a state of delirium accompanied by hallucinations—often under the influence of psychotropic substances.
but she doesn't want to sedate herself, she doesn't want to block things out or shield herself. she feels that something in her is finally awakening. this might be her last chance.

pais - the ground. motherland. the locals keep asking about where she's from, what it's like in her country.
yo soy - i am. who really?
koan - who am i?
koan is a place where there is truth. the mind can't capture it. the body has to live it.
who am i?
the men come back in the evening holding their exhausted machetes. after bathing, they flutter like white flags over the water in their clean

shirts. hegner brings her another piece of furniture. yesterday it was a clothes hanger, today, it looks like a bird feeder. bela, he points to the candle on the table. she can only think of bela and sebastian. hegner is hammering the bird feeder into the wall, and he lights the candle he has put inside. ama is watching his expression. she's touched by the amount of effort he is putting in to please somebody who doesn't exactly want to be pleased. or maybe she does. actually, she can't wait to find out what he'll bring her tomorrow. maybe he'll carve out a tabletop cooker next time.

03.28.08

paradise on earth. another sleepless night. the heat and cargo trains of thoughts. paradise on earth. say it again. her hand is stuck to her face. paradise on earth. bug bites all over her body. a person could die here in many ways: she could jump into the boiling river, she could scratch herself to death. say it again: paradise on earth. death by itching. in this shitty paradise, a death like that is quite probable. the morning bath is a soothing balm.

reason is hiding somewhere, not letting anyone know where it is. it only strikes during vulnerable moments, again and again.

you're certainly ripe for the loony bin.

that thought has been overplayed. isn't there any new material available? naturally, there isn't. ama finally realizes that rational opinion can only go where it has been before. the situation has to be analyzed according to predetermined schemes and regulations. therefore, rational opinion can be realized only in the realm of what is known and what has been verified. experiences that can't be cataloged are disregarded and nothing new is ever thought up.

intellect is only good for remembering a few words. so snap, snap, get on with the next lesson in spanish. *el paraiso* - a garden of paradise. *calor* - heat. in this heat, her brain is tomato soup.

switching gears would do the job, escaping into another story, another daydream. imagining things makes her feel more alive.

how wisdom raced with light

there is no "once upon a time..." this story just happened. one fine day, when wisdom got the feeling that he had gathered all he ever needed under his roof, he relaxed and hung out. he would kill time adding and subtracting, calculating the square roots of numbers. then he would prick up his ears, belching from boredom. what was he going to do now? he had to think of something or he'd go crazy. in the corner of his eye, he noticed light flying by like a squirming worm. in that moment, it dawned on him—the notion that he could beat light excited him so much that he started sweating. as soon as he cooled down a bit, he paid light a visit and said, hey, let's duke it out! i heard some real numbskulls claim that no one can outrun you, and i'd like to look into that. let's race, and let the best man win.

light felt as if he had just been tickled. he started laughing and shook his head. - oh, my dear wisdom, you must be burdened by the wheels turning inside your head. how could you possibly outrun me? but wisdom was determined and undaunted. - don't patronize me, i don't put stock in that kind of language. - all right, said light, if you insist. wisdom was happy. he put on flashy track shoes and hit the starting blocks: three, two, one, go!

at that moment, light flew in every direction. wisdom just froze. which road should he take? he began to pace back and forth, weighing, analyzing, until he chose, according to the rules of probability, the most probable direction from all the probable directions there were. then he took off. he ran and ran, through every crossroad, he blew through every traffic light, he sprinted faster and faster, until he reached the roundabout in dejvice that linked evropská with československá armáda avenues. he contemplated how to proceed. he was spinning in circles, faster and faster. he began unloading weight, all the quarks, planck's charge, around and around until his head started spinning, too. everything was flashing in front of him, blending together. his head was spinning more and more until it twisted off and fell to the ground. in that moment, wisdom realized that he had grown wings, so he flew over the hills and far way, through the heavenly gates, across the constellations. he whizzed through the galaxy to the right of andromeda's hip and dashed along, picking up speed, until it seemed as if he was going to catch up with light. wisdom could not recognize himself. he was so fast, and he wasn't stopping to think. he was breathing down light's neck, stepping on his heels. he surged forward once more and caught up with light. in that moment, wisdom became light.

the indians are arriving, carlos and lus, diego and linda. they're in a hurry, almost running, afraid that they won't get there before the sky pours down on them. the afternoon roars, massive rain, matted pathways. the jungle takes a deep breath. the men are doing repairs to the roofs. the women are singing, casting spells. lus and linda are artists like their mother, and the mothers of their mother, like the majority of shipibo women. they cut, sow, embroider, draw patterns on colorful fabric—sacred symbols, the geometry of the universe, unique shapes that are passed on to them like genes. ceramics hatch from their hands without a potter's wheel. they coil a smooth snake made of clay. one spiral after another. containers that are light and seamless and thin as paper. complex patterns speaking an ancient language, outlining the river of the jungle, the curves of the anaconda, and journeys to the stars.
linda takes out an embroidered skirt, colored red by the bark of caoba. the fabric has to be soaked several times in the dye from the bark, and then it has to be sundried so that the color can reach its fullest tone. the patterns pour into us like the rain. the spirits of our ancestors lead our hands. our cosmology is an imprint of our thoughts, of the landscapes that lie within us.
manu and carlos walk on the beams as if they were acrobats. they are balancing their weight on the upper ridge of the roof, inserting fresh palm leaves in places where the light is piercing through, tightening the bast fiber ropes. ama draws their faces, their movements, their voices. manu shimmies onto a log. there's a six-meter drop below. his hands are sculpted. tight knots on his arms and a tattoo on his shoulder. he smiles when he sees ama sagging over her food with a sour look on her face, as she looks at her boiled plantains and listens to enrique's yapping about its incomparable, inexhaustible but ever so exhausting benefits.

dawn is the ladder the insects use to climb out. giant ants flood in along the railing, two winged creatures fly inside. she doesn't know what type of pests they are. maybe roaches. how could she know, when she's never seen a roach in her life? the candle is burning and hunting with its flame. it catches the seam of the transparent wings. the glistening fly gives a crackling noise, burns up and turns to smoke. others continue to circle around. they're relentless.

domingo 03.30.08

sunday is easy to recognize. nobody works. just reina and i have the same routines for the day. she cooks and does the laundry, and it's my duty to entertain myself, which can be quite exhausting. even after a full day's work, the natives are nowhere near as tired as i am. today's agenda: analyze doubts and other catastrophic scenarios. take a step back, climb up a tree or a roof, and observe whatever a frightened brain can think of.

she comes to an important conclusion. the terrible tropical disease that has been multiplying in little bumps all over her body, day in and day out, is called "ants." ants are in her bed, ants are everywhere. ok. a person can survive ants. but the question remains, is that good or bad? the mind is a spinning wheel. damn it, ama knows well what the three spinsters[4] looked like. one had a fat lip, another a huge thumb, the third had a foot as flat as a tortilla.

reina washes her clothes on the washboard. ama doesn't know where to start with a washboard. whoosh. a white shirt falls out of her hands as she's gathering the clean laundry. it's being mangled there in the mud. oh fuck! it's a do-over. another round of rinsing and her thoughts resemble the shape of her wrung-out t-shirts and her socks with holes in them. why do we no longer live this way? what did people not like about this? it's quite lovely to wash your clothes in a river on a washboard. any fool could stuff her laundry into a washing machine and press a button.

[4] *Translator's note*: The "Three Spinsters" is a fairytale collected and retold by nineteenth century Czech writer and folklorist Karel Jaromír Erben.

as she's connecting the dots into a context, the same words keep coming back to her: *acceptance, atonement, fool.*

her worst problem is impatience. how can you make a friend out of an enemy? eliminate resistance, resentment, retaliation.
as always, the king sends the hero on a dangerous mission in the hopes that he will never return. the hero gets valuable advice from fairy godmothers, elves, from the animals and other individuals discredited by science. all he has to do is believe.
so, which way to go?

she's starting to learn how to read the local signs. the eyes of the jungle screams with colors. but everyone has to forge their own path.

all quiet on the plaza of spirits. colors of salt, formations like a miniature rotorua. everything keeps repeating itself. stalagmites of salt, holes in the ground, and the smell of rotten eggs in the air. a crowd of scarlet inchworms thin as hairs are swarming in one of the hot puddles of water. how can they possibly survive in such an environment?
ama is jumping from rock to rock, all the way to the middle of the river. she takes off her rubber boots, then her clothes. she lays down. the rock embraces her in its powerful arms. the steam surrounds her, caresses her, and casts its spells. vapor. in a few minutes, she evaporates, the rock breathes her in, swallows her, and whispers a memory. when she was a child, she knew the language of rocks, its gentle syllables, its silence that thundered. she spoke to them, to nations of rocks with the slow burning flame of silence. they are like humans, they can just breathe deeper, carve deeper notches in their memories. she loses herself among the rocks. she chips away little monuments, crushes and squeezes the discarded forms. the rocks whisper back in lengthy waves, ttthhheeeyyy aaarrreee ssspppeeeaaakkkiiinnnggg rrreeeaaalllyyy sssllloooowwwlllyyy. she pours her atoms into them. she feels the rocks inside of her. they become one, intermingling. one breath takes a million years. she sees the beginning of time as the rocks have seen it. time—before the earth latched onto the sun.
when she sits up, everything starts to spin faster and faster. okay, calm

down, don't move or you'll fall in. how quickly can a person boil to death in this water? what an atrocious death, but a quick one. the worst is death by fear.
so sit down, get dressed, and try to hop back to the riverbank on one foot without getting wet, you dumbass.
there's a handpress behind the kitchen that's starting to grow new branches. the shaman explains to her how last year, old luis accidentally lit up a small field of sugarcane on the hillside overlooking the santuario, when he tried to smoke out a wasps' nest. they salvaged what they could. in the course of a day, they carved two serrated cylinders out of wood using just a hammer and a machete. they needed to extract all the cane that could be salvaged from the burnt yield before it started to mold. the next day, everyone worked on extracting the cane juice till late into the night, until the job was done.

pescadito for dinner. salty fish. the day she arrived with gloria, they both agreed that it was inedible. now she is stuffing her face with it, chomping like a frog. true, the fish is as salty as herring, but it beats having *arros y plantáno* over and over again, damn it!
folks in the jungle know how to preserve fish without power, without a refrigerator. they just throw on some salt and then dry it in the sun. before they cook it or bake it, they rinse it off a bit, but the salty taste still lingers. this one has as many bones as a sardine. but if she were of sound mind, she'd never have tasted the thing in the first place.
a chicken without legs bounces its way to the table. it just has two stubs sticking out, like two little stunted paws. can chickens have paws? what does it matter? reina laughs. back when this chicken was just a chick, it flew into the river. by the time enrique managed to get it out of there, its legs were looking like boiled chicken necks. it seems to be quite the funny tale. the locals are laughing their heads off, occasionally slapping each other. the chicken is bouncing up and down like an acrobat in a circus tent.

reina explains many things to her as if she is a child. when you don't know the language, most of the locals think you're stupid. but who cares? playing the part of a half-witted child is fairly easy. while she's connecting the dots to get the context, the same words keep coming back: *acceptance, atonement, fool.* she once covered the word *pitomec* or *fool* in her old church slavonic class. *pitom*, in old church slavonic means to feed or take care of. pitomec could be a chicken, goose, duck, or any other domesticated animal. a fool was someone who needed to be cared for or fed.

why is she thinking of this now?
they are taking good care of her here.

03.31.08

it's nighttime and humid outside. inside, it's blazing hot. she wants to scream, curse, jump out of her skin. she's lying on a burning anthill, in a sea of gnawers, and she's trying to come to terms with it. skin scratched to the bone. maybe it will help her. her thoughts are rushing like the crowds at prague's main train station, but they don't know which way they're heading. it's too hard. raven, i give up. tell me the way to end it quickly.
go to the source. don't be lazy. just go to the source.
fuck your source. i'm lazy and a coward, and i want to die.
she's grasping for light, fumbling, she doesn't know what to do, she just wants to get away from this stranglehold. please!!!!!!!

plead and you shall be heard, beg and you shall receive. is anyone even listening?

a white light. her eyes can't see it but it's there, all around. darkness is all around, too.

don't go do your laundry by yourself, *mi niña,* you have to rest. mama reina will do it for you. this is not the right work for you. it is not good for you to carry water from the river. mama reina will take care of everything.
thank goodness they don't have electricity. reina would most likely iron ama's clothes in this heat. this thought reminds her of someone. *mama reina will take care of everything.*

reina, where's franco?
he's back in pucallpa. he goes to school there. he's very smart, you know. he comes here only on vacations.
reina keeps talking and talking, until she can't talk anymore. tears flow from her face onto her hands and then into a dirty rag. franco's father was a fisherman, you know. my son. he died almost a year ago. he jumped into the water—like this—and never came out. then, when they pulled him out . . . he was only twenty-five.
she carries on, gasping, swallowing her tears. ama doesn't understand a word but it all makes sense to her. mama reina's words are melting, molten, becoming a melody, and she begins to sing a prayer with the scent of cinnamon and lemongrass. she covers the sky and her song is beautiful, sorrowful, and soothing.
a song for you, *mi niña,* for you and my son.

04.01.08

enrique and hegner return from pucallpa. the men are carrying their cargo. reina is cooking. you have beautiful hair, amita, she raves. you look like a doll. manu is laughing in the hammock with a cigarillo in his hand. he asks her if she likes kids. yes, manu, especially yours. i could just eat them up.
hegner brings manu's son and ex, just for a few days. they will sleep with hegner in a shack beyond the river. so, it turns out hegner stole manu's wife from him. how that happened is beyond her. who is this woman that picked hegner instead of manu? who would trade a volvo for a moskvitch?[5] somehow, it doesn't add up.
reina sits behind the table. reina lus flores paredes melendes is making chapo. she is squeezing a sweet banana in her fingers, working it, kneading it, rubbing it, turning it into a mush, a slop. she adds a drop of water and then pours her story into it. a life that travels from one river bank to another. a cycle of men, children, and places where she treads the ground with her bare feet.

reina lus flores paredes melendes

mama had ten of us, in a village where electricity was just a dream. it was not far from tourna vista. tourna vista rustled with an exotic air. it always put on such airs, like a shaman's magic. when i first stumbled into its deafening market with a basket of herbs, i had a feeling that all that beauty could vanish at any moment. livestock was howling in the port: cows, pigs. people were grabbing them by their tails, lugging them out of boats. you could hear them squealing and stomping their hooves. the cows were mooing fear. i met enrique when i was sixteen. he stared at me with that look that made my hips melt, but i couldn't want him. i didn't have any room for him. not in my stomach or in my life, which is essentially the same thing. that kind of thinking didn't dwell in my head back then. it dwelled in the damp cellar below my bellybutton. enrique's eyes would sneak up inside me, but another child was already happening inside me, my daughter, she was growing and rounding out. her hair was caressing my inner walls. my two-year-old alfonso was climbing up my leg. he was the spitting image of his father, and so enrique disappeared once again. he left me to tend to my children and treaded a path of his own. he was just like my husband, who never meant to keep me warm for long. all he left me was a few pairs of shoes and two little cubs. alfonso's father was a sharp-toothed cayman. i was just thirteen years old when he tore me apart. i gave birth at home, you know, at my mother's. where else would i go? my mother knew well what herb i needed to inhale and how to sing to my belly, how to cast a spell that would lure babies to swim out. little lusita was a friday child. she dropped out with a ruckus. she was boiling and cursing until she gasped from her own bitter tears. mama put her in a bucket of water. well, lusita, you got the shit end of the stick when it comes to your father. he took off, so what can you do about it? stop whining, so you don't attract a hot wind that dries up the harvest.

my cayman disappeared and never saw his little girl. i would roam about, finding work from place to place, but i would always come home to mama and my sisters, to my children, who were multiplying.

mama would rip into me with her sharp voice and carve a piece out of me as soon as i walked in the door. man number five and six kids? get out of my sight!

but then she would calm down, and go back to spinning threads and mumbling under her breath after she lured another screaming child into the world with her singing. how are you going to support her, you tramp? you always had two left hands when it came to men. and now your insides are like a badly patched beggar's sack. what am i supposed to do with you? i don't know how to sort out such a mess, myself.

my stomach started getting rancid, then it became inflamed. pus was pouring out of me in clusters like porridge. death will soon come for this little weakling, mama lamented. i have to find a medicine man. you can't just leave me behind with six orphans.

and then he showed up. i don't know how my mother found him. he was just suddenly standing there in the doorway. enrique. he had been a shaman for years. there was a strength coming out of him. he put his hand on my belly and immediately knew what was going on. he gave me some herbs, wrapped me up. i drank his concoctions. he came back day after day until the walls of my belly tightened, my wounds healed. then he asked me if i wanted him. of course i wanted him. he was my love at first sight. i'd kept a vision of those eyes hidden inside me like an amulet. mama liked him. he rarely talked, and she appreciated that. she trusted men more when they hardly spoke. stay away from men who like to sweet-talk you too much. you can't cut a log with words, or hunt animals. that shaman was sent to you from heaven.

enrique blew the spirit back into my body. i grew new leaves. my hair grew fuller, and it shone like *datura* seeds. there was a certain calm about him, and it would pour into me as well. he taught me how to sing, how to merge with the plants. we would cut down everything that lay in our path. it was easy to go with him. rough roads were easier to walk on. people would come to us seeking a shaman, and after, they would thank him with trembling voices.

santuario hatched out of our prayers and sacrifices. it bloomed, it emitted a sweet fragrance, it touched my heart. angels began to come here. we worked hard, that was a given. you can't soften the ground without hard work. and at least i felt useful for a change. i always knew how to work hard. when antonio died, something broke between us. another piece of my soul flew away. we took in my daughter-in-law, nai, franco's mother, at least until the girl worked out her worst misery. she is smart, you can see that right away, words just flow from her lips when she starts talking. but back then she was in a jam and was grateful for a few *plátanitos* and a soothing song. and enrique said that he would try her out, make the girl his apprentice when she lived with us anyway. she didn't last long. she wanted to get back to the city. now she's pregnant from god knows who. a young widow. well, i too was wild back in the day. but she won't escape her sorrow. i know something about that. i won't stick my nose in her business. i just wish that franco had a father, and what can you do when he's up in heaven? you can't pull him out of the ashes, and your tears won't bring him back to life.

little julio is standing on the other side of the river. he's shouting, begging. ginder carries him across the water. reina nods with her hands on her hips, her eyes shining. the boy is just three years old, and he, too, should have a father. you know. the boy's mother has another partner. and manu? well, manu is a lone wolf.
manu finally comes out because of all that noise. the child in his sandals, the mud squeezing through his toes, toddles towards him. manu picks him up. he examines his little feet and sits him at the table. julio wants to play but there is nowhere to go. the rain is everywhere. he sees ama in the dining area. he climbs into her lap. *the itsy-bitsy spider climbed up the water spout*. the boy begins to shriek with all his might. ama continues to sing. *green, green grass, you are my precious thing*.
for dinner, *pescado con hormigas*, fish stuffed with red ants. at first, ama tries to separate the insects from the fish, but she soon gives up any capricious notions of grandeur and devours the food any way she can. at least they're dead, they won't be eating the insides of her stomach. it's getting dark in the cafeteria. the kerosene lamps are flickering. reina is puffing her *mapacho*. julio is fighting like mad, he's screaming, rebelling, squirming. hegner is trying, he's getting tired, the child slips away and escapes. he doesn't want to go back with his stepfather to the other side of the river. manu is silent, his arms folded in front of him, watching

like a wild beast ready to pounce. hegner gives up and crosses the water by himself. reina squeezes the wild child to her bosom like a bundle of laundry. you want to go to sleep at your daddy's, don't you? the boy begins to shine through his tears when manu lifts him up and throws him over his shoulder like a sack of bananas. *buenas noches*.

04.02.08

there are some books here, would you like to see them? hegner, who is considered worldly in these parts because he knows how to read and write, hands her a pile of about a dozen books. most of it is pulp, and all of it is in spanish. but on the bottom of the pile is a worn-out paperback in english. carlos castaneda: *tales of power*. ama breathes in the moldy smell and opens the book.
excitement within. the curtain opens and everything around goes silent. only the river quietly exhales in the background. something is about to happen. your knees begin to shake. you have embarked on a journey of power and there is no turning back. the rain is hanging from the sky like tiny nooses.
"the best of us always surfaces when we're up against the wall."

at times, she feels that she knows what she is searching for.

"the life of a warrior can never be cold or lonely and without feelings, because it's based on his affection, his devotion, his dedication to what he loves. this earth, this world. for a warrior, there can be no greater love . . . he roams on the paths of his love, and, wherever he is, he is complete."

something is different. she's seeing things differently, recognizing shapes and patterns. chewed out papaya leaves. fibrous noni, fruits with beige eyes. the rain is pouring down outside like sifted flour. and inside of her, she is walking on the blade of a knife. can a person even carry such a load? she starts touching her face, her left side is drooping, collapsing. she has a burrow in her body, and slowly but surely, the animal living inside is waking up. the jungle is silent between downpours. the

mosquitos slow down. she manages to kill one of them in flight. a green bird with a red belly is shrieking somewhere nearby.
can she love the whole world and still kill mosquitos?

the river shrugs its shoulders. the stones on which people cross over to the other bank are disappearing under the surface. i'm thinking of you. how are you doing? you don't have it easy, and also, you have me. mom, sometimes i pity you because of me. a bird in a yellow cloak is sitting close to me: theeeeeyuuuu. we look at each other eye to eye. i repeat after him: theeeeeyuuuuu. he's quiet for a little while, but then he decides to answer. we exchange strange sounds back and forth. somehow it changes us, turns us inside out, reshapes us. sometimes i dream about the language of birds. in the morning, i wake up with feathers on my temple.

04.04.08

"if you don't act impeccably, if you begin to fret and get impatient and desperate, you'll be cut down mercilessly by the sharpshooters from the unknown."

she adopts the local pace. no rush. today is a day to frolic. julio is frisky, constantly trying to climb on her. like a true male, he immediately reaches for her zipper. ama zips him up in her jacket. the boy is poking out of her cleavage like a baby kangaroo. he asks her about many things. she can't understand most of it. *yo no se*. i don't know. *señora, yo no se*. she is slow-witted. but that doesn't dissuade him, he's guided by his heart. he likes her. and even if she is missing a few screws, he wants her to sing the nursery rhyme, *it's raining it's pouring the old man is snoring*.

here, she discovers someone new. who it is, she doesn't know. she takes off her socks. with her bare feet, she sinks into her own skin, into the clay. she throws her shirt to the side. she is flowing. she is the rain, a leaf, a light green leaf, yellow veins on her skin. raindrops splatter on her cheeks and the sky falls on her head.
pilar comes to visit. she crosses the river. she has a lighter complexion,

and her hair is different. she stands out. she smiles as she talks. she asks questions, she's twittering like a bird. pilar is a princess, a trophy for a winner. she knows this. women of her kind beautify the ground, the arms of men. they know how to hold the reins and lash out with a single look. pilar can transform from a mother to a lover. she drapes her bangs over her face. manu is the lingering aftertaste in her mouth. ama feels the bitter taste of weed, of burnt pots. the campfire is still smoking. they are on opposite banks. between them, a steaming river and clumps of fog. she isn't indifferent to him. ama collects herself and clears out. she can see all the charred promises between them, the birds with beaks as sharp as a knife.

screaming. in the middle of the night. it's reina. before ama gets out of her loft, before she can get up on her feet, she hears manu. both voices carry into the night. one agitated and tearful. the other deep and calm, cradling, soothing. then reina begins to sing. it sounds like a prayer.

it was an evil spirit, but manu cast it away, reina explains during breakfast. julio is twitching, he's restless. he wants to go to the other bank and then back again. he can't settle on which side he prefers. the river intensifies his screaming. manu goes to pick up the child once more. he speaks to pilar, sounds coming back and forth in a crisscross of pantomime. ginder is uneasy. from the table in the kitchen, he watches the silent film showing across the river. pilar and manu—between them, fire and arrows. the events unfolding do not concern ama, and yet her breath grows heavier.

may i sit down? hegner's tearful eyes and trembling voice. pilar has broken up with him. he is deeply hurt. he points to his heart. we had problems, he says, stuttering, almost sobbing. then she said she was going back to manu because of the boy.

a quick exchange. the spectacle is over. all evaporates above the surface of the water. pilar carries a large bag, manu has a rucksack on his back and the boy on his shoulders. hegner continues to shout something incomprehensible, but pilar moves on, doesn't look back, or even answer, for that matter. the jungle closes its jaws. the three of them are gone.

hegner starts chopping wood for the fire. then he stops by ama's with a flower. he needs a shoulder, or a basket in which he can fall to pieces. he is wailing, lamenting. it's hard. the boy wants his father. he keeps on telling me that i'm not his father. pilar isn't sad about the split. she doesn't care for me. but i care for her. i'm the one who's hurting. right here. so, so, so much. and manu is pissed off at me now.

ama?
enrique suddenly appears from behind her like a ghost. come with me. i want to show you something.

how to sing to a princess

princesita looks like a haystack. a pile of branches. carlos is beating it with a mallet. the branches are breaking down into hair-like threads—into fragrant streams. threads that darken once exposed to the air and curl a little. a bit of *chacruna* is added into the ayahuasca. the kettle is boiling. it is the womb of the universe. the shipibo know that people come to this world on snake-canoes, and when they drink ayahuasca, they travel back to that cosmic moon—the source of all things. to drink ayahuasca means to drown, to die. time travels backwards all the way to the embryo, to the beginning, to its own birth. to the moment when the universe was born, where only darkness was all around. diego is singing songs to the princess that reach to the stars. the flute made from sugarcane is gently convincing the herbs to dissolve.
the shipibo are hunters, fishermen, and craftsmen. in their settlements along the ucayali, they hold on to their ancient customs and traditions. their shaman transforms into a jaguar or anaconda to duel the demons. sometimes he has to fight other shamans, who try to deprive him of his strength. ayahuasca is like a woman, the men laugh around ama, you never know what it will uncover. each time it has a different strength, a unique pull that affects you in another way. ama rolls it in her hands, leans over to smell it even though it is everywhere in the air. she tastes it. you won't feel your tongue, enrique says, laughing, fresh ayahuasca is a powerful anesthetic.
the shaman understands plants and people. he first tests each herb

on himself. he will start off in small doses, and then he will go hardcore until the plants turn him inside out.
the night carries words with a strange cadence in a voice she can't recognize.
why me?
darkness starts to pour into her.

"without the awareness of the presence of our death, there is no power, no mystery."

sueño, mi niña.

04.06.08

depression. it squeezes ama to its bosom, like a mother.

death is not defeat. defeat is when you waste a precious opportunity.
oh, fuck you and your opportunity, old raven. i've had it up to here with you!
you don't understand. it's not what you live, but how.
thank you. that sounds like a line out of a handbook for practical housewives.
that's just the thing you need, amazon princess. happiness and tragedy are both human categories that make no sense. one experience is preferred, the other is rejected, but at the same time, they are alike. on her way to the river, she kicks away fallen nonis that leave a light beige slime on her rubber boots.
what is your point? do you want to learn something or just get a merit badge?
merit badge? what do you mean by that?
the goal that you set for yourself, and that you're scared you won't finish. you're running up a tab, but who is it for? you want a reckoning, but for whom?
i don't know. could it be for my ego or something like that? and stop cackling!
it could be. what else? who are you trying to please? are you afraid that

you might only disappoint? that you might cause pain? of course i am! and that's what's holding you back—your mother's tears. if your recovery becomes your only goal, then your true purpose has already passed you by.
yeah, yeah, yeah, i'm writing it in my diary so that i don't die a complete idiot. now let me be.

the breathing helps. it pushes the depression down into the cellar. into the underground pipes. she lies down in the light and unwinds as she stretches out over the landscape a thin layer of netting, a membrane. her body is building back up—organs in no particular order are gradually disappearing in phases and intervals. she becomes an eye in this space. a moving cloud, trying to get a feel for its size. next time she will reach for greater heights. she begins singing while doing her laundry, and she stops caring about how her life will end.

she is standing on the threshold, and she doesn't know if she is in the right place. her hut has become a gallery, her personal exhibit of shipibo indian artifacts. masks, candles, beads, and a rain stick, a colorful tube filled with rattling seeds. when she points it down, it sounds like rain. reina is laughing. do you like it? of course i do. *linda sopresa* - a nice surprise for our princess. yes, *princesita*. she feels exactly like a princess when she looks into reina's eyes. she is touched by the way people here try to make her feel at home.
happiness comes in the shape of empty seeds, hollowed walnut shells, and fragments of seashells.

the evening escapade with manu and pilar seems like a minor étude. darkness cradles memories and then the stress comes back. what will they say at home? do you really have to satisfy their impatience? that constant feeling of never doing enough. that fear nipping at her heels. fear is her achilles' heel.
when she listens to the sounds of the jungle, her inner voices disappear. it's exhausting to listen to that constant yapping, commenting on everything all the time. she looks at the sky, and the blabbermouth in her head says "sky" or possibly "blue sky" or "cloudy." when she aims

her eyes towards the crown of a tree, she hears "tree crown" or "large leaf, filled with holes, unique shapes." oh, just shut up! can't you just look around? does it have to be so complicated?
her internal monologue quiets down when she listens to music or when she reads. when she wants to find an answer, she grants herself the power to open her story to any page, and there it appears, falling straight into her lap. the words she hears from the raven when it ridicules her in the morning ". . . life is an endless challenge, and challenges cannot be possibly good nor bad. challenges are simply challenges."

hooyahh! hooyaaah! someone keeps shouting. calling for help. a bird or a monkey? voices in the shadows of the night, a messenger, breathing heavily, brings news. enrique is waiting at rio pacitea with its cargo and visitors from far away. they arrive in the middle of the night: two bridgebuilders from the czech republic, šimon and jáchym, nicknamed lech, with little filip, jean, and his beautiful dolores, and finally dimas, who has guided everyone here. reina is cooking as if it were daytime. everyone is sitting at the table, drinking and feasting. in just a few minutes, *santuario* has turned into a regular babylon.

7.4.08

a day of death

the table is full. people, food, and the cackling of chickens. hegner is chasing one. most likely, it will be for lunch tomorrow. dolores is exotic, gracious, and graceful. the men leave for the river. they begin measuring and taking pictures, contemplating where to build the suspension bridge. the presence of this expedition pleasantly distracts ama from her own thoughts.

the camera captures the opposite bank. two natives suddenly emerge from the jungle. they both carry bundles over their shoulders. they cross the river, followed by a dog. a black mutt. it begins crossing the water, balancing on the logs of trees that create a slippery footbridge a quarter way into the river. the rest of the way, it is hopping from one rock to another. everyone focuses on the two men with their loads who shout at the dog to go back to the bank. the mutt hesitates for a moment, staggering, but then continues across. it just takes an instant, a single whimper. the mill wheel stops. the onlookers hold their breath.

death is quick and hot, like the water. ginder heads out to retrieve the dead body. its head is lolling to the side. its body is swinging in ginder's arms as they disappear into the jungle. the air is stuttering, turning, the salty taste of uneasiness. and then everything stirs up again.
damn, that was fast, šimon breathes. lech nods. yeah, that's why i came here to build this bridge. only jean is laughing. so, the bridge marks the spot where the dog died.

another bouquet of flowers from hegner. the chicken he was chasing this morning is on the table. šimon talks about the dog. how it looked when they fished it out of the water. he won't stop talking about it. the way its teeth were showing, its eyes popping out, and its final expression of total fear. and then the chicken that was clucking away in the morning, and now is spread out on a plate. death does not hide itself here. it is present, every step of the way.

the sound of swishing—the night sky and bats. the inner dialogue is growing smaller and smaller. the eternal critic goes mute from time to time. something is approaching in the silence. it is getting closer—a gust of wings, a purple ripple. come closer. a needle in the spine. a string that unspools. higher and higher. windlessness, timelessness. silence. only the sound of movement that nobody is making.

lech sits beside ama. hey gorgeous, what are you doing here? what has brought you to *santuario*?
ama thinks for a while. without a doubt, she ended up in santuario because of her crazy friend, jára.

somehow, she doesn't know where to begin. perhaps with the start of the new year, because that was when she was caught off guard. there are diagnoses that come out of nowhere like a food allergy. your entire being goes into denial. you didn't ask for it, you don't accept it. in that moment, something cracks. the bubble around you suddenly bursts, and all the streets in your town black out. their names disappear, all the signposts are gone. all the capital letters in your book fall out, words begin to liquefy and turn into black worms. you don't know where the beginning is, or the end. everything starts blending, feathering out. strict routines fall apart, spaces begin to collapse. all that's left is stress. the overwhelming pressure. those pistons moving behind you, in front of you, from above, from below. pushing and crushing you. it happens when you least expect it, because you never expect such a thing. and always at a time when you feel that you have just started a new life.

she had come home for christmas after three months in iowa. everything was still fresh inside. all her experiences, new friends. she almost didn't know how to process it. after her split with evan, she was free. she could breathe again. she felt that space, and doors were opening for her wherever she went. upon her return, she saw her sister expanding. how she was glowing in that flashy t-shirt. she looked like a big orange whale. the infant's hands and feet were forming mountain ranges and hills out of her belly. ama couldn't wait for the baby to pop out so she could play with her, teach her stupid stuff. on new year's eve, five minutes before midnight, she first felt a lump. happy new year!
in that moment, it became clear to her, though she tried to deny it, to comfort herself, because it didn't have to mean much. it could have been anything. there was always more than one possibility. but she knew, even as she tried to talk herself out of it. she knew very well by the way it affected her, the way things were happening inside her.
the fear that overwhelmed her. she had encountered it once before. it was dormant in her blood, waiting to hit her out of nowhere. the

word reappeared. she was too afraid to use it. she didn't store it in her vocabulary. it was an outdated word, one that had lost its smell but it kept coming back to her. a word that was linked to superstitions and old wives' tales. every time she ran away from it, it would catch up to her. a curse. she was only fourteen when her mother told her she had cancer. and now, after a quarter century, she had passed the baton, her inheritance. the same diagnosis at the same age in the same part of the body. a carbon copy. today, they call it genetics. it used to be called a family curse.

shortly after my diagnosis was confirmed, i lay down with a fever and he appeared, stood by my bed, hovered over me. i knew who he was without an introduction. the raven spirit. a cloak made of black feathers, wings on his head, a cane in his hand. a bonfire roaring behind him. surrounded by a circle of the dead. ancestors in a sacrificial ritual, stomping so that the earth would give shape to their brood. you will embark on the journey of the raven, he said. he did not ask if i agreed. i tried to object, to say that i was not sure, but he hit me with his cane until he cracked my skull. he came back a few days later when the fever was gone. completely sober, i spotted him standing over a cauldron. he mumbled something, mixing a potion, casting a spell. i saw myself lying in a hut with animal skins beneath me. he came closer to me with a dagger, he carved up my chest, and then he opened the palm of his hand like a leaf. he shoved a crystal into my flesh, and he covered it with his hand, and the wound healed as if it had never been there.

my friend, the psychologist and amateur shaman, said that this was normal. it was a textbook case. a classic initiation of the apprentice. be prepared to take a long pilgrimage. you have no choice. either you will go, or—well, you know.
as a raven's apprentice?
somehow, she doesn't know what to say to this. the world of shaman drumming and fox tails has never been her cup of tea.
read eliade or kalweit. there's a ton of books on this. if you'd like, i'll bring you something on it.
will that help?

you won't be so scared. have you ever seen spirits or spirit animals before?
no!
late at night, it comes back. the ceiling is collapsing. it buries her in memories: when she was young, she used to see a wolf. he was friendly and always walked beside her like a dog. he would sometimes growl at people. but usually, he was calm. when she was alone, he would come and play with her. he would speak to her. he was real, as real as everything she saw around her. she can't remember when he disappeared for good.
maybe she can summon him once more. she starts raking through her thoughts, fishing for the wolf's name. she knows that he had a name of some sort. perhaps he is still with her.

01.18.08
friday, the unlucky day

morning. she can't get up. right there at the edge of her bed, the world begins but she doesn't want to enter. and so, she lies there and all kinds of crazy thoughts spin through her head. she tries to imagine how all that stupidity would sound if only she could record it—she can hear how her thoughts are crisscrossing each other from within.
apparently, cells have memory. not too long ago, respectable scientists proved that treatment at the level of a single cell can eliminate defective material throughout the body. this idea goes beyond the reach of logic. if it were possible to think this through logically, we would have harnessed it long ago. clarity can only be found at the subconscious level. that is where a person finds the answer why.
that is true, but you'd have to have the will. the will to do what?
the will to live.
nailed it. hands-free applause! that's something new, to want to live. sounds like pretentious bullshit. she's looking around, searching for footing, a safety ring, a life vest, a floating mast, a reason to live. i want to want to live. how can that happen? start by writing it down.

*i **want** to want to live, i want to **want** to live, i want to want to **live**.*
*i **want** to want to live, i want to **want** to live, i want to want to **live**.*
*i **want** to want to live, i want to **want** to live, i want to want to **live**.*
*i **want** to want to live, i want to **want** to live, i want to want to **live**.*
*i **want** to want to live, i want to **want** to live, i want to want to **live**.*
*i **want** to want to live, i want to **want** to live, i want to want to **live**.*
*i **want** to want to live, i want to **want** to live, i want to want to **live**.*
*i **want** to want to live, i want to **want** to live, i want to want to **live**.*
*i **want** to want to live, i want to **want** to live, i want to want to **live**.*
*i **want** to want to live, i want to **want** to live, i want to want to **live**.*
*i **want** to want to live, i want to **want** to live, i want to want to **live**.*
*i **want** to want to live, i want to **want** to live, i want to want to **live**.*
*i **want** to want to live, i want to **want** to live, i want to want to **live**.*
*i **want** to want to live, i want to **want** to live, i want to want to **live**.*
*i **want** to want to live, i want to **want** to live, i want to want to **live**.*
*i **want** to want to live, i want to **want** to live, i want to want to **live**.*
*i **want** to want to live, i want to **want** to live, i want to want to **live**.*
*i **want** to want to live, i want to **want** to live, i want to want to **live**.*
*i **want** to want to live, i want to **want** to live, i want to want to **live**.*

no response. just a black hole, lamenting planets above. the sun strikes her with a white flame.

she doesn't want to go anywhere. she would rather crawl back into bed. it would be better if she didn't exist. she needs some reassurance. her eyes chase around the room, jumping from one book spine to another, over and over. *that's it.* siddhartha. that book opens up like a window.

"kamala owned a rare bird in a gilded cage. he dreamed of this bird—that the bird, which sang to him every morning, had become mute. wondering about the cause, he approached the cage and looked inside; the bird was dead and lay stiff at the bottom of the cage. he took it out of the cage, held it for a moment, and then threw it out onto the street. at that moment he felt terribly shocked, and his heart pained him, as if with that bird, he had thrown away everything precious and good.
awaking from this nightmare, he was enveloped by deep sorrow. it

seemed to him that the way he had been going through life was worthless and pointless; nothing alive, nothing of any worth or permanence had been left to him. he stood alone and empty like a castaway on the shore."

she's holding a fistful of feathers in her hand, death is growing inside of her, worthless and pointless.

massive traffic jam. the strahov tunnel is closed, so she takes the tram across letenská field as if her life depended on it.
come on in. i don't have good news for you. it's malignant. an invasive carcinoma, which means that it is growing quickly. treatment must begin immediately. blah blah blah. blah blah blah. chemotherapy, surgery. chemotherapy, radiation. i'd say it will take about ten to twelve months.
ama is counting, swallowing spit with metallic taste. she pulls out a bottle of water. two gulps to escape, but the doctor keeps at it.
your hair will fall out. your health insurance will cover the cost of a wig. you'll also be eligible for disability.
excuse me, can you open the window?
of course. are you feeling sick? as soon you pull yourself together, the nurse will show you what to do next.

the nurse guided her through the ward, the infusion room. hairless faces, colorless, wearing bandannas or not. iv bags dripping above their heads.
her legs were acting up again, damn her knees. she should have had her knees checked, too. there had to be an emergency exit somewhere. dear god! how am i going to do this when i get sick just at the sight of a needle? and this place looks like a concentration camp.

hey mom, guess what? i can join your club now. what did they tell you? should i come visit you?
that would be pointless, i'm heading straight for the nusle bridge.[5]

---

[5] *Translator's note*: The Nusle Bridge passes over the Nusle district in Prague. It is known as place where people jump to commit suicide..

she's driving home with her car full of chatter. if you concentrate on a problem, it's hard to find a solution.

perfect. could there be a perfect, elegant, quick and painless solution to this problem?
sure. how about just driving into that crash barrier?
the better solution would be to get on the highway, put the pedal to the metal, take it to the max, and fly. a gorge or a ravine would be best. a cliff. that would be a flight. she could see it before her with her eyes closed. someone is honking. where the fuck are you going, you stupid cow?! sorry, shithead, i don't know where i'm going. what can you expect from a stupid cow?
maybe it's better to swallow some poison. you won't get so beat up. it's more aesthetically pleasing when you're still recognizable. it's important to look good. to kill yourself with grace.
what about a bathtub? slitting your wrists?
out of the question. she'd pass out just at the thought of that.
euthanasia! they just legalized it, didn't they?
sure, and if they haven't, chances are they'd legalize it just for you.
she will find out. she'll google it tonight, and if they don't do it here, they'll do it in holland, they're always a step ahead over there.
euthanasia, such a lovely sounding word. almost like ecstasy or euphoria. you could sing it. has anyone written a song about euthanasia yet? or a poem? she could write something. a musical. *euthanasia*! it would be a box office hit. lucie bílá and daniel hůlka could be the lead singers.

01.19.08

"to be seen is the desire of ghosts. to be remembered is the desire of the dead."

—norman o. brown

how do we break a curse? by descending into the underworld. ama knows that millions of people have lived through this before her. some of them left traces, like a manual. but everyone has to schlep down this road on their own.

books were medicine. she picked out *waiting for the coyote – a contemporary native canadian drama*. she discovered shirley cheechoo and *the path with no moccasins*.
"i'm waiting for the sun to rise. you too? i'm here to let go of my old self. i don't know how but i figure i'll find out here. you're supposed to have visions here on dreamer's rock."

in the evening, peru pops into her mind. it is as if someone whispered in her ear to do it. you will go to peru. what sort of bullshit is that? if she were to go anywhere, it would be india. she always wanted to go to india. also, she has friends there. she doesn't know the language in peru, and she doesn't know a soul. what would she do there? she puts a cold compress on her head and hits the sack.

01.21.08

there are moments when she has the feeling that she is being guided by something, and she is ambushed by other voices, other rooms. madhouses are full of those guided by something.

mistletoe is not incompatible with classical medicine, said the neurologist, who knew a thing or two. if you would like to try it, you could begin chemo with injections of mistletoe. you'd have a fever for about one or two days after getting the shots, which is expected. after three or four doses, it will pass. the body will get used to it. so, shall we proceed?

that evening, she's in a downward spiral. this is hell, not knowing what comes next. and whoever knows that? but that's the point. it's pure fear, rarely acknowledged because we live in an illusion, hidden behind the plans of mice and men. the question is, how to live without illusion and not feel scared shitless?
outside, darkness. inside, greater darkness. fear carries the stench of sulfur. it hides in cracks and holes. it oozes down walls. no one can air it out, suck it up with a vacuum, or throw it in the trash. so stop. take a look. find out what you're afraid of.

when she closes her eyes, she hears thunder. the roar of war. she marches across battlefields. the sound causes pain in her chest like a broken rib. her stomach her head, her toes begin to whirl.
death is your fear.

a woman comes in and sits in a chair across from her. she stares with half of her face, with one eye. the other half is just exposed skull and a sharp jawbone.

02.01.08

the way of love is not a subtle argument
the door there is devastation
birds make great sky-circles
of their freedom.
how do they learn it?
they fall, and falling,
they're given wings.
—rumi

the landscape on the journey to lažany looks like the scenery inside her: dark fog, sinister fumes. the doctor recommended anthracycline. that sounds like "xyclon b," the gas chamber. and her thoughts crawling over one another like ants. but ants at least know what they are doing. or maybe they don't, but anyway, they follow direction, build something, always constructive, which she certainly can't say about her own thoughts.
the seminar, the art of dying, which she signed up for last summer, now takes on new dimensions. it's as if a light designer is directing the spotlight into the darkest places. she thinks about death and wonders if it all isn't just a dream. the vision of the grim reaper seems appealing to her, but the act of dying leaves a repulsive stench. she could just kick him in the ass for getting on her nerves so much. this is the time for the atheist to start looking for god.

if you die tomorrow, what will you leave behind?
if you die tomorrow, what will you regret the most?

if she died tomorrow, she would regret not frolicking more, not laughing, not dancing more.

02.03

the thought of peru keeps visiting her more and more often, annoying her. she tells no one. it is a stupid thought, so why bring it up? but then jára stops by, and somehow, it pops out of her mouth. then she immediately adds that she isn't planning on going anywhere.

the next day, jára phones to say that when he was on his way home from her place, he met a friend who just got back from the amazon. what a coincidence! he had visited a shaman for a few weeks, and even now, he was still out of it. he looked like the trip had left a mark on him. he was still really thrilled by the experience. would you believe that my soon-to-be mother-in-law, radka, is currently teaching in pucallpa? she studied herbology, and she knows all the shamans in the area. radka is in prague at the moment, and i have her number.
oh put a sock in it, you clown, i'm not calling anyone.

a few days later she is sitting at radka's place, listening to stories about faraway places over a cup of lemongrass tea. and when radka pronounces that name, it sounds like an incantation, and she is almost certain she will go. the name is santuario huishtin.
okay radka, write a letter to the shaman, ask him what he thinks about me going there. no strings attached.
okay. it might take a while for the mail to get there. he travels to the city about once a month.

02.14.2008

yesterday, i had a strange dream. i was teaching you how to swim, but you didn't want me to. you didn't want me to go in the water. finally, you started running and then flying. you were flying. are you okay? write to me. jeff

jeff, the truth sounds too simple, just like any diagnosis. a few scholarly words. it's almost like your equations. skype?

ama: ciao, professor. i'm asking you, not as a friend, but as the closest qualified authority i know, an expert who has the stamp to prove it. can you please tell me from that eminent quantitative-paralytic empire of yours, how things really are? and don't bother me with theory, or you'll piss me off.

jeff: even though i'm twice as old as you, i still don't know how to react to certain things. so instead of letting out a few empathetic sighs, i'll send a few books. remember when you told me that david bohm was a spiritualist dressed in a quantitative costume? the books that i packed for you take that theory even further. you'll like them. a person is born with the knowledge that the world around him is not a predictable mechanical device. and then we grow up and some of us forget. therefore, we need science to tell us how things really are. an image of a mechanical device gives out a sense of safety, and it's very soothing and deceptive. i can sense that you're standing on that threshold of exploration, determined to find out how things really are.

ama: i look forward to reading those books. i still feel a sense of gratification that you admitted i was right when i called bohm's quantitative wave theory pure mysticism planted in a little garden of science. i just finished reading quantitative thought by arnold mindell. it also totally goes beyond that box of acknowledged reality. he quotes bohm, of course, but he calls his pilot wave, the strength of silence. if i could manage to experience just some of that in real life, i'd consider myself lucky.

new phrases such as "we'll see" and new mottos such as "let it be your will" are helpful.

evening. chapelle royale, conducted by phillipe herreweghe. heinrich schütz. he lived during a time of death. he buried his parents, brother, young wife, two small children. hallelujah. death. he knew it so well. he had to love it. he lived in a time of open wounds. war. plague, broken justice. time didn't even exist. what comes first: minutes? seconds? or the rhythm of seasons, the invention of the modern man. and in the nearby villages, witches were burned at the stake. what did he mean by mentioning his nearly destitute existence? he stares, eloquently silent, from rembrandt's portrait. heinrich schütz is praying, a rhythm behind the embrace for the church's walls. a cool wind in a time of fever. *"ich bin nackend von meiner mutter leibe kommen, nackend werde ich wieder dahinfahren. der herr hat's gegeben, der herr hat's genommen; der name des herrn sei gelobt."*

it keeps coming back to me: "the lord giveth and the lord taketh away; blessed be the name of the lord."

02.19.08

someone has left her a copy of *love your life*. apparently it has medicinal qualities. someone by the name of louise hay has written that it took a lot of work for her to stand in front of a mirror and say, i love you, louise.
christ, this is ridiculous, you can't be serious. i love you, louise? that took you a lot of work? go fuck yourself, louise!
ama stands in front of a mirror and doesn't even let out a hiccup. it doesn't matter, it will take time. in the meantime, she can try it: i love you, louise! or how about, *you cow*?
yeah, that works. i can deal with *you cow*. i can even shout that out. i love you, *you cow*!

ama knows a simple recipe for getting rid of depression: it has to be trumped with something that doesn't have a shape yet, that's even worse. it works every time. she injects a shot of mistletoe under her skin; the depression will burn out with the fever.

a fever is a mountain climber. i see you again.
who are you, raven?
i'm the messenger of emptiness. everything that hasn't yet formed is in my world. my road leads along the edge of time, straight into a huge mystery. i'm a black hole. i am the current and the source. i bring changes to consciousness that turn sickness into power. i bring a message from the ancestors.

so why am i so afraid?
you don't want to encounter the demons that you yourself created.

the fever pushes me against the stubble of time, back to new york. i'm standing with you in a townhouse in brooklyn heights, and i'm staring you straight in the eyes. i'm holding a weight in each hand. two heavy dumbbells. i'm trying to let go of them, but i can't. it's like when a movie projector gets stuck. all of a sudden, there's a click and something happens. images start to flicker faster. one of the dumbbells flies out the door. bang! the glass is in pieces. the other dumbbell heads straight for the wall and goes right through to the neighbors' mosque and lands among men of islam. and then a gorgon appears on the scene. it is angry, hyperventilating, hectoring fear, and at the same time, it seems a bit comical in its insanity. it's banging chairs into the dining table, which has now turned into a pile of kindling. it is surging out, smashing everything in its path. pieces are everywhere. ruins. remnants. and then it calms down.

i am standing in front of you, and i am looking you straight in the eye. i point toward the gorgon. fire is coming out of its mouth. its tongue is sticking out all the way to its chest. i apologize. i never showed it to you before, but it's part of me.
it's done. i needed to tell you that. there's no need for shame or apology here. just the facts.
i stand in front of you, among the bits and pieces of wood and glass. there is a pile of logs next to the fireplace. it occurs to me that it's time to heat up the place. everything goes up in flames.

sean pleads with her to write, let him know what's going on, like so many other people. i don't know why you're not writing and i'm worried. an email filled with dozens of messages, shout-outs, pages with recommended medicines, doctors, healers. panicky interrogations that are choking her, beating on her, intruding. how can i help you? should i fly out to prague? do you want to come to america, argentina, to mars? i will find you the best of doctors. be sensible and accept my offer. please! pretty please!

silence is the language of rocks. she has so much in common with them.

03.02.08

what your teeth are mauling is not medicine. medicine can't be seen. it has no tangible form. it is an expression of power.

—paracelsus

the head physician, skovajsová, speaks forcefully. start chemotherapy while there's still a chance. when you get through it, you'll grow stronger. i have a lot of girls here who start crying that they should have listened to me three years back. it's terrible to watch them. please, stop this denial. alternative medicine will not help you.

and you have a rock solid solution, ms. head physician?

she still doesn't know which way to go. there are so many paths, and none of them look like you can come back to them. she doesn't know how to decide. maybe she can write down all her possibilities on a piece of paper, throw them in a hat, and pick one solution by chance. it would just be a game of russian roulette.

ama, as soon as this snow melts, i'll build you a sweat lodge on the grazing field behind our house. it'll be on the spot where you always used to sit and write. i'll do anything to keep you around. i want you to stay. i'm sitting next to the river, and i'm staring at a nest of bald-headed eagles—it's their time to spread their wings and fly. should i fly out to visit?
no, sean—just send me the new pictures of the zapatistas that you took in chiapas.

03.09

i don't know where to look or how or why. the role of the prologue has long disappeared from modern theater. maybe that was why she was so disoriented. maybe the time had come to speak directly to the audience.
if you think that now some competent guide will appear after this shit show and trip to other galaxies take you by the hand and tell you where to step, what to pack, lend you his flashlight, and properly explain

exactly the way things are—then you're mistaken. the best that can happen is that a gang of inner voices will emerge and start haggling with each other. whose fault is it, who's the greater idiot? the resemblance to a primary election is just a coincidence because i'm not fighting for votes here, but for my neck.

the first event is a live target round. you hold a kalashnikov in your hands, but unfortunately, you are the target. you have the words "DON'T SHOOT" tattooed on your forehead but because your inborn shortsightedness impedes you from seeing that far, it's "fire!"

she saw a shooter fall into the sea. the flash of light from the last arrow stayed lodged between her ribs. his eyes swim towards her whenever she comes closer to water. in the meantime, it is hidden, safely buried on the bottom of the ocean, the fire she doesn't yet know how to harness. one day, she will lift it up to the heavens.

i have to get out of here. i'm surrounded. people are looking at me as if i owe them something. they're whining, give us back our millions. i want to yell back, but i have no debts, so just leave me alone.
it's exhausting for a person to constantly try to defend her basic human rights. the right to choose her own road. to make her own decisions. to make her own mistakes. and even further, the naked right to choose her own death. i don't owe anything to anyone. so, i have the right to die as i choose, don't i?
i have to leave. get away from this stranglehold. somewhere far away, where i won't be bothered by these nosy and stubborn creditors.

on the train to zlín, a group of romas. across from her, an old man with wrinkles and blue eyes. grey stubble, the charm of an aged complexion that put her in mind of samuel becket. the smell of tobacco mixed with mustiness in this enclosed, airless space, more uncommon than unpleasant. the train arrives at the station. the roma get up, throwing their bags over their shoulders. the old man asks ama whether they were already in přerov.
no, we're in olomouc.

he snaps at the men, growling as he nags at them with his raspy voice, they all return and quietly sit down in their seats as if they are at school. the old man shakes his head, then he smiles at ama. they're like italians.

nursing time. so, i'll finally get to see you, my little hedgehog. your changed body, the gentleness in your eyes. your new year's baby. i finally get to dance with him to the vltava[6]. i'm letting it all hang out with you, you have no idea, but i have to, because there is simply no good time to say something like this. i have to go to peru, so i can write about it. do you understand? salty cheeks, both yours and mine, press against each other. don't worry about me. you're crying out loud, and the little one is gobbling you gluttonously. he doesn't understand the shadows hovering over his head.
i'm afraid. i'm terrified that if you leave, i will never see you again. that's ridiculous, i say, but at the same time, i feel my leash tightening.

3.13.08

"where there is no hope, it is incumbent on us to invent it...or commit suicide. misery...offers no truths."

—albert camus

radka calls. the shaman had written back to come as soon as possible. if you could make it by easter, he would wait for you in pucallpa. that's a bit sudden, don't you think? i'll think it over and let you know. never mind, write that i'll come for sure, and i will try to make it before easter.

would you believe it? i have to go. i'm screaming from the window into the street. i'm going to peru! mom is smiling even though she isn't looking too happy. yep, workers of the world, beware!
yes, i feel so relieved, mom. i feel so much more relieved.

---

[6] *Translator's note*: Vltava is a symphonic poem by Czech composer Bedřich Smetana. The score was inspired by the Vltava river, which runs through Prague.

lara stopped by and looked straight into ama's eyes.
how can i help you? if you need money, don't hesitate to ask.
i'm good so far. but i could use your backpack and your swiss army knife.

the tambo • when it rains monkeys and there is darkness inside

04.08.08

finally, it's decided where to build the bridge. santuario is empty. all the men have left for pucallpa to get materials. it's suddenly peaceful. ginder offers to take her to the cascades. it's quite a distance, if she's up for it. ama grabs her hat and her water bottle.
vamos?
up ahead, ginder is cutting sections of the path with a machete. be careful where you step. most of the time, she doesn't know what she's doing. it's slippery, slimy, and she's up to her knees in mud. she continues uphill, downhill. she crosses several creeks. when she stops to admire the local habitat, ginder suddenly disappears. the jungle swallows him whole. like everything else, it grinds you, cuts you to pieces, and puts you back together in a different shape. damn it! her foot is stuck. *lianas* are creeping, crisscrossing the jungle like snakes. ginder comes back and releases her from the mud hole. that constant grin of his. *cansada*? no, i'm not tired. but i'm better at walking over cobblestones. ama doesn't know how to say cobblestone in spanish, and she probably won't be able to explain it to him anyway. he would probably picture a shrunken head instead of cobblestones. after two hours, she is out of breath, sweating, dirty, and bleeding. some of these plants burn and cut right through your pants. ginder, what type of plant is this? *patikino*. the leaf is in the shape of an isosceles triangle. its sides are over a meter long. and this is *higuerón*, he points to a tiny tree. - its sap is poisonous—we dip our arrows in it, you know?
they walk through all the noise of the jungle where, once in a while, a bit of the sun falls through the heavy growth. a set of wings flashes by, and something lets out a quacking sound.
look, this is the route that enrique takes.
ama follows where ginder points and tries to see something that could

possibly resemble a path. she is unsuccessful, so they both continue on this invisible path made only for those who can travel it blind. if ginder left her here, no one would ever see her again.

"you are the way you are, because you tell yourself you are that way."

i am constantly trying to write to you about where i am. then i have this feeling that everything is completely different from what i want to describe. the jungle swallows you. it entangles you around the hips, hangs around your neck like a necklace made of colorful seeds. there are hundreds of eyes here. they come for the body. they want to be there and see that struggle for balance between the human soul and the rainforest's gluttony. and at the same time, there's this awareness that it's all just a bubble. we're living in one like it. not everything we notice around us is part of the surrounding world, but rather, it's our own reflection in a distorted mirror.

"we think we decide, all we're doing is acknowledging that something beyond our understanding has set up the frame of our so-called decision, and all we do is to acquiesce."

and that's exactly how she ended up in santuario. she's not the one who made the decision, because if it were her doing, she never would have come. even now, the thought of it seems crazy. it would have been a lot easier to get a hospital bed at zelený pruh[7] or take the trip to the clinic in munich, but she is afraid of that, too. she's afraid of everything. somewhere in some hidden corner, she admires people she sees in hospitals. the way the chemo drips through them and how they manage to live through it. she has run off to the jungle to hide the fact that she's a coward.

04.09.08

an exercise in self-control. don't scratch. above all, do not scratch. she's bitten all over, like someone with a pox. cicadas screeching above her head like a high voltage wire. in the distance, bells cut around corners,

[7] *Translator's note*: Zelený Pruh a neighborhood in the Nusle district in Prague, which is home to a university hospital.

precisely and sharply. sounds are blending, overlapping, they have a rhyme, a unique length. some of them shoot out in one big cluster, and then they're silent for a long time. some sounds are constant and consistent, a staccato; other sounds are muddled and then comes a quick rain. *llubia.*
reina begins to laugh. every time we hang our laundry, it rains. ama sits on a bench. in the distance, another batch is heading over. maybe it's simply that it rains here all the time.

"the moths are the heralds, or better yet, the guardians of eternity. the moths carry a dust on their wings...a dark gold dust. that dust is the dust of knowledge."

why is it so hard to remember? you're born with it, but then you forget. when does that actually happen?

she always had many selves inside of her with different figures and voices from different ages and epochs. she also carried different animals inside her. she often walked through the landscape that is called a dream. in some of her dreams, her selves, voices, and animals met each other. in other dreams, she inhabited different universes. some universes were extremely loud. they didn't hold planets but only sounds. there were universes where only wind existed.
she liked her purple selves, her white and golden ones, with a vortex of light over them. when she was little, it was easy to touch a rainbow, run in slow motion, and live in the branches of the spruces. she did not see people around her, but bubbles. people were wearing space suits, they moved about in balls of colorful mist. animals too, the trees, rocks, everything lived in pastel clusters of light. she would talk to them. forget-me-nots would strut about, gossiping among themselves. the silver birches danced in a whirlwind like ballerinas. she would notice dots in the sky. transparent dots that would pass by, circle around her. when the air was clear, the dots would flicker faster, leaving silver sparks behind.
they would laugh at her. she liked to imagine things they would say. the adults would say that they had stripes on their spacesuits, as if they were in a cage. in a tiny, mobile cage. many people had large heads,

much larger than the rest of their bodies. she would often wonder why they did not fall over. she stopped talking about it, and then she stopped seeing these things.

the house is humming like a beehive. josie is moving to manu's place with the baby. the giant black ants are covering the railing with a four-lane highway.

josie is enrique's niece, reina says. we took her in to help us with the kitchen, now that we are building a bridge over here. the ten-month-old, calet, is gurgling in a sling. josie takes him in her arms and pampers him, sings to him. the father of the boy is in lima, attending university. they don't see much of each other. she claims that she's not sad he's gone, but there are clouds in her eyes, waiting for a downpour. the child is sitting on her lap. josie is putting on clean pants for him that she wove at home. children in the jungle don't wear diapers. they piss and shit straight into their pants. in a few minutes, it's pouring out of him through the pants, right onto josie, and down the chair to the ground. the puddle starts spreading over the floor. josie just pats his wet pants with her hand and continues to sit and talk. calet is screaming. he starts climbing up his mother, reaching out to her, cuddling with her. josie is laughing. she squeezes him to her chest.

amita, come with us into the jungle to gather herbs.
ginder with a machete, then ama, followed by reina. long steps. expeditions with reina are always long and sluggish. she smokes her pipe, stops at every tree and explains all its medicinal qualities. ginder moves quickly, without effort or fear. he sizes up the ferns with his eyes and clears away the bushes and leaves. once in a while, he moves a fallen branch or a giant *patikino*. after a few hours of walking through the sludge, he stabs his machete into the mud, lights up a *cigarillo*, and points to a cactus-like rope. *starsa*. he starts digging for the roots, brushing aside the terrain. liana, with her sharp thorns, resists. ginder takes her on. he's chopping, untangling, once in a while he pricks his finger and hisses as he squeezes out the blood. after an hour of struggle, his palms look like christ's, and his bag is filled to the top.
on the way back, the usual stop—a siesta in luis's shack. luis is not at

home, but the fire's still smoldering. above it hangs a beat-up old pot with a lid. ginder takes off the lid. ama lets out a scream. mono. a boiled monkey, the tiny body with its head, its huge mouth grinning from ear to ear. ginder and reina are laughing their heads off. yep, luis loves monkey. you should see how he lights up when he manages to catch one. great! shall we go? *vamos*. they all head to santuario. the last steep climb, she's out of breath. she can't get the image out of her head. it's like a bad aftertaste. a pot with grinning teeth, a monkey's grin.

the bridge builders are back.
no one's using concrete. we'll secure the bridge to the trees about two hundred meters against the current.
what will enrique say to this? didn't he want the bridge here?
lech waves his hands. yeah, i wanted that too, but in the end, simon and jean convinced me otherwise. that concrete was useless. the river had corrosive minerals in it, and there were other issues, like with this soil. we would have to dig much deeper until we hit something more secure. i still think that we could have made it out of concrete, but i gave up. enrique had to choose. either we would have a bridge hanging from the trunks of trees a few meters way from here, or nothing at all.
it's settled then. will you stay long?
no, just a quick run and we're heading back. here are the things you wanted. notebooks, pens. i sent that note for your mother on the first night.
you're an angel.
yeah, a fallen one. oh, radka says hi. she won't be able to come for a while, but she might make it by the end of june.
simon shows her his hand.
do you know by any chance what this could be? it looks like a nettle rash, but it really itches.
yeah, it's those little flies. whatever you do, try not to scratch it. it'll spread, and it will burn like hell.
these fucking insects are getting the best of me. how the hell did ikmund and hanzelka[8] ever manage?

---

[8] *Translator's note*: Jiří Zikmund and Miroslav Hanzelka were two Czech adventurers who wrote several books about their travels around the world in the 1940s and 1950s.

white sharks emerge out of the flowers. she has the runs. the morning is trying to bring in the light, but she can't sweep out the darkness. at noon, she is hanging over the railing, fluttering and smoldering. trying to create wind with her eyelashes to cool herself down. a butterfly the size of a horse flutters by, making waves like ripened wheat fields, fanning her.
and then death. the closer it is, the more transparent. it overflows, leaving just a pale breath behind.

04.10

tambo. apartmá separé in the jungle by the river. most of the structures in the jungle do not have walls. just a floor and roof made of palm leaves held by columns. the *tambo* has hardpacked clay. enrique says that time spent in the *tambo* is necessary to gather one's energy and strength. *concentrado, tranquillo*. he doesn't get this from books. he has never read a single one. people here are proud when they know how to sign their own name. enrique writes emails on a computer, so he is considered a learned man. his helpers sweep through the surroundings, clear a path to the creek, and the hole in the ground that they call a toilet. a turkish toilet in the wilderness. you will be here completely alone. they look at her, guessing how small the little soul inside of her is. are you afraid?
ama doesn't know, and to be honest, she doesn't care.
but i do want you to do something with that huge termite hill on the ceiling, and with the rows of ants along the legs of the bed and the bed i'm supposed to sleep on.
she calls it a bed because she doesn't know how to say plank in spanish. the legs of this plank are made of thick branches, all of them are the same length and because the structure dwells on a slope, the difference in the height between the head and the foot of the bed is about 25 centimeters. the architecture of the rainforest doesn't bother itself with such details. design à la *pat & mat*,[9] a turnkey home: where there is no door, there is no need for a key.

[9] *Translator's note*: *Pat & Mat* is a Czechoslovak slapstick animated TV series.

si si, hormigas, hegner laughs.
yes, ants, hegner. i don't understand why you would laugh.
you can write here.
he points to another one of his creations, a rough desk with a sea of splinters and two little stools. boards nailed to thick branches, standing on a slanted floor, and above it, a fancy roof built in early gothic style. after three weeks of sitting on these wooden benches, she develops quite the callouses on her ass.
and here is your kitchen. a fire circle and a few logs. you'll get food once a day. ginder will bring it to you.
understood. or she could catch something if she needs to.
enrique takes out a bottle with some liquid. this is for you. it's strong medicine. if you don't follow a strict diet, you'll start developing lesions on your skin.
great, *muchas gracias*.
have a good time.
the moon hovers over the courtyard like a phantom. through the liquid darkness, birds are pounding on the walls of the night at regular intervals. how long will they last? long, long. and then suddenly, it stops. the monkeys attack the branches, and the god of rain is squandering his coins. thunder behind the curtain. hunger, hunger, bitter hunger. she's lying there and feeling every bone in her body, probably because her ribs are showing. *tranquillo medita*, blah blah blah. she can eat cockroaches. calm down. you're forgetting to breathe from all the anger, amazon warrioress. the jaguars and pumas can smell you a mile away. but they'll keep their distance.

oh raven, for godsake, how long will this take?

until you stand up for yourself.

04.11

good morning, i bring you food. here is rice and six *platanos*. it's for the whole day—three meals.
ginder holds up his ring, middle, and index fingers.

today is the last time we see each other. i will just leave your food here. during your fast, you can't speak to anyone. you know that? not even me.
that doesn't bother me. i can't understand half of what you're saying anyway.

for lunch, a fairytale. well, they don't cook with salt here either. and besides, everyone has run off. she has to convince herself somehow, coax herself to keep sane. she doesn't intend to feel hopeless three times a day for the next two weeks. so how about grandma's priceless motivational slogan? *in africa, children are dying of hunger*. a useless strategy through and through. it won't turn the plantains into sushi or eggs benedict. so use your imagination, ama. *schola ludus,*[10] use all your senses. how does it taste, what is its consistency, its texture, is it dry or damp? how does it react to contact with saliva? how does it taste in the front part of your mouth, in the middle and on the sides, in the back? coming out of your ass or inside your stomach? pretend that you're a connoisseur. a connoisseur is a person who can determine the flavor of something that doesn't have any taste. a local kind of jay is shouting down at her as if it were obsessed. just calm down, you hysterical old cow.

the sun retracts its claws and that hysterical screaming persists. it sounds czech, as if something has happened. something really has happened. ok then, scream. i'll go sample the rice and *platanos*.
ama is trying. she's trying, swallowing, but after a few bites, she gets the hiccups. rueful and heartbroken like that jay above her, she's catching tears on her plate to salt her meal. the entire *tambo* situation would be a piece of cake—the open shack on a chicken foot, the night in the forest, the bath in the local creek, the hard bench, the bent assbone—except for this saltless kingdom. this fast, *dieta*, in comparison to it, all her housemates, spiders, lizards, beetles, grasshoppers, mosquitoes, flies, sorry if i left anything out, are sheer joy.

---

[10] *Translator's note*: *Schola ludus,* the Latin term for "school is play," was first labeled by Moravian scholar and father of modern pedagogy, John Amos Comenius, who advocated for creative and engaging teaching methods to achieve better results in learning..

how to be happy, here and now? by shutting down that inner dialogue, that constant babbling.

at night, she needs to pee, but she doesn't want to get wet. that's a puzzle, even for a really intelligent person. so far, she's learned how to blow her nose without a handkerchief, just like a construction worker. she's really proud of that.

04.15

the bowels of the forest, the plopping of juices, the folding of cilia. on her way to the creek, she is screaming at the wet trees. then, suddenly, everything stops. hymenopterous silence billows. just two or three breaths before the day breaks. in that moment, she hears the gears of her mind squeaking as they turn. it's entering through her feet, through her soles, like the sprouting of vines that grow through the body into all the corners and capillaries. it is the rhythm of the earth.
she knows this place. glancing at the roof made of palm leaves, the *lianas,* the fire, something moves within her. something ancient, the smell of a different epoch. she is standing on one bare foot at a single point where ancient history overlaps the present while the birds screech out the *mañana* song. *mañana* is the most frequent word spoken here. when someone doesn't want to do something, they just say *mañana*, with a smile on their face.
she finds a note with her daily ration of food.
we were here just for a bit. we have to go back to pick up a cable. back on wednesday. we'll see each other on sunday, much strength to you. - lech

here, a person can quickly become close to someone she has never seen before. the jungle washes away all labels. it breaks down all the tiny barriers. everyone here is barefaced.
the butterflies are unusually quiet today. no one is talking to her now. and the rain in g major is happily riding it out. she should be careful.
hi, i hope i'm not intruding.
a yellowish-black grasshopper is munching on a chestnut that was

already in a desolate state. it looks like it's wearing huge black sunglasses. it's a cool design.
ama is splashing in the creek, the muddy steps are slippery. she's washing dishes in the murky water. other than that, she'll waste the entire day.
so what? are you in some sort of hurry? is someone after you? just that bitch with a scythe.

generations of women in a row, walking, carrying a burden. the load is breaking their backs. they're shoving one another forward, toiling, trekking. behind them, a bonfire. they put down their load one after another. a horologe of women. the fire sizzles, grabs with its tongue, sputtering, swallowing. and above them, your cackling. you're juggling a dozen weights. in your hands, they're turning into tomatoes, peppers, cucumbers. you throw them into the pot on the fire. the water is bubbling, smoking, overflowing. the kinswomen are circling the bonfire. seven generations. lifted skirts, strength, an evolutionary movement. come join us, they beckon. the smoke and the scent of their ancestors' soup is in the air.

the day catches its last breath and hands the relay off to the night, dressed in a purple smoking jacket and a lazy rain.

04.17

santuario is a place that a person sees in her dreams even before it appears in real life. she wakes at night and doesn't know whether she's just in another dream.
in the morning, a metallic blue beetle promenades on the table in front of her. it's loitering around her crayons. it likes the pink one. just as it takes off, here comes its comrade. *comrade*, such a waste of a word. such a beautiful word, and boy, did the "comrades" make it ugly. they buried it, irrevocably and completely, for future generations. quite possibly for all time. the matches are gone because she forgot to put them back into a plastic zipper bag. the lighter has died out too, so no fire today.

for the first time, she has the courage to go alone. a long hike with a dull machete. rio tibio is the destination. the *lianas* are avoiding her, she's wading through the mud, the sound of birds and leaves. she's keeping track of landmarks, breathing in the fragrances, searching for direction. the spirits in the rainforest are masters of deception. they scramble the branches of trees, turn pathways inside out. they make colors fuller. they have fun when they mess with the imposter's head, her legs, as they stupefy her. at moments she is uncertain. she doesn't know whether she needs to turn left by that fallen trunk of a tree. suddenly she stops. she freezes. a snake crawls by her foot. the green skin starts to hiss. it raises its head and flicks its tongue.

it happens in the blink of an eye, a split second. an invisible motion. the speed of a thought. the swoosh of a machete and the snake's head is without a body. *a body without a head. on the poplar tree by the cliff.*[11] she glances at the hand that holds the machete. it extends from her body, but it can't be hers. she swears to god that the hand doesn't belong to her but nevertheless her right hand, one of many, has tens of arms like durga. oh my god, that wasn't me. i didn't kill it. i'm not capable of killing.

it was someone she doesn't know. around the twinkling wonder of dragonflies, the trees raise their brows and sigh loudly. a salty taste on the palate and a cramp in her palm. tears on her face for the fate of the snake that lies in two pieces at her feet. for the amazon warrioress that dwells within her, for the city girl who came here, to the rainforest, to break a curse.

voices start swarming inside her head, running around, screaming. you killed it! maybe it wasn't even poisonous, maybe you killed an innocent snake!

he just got in the way, right under my feet—

you don't have to kill everything that crosses your path.

fear? she didn't feel any fear. there was no time for fear. it was something much quicker than that. prehistoric lizard brain. she has killed a snake. if only she could wake up in another dream.

[11] *Translator's note*: Verses from the ballad, "The Watergoblin" by Karel Jaromír Erben.

04.22

her solitude ends. the construction of the bridge continues.
simon hands her a tube of cream. he has long hair, and his shoulders are pink. he has a pale stripe on his chest from wearing his camera on a strap like a mail carrier.
can you put some of this on my back?
sure, give it here. with that stripe you look like a musketeer.
his skin is soaking up everything under the palm of her had. it is stretching, thirsty. the cream disappears in the shrubs of his capillaries.
you look a lot like this friend of mine.
hold up your hair. really?
i was fifteen, when we first met. she was a witch, a pythoness. she would teach me how to meditate. how to relax. how to shut down. and then i went crazy. first i tried aikido. then no-touch kung-fu.
impressive. did it work?
yeah, it worked so well that i made my friend's heart stop. they jump-started it again, but i ended up in bohnice asylum. i would like to try the ayahuasca, but i'm a bit scared. i have respect for drugs. i've taken quite a few.
there, it's done. i don't blame you. my knees were shaking as well.
will you rub it into my chest?
ama starts to laugh.
you can do that on your own.

simon is asking enrique. the shaman smiles. ayahuasca is like a woman. you have to court her, respect her, but you can't fear her. ask ama here. she can tell how she lived through it. at the beginning, she was spinning, vomiting. the ayahuasca knocked her off her feet, threw her to the ground. turned her inside out. and during the last ceremony, i saw how they became friends. ama doesn't fight it anymore. she stopped being afraid. that's how she gained control of the *princessita*.

mom, it's strange, this friendship with an herb. it holds me by the hand. i can still feel its grip; something inside of me comes alive. don't forget, it told me, you yourself are a flower—do you remember how flowers would grow out of you? how can i forget? tiny flowers are pouring out of me, spilling under my feet in all directions. they are green with a golden center, like thick moss it is growing inside of me. it flushes upward. i get lost in the flowers.

suddenly she remembers that some time ago, she knew how to be a plant.

04.23

the construction of the bridge isn't going according to plan, because there is no plan, but it is slowly taking shape. the only professional on the site, a native foreman, an expert on suspension bridges, has his hands full keeping a rein on the whole project. the men are flickering in the mist. the steam from the river is like a bad omen. one of them falls in...
in the afternoon, the czech expedition leaves, but they don't want to give up until the last minute. just the final tweaks at the bridge. simon attaches about a dozen boards by rope. lech pays the workers. you'll get the rest once it's finished.
ama packs her things. she's going with them to pucallpa just for a bit, to hear the voices of the people that she dreamed about here.

evening at the hotel los gavillanes. a bed. a real bed with a mattress and white sheets. maybe it, too, is just a dream. a spacious bathroom with a tub, light blue tiles, white towels, and a mirror. it's been so long since ama has seen herself in a mirror, she is almost startled. she's never seen this woman before. she looks beautiful.

04.24 pucallpa

mom, i don't have to call you to talk to you. but i do love hearing your voice.
and i like hearing yours. your grandmother had a dream about you.
you were guiding her through the jungle. she said you seemed to be at home here. then you told her that she had to go back before nightfall.

it's true. i am seeing granny a lot. and you? how are you doing?
people are asking me about you. family and friends. i'm bumping into people who are just shaking their heads at me. they're looking at me as if i were crazy. some of them are blaming me for letting you go. i was supposed make you, even force you to start getting treatment. for god's sake, i've worked my whole life in healthcare. i know how these things go. i lived through it myself. i got treatment, too. people keep telling me that i should have forced you to get treatment.
that's absurd. how the hell could you have forced me into treatment? am i a dog that you can just order to sit and stay?
i know, it's pointless to explain anything to anyone. i've known you since you were born. i know how you are. i know that when you decide to do something, there is no force that can dissuade you except you. they don't know that the only thing i have left is to stand beside you and respect your choice, no matter what it is, no matter how hard it is.

a postcard from pucallpa. a sad, fusty kitty, thin, hungry. mongrels everywhere, a sleeping vendor at the market stretched out among the piles of vegetables. a motor cart decorated with murdered chickens, bundles of colorful feathers hanging by the legs one after another, their heads swaying back and forth to the rhythm of the wheels. an overstuffed email inbox.

ama, i remember a long time ago, when i read burrough's the yage letters. i have the feeling that yage and ayahuasca are just different names for the same thing.

jeff, ayahuasca will show you true reality. if you give it space, it will shatter the screen of your home theater into pieces. but in that moment when i try to describe what a person experiences during a ceremony, i come to the bitter realization that my words are from this flat earth and don't have the dimensions to do so. they simply don't measure up to

the world of ayahuasca. and you just can't define it with an equation. sorry. "there's no point in defining the undefinable."

stop the dilly-dallying, ama. i don't buy it. especially not from you. i expect a better answer.

okay. imagine that you're stretched out across the entire planet like pasta dough. you're a colorful chunk of wax that's melting, dissolving. you feel it physically. it's happening to you. you are a *liana*, a jaguar, a dragonfly. you're the planet. i mean, it's really like that. you can put your hand through a wall. the molecules of your arm blend into the molecules of the plaster. you don't know where you begin and where you end. you're an observer and at the same time you're a part of everything, you're getting through it all but you solve nothing.
you can stare at the moon through the palm of your hand, and the moon is flipping you off. it's laughing at you, and it talks to you like a person would. you go to maloca, to the cafe on the river, and it's far away, but you still hear the shaman's singing. it's logically impossible, but still, you can hear his voice. his spirit watches over you, calls on you, something inside of you wakes up. you're no longer yourself, but rather, someone else. it crashes over your head. it enters your body and takes over. it picks you up and you follow, and though your head is completely spinning, you're marching majestically like a marionette. you're a programmed machine, like those monsters in star wars. a soldier's march. a confident smile. stop! you scream at yourself. you moron! halt! the shaman is standing in front of the maloca. c'mon, he says, let's sing together.

life doesn't belong to you, but your soul can go anywhere. everything begins in darkness. our bones lie in the ground, and you soak up strength from the soil. your body becomes overgrown with flesh, you're a predator, you control every muscle in your nose. you register every cell. you air out your blood, and you start to smell everything. you know that you have a key to go anywhere. you go to the realm of dark powers, you dress up in the force of a volcano. you're a tornado. you're moving fast, spinning over the landscape. everything is spinning inside you. you climax with an explosion. you disperse in a wave and spread out above the earth like an atomic mushroom.

your body is a container, a hallway, a rental tuxedo, a period costume, and above all of it, the timelessness of feeling, the feeling of timelessness. you can be whatever you want. it's all within reach of your mind. you can go anywhere. you see perdition, your own ability to be a coldblooded killer. you see images of the world. they are true, flawless. everything works together, blends together, falls into place. you fly to the planets, you pass galaxies, you take in the speed, the flickering of lights, and from that distance, it's all ridiculous and small. human toil, the absurdity of our wishes.

a person gets dizzy when she realizes her limits. i don't know how to explain it at our level, i don't know what i can compare it to. perhaps math, complete equations, feynmans' diagrams. it's like when gould plays bach, and you stand there, amazed by the capabilities of humankind.

in the evening at the hotel, by the pool, lech brings a coconut. he passes it around for everyone to take a gulp of its milk, until it's empty. and then he smashes the nut on the ground like a caveman. the marrow smells sweet. all around, there are waiters in white shirts, a sticky darkness, heat and music from the local bar. filip has been jumping in the water for hours. look, this is a cannon ball! splash! a body inside a geyser. brilliant! and now i'll do the tornado.

ama! simon! can you throw me in the water?

sure thing. simon by the feet and ama by the hands. on the count of three!

simon hesitates at the last moment.

do we throw him in on the count of three, or is it one two three, then go?!

are you three sheets to the wind, or what?

yeah, i had a few. ok, on the count of three!

filip is a fish without fins, a blue-eyed blond with a tooth already missing. he jumps in and swims out. the men throw him a line. ama doesn't water ski, she'd rather go to bed.

i meet my demons in the night. they are my strength.

04.26 santuario

the men are goofing around in the hammocks as if it were sunday. enrique arrives, carrying the wooden tobacco box that lech gave ama in pucallpa to bring to him. the box holds the money to give the workers when they finish the bridge.
ama stands between worlds.
but the bridge is not finished.
it isn't. there are no supplies to finish the job.
that's strange. could lech have miscalculated? what supplies?
we don't have rope to finish the railing.
so why don't you buy rope?

because we don't have the money.

but this money is for days you haven't even worked yet.
they're trying to explain it to her. they're gesticulating, squirming. ama doesn't know the meaning of their words, but slowly she begins to understand. they have no intention of rebuilding the bridge where it stands. they wanted to build it here, and not where it currently stands. the bridge is too far away, and it is dangerous. it was all just rushed. ginder explains excitedly how, during the construction, one of his friends fell into the river, as if everyone there didn't already know it. how his leg was burnt all the way to his knee.
only ama wasn't there. it is for her that he retells the story and fills the air with pain. all her life, it has seemed as if she were walking between worlds, between *paravanes*. she glances into compartments and boxes, and she's trying to make sense of the fences and the barbed wire. and then it comes to her: this is about how the world is divided into white people and everyone else. enrique orates. he shows her where they'll build the bridge, the one they really want. ama is looking into his eyes and trying to understand him. the eyes that live in the second world.
the wooden box with the money has released a dragon, and ama pokes it one last time. so, should i return the money to lech? ginder is boiling. a few others are angry too. they're here waiting for their pay, they can't be bothered with the bridge and the czech *gringo*. and ama is sitting on a fence with its pickets dividing her butt cheeks. a world divided into us

and them. it was never about this bridge. they wanted another bridge at another location. not here, where the gringos built it. not so high and not so far away. does it make sense? yes, the construction of the bridge is an opportunity to make some money. under the circumstances, it's the most logical reason. ama adjusts her attitude. she tries a different perspective, the voice of another storyteller, until finally she is standing with them, wearing their rubber boots, and she puts on a straw hat. now it's clear to her. the gringo has money, and i don't. i don't care what's going to happen in one month or one year. all i care about is what happens today. how will i feed my children tomorrow, the day after, and maybe next week? further on, i'm not concerned. i won't look that far. looking way ahead into the future is a luxury, a privilege of the rich, those who have plenty. and if i can earn some money for honest work, i have to take it, even though i know that the bridge that i'm building is bullshit. i'll give an impression that it's the greatest thing, until i get paid. i won't try to resolve what's going to happen in a year when the gringo will possibly return for a few days. and what's that great white man going to do?

ama watches as they divide the money. ginder's voice makes an impression on her. his lamenting tone. now, my friend can't walk. he almost lost his leg. she could see the boy: his leg burnt to a coal, it looked ready for amputation. which insurance company would pay for the doctor, sick leave, compensation—united amazon snakes and scorpions, inc.?

enrique has been given a choice: either they get a bridge like the white boys want, or they get nothing. should he have sent everyone home—all the people who he brought together, who came here from all over the region at the invitation of the shaman?

ama returns to the *tambo,* to the hut in the middle of the rainforest. to a place where "they and we" blend into a single bat yawn.

death by bug

gallo es muerte. the rooster is dead. he pecked at a bark beetle, and it got lodged in his throat and choked him. if the bug was going down, it was taking the cock with him. the rooster drama started when she was still in pucallpa. so, you're finally at peace, gallo. the men have surely

had a tasty dinner. and he was a looker. feathers like fireworks. he was loud and aggressive—she had to show him who's boss once or twice; now he's crowing in a heavenly henhouse.
ants, like little specters, are crawling out of the sweat-saturated shoes she wore when she first arrived here. each one carries a snip of foam from the padding inside. they are flickering like a digital image as they have removed all the padding at the toe of the shoe. it's time for a new pair of shoes.
she treats herself to a pear that she brought from pucallpa. she offers a piece to reina, who is cleaning off the table and is ready to do the dishes. would you like a taste? reina goes crazy when she sees how ama is cutting off pieces from the bruised pear. can't you see that you're wasting so much flesh, amita?! she starts to pick out the scraps from the trash. in santuario, nothing goes to waste. everything is consumed. ama is constantly learning.
the fire is dying out. no cooking or eating will happen in the afternoon. the evening will contain another ritual. at twilight, the shipibo emerge from the jungle, and reina sings *amor amor medita con amor amor amor.* it's a catchy tune that easily brings tears to her eyes.

ayahuasca arrives with the darkness, the sky pinned with stars. i'm standing in front of the *maloca*, above my head, a dome as if santini himself built it. stars with a pink southern cross. slowly i swallow it, and i take a ride on the milky way. i'm flying with you, and i'll crash into your dream, if you don't mind. in case you don't know by now, you can jump out of your body through your head. that's why the dead turn their eyes up.**04.28**

a backpack is called a urinar

i want not have wash sock. ama realizes how deranged she sounds when she expresses herself. but sometimes she forgets, she gets carried away and wanders off, far beyond the borders of her capabilities. the only exceptions are the rituals. after a shot of ayahuasca, foreign languages flow. an example that brings this to light is the episode with the backpack. during a conversation in the candlelight, stories are landing on the table

like cards during a game of whist. and without really realizing how, the conversation turns into a debate about the usefulness of a backpack, which in spanish is *mochila*. ama eagerly explains to reina and hegner that the same word in czech, *močila*, is past tense of "to pee." she leaves out that the conjugation of the verb is feminine in czech. those details are never discussed here anyway. a few days later, she finds out that her explanation has gotten slightly out of hand, and the jungle people have understood from her linguistic excursion that the spanish verb to pee, urinar, is the czech word for backpack. when she returns to pucallpa, hegner asks her during lunch, how much was her *urinar*?
my what?
your *urinar.*
he points to her backpack. *mochila*. how much did your *urinar* cost? flashback. oh, okay. she realizes what she did. rather than explaining the semantics of the misunderstanding, she tells him that she doesn't know how much her *urinar* cost, because it isn't hers. it's her friend lara's urinar.
in reality, she has probably said "my *urinar* is my friend, lara," but he looks like he understands. he nods, and in the background, the jungle rustles on. santuario is abandoned. the bridge builders, investors, workers...all of them are gone. the only thing left is a pendulous bridge without rails, its planks made of cedar randomly hovering in the air like gloves.
ama is singing in some made-up language, but it sounds great. the river is accompanying her with clusters of neologic variations. it's steaming. two dragonflies are sunk into each other on her body like a piece of jewelry made of rubies. on the *plazo de spiritos*, she opens a basket and tears out the meat, a bubble of light floats towards her. she climbs into it like it's a ship, and the bubble bursts. the steam over the river foams upward, and a genie appears. he dwells here. he spreads out below the dome.
your wish is my command.
ama is wondering how she summoned him, and she doesn't know what to wish for.
anything. your wish is my command.

are you good or are you evil?
i am what you make me. you alone can modify me.

she's dreaming about a *wacra renaco*, a tree from which comes a medicinal sap. it enters her dream like a ghost. enrique once brought her to one.
she's rolling her head in front of her down the path through the jungle. she's thinking, pondering, after an hour of hiking, the giant tree stands before her. roots above the ground waving in all directions, crisscrossing one another. one chop of a machete, the wound is bleeding white. using rolled up leaves, the shaman collects the milk into a bowl. he quietly mumbles. *wacra renaco*. ama touches the sap, rubs it between her fingers, smells it. don't be afraid. taste it. like cream. sticky and agile. it pushes the tongue to the upper palate. she feels sorry for the bleeding tree. she worries that it feels pain. she puts her ear up to the soft skin of the trunk and listens to the tree's voice.
i know nothing about pain. i only know the way things are.

05.01

it was the first of may, a time of love.[12] but there are no doves here. the trees stare at her as, in the middle of the night, she prays to the water to wash away the heat from her body. her fingers feel like rubber toys. in the morning, the sky tears open. finally. it is late night, the first of may. at the end of macha's "may," everyone is dead. the prisoner prays to the heavens while on his pilgrimage, and he greets his country: *oh, my beautiful country, my beloved land . . . my cradle and my grave . . . my heritage bestowed . . . my one and only home.* maybe she's homesick.
the river is busy. men emerge with cargo on their heads, their backs and shoulders. they're balancing it all. it often seems that they're carrying more than they weigh themselves. belisario arrives. even luis

[12] *Translator's note*: The author is referring to the Czech poem, "May," by Karel Hynek Mácha, '*Twas late evening—on the first of May/ twilight in May—a time of love/ tenderness beckoned in the voice of doves.*

shows up. everyone gathers for lunch. enrique discreetly mentions that there are natives in the jungle who feast upon human flesh. luis gives him a toothless laugh, reina encourages everyone. *servido*. she's adding seconds to tin plates, topping off their fresh tea. the men begin debating. they're preparing to repair the *maloca*. the roof is leaking, and some of the floorboards need replacing. they want to begin in the afternoon, but it looks like it's going to rain hard, so they'll start tomorrow. they're all in sync. they all agree. of course— *mañana*. during the afternoon storm, diego arrives, and three women with him. three generations of shipibo natives. the grandmother and her granddaughter have the same chubby and radiant face. both of them are giggling with unbridled lightness. but linda is gloomy like the day, as if she were carrying three generations of sorrow and wrongdoing. only when she hugs reina does her face light up for a moment. the mischievous she-devil in reina transfers to her, even if it's just for a bit. the women spread their work on the floor and sit in a circle. they're stringing beads. linda is picking through reina's hair, and what she finds, she puts in her mouth. diego notices that ama is staring at them. perhaps her jaw has dropped just a little. that's our culture,our tradition, you know? ama nods. she tries not to look disgusted. it really isn't such a big deal. bugs are quite a decent source of protein. it's a healthy tradition.

grandma norma heats up a pot in the kitchen. every other minute, she sniffs in, snorts a loogie that breaks up and rises to the back of her throat, then she lets out a gargle, a belch, a cough, leans over, and spits. a duck runs over and slurps it up. and that goes on over and over in waves. it takes on a rhythm of its own.

reina is dyeing linda's hair. they have mixed the black color from the marrow of the unripe *huita* fruits. ripe *huita* is added to sugar-cane moonshine. its juice is also good for the blood, and it helps digestion. reina braids strips of linda's hair, and from time to time, she finds a moment to take a puff from her pipe. ama is watching. diego is singing songs of his tribe, and then he gives a lecture about the shipibo language. ayahuasca is called *oni*, a woman is *ainbo*, water—

onpash. a rock— *macan*, the sky is *nai*, house is *shobo*. diego's friend is a professor at london university, working there because he married an englishwoman. diego says he would also have liked to marry an englishwoman and move across the ocean to europe. and then he proceeds to ask ama if she would like a full-blooded shipibo indian.
but i'm not an englishwoman.
diego wouldn't mind, he says. he's generous. he'd be willing to marry a czech.
but then you wouldn't have any full-blooded children. why don't you just sing something? you sing very well.

05.03

diego has been stung by a black scorpion. he shows his calf during breakfast. it hurts terribly, and i'm having a hard time breathing, but i'll survive. i treat it with *sábila*. i'll be fit as a fiddle in a few days. here, i caught it and put it into this box. it's still alive, so don't open it yet.
ama gapes at diego and then at the little box that is sitting on the table next to a bowl of salt. she's looking forward to her solitude in the *tambo*. another 14 days. she's quite in need of it. there are too many people around her. after a few days, she's feeling claustrophobic.
i will give you the *uchu sanango*, *medicina fuerte*, says enrique. you'll be watched for two days. if you don't freak out, another world will open up to you. you have to realize that mother nature heals everything, but you have to believe in her. you can use herbs for anything, for medical treatment, black magic. their effect is always based on the way you think. if you think positively, you'll have a positive result.
ama nods slightly, she understands those words, but their meaning somehow escapes her. to think in the language of the white tribe means to judge, sort, dissect, and over-discuss everything.

in the evening, it awaits her on the mosquito net. it looks like a toy from a store. nothing moves. neither ama nor the tarantula. it's pretty big, black, and furry. what am i supposed to do with you? i'll wait until you crawl somewhere else. just don't crawl anywhere near my bed. i hope we'll both come to some sort of agreement, since we share the same planet. the people of the jungle resolve this issue directly, that means they use the machete or they lite up a mapacho and blow smoke at the creature. i don't have a mapacho so i will go get my machete, and in the meantime, you'll get lost. if you're not gone by the time i get back, there will be a massacre, which i would really like to avoid.

the female tarantula knows that the future is woven from the threads of the past. most of the time, she lives alone. her dwelling is entwined by silk thread, and there is a woven doormat at its entrance that vibrates like a guitar string when something approaches. during mating season, the male looks for a partner. as soon as he arrives at the welcoming door mat, he plays on the string. he sings and dances to entertain his chosen mate who waits inside. depending on his performance, she will invite him in, or she'll refuse him. in both cases, he will most likely end up as her dietary supplement because the female needs proteins to feed her offspring to health. the tarantula also eats bugs, grasshoppers, lizards, and mice. sometimes even small birds.

ama returns with the machete. the tarantula is gone. only sapo is munching on his evening celery. it's strange, after a while in the jungle, a person calms down. stops being so alert and has the feeling that nothing can happen. how many times has she put on her rubber boots without turning them over and shaking them out? that's what you call negligence. so, stop slacking off, always wear a headlamp, and watch where you step.

"strangely enough i was less afraid of being afraid than of being unafraid."

exactly. a person is afraid not to fear. that straitjacket we've gotten used to can seem better than freedom, when we don't know what to do with it.

a scorpion's teachings • every banana speaks a different language

when she comes out in the morning, enrique is sitting on the bench in front of the *tambo*. he's carving out a piece of light-colored root. u*chu sanango*. he's shredding it like horseradish. he explains that it isn't good to combine medicines. you have to start with one plant, then another. some herbs are simply too strong and can scare away the spirits of other herbs. herbs are like people. sometimes they try to push each other around or they get jealous when others are making love. these uber-herbs stay inside you forever, they'll always be your allies if you open yourself to them. but when you first welcome them into your system, you have to adhere to a strict diet, and you can't mix them with anything else.

in the meantime, ginder is setting up the buffet, two bowls with plantains and clean water. no, no, the shaman says. you will not eat yet. you have to take your medicine. he wraps the grated horseradish in a cloth and squeezes it hard above a glass. here, drink it.

he gives her the shot glass. great, cheers. after she swallows the drink, her engine stops. oh shit! her throat's on fire. her diaphragm is like a trampoline, her voice is incinerated. water. hic! water quickly! but enrique shakes his head. he doesn't want to give her a drink. he tells her that it will pass. the words "it will pass" are also a local incantation, *it will pass* is just like the word *mañana*. it will pass. of course, it will pass! everything passes in good time. hic! the shaman shows mercy and hands her a tin cup. just one sip. two gulps sizzle down to no avail. she's still braying like a donkey.

it'll pass, he nods soothingly. it'll kick in soon. you'll start feeling dizzy and you'll get a fever.

how do you feel, *mareada*?

well, the stuff made a unique entrance. it's probably kicking in.

she lies there passively and *uchu sanango* is shooting through her veins, burning out her bones. enrique and ginder tear down another termite colony. there are corpses lying all over the place. a crowd, mass graves, a concentration camp. dear god, turn it off. turn it off. insects are flying in slow motion. she swats a fly in the air. the *tambo*'s spinning, tripping over its own feet. so she'd rather lie down, but that doesn't help much, either. her temples are banging and her head is like a smoking oven. her hands feel like they're in a deep fryer. her heart is being ground into a burger, just her legs walk away. she thinks she's groaning and moaning. ginder leans over to her and touches her feet. does it hurt?

i see two of you, ginder.

you have a fever, i'll lead you to the river.

no, i don't think i can walk.

that'll pass.

he says that he needs to go somewhere but he'll be back, and he walks away, emphasizing the word, *ahorita*. immediately. another word from the family of *mañana* phrases.

she passes out and sees scribbles on the roof. thousands of beetles. her thighs and calves are cast in cement. ginder is here. did he get back that fast or did time slow down? come, you need to pour some cold water on you. it'll feel good. can you walk? i'll try. whoooh! how is she going to fit her two marble columns into her rubber boots? the steep access to the river turns into an actual cliff, a neck-breaking fall off a quarry. she just can't understand it. the cold water helps, especially for those two heads of hers. if only one of them would fall off and swim away. she acts normal while she's putting on her clothes. she stands on a rock on one foot and puts on her sock. the only thing is, she can't tell which of her four feet is the target. the water is blurry on the rock or is the rock blurry in the water? she can't tell which is which. balance kicks the chair out from under her. her socks and her pants jump into the mud. ama falls, she almost sprains her ankle, wrist, neck. ginder helps her back to the hotel. she asks him to tell the receptionist to finally turn on the air conditioning.

does it hurt much?

what?

your feet, your calves? do you want a massage? no, i don't want a massage. i want to be alone. ok. can you handle it on your own?

she's sitting on her bunk and staring. when she tries to focus, everything seems to feather out. she is surrounded by memories. they lie there like bags filled with garbage in the streets of manhattan.

the garbage strike in the middle of the hot summer caused the new yorkers to lose their cool. garbagemen of the world unite! the rest of you can go fuck yourselves! the big apple was rotting in garbage, a medieval stench shoved its way through the metropolis like a workhorse. a big feuding apple. we wanted to be together but we were on different continents. you loved that fruit, but i couldn't bite into it the right way. our two-years-too-long three-year relationship—we were connected by a river of love, a sea of promises, and buckets of good will, and later on, by credit cards and shared friends. but the atlantic finally won. it wedged itself between us, just like your mother, father, the holy spirit. your inheritance. amen.
the daughter's bittersweet return to the hundred-spire mother.[13] in mid-march she goes to the ruzyne airport and tries to convince the customs officers that those elegantly packed crates and boxes are her personal items: books, flippers, neoprene. nothing to declare, gentlemen. only the knife that's sticking out of my back is not mine.

your promises faded before my eyes, like the skin of corpses in a morgue.

she looks at her tattered fingernails. she could use a manicure. she takes out her nail clippers and clip, clip, but she can't tell which finger she's grooming. her fingers, spread out like a fan, are blending together, fading into one another. it seems like someone is laughing in the distance. she decides to continue with her toes, but luckily, she can't bend her legs so today's treatment is over. the beauty salon is now closed. the spirits are creeping closer, spreading dusk all around. no food, only hunger. the dinner table is set. the plate chatters its teeth at her. silence. i want to eat in peace. and on the plate, blurry snakes cut into pieces, creamy with a thin black spine. they taste like flour and water. raw dough. someone else is biting off the food in her mouth, someone else's teeth are chewing the mouthful. her tongue can't reach anything. she decides

[13] *Translator's note*: The author is referring to the city of Prague and its many towers.

to complain that the portions are too small. damn it. if she has to eat snakes, then at least she wants to fill her belly.
the food has helped. the sea calms down. her eyes can focus in a single spot again. she has a content feeling in her stomach. four *plantanos* deposited like money in the bank. or maybe there were only two.
the nightly roof-munchers are doing a classic number. something nearby is walking around making noise. probably a monkey or a capybara or perhaps the *ajaroro*?[14] impossible. that horrific gobbler lives on the island of the blessed, and even if this place looks like a paradise, it is definitely not an island. she feels too queasy to go out and face it, so all she does is shout.
get out of here or shut up! suddenly, there is silence.

05.06

in the morning, she cleans blood off her white pants. this seems to fascinate her. *zancudos* can bite through a wool blanket. how do they do it? she needs to wake up her legs from their morning stiffness. she shuffles her way to the plantation. it always smells different. today, curry and fresh coriander dominate. perhaps she's overestimated her abilities. she's overheated like wagner's parsifal and collapses at the first banana tree. so, a retreat it is. on the way back, she picks up a flute, and she whittles it in the *tambo*. flakes of sugarcane look like human skin, with hair and veins soaked in juices. she sucks a freshly cut piece even though the shaman has forbidden it. she isn't supposed to consume anything with sugar in it. no cakes or pastries. she could really go for some pancakes or crumpets with blueberry sauce. the sweet taste of sugarcane wakes up her taste buds. she brings out her hidden files; something will blow her way.

ama stands at the main boulevard in zlín by the czechoslovak airlines office. she holds a lollipop in her hand.

---

[14] *Translator's note*: The *ajororo*, the "horrific gobbler," is an imaginary creature from a short story by Jaroslav Hašek, titled "Natural Science Journal" about the new editor of a nature magazine who decides to invent species to attract new readers.

daddy has to go to mongolia, you know? he's going to build a factory there. so that girls like you can wear shoes. he'll be back in two months. the bus takes off with her father in the window. her mother beside her. liquid dragonflies on her eyelashes fall silently and turn into tiny dots on her violet dress. don't cry, amalie, you're making it harder for him. he'll feel sad. ama waves goodbye, with sadness just half a sigh away, she holds it behind her jaw, she swallows it, never to let it out again.

at last it pours out of her, all those little dots that she's been saving for all these years.

the word level sounds different in different tongues and ears. after a customer service call, they send an expert to fix her bed. they have never heard of a level. that's why all the structures, especially staircases, look the way they do. ginder bends over and looks at the bunk. when he stands up, he proclaims that the bed is straight. look, all legs are the same height. he smiles.
what can you say to that? if all the legs are the same height, it has to be straight. that's just logic.
that's true, ginder, but the ground is slanted, so these legs have to be shorter than those for it to be entirely straight.
he doesn't quite see her point, but he finally does what the *gringa* tells him to do. the result is ginder's eternal smile, followed by a smirk that would make jack nicholson proud. as good as it gets.
the sutures on her skull are cracking, contracting, creaking, her bones are dissolved, she has no control over her body. how do you say oh fuck in spanish?
the creek. she has to get to the creek. the cold water sizzles in her hair, spins her around, undressing her out of her fever. there's only one thing: she can't bring herself to climb up the steep steps that are really not steps at all. ama just calls them that to confirm that it's possible to elegantly run to the top. she's graciously digging in the dirt, grabbing onto a clump, a branch of *liana*. the mud is slipping from under her feet. but that's not the reason she fails. you're going to die here, amazon warrioress. go back to prague.

she's incredibly hungry but has no craving for plantains. what are her options? why, she'll have more plantains. the thought of ginder keeps coming back to her—his permanent smile. what kind of man is he? he's constantly grinning. dear god! how is that possible? it's not human, a creature that has the ability to look happy from morning to night. and it's quite possible that he grins in his sleep. he never falters, he never gets a cramp, never passes out from exhaustion. he can't possibly be human. these natives are all deranged in one way or another. back home, in her country, no one grins like that, because for someone to laugh or even smile, they have to have a reason. and it has to be a logical reason, at that. smiling all day long is just not humanly possible. certainly, that can be proven scientifically. a normal human being doesn't grin like a fool just because it's morning, and she has something to eat and a roof over her head, or because she is just seeing what she saw yesterday and the day before that. a person with a smile like that is suspicious and gets on every normal human being's nerves. it's a lot more reasonable and natural to be in a bad mood, to be pissed off, to complain and curse. you could almost say, the more pissed off a person is, the more intelligent she looks, and if someone keeps smiling all day for no reason, that person is an idiot.

the lightning bugs are waking up to go to work. ama is browsing through the latest edition of *house & garden* published by the local flora and fauna. an evening in style. though that unblemished reputation of our supreme scientific-narcissistic civilization is tarnished a little by blondes. jeff, you would like this. a story unexpectedly emerged from the ultra-prolific uterus of the jungle.
it's getting dark. the jungle blonde attempts to light up a kerosene candle, a *lamparína* that looks like a beat-up can of condensed milk with a burner attached. fortunately, the blonde knows not to drink it. otherwise, this joke would have ended way too soon. she holds the can in one hand and a lighter in the other. and yes, the blonde also knows how to use a lighter. she runs her thumb down the serrated wheel, and voilà! however, the blonde does not bring the flame closer to the wick, but rather leans the lamparína over the lighter and then freezes.

what the hell is happening? is this another moronic lesson in the law of physics? to hell with that tacky ol' newton and his gravity. the kerosene is pouring down her arms, onto her rubber boots and to the floor of the *tambo*. is she supposed to sleep in that smell? she could just light a match...it smells like a gas station and a sign above her head says *greenpeace forever*.

"a warrior accepts in humbleness what he is."

some people really get the shit-end of the stick.

05.08

a state holiday, to mark the end of the second world war. no one here has a clue. here, it depends on which sort of world you're talking about. and that concludes our world news for tonight.

my bones are melted. i can't do anything, so i'm sucking the marrow out of raindrops and stuffing myself with them.
hey raven, i'm having dreams of food. what should i do with them? embrace them. hunger is just a feeling that can be controlled. learn to master your feelings. you should know, the raven doesn't fight. the raven wins. imagine that you're eating and then relish every bite, color, smell, taste. feel it with every cell in your body, with all five senses. when you figure out how to fill yourself this way, your cravings disappear.
advice as good as gold. but why not try it, just to see if there's a chance it works? she's got nothing on her plate anyway. after a stint of buoyant fantasies and the empty chewing of imaginary bites of freshly baked bread with butter and a soft-boiled egg, her gluttonous twitches don't disappear entirely, but their curve of effect is drastically reduced. quite interesting.
besides *platanos verde* that taste like a mushy potato, sweet bananas grow all over the place. those are forbidden during her fast, because most strong herbs don't favor bananas. *platano seda, platano isleña,* and *platano moquicho*, ama's favorite. each one of them uniquely rolls on the tongue. they each speak a different language to the taste buds

when she imposes her own stories on them, her memories of a sweet life. there are sixteen different types of plantains, enrique claims, but ama counts about six. she could be wrong, though, or she could have misunderstood. no one eats before the ceremony. at most, just a quick lunch and then a fast until evening. especially no bananas. the goddess ayahuasca can't stand bananas, she will scream them out of you before you can cough up a pasqueflower.

there are fires here, in the trees, the roots, they're searing through, separating the bones from the skin. the ghost *uchu sanango* clusters and seethes, seven voices and nine heads, an infinite number of arms. i will warm you up. i flow through your bones, i heat up your blood. i sear all the nooks and crannies. swallow my breath, and the sea will begin to boil within you. *planta fuerte*. for two days, her extremities have been brittle. something between atrophy and extrrreeemely strained muscles. today she is walking like a human again. she even dares to do her laundry in the creek. her white shirt flutters in the clear water. she stretches the fabric out in the sun.

in the afternoon, she folds the clean shirt. her veteran shirt. her globetrotter shirt. she has shared everything with it: australia, thailand, mexico. in the summer, this shirt will turn 15. when she bought it in '93, that thin, luxurious fabric for which she spent an ungodly price, she didn't expect how much it would pay off. but it served its time in the corporate world, and then it climbed up mountains, pyramids, walked through deserts and beaches. it's still in one piece. this shirt is a symbol. it should have its own name. perhaps she will baptize it before she parts with it. it's the best piece of clothing she ever had.

we bought it together, lara, but you probably don't remember that. we knew each other only briefly. a moment of infatuation. your story and your apartment on maislová street. the grace in your culinary skills, your vegetable salad with rice and shrimp. what should have been years of friendship and sharing, laughter and wishes, were only a whisper before they were over. suddenly, like a lovers' breakup, the razor harshness with which i cut you off condemned us to years of silence. how long does it take for a person to let off steam, to soften up, to cool off before she forgives?

and now you're with me, as if you never left. you were always with me, just like that shirt, accompanying me everywhere. and now i can finally let go of you. my face afloat in tears. i'm releasing still waters from prison, they're forming letters as they drip through the bars of my graph paper journal. lara, i had to lock myself up in a *tambo* in the middle of a screaming forest, to pull the marrow from the bone and the rustle of the palm trees, and let it flow away to the opposite bank. i'm not asking you to forgive me. this is my doing; this is on me. i have to forgive myself. i'm sitting under a mosquito net among clumps of snotty toilet paper and raven feathers. if only you could see me, you wouldn't know whether to laugh at me or join me. that shirt is lying on my pillow, folded almost as if it were ironed. it still looks fantastic.

it's the hour of bats. their caribou-like heads making smoke rings in the trees with their clear blue silhouettes. time flows by like liquor, the bats are soaking it in, climbing across the sky, where the darkness falls off them.

05.09

i'm waking up again with an old head. i can't stand that feeling. an old head. i can't put it away, because my new head is off somewhere, and today i simply can't afford to be without one, because it's pouring. i don't want to be full of water again. i'm already filled to the brim. and wildflowers are blooming inside my mind.

the scorpion knows

a lizard is sitting on her notebook, watching as she writes. it licks the date and wags its tail like a dog. a blue-eyed butterfly lands on her hair. she likes that moment when she blends in with her surroundings, when the bugs and birds stop taking notice of her. it's happening more and more often. lizards slide over her, butterflies sit beside her and chat. in a moment like this, everything flows. she knows, even time needs time to itself. she must keep thinking about the black scorpion that's been

trapped in her box for the past few days. she knows that it's still alive. she hears it in the night. she feels the creature resonating inside of her. its voice circling around.
the scorpion is a mystic, but as a true mystic, it doesn't get hung up on its mysticism, it doesn't blare it out at the universe or all the dimensions where it dwells. it doesn't feel hunger, and it doesn't mind waiting. it meditates, and it looks forward to shedding the skin it has put on for now, ama sees its magic, its spells, when its soul passes through her dreams. it turns arrows into thistles, pebbles into rain. before she enters her door, she will let out her genie to paint the place with rollers of light and, in the blink of an eye, it will change into an eagle that instantly stops a storm. she recharges her palms over a fire as she sings to it. she shares everything with the fire. she picks at her food and offers it to all the languages around her. she doesn't talk much about herself. the scorpion knows that "me" is just a necessary linguistic tool, even though it indicates something that doesn't exist. when she says "me," she doesn't really mean "me" because there is no such thing.
i must have gotten into the head of that white girl, she hears the scorpion ruminating. she could come and join the game. she could turn everything upside down in one move. i can hear her. she's thinking about how she's going to save me. people in the jungle don't dwell on things like that. they accept how things are. but she keeps turning everything over in her mind, planning her actions while wrapped in explosives like an assassin who believes that she is on the shortest path to god's canteen. rescuers of the world, unite! she blames her most recent rush of guilt on the snake that got underfoot. she has it engraved on her forehead in capital letters: i killed an innocent snake! but in secret, she believes that her score will improve. oh karma, karma, a classic fabrication of the human race. how crazy they go trying to game it. she's on the move, coming closer, her rescue squad is in full gear. she's just a bit scared shitless that i might sting her.
ama crosses the river and sneaks towards the kitchen so no one will see her. she grabs the scorpion. i won't cut you, slow girl, even though you're doing me this disservice, because "i" am generous. i don't know the laws of revenge. i hear your heart beating, your head throbbing. you have good

intentions, after all, i know. i stung diego because he had it coming, but if i did it to you, at this point, it would make no difference.
ama opens the box and quickly jumps away. she watches as the scorpion climbs out awkwardly. if you save one life, it's as if you've saved the whole world, they say.

05.10

a week of rain. the sun is rotting somewhere on a compost pile, and the local gossip mongers are sounding off in the trees. a morning clash with a spider derails her a bit. though she thoroughly shook out both of her rubber boots before she put them on, it lingered in there like a blockhead. maybe it fell asleep. she almost had another corpse on her conscience.
i hear your voice all the time in the crowns of the trees, derek walcott. love after love: *feast on your life*. life is a feast and i am fasting. when a person fasts like this, her senses intensify, everything becomes clear, with sharp outlines. every detail leaves distinctive prints someone is screaming that something has just happened—a bird. it sounds like a loud, squeaking door. the natives call it the *tatatoo*. in the distance, it reminds me of a lament, an endlessly stammered tao in the amazon, announcing the arrival of the next train. it'll be here in a minute or two.
a downpour like a bull in a china shop—no restraint. it knocks off the roof. strips of palm trees, broken branches, trampled flowers lie there on the ground in the mud. ama writes a note that her all-in-one banquet hall and office are now without a roof. she uses present tense because she hasn't learned past yet. and also, she understands that by definition, past tense is no longer relevant. it's time to completely give up on the past—so she doesn't even need to bother with the past tense.
ginder has come to fix her roof. he isn't speaking, because the highest shaman in this neck of the woods has forbidden him to. but in the evening after work, he sits down for a while on a bench and then, suddenly, smiles. ama jumps up and screams. i can't believe it! what did you just do?
a quick swing of the machete and the lizard is cut in two. its tail is

squirming before her, but the lizard disappears to safety in the closest bush. ginder's infinite smile. the civilized white amazon warrioress's disappointment. she yells at him in czech, and it's clear to him that she's not giving him a compliment. he begins to explain something. probably that the tail will grow back. maybe that it's good for the lizard, that it'll be stronger for it, or something like that. but ama is not listening. all she can see is two pieces where one body used to be. she doesn't want to see ginder. she doesn't want to share the same sky with him, this day that's slowly sailing away.
go away. i want to sleep.
he gets up.
don't you miss your friend? *pareja*.
no, i really don't.

he confides to her for the hundredth time that he has no lover. he has to be without a lover for a year to absorb energy so he can become a shaman.
go on absorbing energy. clearly, you're about to burst.

the fog flows through the forest. something is coming, forming in front of her eyes. silhouettes, stones in the lake. it grows clearer as time goes on. she's drowning in it. she's walking through a desert, sunlight seeping through her skin, fiery blossoms springing from her head.

05.12

in the morning, she snoops around. someone has been here, but she didn't hear anyone coming. the water in the creek smells like fish. around the *tambo*—a total lunatic asylum. everyone here is busy in some way. a fly plays the cornet, it's striped like a prisoner with a red trumpet. a carpenter bee has made a home out of one of the sticks holding up her writing desk. it's buzzing a lot, bothered by the white girl who keeps sketching and scribbling. apparently, the whole wide world can fit into its heart. is there any room for a little drag of a girl with a rigid smile?

the heart is a strange place. sometimes, it's so small that not even a single person will fit in there without her legs, hands, and head sticking out.

her old friend is on the laundry line—a giant praying mantis. this time she has a lover on her back. the male, half her size, is embracing her and holding on for dear life, embedded like a nozzle in a gas tank. an hour of filling up. they have chosen ama's underwear for the deed. glad that i washed them for you. the female, unaroused, climbs about, munching on the underwear elastic. the male is holding on. *do you know, young man, what awaits you as soon as she gets her fill*? she looks like a dry stick. he looks like a thin green twig. such a pretty couple. "i don't want to marry you," he assures her. "you had your chance but you missed it." "yeah, yeah," she laughs. it seems appropriate. good old fitzgerald, right here in this jungle.
an unusual fragrance of dry land and plants fills the plantation. the rainy season is gone. there are fewer mosquitos. but still, shadows are circling around her. the spirits of the rainforest. to be or not to be, the answer is clear. it's beautiful outside, but inside, it's d-day. d for depression.

"the world that we perceive is an illusion...created by a description... we are complacently caught in our particular view of the world, which compels us to feel and act as if we know everything there is to know about the world."

what a mess! her grandma would say. the rice spilled on the ground like a broken rosary. it just slipped somehow. what now? she picks up what she can, dusting off the soil. it's probably going to be crunchy between her teeth. it doesn't matter. she won't die of hunger. she'll sweep the rest of it into the bushes so that the ants won't build her a highway on the floor.
they're celebrating halloween on the other bank. ripened papayas with windows eaten out of their faces. all it needs is a candle. the river's surface looks like a rock concert. light beams and smoke. an overgrown iguana stretches out by the bank closer to her. it has climbed out of

the stone age. she almost forgot how ancient its tongue is. i want to live fast, to be with you, someone says inside of her. rain inside me, or outside. where exactly is it raining? where am i standing? on the bank. between us, a river flowing through your watershed. i'm staying here, daddy, tearing myself to pieces. i know her, that girl who wants to go with you. she's paddling toward something she could never reach. by midnight, she is running against the current of time, distant from only herself. the smell of foreign lands and strange bodies. my old lover, rei, reads poems to me so i can fall asleep. i cry in his arms for my father. i'm missing him in every embrace.

05.17

"if you don't understand, then you're on the right track, it's when you think you understand that you have a problem."

in that case, i'm on the right track.

reina is teeming with fairies who are constantly talking, roaming about, they can't stay still in one place. she picks off two banana leaves and heats them over a fire. she pinches off a piece of dough and rolls out a tortilla with an oval stone that looks like a large cucumber. *kachanga*. a tortilla made from flour and water. she puts the flat bread into the banana leaves like a letter in an envelope and carefully puts them on a grid above the hot coals. reina creates a whirlpool of sounds like a jacuzzi, she's kneading and mixing and making a mess all around her. she takes out the tortilla from the envelope and throws it back on the fire, waiting until it inflates and dark spots start to appear on its body.
mira, mira!
i'm watching, but i can't see. i want to be alone, reina, i just can't tell you that without hurting your feelings.
don't be sad, amita. i'm your *mama de santuario*. don't be afraid.

death has the rapidly fluttering wings of a hummingbird, a snowflake sizzling in the steam above the river.

i'm lying in the *tambo*, and i see no end in sight. i want to curl into the fetal position at death's feet, but in reality, i am searching for you. you're standing in an horologe of women, they're pouring out water from pitchers that they're handing from one to the other. they are spilling life and death. mom, i'll take your smile and some of your potato soup.

sometimes i'm so far away from myself that it's unbearable.

aya is on a roll, she's funny and frisky. ama hears laughter. *uchu sanango*. it's looking over her shoulder, into her cup. it's still in control. it occurs to ama how those two roosters would settle inside of her. aya is turning her stomach inside out. a pair of eyes is staring at her from inside a bucket. the eyes give a wink, she's looking good. a cramp behind her neck, it clenches its claws. pecking at her scruff, turning the world upside down. mass graves, lime and gas. soldiers are dying, surprisingly they clutch at their young lives, their organs eviscerated, calling for their mother. which mother? whoa, everything is moving too fast. her hands are locked onto her head. someone is leaning over her. how do you feel? i'm cold, and i'm sad.
why?
i'm homesick. i miss my country.
ama doesn't understand what the shaman is saying. she isn't out of it enough. what does *llorar* mean? i don't know that word.
when water flows from your eyes.
aha, i don't know spanish. to cry. no, i'm not crying, enrique, but i would like to. i see through your body, clumps of light twirling, changing their colors and shapes. it is good to cry. crying extracts salt. when you feel cold, call upon the ghost of *uchu sanango*. he will warm you up. he is inside of you. he might come if you sing to him.
uchu sanango. ama thinks about him and possibly wants to sing, but before she opens her mouth, the spirit is already in her, breathing flames. parts of her body are swelling and retracting and turning inside out.
ama is sitting and hugging her knees, swaying back and forth rhythmically. no tears in sight, as if the ghost forgot about her. a little girl comes and stands in front of her. she has large eyes and long eyelashes. she watches

ama intensely. she is lovely, just standing there and watching. ama watching ama. and finally, it is here—the river she has been waiting for. you're crying? why? the girl has a coneflower in her hand with a large, brown center. she puts it in ama's hair. and suddenly ozzy appears in the middle of the maloca, screaming across the jungle: *mama, i'm coming home*.

18.05

"power showed me that you had to be pushed mercilessly or you wouldn't lift a finger."

that made her laugh. she is having panic for breakfast and depression for dinner. still, she can feel the hand that guides her.

hegner is coming from the river carrying plantains. reina is singing to herself in the kitchen as she glides back and forth from the fire to the tub. she is cooking *sudado de pescadito*. water is boiling in another pot for tea. i'll make you malba[15] to calm your stomach, *si, mi niña*? over there, in your country, do you have *malba*, too?
yes, on the walls and on the ceilings, but that would be hard to explain. *malva* is a bush. you brew up the leaves and it tastes like slime. no reina, we have other plants.
the same plants with other names?
no, completely different plants, malva doesn't grow where i'm from. these folks don't understand that there are places where bananas don't grow. how do you explain that? how can you explain snow?
and everything here is a diminutive. amita, *queres sopita*? do you want a "little" soup? *calientita*. a "little" hot.
yes, amita will have a "little" soup.

enrique is in a good mood today. he's been cooking ayahuasca all day. when he found out that ama ate yuca, he gets mad at reina. don't you

---

[15] *Translator's note*: The Spanish word for "malva" phonetically sounds like "malba" in Czech, which means painting. The author was playing on the phonetic similarities of the words and their different meanings.

know that she can't have any yuca? *uchu sanango* can't stand yuca, she'll have stomach cramps!
reina calms him down. it was only one bite.
she can't have even that one bite. *uchu sanango* is too strong of a plant.
ama tells herself that it can't be that bad, but after a few hours, she's sprawling.
the shaman makes her a concoction of herbs. sip on this, but don't take big gulps. the tea is bitter like centaury, her eyes are bulging out, but in twenty minutes she feels relief.

dawn brings fires and a sheer, full moon that is stuck over the river and will soon be cooked.
the air is getting darker and thicker, and a flame flares beneath a family of withered and burned-out pots. the logs are speaking, a kerosene lamp sits on the dining table. enrique is wrapping mapacho, he has a tool for it that looks like a little flag. through the scent of tobacco, he tells a story about how during the last ritual, ten evil ghosts came to him and sent the local *curanderos*. he was clinging by a thread, but at the end, he defended himself. just in case, he would fast until tomorrow, until he had more strength.
life is liquid, elusive, eternal. when i turn off all the babble, the wide screen opens up and projects. at night, i am back in that same place, in a different universe, where i speak a language that i do not know. i don't know what i'm saying, but everyone understands me. before daylight, i'm falling from a bedrock into a waterfall. i climb up a cliff, scratch my way up, and the spirit of *uchu sanango* pushes me. i am flying head first, down into the gorge.

you see, i told you that *uchu sanango* does not sit well with yuca. it will catch up with you. if you don't stick to your diet, the spirits of strong plants can turn against you. but all is not lost. you have a few days without salt and *uchu sanango* will calm down again.

uchu sanango. ama knows that is the truth. during the last ritual, she felt for herself how it broke her down.

05.21
sex with yourself is still sex

the cafeteria is crowded with little fuzzballs. sweet baby chicks. they are still featherless. they just have a funny-looking down. they are chirping. reina's eyes light up when she looks at them. - yes, we'll soon have more chickens. ama embraces them in her lap. she pets them and teaches them their first words of czech. you're growing for the cooking pan, my little cuties. mama reina sits down in this commotion of chicks. at the table, she picks through the rice, cuts peppers, and gives advice. everything that you ever wanted to know about sex is presented vividly and clearly. ama is feeling frisky, and so she begins to ask. reina loves to point out that sexual abstinence is included in the diet, and she explains the importance of celibacy, the relationship between herbs and sex life. ama is amused and listens. she writes in her diary. she nods, and once in a while, she manages to contribute to the discussion, once they've covered the basic provisions and universal regulations, she asks if sexual abstinence includes autoeroticism as well. reina is thunderstruck. her eyes bulge, she clears her throat and stands up to the orator's podium.

síííí, mi niña, sex with yourself is still sex! she raises her index finger and wags it at alma. you little wild child. i wouldn't have expected that from you. but the devil is cunning and plants traps everywhere. that is something he knows how to do well, that's a fact. so be careful, for instance, at night when you're tempted, run to the creek. *andele, andele, ariba, ariba.*
reina starts pacing around, she is rushing, dashing. and there, you pour cold water on yourself, from head to toe. pour water on your private parts, and just like that, the feeling is gone.
while she is saying this, she is standing by the dining table with her legs spread open and her hand digging into her crotch like a dog that just buried a cut jewel. then she turns her back to ama, splashes a bit on her butt. splash, splash, and she begins to waddle like a duck. *claro*? is it clear to you, sister *claro*? come and ask anytime and anything. mama reina will advise you.

ama is grateful for the spectacle. it has been so long since she went to the theater. and this performance was flawless.

05.25

"your shortcomings are your road to power."

the fog is chaperoning her today. it forces itself into her view. she can't reach anything, everything is behind a glass wall. she doesn't even feel like pressing her face against the glass, as if that beauty outside never belonged to her. she's hanging out in a bubble about half a meter above the ground, and she's waiting until the bubble bursts. the trees are moving slowly. they are waving at her. finally, rain. she's catching it in the palms of her hands. the reflection of the trees in the sky comes closer. it's at arm's reach. she hears their voices. this is all here for you.

don't think about anything, just believe in the herbs. their effectiveness is measured by your love and your belief. plants are like people. when you love them, they will reward you. ayahuasca doesn't heal like ordinary medicine. ayahuasca forces you to surrender your illness to a greater being. it's better to consume it sitting up, you'll be able to focus on it better. when you take it lying down, the spirits think that you're asleep, and they ignore you.

i'm opening my eyes. the shipibo are playing the flute. it's thundering outside. i have to get out. enrique follows me. i know that he's watching over me. his silhouette lightens against the jungle background. i'm lying on a bench surrounded by the steam of the night. he's standing there, not doing anything. he simply exists, he guards me. the spirits are lurking in the distance. no one dares to come closer. when he turns slightly, the world turns with him. i can't lift my arms. i'm fading again, not breathing. is this death? i hear a voice pouring over me like stardust. ama? it's soft and firm. focus on your strength.

i'm climbing into my own body. the shipibo are singing, *heya, heya, hey, hey, hey*. they're calling upon their ancestors. their voices are the bats.

i stand above the morning in front of the malorca. i press the darkness into the ground, and the rainforest is washed with light. someone's breath marches loudly across the sky.

05.28

flying toys in the crowns of the trees. chattering creatures. hey girls! you're just adorable. what did you come to tell me? that it's going to rain for many days? yeah, it sure looks that way. it's hanging on to our ceiling in colors from michelangelo. would you like some rice? or a *plátanito*? then come and get it.
the snack is accompanied by thunder, inside and out, water currents. she begins to feel very sorry for herself. she wants to go home and live a normal life.
and what is stopping you? you can leave tomorrow. live a normal life? is that a joke? as if you've ever lived a normal life.
i need a break. at least for a while. i want my old world back, my well-worn shoes.

it's strange. yesterday she discovered her center, and today she is at the limits of her strength.

so, what now, with this disheveled life and a scruffy mind?

jeff, last time you asked me to write to you, but even when i'm not writing to you, i am doing it in my mind. a person sees everything differently from the end of the world. the comedy of our lives, the absurdity of hard work, neurotic ambitions, inscrutable bus schedules. in the morning, you'll walk through the jungle to rio pachitea, you'll sit on the bank and watch and wait for a boat to come by. and if it does, then you will travel. if it doesn't, you'll stay put. when it rains in the rainforest for a week, none of the natives goes hunting or breaks their backs on the plantation. it's we who insist on keeping up the chase. we pretend that time is chasing us, and then we are chasing time. we try to catch it by its tail. we chase and chase from the front, from the back, though we don't know why. but the main thing is that we're chasing after something. it's amazing, jeff, what we are capable of creating.

i have a new medicine. jergon sacha. it's a bouncer and a dj at the same time. it takes away the pain, and it releases emotions, a person's forte. i gradually drink up this dark blood from a half-liter bottle labeled *vida*, but it's pronounced "bída."[16] *vida* means life. *mi vida.* my life. i'm drinking myself back to life from the ground up.
the trees are straightening their spines, cracking, and quietly moaning. jergon sacha is affecting me, i feel ants racing in my fingertips.

dealing with the jungle is like dealing with any other thing or person: either you constantly fight it, or you blend in with it. i like the moment when i don't stick out, when i'm no longer in the way. when i become a resting place for butterflies, or a slide for lizards. the desert keeps coming back to me. that indian in a flash of light. an old face and long hair. he is coming closer, nodding, beckoning me as the crimson hills and mountains outline his wrinkled silhouette.

you're never whole without your roots. you can never see the wind, but you know it exists. you just can't catch it. like nevada. she knows that she'll go. she's gradually changing. maybe the jungle is inside of her now. she smiles, and they all smile back: reina, ginder, hegner. there's strength in her movements, in the tone of her steps. she's no longer a blinding light, she's inconspicuous, not on display any more. she simply exists.
beside the river, she takes a knife in her hand and a wooden plank. she pulls out a carrot and a stalk of celery from her bag, she even finds the last of her leeks, and she starts cutting.
what are you doing, amita? leave it, mama reina will take care of it. i want to cook, reina, i miss my kitchen.

in the evening, i'm crossing the river. the darkness behind me extends all the way home. the *tambo*'s roof has turned crimson, and the trees have grown new faces.

i'm lying in the ground, rigid energy mixed with the smell of worms. they multiply, survive, clean the clay of my flesh. a darkness without

[16] *Translator's note*: The meaning of the Czech word *bída* is misery or poverty.

borders. their breath is now mine. the roots are growing through the soil where i'm kneading a new body with hundreds of hands, cliffs, rocks. i'm pulling them out of lakes and oceans, from the entrails of the deserts. i'm spreading out through the land, the fallen leaves and honeycombs in my hair.

05.29

when i have white light for breakfast, i feel relieved. a small papaya blossoms near the *tambo*. you smell nice, you know? what i don't understand is how you can grow so fast. it laughs at my questions, like a child laughing at adults who waste her time with their nonsense.

"your only chance is your impeccability."

ama celebrates every bit of success. after she bans all internal bullshit, the poisonous voices truly disappear. then she realizes she has started singing to herself. song replaces bullshit. bravo! *if you're going to san francisco, be sure to wear some flowers in your hair*. her san francisco. the man who pulled the ropes of the street cars. perhaps he was an indian or of mixed race. his muscles, shirt with no sleeves. his smile. and the people next to her, smiling and wild. she is in san francisco once again. this is my house. you pull me across the street and knock on a door. an older man lets us in. he tells us stories and makes coffee. a little schnauzer getting underfoot, if you're going to san francisco . . . that's our destination. chinatown, greek restaurants, a russian shop on the corner where they sell salted caspian roach. why are you laughing? the golden gate bridge in the afternoon sun. our fascination with bridges. at night, you captivate me with the tip of your tongue.

it gets colder. tea would be perfect right about now. a raincoat is a great insulator, even though a person is always mildly sweating in it. the birds are beginning to do their magic, which in the language of the jungle means that it might stop raining. dressed in everything imaginable, she crawls into her damp bed to get warm. grandma would have called it sodden. over here, dear grandma, soddenness is ingrained in everything. it's an intrusive local creature. soddenness omnipresent. and to make things worse, my toe is sticking out of my sock.

that's nothing. that's an easy fix.
grandma pulls out a wooden mushroom and stretches the sock onto it. - come here. i'll show you how to patch a sock. ama watches, but she doesn't see, she really likes the wooden mushroom, though. grandma's hands and her words: this way and that way, and then we sew it here a bit. everything back then was mended and patched. mother would even send her stockings to be mended by a grey-haired man in overalls who cultivated the smell of leather and glue among his wooden lasts.

maybe i'm beginning to understand something here. our ability to move through time. how it actually works—your own quantum physics in practice. i'm sitting in the jungle, surrounded by rattle and hum, and i'm going back into the past, digging into my memories, bringing images back to life. they appear before me, expand, gain color. one by one, i hang them on the *lianas* and then sit back and look at them. and in that single glance, something starts to change. jeff, i'm changing the past, turning its contents upside down. i'm mixing it all together over and over, and then i'm spreading it out on a canvas. completely different images come out of it, different realities, different pasts. when we meet face-to-face again, touch will feel like a brand-new shirt.

06.01

the *curhuinzi* are swarming about, those motherfuckers, they're everywhere and eat everything that comes their way. they riddle the leaves like bullets. they weigh heavily on enrique's mind because they liquidate the mango plants and yucas. he has sprayed the plants with juice from *piñon colorado*, a plant that provides a poisonous layer, but it hasn't helped much. *curhuinzi*. ama didn't see much of them around the *tambo*. but the monkeys had a party at the creek. you're making a mess in my pool, you flea-infested bastards, you better watch out for me.

oh, how i would really like to hear bach, the well-tempered clavier, gould's hands humming over the keyboard. how long since i've heard him play? watch out for the palm trees. another decapitated head falls to the ground. i would really like to hear some bach. the art of fugue. i'll have some rice.

instead of the fugue, i hear the rain. from a distance, it sounds like a train.

i want to feel it, liquefied mud on the bottom of my feet, on the pillows of my toes as they sink into the crust of mother earth, into her creases and pores, as she pulls me into her nest where warmth and darkness lie.

i'm standing, my feet sunk into the ground, and i'm moving the clouds with my hands. each one of my fingers has a piece caught under its nail. i'm running in circles, mud up to my ankles, and i'm leaving muddy palm prints all over the sky.

after the rain, everything starts moving, pumping. along with fresh new sounds, the beast comes back again. it takes control of her. it straps a saddle on her. she is bursting out of her throat, wailing in her bones. she wants out. as she staggers through the jungle, the howls, the shrieks come from that beast that broke out of its chains:

HAAAAAAAAAAAAAAAAAAAAAAAAAAAAAAAAAAAAAAAAAAAAAAAAAA
AAAAAAAAAAAAAAAAAAAAAAAAAAAAAAAAAAAAAAAAAAAAAAAAAAAA
AAAAAAAAAAAAAAAAAAAAAAAAAAAAAAAAAAAAAAAAAAAAAAAAAAAA
AAAAAAAAAAAAAAAAAAAAAAAAAAAAAAAAAAAAAAAAAAAAAAAAAAAA
AAAAAAAAAAAAAAAAAAAAAAAAAAAAAAAAAAAAAAAAAAAAAAAAAAAA
AAAAAAAAAAAAAAAAAAAAAAAAAAAAAAAAAAAAAAAAAAAAAAAAAAAA
AAAAAAAAAAAAAAAAAAAAAAAAAAAAAAAAAAAAAAAAAAAAA!

the glass in the sky is breaking. its shattered pieces are falling on her head. they are cutting new seams. she hears engines revving in high gear, howling from the bowels of the earth, from the pelvises of mothers. a greeting sent from the beast that resides inside of her.

never has she screamed like that before.

she's laughing in this downpour. water is rushing into her from all sides, shattering bedrock. her voice is splitting mountains. all a person

needs is one solid scream, and she'll fly to the moon. i'm no longer just *poco loco.*
they had to hear me from beyond the river and see that trampled plot of mud.

don juan said that the howl of a warrior is one of the most important tools in mastering magic.

when she lets out her howl, the jungle becomes quiet. only the insects are swarming, but for a few long moments, not a single mosquito dares to land on her skin.

06.02
in the name of the balls: father, son, and holy ghost

the definition of a ball:
a ball or sphere is a body of matter on which all points on its surface have the same distance from its center. a ball can be used for shooting, for playing—for example, bowling or billiards—in card games, and also for sports and as weightlifting equipment. in the past, balls were used in prisons. nowadays, they have been replaced with other equipment. in life, when a person drops the ball, she can expect an assessment of complete failure.
after defining the ball, a lesson in callousness follows. when she started in business, an older colleague advised her that, if she wanted to move up in her career, she had to put on some armor and be tougher than a man. otherwise, she would be eaten alive and trampled upon like a rag doll. *it's just bullshit,* she thought to herself. some things a person has to experience on her own. and so, after a few years, she left. she didn't want to cultivate a shell, to sharpen her elbows. she wanted the softness of lamb's wool. she wanted to knit stories like a sweater, to weave them like the webs of railroads and train stations.
when she wrote a short story about "the call of the bones," the editor said he agreed with two other readers that the story had no balls. what can you say to that? the patriarchal triumvirate had cast its judgment: the father, the son, and the holy ghost.

she doesn't have balls. that mean she's unsatisfactory. she gets an f. uninteresting, unimpressionable, because dear ladies, in this day and age, there is no room for anything without balls. the criteria of evaluation depend on callousness and standing erect all the way up to the heavenly heights. and so, dutiful daughters, in this patriarchy, kneel, bow down, and slave away. they try to jump over the lath, to please their fathers—they are daddy's little girls. whatever you do, don't act hysterical. hysteria is a uterus. what does that even mean? don't behave as if you had a uterus. leave your emotions out on the street. don't make a scene—be *reasonable*. i mean, reasonable. an incantation. that universal spell cast when you are still in your diapers, under the whip of wisdom. woe to women who are ruled by the wisdom of men.
but there in the underground caves, it still remains—that yearning for the treasure that great grandmother sang about. no matter what, somewhere there is still a power that is soft and flexible and that flows; it falls from the heights into the valleys, lower and deeper. it doesn't crawl its way to the top. it just exists, without striving, without struggle. i'm not the one crying, it's the womanhood i tossed away. like in that fairytale about the maiden who cried softly. i'm lifting my head. the sky is falling into my eyes. i want to be mud, naked on the damp body of the earth, soft and flowing, gathering up, spreading within, kneading and swallowing. this is a book of searching. searching for peddled womanhood, enslaved in the name of a ball. womanhood with a ball and chain at its feet, clamped in iron shoes, wearing reins, with blinders over its eyes. just this way, please. a womanhood that is plucked, beaten, abandoned, blinded, wearing a straitjacket made out of wisdom.
a dress with a veil embroidered in silver, but she's no princess, my lord.[17]
what now? you painted yourself into a corner.
now would be a good time to point a finger.
but toward what?
the trees are standing by, and once in a while they let out a chuckle. what is there to laugh about? this is serious. she needs to find the right catch phrase, something like: it's raining again—those fucking communists!

---

[17] *Translator's note*: A quote from the Czech film *Three Nuts for Cinderella*, a popular fairy tale, which airs ever year on Christmas.

that would fit in rather well here. but it might need to be something more subtle like: *it's all my parents' fault.* no, that's even more clichéd. you can get a stamp for that from any psychiatrist. it's all because of those feminists. that's it! the feminists. they turned everything ass-up. in the last hundred years, they fought like hell for equal rights—just so that women can be like men? what a win. professor higgins sang to pickering: *why can't a woman be more like a man?*
we came a long way. today, a woman has the same rights as a man—to be a man.
what do you do?
i'm a mother. and your profession? aha, you're just a mother. and you want applause for what? what have you done for humanity? what sort of mark have you made in history, in the call of conquerors, discoverers of new worlds who pillaged every continent they debarked upon?
i'm standing in the rain forest, and i'm applauding and bowing down to all mothers. all mothers who ever were, that are, and that ever will be. the tropical rain is falling on my knees, splashing on my face. every leaf in the jungle begins to clap in honor of motherhood. unembellished womanhood, full of strength, but also soft, like a ball of yarn made from lamb's wool. i raise my shot glass high, i drink a shot of jergon sacha, a blood-colored potion. cheers to womanhood, the emancipation of women's bodies—soft curves, dimples, buxom calves. i drink to the resurrection of suspended dreams. bottoms up.

enrique heard her scream yesterday. it was quite dramatic—it must have been heard all the way to the honoria, he laughed. ginder was worried about you. he wanted to run after you, but i told him to calm down, that you were alright.

06.03

it's building up inside of me. gathering. i'm waiting as the eyes of my killer appear above ground. they always show up when the ground is burning. i exist in layers. i create my layers quietly, in the chirrup of the rainforest, and i'm quietly sweating, sweating quietly because i'm quietly sweating.

am i losing my mind? that is the question. i would like to know whether i have already lost my mind or if i am just waiting for it to happen.
and please take away these horses. they're trampling my english-style lawn.
i'm on a roller coaster. at the top, i'm ecstatic that i'm alive, and at the bottom, i just want to kick the bucket. this schism is exhausting and leads nowhere. most of the time, between breaks and hiccups, i'm fucked. so, the song sounds a bit like this: hic – pause – hic – ecstasy – chaos – death – chaos – death, and so on. let's sing.
i've read about people who died from the hiccups.

i'm riding my doubts, wildly, foaming at the mouth until it tires out all my layers to the point of total breakdown. i doubt the whole universe. what the hell are you exactly about, universe?
then, suddenly, i hear a voice that doesn't belong to me, and it comes up with a brilliant solution.

then go someplace else! divorce this universe, if you don't like it. find yourself a better partner!

and meanwhile, behind this far-reaching confusion, something immobile still stands, something unexpected. a feeling that everything is alright. a feeling that everything that happens is just a façade, and that in reality, nothing is happening at all.

don juan says that we have a habit of adjusting our reality to suit our own thoughts.

"knowledge comes floating like specks of gold dust, the same dust that covers the wings of moths."

06.06

rio tibio

when you fast without salt, your body begins to change. it waits until you get knocked to the ground so that it can bounce back. but the ground could also break, and the body could continue to fall. maybe underneath the ground there is more ground—but what if it's not there at all? what if belowground there is no ground?

she could show her strength by heading into the jungle on the path that leads to the rapids, and farther down to the cold waterfalls—and letting out a powerful scream. in the meantime, she is just lying down and begging. god have mercy. *kyrie eleison, christos eleison. krleš krleš, krleš.*[18] keep calm, my daughter. fear is acid. it will devour you in an instant.

and so, it's time to get up and go. a machete, hat, water, *vamos*. sometimes she doubts whether she has taken the right path, whether she'll reach her destination, because the jungle is thickening everywhere she goes. here, next to this fallen tree, she needs to turn slightly left. next to that molding stump, turn right. he remembers the work of ginder's machete, quick cuts to a few thickets. this stretch is a bit breakneck. it's almost impossible to pass through. aerial roots intertwine with *lianas* sprawling up and down, no one can tell which is which. and here comes the fallen palm tree, then the partially decaying stump, then sludge. there's more mud today than last time. a turn to the left, then a stretch fit for a tightrope walker, a narrow tree trunk, a steep drop below—better not look down.

a slip-and-slide. you wouldn't believe how slippery the soles of your rubber boots can be. a question for this task: is it better to go around that huge tree trunk in the way, or just climb over it? definitely climb over, even though she'll get as filthy as a pig, because no one is around to pull her out of a bind. what next? this time she doesn't have a clue. should she make marks on the trees to find her way back? scatter rice grains or reel off a string? why didn't she bring strips of rags? or, ideally, psychedelic spray paint.

at the crossroad—the *lopuna colorado*, the tree of teachers. finally, something shows her which way to go. they call it the witch: a tree trunk bulging out like the belly of a giant. gigantic ceremonial drums, *manguaré*, are carved from it, they were used as telephones in the

[18] *Translator's note*: Verse from Old Church Slavonic poem, "Hospodine Pomiluj ni," or "Lord Have Mercy on Us," the first documented Czech hymn, from the 10th century.

jungle, their resonant sounds carrying a dependable message to the friendly tribes in the far regions.
after two hours, she walks through the riverbed. the overgrowth around it is too thick, so she has to move upstream. she's slipping on the rocks, climbing up the rapids. she's wrapped in heat and salt, like a steaming river. once she makes it through the riverbed, she clears a small passage along the bank.
at last, a laguna, only mildly deep. a pallet of noni fruit and overripe *papajas*. a silver waterfall looming above her. ama stops, undresses, a bent tree willingly functions as a hanger for her clothes. in front of her, a five-meter wall of bedrock with moss stubble. water flowing over it. she finds a liana, pulls to see if it will hold her. she goes hand over hand, her feet slipping on the smooth surface. step, slide, step—the damp *liana* and the grip of her palm. she is climbing all the way up to a tiny embankment where she can stand. the cold sky is falling over her head, the hair of the goddess shiva. it tells ancient myths. they flow through her body, this space. her hands are burning, they're catching the rush of the current. with her eyes closed, she sees as if inside blown glass, her organs, clear and brittle. she sees the trees above, the bedrock at her back, and water flowing through her head, her legs. she hears her own voice that isn't human anymore.

she has never heard herself laugh like this before.

the muddy sun is boiling in the pools amid colorful salts. a lagoon of smells, a cave adorned with the dreams of bats. dampness and darkness. she is sitting and watching. suddenly, she feels a gust of wind. a strong gust. a smell coming from nearby. birds stop singing in the middle of a measure, and the leaves turn to stone. not even a shadow is moving, just her inner eye. so, show yourself, she whispers to herself. her inner eye is watching, looking around, sniffing. i know you're here somewhere.

ama is listening. she becomes the creature that is watching her. a jaguar—his story begins to resonate with her. his eyes reflect a light as colorful as wallpaper. it sees through worlds, penetrates the darkness, every turn or curve. every movement. he walks in the sky at night, and the stars latch onto his fur as he carries them. he hangs up the constellations, moving like water, and people interest him very little. he knows that everything light up above is dark down below, and vice versa. when he wants to, he descends, and in the corners of the earth, he hunts. he carries the consciousness of the world on his fur, the cauterized stains of their bodies. his skin smells of ashes.

she heads back through the riverbed, hopping from one stone to another. the entrance to the forest has to be here somewhere. she tries to remember, but she didn't pay attention. that's a major mistake—she let her guard down. she searches for the entrance for a long time, the steep decline that brought her here. a few times, she tries to climb up a hill but the thick overgrowth clutches at her, grabs her by the legs. the clay beneath her is slipping. she goes down on her stomach and falls straight into the river. one time, she almost stabs herself with the machete. she continues to search, to prowl, desperately trying to remember where the hell she came out. she's afraid that it will get darker, and she won't find it. she hasn't even left a message that she took off. if she doesn't return, they will notice it tomorrow. she has to find it, there is no other way. no, even this isn't it. i have to find it.
she starts screaming at the entire forest. a few birds wave at her with their wings. someone cackles. there are thousands of spectators that don't understand what is at stake here. could it be here? the fourth time's the charm. finally, she remembers. it's by the rock that looks like a double bed, a leaning tree with hair like a linden. it's slippery, as it was before, like it is everywhere, but there's a little more room and a few tree trunks she can hold onto. she's relieved. her breath resumes its normal pattern: in and out. she marches and gently adds speed to her steps. the sun is on an incline, and she doesn't want to spend the night here. the jungle has signs all over its body, if you know how to read them. turn left at the *lopuna*, right at the fork. the *lopuna* with round hips like a massive flask. petals that look like chewed-up leather tell where to go this time. step on it. when she gets closer to the *tambo*, she becomes nervous. she should hear water flowing. there has to be a creek somewhere; cauterized palm trees. but it is dry season—instead of a loud flow, there is a sleepy trickle, like a weak whisper. she's glad

that she slipped. ginder slipped on that same rock when they were here together. that's good. it means she is home. she has an imprint of a tree on her damp pants. the landscape is reaching for her heart.

you're with me this whole journey. i'm carrying you on my shoulders. i would like to show you these parts, mom, this world's end where everything seems to be beginning, where trees are not afraid to grow and the lizards will sit on your knees like children. your scent is falling from heaven, the softness of your skin. you carry time in your hands.

06.07

"death is waiting for you everywhere and nowhere."

the white tint in the air pushes me to the ground, onto my knees, my head in the wet soil. death is infinity, and i want to go to it. to wind around its legs like a ball of yarn, but i can't move. look at me. look into my eyes. death says nothing, but i can hear it all around. i am watching forever, because infinity is timeless. it has no eyes. it nods, turns around, walks gracefully away, and vanishes into the bushes.

something is driving her, she can't stay still, she tries to calm her skittish horses, to pull on the reins. nothing helps. and so, the solution is water and a backpack, a headlamp just in case, and forward, march! to rio pachitea. she is rationalizing on the way, trying to figure out what's chasing her and why suddenly this desire for pachitea. finally, she realizes that she is just like carlito, who pissed her off, always with a notebook in his hands, writing everything down, his hundred-and-one different questions, with which he bombarded don juan during his tales of power. ama stops halfway up the hill, her sides splitting, she has to laugh about how we learn to name everything. how we learn to negotiate, how to chisel words, how to convey ourselves in simple and compound sentences, complicated inversions and loopholes. how we learn to wrap our thoughts, how we bathe in rhetoric, debate, discussions. we fight with words, we live by words, we fortify ourselves with words, and then we end up face-to-face with the grim reaper, and all that effort is worth shit. she is getting closer

to rio pachitea, the sun is turning blood red in the west. she becomes one with that image, locks away the desire that made her restless. she wants to be on the other side of the ocean. she is sitting beside the river, and suddenly, she is home.
she is sitting at the table in the kitchen, watching her mother make coffee. she prepares a cup, scoops a spoonful of coffee, the kettle starts whistling, and then suddenly, one wrong move and crash! the sound of porcelain breaking. mom sweeps up the pieces. tears.
are you crying, mom?
it was my grandfather's cup, you know?
deep inside it suddenly stings. fragments too big for a child's eyes, mommy don't cry, i'll buy you another one.
don't be silly. where would you find the money.
ama runs into her room and grabs a piggy bank from her shelf. here, see? I have money, i've saved some crowns.
keep those for yourself. you can buy something with them. maybe some new puppets.
no, i'm going to buy a cup for you.
she is standing in line at the store, holding a change purse. her head doesn't reach the counter. she can't see. the saleswoman leans over. which one would you like?
that one.
she points. she can't keep her eyes off of it. the saleswoman takes her change purse, pours its entire contents onto the counter, and starts to count. ninety-three crowns, her life savings. mom tries one last time to stop her.
look, you'll have nothing left, only four crowns, just enough for three ice creams, nothing else.
ama is not listening. her eyes are fixed on the cup. she sees nothing else.
writing is meant to be shared. poetry is a quest. people are most impressed when they catch glimpses of their own greatness, because it usually surprises them.
she arrives at the *tambo* along with the dawn, a bird that whistles like a train conductor is close behind her. one train after another—today, they are all arriving for her.

06.08

"a warrior is always ready...to be one is and endless struggle that will go on to the very last moment of our lives."

ama has a twig, a shoot that sprouted. it could possibly become a tree that could one day be covered with birds, its dry branches turned green. a piece of *liana* on which she will hang her socks. it already has two sprigs. she plants them in the dirt.

she causes a commotion in the *santuario* dining hall.
amita, where did you get that scratch above your eye? and you have another on your neck. you're all bloody.
when she explains that she was in rio tibio, ginder raises his eyebrows. alone? you shouldn't do that. it's dangerous. you could run into a *tigre*. a jaguar.
enrique is not here. lately, he is often traveling. she wonders whether he has another woman. he seems uneasy, as if he has run out of strength. she sometimes sees herself in him. the more he turns up his nose at modern medicine, the more comical he seems to her. ego is a vain princess. healers and doctors are the same at their core. they just don't see it. they lack humility.
"the humbleness of a warrior is not the the humbleness of a beggar. the warrior lowers his head to no one, but at the same time he doesn't permit anyone to lower their head to him."
that is the moral of all fairy tales. even our good king miroslav said: cobbler, never raise yourself above anyone and never lower yourself to anyone.
"you like the humility of the beggar," he said quietly. "you bow down to wisdom."

06.10 pucallpa

reinita? i'm heading out today to pucallpa to extend my visa.
i will be sad without you, *mi niña*. when will you be back? here, i'll pack you something to eat.

since the day she arrived, *santuario* has changed beyond recognition. you could cut the tension with a knife. hegner is silent. enrique and reina, the old tiger and his mother, are barely speaking to each other. is ama's assumption about another woman correct?
there's an argument in the honoria at the tiger's place, they are yelling at each other. a door slams, cooking pans fly and crash. ama waits for a *collectivo* to appear to take her to the city.
in the afternoon, her patience is rewarded. calm returns to the tiger's. the toyota gets stuck in the mud several times on the way. no one can just ride up a slippery hill, so everybody, get out and push! the driver is the man. he has a plastic sheet in place of his back window. instead of a back door handle, he has a rope with a knot that opens when you pull on it. instead of a lock pin inside the door, a rusted old screw is sticking out. on the other side, the lever is completely ripped out, so the door can only open and close from the outside.
the streets of pucallpa are thoroughly parched. she walks through the city and notices all the pregnant women, she buys pomegranates from a pretty woman wearing a dirty apron, whose stomach is as round as the fruit she is placing in the bag. - *dos soles. gracias*. hunger is like a hunting dog. it runs until it catches something. in front of the restaurant *el paraíso* lies a hairless dead dog covered in bugs. the stench is everywhere. in spite of what she sees, she never loses her appetite.
the yearning to create rituals is strange. going to the same places, like an animal marking its territory. she's sitting in the lounge on plaza des armas, on a barstool in a glass booth, dialing a phone number that's ingrained in her memory.
finally, i can hear your voice.

late in the afternoon, she gets into a go-kart, and on her way, she stops by enrique's sister's to relay a message. merthy welcomes her, she offers ama a chair and asks if she is hungry. ama shakes her head, her eyes scanning her surroundings. the kitchen has a view of the ucayal, the rumble of engines on the wooden boats carrying cargo and cattle. living in the city. hard-packed clay, someone is washing dishes in the courtyard, next to the toilet, a wooden booth covered in black plastic, out of which runs a rat the size of a dachshund. the apartment walls are

decorated with magazine pictures instead of wallpaper. the kitchen has two hotplates on a wooden table and a few aluminum dishes. the mud under the table is squishy and sticking to the bottom of her shoes. six daughters and four grandchildren live with her in these two rooms. no flushing toilets, no running water. the household is ruled by the television screen, because the place has electricity. two four-year-old boys run up to her. timidly, they observe the *gringa*. they look like twins. joel and roberto. - *encantada*. ama gives them the fruit she bought at the market and asks merthy whose boys they are.
joel is my grandson, manuela's son, and roberto is mine, my sweetheart. they were born two days apart.

the handsome man at the immigration office bombards her with an array of typical questions—beginning with whether she wants children and how many. ama starts laughing, she's finally getting used to the local customs. folks here interrogate with no boundaries.
it'll be done tomorrow, *señorita*.

this will interest you, jeff. during an ayahuasca trip, i fly to visit se jára. he has recently moved and now lives somewhere in prague 6. i've never visited his place, but i find him anyway. i see a room on the ground floor, a bed across from the window, a small room where jára is sleeping. i sit on the bed next to him and wake him up. i say nothing, i'm just staring at him.
then today, i spoke to him on the phone, and the image i saw of his room is accurate. he also said that he dreamed of me. he didn't exactly know when, but i do. apparently, i said nothing, i just sat next to him for a while.

06.11 pucallpa

a city cast in concrete. *mercado*, a market full of smells, fresh fish next to bras and baseball hats in imitation of famous global brands. an old indian woman selling spices, she has beautiful wrinkles, calloused hands, and patches on her dress. ama buys cinnamon from her. a linen bag for one sol.
here, *señorita*, *canella* for you. god bless you.

a storm and then rainfall. her trip back to *santuario* has to wait until tomorrow. at least she can write a few emails in peace.

i would like to send you a few sounds in which i'm drowning. when i wake up at night, i know the exact time by the sounds of the jungle. midnight carries the same darkness as the moment just before morning. you can't see your hand in front of your face, but the sounds reveal everything. the howl of a bird that chases away the darkness. a brief silence just before the break of day, that strange moment when everything stops for a little while. it happens twice a day, at dawn and at dusk, the changing of the guard, two measures of silence. i would like to give you my hands. they look like mine, yet they belong to someone else. blue veins are sticking out like inverted riverbeds. i look at my palms, and in that chaos of lines, i see traces of my ancestors, their fate, their laughter
i smile, too, when i have a good day. sometimes i want to scream until i lose my voice. i learned that here as well—to scream. that roar is an animal. it's transparent, almost gentle. when i roared, the boiling river froze. trees lost their speech. in that moment, something lifted me up and began to rock me a bit. i don't know. i don't know how to describe it, how to translate it into words. i don't know. maybe you understand me.
a person's senses sharpen while living in the jungle. i wake up at night, and i sense the monkeys even before they start rustling up in the tree crowns. i can recognize the smell of capybara before he gives himself away with his panting. your ears turn into radar, your eyes scan the wide horizon. i see myself from the inside and out. i am getting to know my new faces.
strange things, and yet quite simple. no pageantry, no luster. i feel the creek in my hair, and i don't know what day it is.

06.17

the tree of wild bees

enrique and hegner are waiting, ready, tools hanging all over them and holding a snack.
ama! are you coming with us? we'll pick up luis on the way.

the sun is hissing in the sky. the black rubber boots are like steel mill furnaces, sludgy inside and out. the men pick up the pace.

hermano! where are you? luis emerges, toothless as an ant eater. he laughs and nods. come on, i've got something here for you! he's boasting about yesterday's catch. *carachupa!* ama looks down and sees an armadillo. hegner holds the roasted animal in the air. armadillo, he says. luis is a cannibal, did you know? hegner laughs and feels the carachupa's claws. he eats everything, even monkeys. admit it, doesn't he look like a monkey?

luis is making faces. perhaps he's trying to look like a monkey, but he looks more like a dried up and hungry old man.
vamos?
off they go. it's really hot, and she feels something spinning in her. perhaps the aya, and remnants of the night, two hours of sleep. she puts one foot in front of the other without giving it any thought, and in the middle of the hike, everyone freezes in front of her. *naka-naka*, they whisper. a brown and white snake slithers on the path. yep, that one is quite poisonous. ama gets closer and peeks through, she is breathing on hegner's shoulder. is it deadly? no, it can make you really sick, but you won't die. enrique spits on his machete, and he sticks the spit under the snake's nose. the snake just sticks out his tongue, tastes it, and that's it. *people don't bother me,* he hisses in his language. but when the shaman pokes at him a few times with his machete, the snake slithers away. hegner nods at her. come on, it's gone.
finally, they reach the river with the fossils. last time, she collected petrified shells. now, she's taking in the scene, feeling the surface with the tongue of the puma that comes here to drink. she is wetting down her hair. the cold water gives her goose bumps. enrique is carrying a bucket for honey in his hands. bend over. he pours water over her head. slowly, gently. it's ice cold.
better? yes. it reminds her of africa.
hegner starts hovering over her. you're still weak after the ayahuasca, he says. he puts on a caring face. he's watching her, lurking, observing

her jagged movements. if he hadn't caught her hand so quickly, she would have fallen backwards into the riverbed, straight onto the rocks. here, smell this. it will get you back on your feet.
he's handing her an herb that smells like mint and lemon. she breathes it in, but the way she's feeling today, she would have to stuff it up her nostrils to make it work.
off they go again. there is no end in sight for this climb. the men with machetes, and an axe she lugs behind her, along with her own weight, stumbling from time to time. look, this is *barbasco*. the shaman shows her a plant. you make poison out of it to catch fish, so there is nothing to eat here. the men chuckle. ama swallows emptily and wipes off her sweat.
after another hour, they finally stop. rest. before we chop it down.
a tree that houses bees, fluttering, humming, resonating. ama listens, watches. the axe strikes into the flesh and exposes the bone. a reddish wood and a bloody pool pours out through the fingers of the forest spirits. ama covers her ears so she won't hear them moaning, lamenting. she leaves so she won't see. but the sound of the blows catches up with her. they're breaking branches, cutting into her skin, she is stumbling over the sound of the axe and she keeps going, her body wrapped in fatigue. the bandage is wrapped around her tightly.
after a while she hears voices. aaaaammmmaaaa, aaaaammmmmaaaa! luis is shouting, sounding his horn. she hears her name through the jungle and returns to the men and the trees. they are levitating in a swarm of bees, they are cutting into the opening of the cavity the bees call home. they are breaking off the honeycombs, and the bucket collects the liquid. the substance oozes down the walls, flows, and then settles. taste it. it's *propolis*. enrique's arms are covered in sap and bees. and this is honey. it's not too sweet. it's rather tangy, less thick, and mixed with fragrance. an unexpected witness runs out from the bottom of the severed tree trunk. the men jump back, and hegner begins to laugh. it's a tarantula. enrique feels the tree to see if it has disappeared.
when they are done, they close the opening; they dress the wound with leaves, and tie it with bast. see? we do this to tell the bees that they

shouldn't return, that they should find another place to build a hive. they already know that. i spoke to them. ama nods, but she is not letting her thoughts out. she is saving her strength for the hike home. on the way back, she can barely drag her feet. she rests. the buzzing of bees is resonating in her head. they are building new homes. something is lifting her. the image of purple fruits on trees reminds her of rowanberry bushes. it's slowly getting dark, the path curled up into a ball. she's resting. if only she could sleep. she recognizes it here. she walks through the buzzing. she knows that they are not far. just a few more hills, up and down. half an hour later, they are home.
enrique pours her a shot of mead. ama picks out the pieces of wood, just a few of them are still floating in it, but who cares, as long as the splinters don't stick to anything. well, cheers! she knocks it back. the men laugh. do you want another? you're going to be drunk.

as evening approaches, she opens tales of power, the book has a strong scent that tells the story of how she got here. a story about travels. she is caught up in a rush, a journey away from here. it's chasing her farther out.

06.21

solstice
ama is waiting for something here, and she doesn't know what it is. trying to wait with no expectations. waiting for a moment of action.

ginder has been gone for a week already. he left for santa rosa to spend some time with his son. the boy is ten years old and sees his dad twice a year for three weeks, sometimes a month.
when he said goodbye to ama, he pressed a piece of amethyst into her palm. the rock calms you. he smiled as he always did. if you put it under your pillow, you will sleep well.
she stuck it in her pocket, and when she remembered about it yesterday, the rock had already disappeared. she never found it. and now she regrets it. when ginder returns, she will already be gone.

"there is no final crossroads, no final step to anything"

reina sits next to her with a cup of hot tea, as she digs out the last bits of food with her index finger that are stuck in the pockets behind her cheeks. then she takes out her tobacco pouch and ritualistically starts packing the pipe that she always carries with her. she lights up, mumbling something as she starts puffing.
lights, camera, action. and once again, the same conversation about members of the family. for the 53rd time. reina asks what her mother's, sister's, nephew's, father's, grandmother's name is. how old are they, what do they do, and are they healthy?
y tus papa?
mi papa muerte.
like a broken record. my dad is dead. he's dead. dad is dead. it's like a practice. she's practicing something. my dad is dead. he's dead. *mi papa muerte*. fuck! he's totally dead. it's been five years. she should be used to it by now. she can't believe that it's been that long. five years. but i live in timelessness.

06.23

reina is wearing jeans, with a rucksack on her back, ready to go to pucallpa. she asks ama if she doesn't mind. she seems oddly sad, irritated, but when ama asks her about it, she insists that there is nothing wrong with her, that she just needs to run an errand. she disappears beyond the river at first sunlight.
two indians emerge from the jungle. they've come for medicine. one is a fisherman who brought a basket full of live fish. *boqui-chica* and a few small bullheads. they are sprightly, gnawing at the table top as if it were the river bottom. they're called *carachama.* the fisherman offers to take enrique and hegner to honoria for the feast of saint john. ama gathers her stuff. i'm coming with you. i want to see for myself how lener catches fish.
she watches enrique's steps. they are unrecognizable. tense and quick. what's his hurry? what is he chasing? rio pachitea has risen slightly. the boat is full of nets. the fisherman bails water out of the boat with a tin plate. ok, you can board now. the seats are a bit dirty. hegner reaches

into his pocket, conjures up something that might once have been a small towel, and spreads it over the dirty seat.
so you don't get you *pantalones* dirty. he points to her pants. ama gives him a smile that she keeps handy for thoroughbred brown-nosers. *gracias.* and off we go! clouds, and above them more clouds; they float by in layers. in the place where the steaming river flows into the pachitea, he takes out his fishing net, and with one sweeping movement, he throws it into the water. a moment of silence, anticipation. one pull. two pulls. and a silver fish, a *lisa.* the fisherman lets out a sigh over their catch. it's a *lisa.* the banks turn red in the twilight. they move on.
she tries to remember the feeling she had when she first arrived. that shivering sensation, the short breaths. well, every adventure turns into routine after a while, when it's repeated a few times. or is it just her and her nomadic life? her restless soul, that constantly drives her to go farther, to greater heights, to the very depths. to go to ground. that first glance at the *santuario* seems so far away.
she watches the currents in the water. the fisherman, lener, is catching fish in the crown of a tree that must have fallen into the river during the last storm. he repeats the trick with his net twice more, but to no avail. meanwhile, the *lisa* is flopping around on the wooden planks at the bottom of the boat, gasping for air. ama looks around to see if anyone is going to tend to the fish. no one does. she contemplates throwing it back into the water, but she would not be able to explain to the men why she'd do something like that. when they reach the bank of the honoria, the lisa is kaput. all flopped out.
the men gather their things. enrique assumes the face of a holy man. you should return, ama. san juan is a big holiday, there will be huge barbecues and a lot of drinking. the whole honoria will be filled with *contaminación*, do you understand? yes, ama, understands. honoria will turn into an infernal barrel house, a tasteless orgy and fireworks, not for her delicate, emaciated, washed-up soul. ama nods. the holy man's overprotectiveness is endearing.
he says he will most likely return late. she replies, *sííí.*
knock yourselves out, gentlemen. you'll pretend that you're returning tonight, and i will pretend to believe you. she knows this game from the

men on other continents. after so many reruns, she plays this role with such skill and grace. *síí́í.* i wish you all the best, boys, have a grand ole time. she watches the men surge towards the raids of the sinful honoria. we will return *mááás tarde*. veeery late, even after dark.
yesss, of course, and do you have any flashlights?
the men exchange glances. i don't. what about you? i don't either. the moon will light the way, enrique says.
ama smiles. of course, it will shine like a pig's ass. right through the three layers of clouds in the sky, shaman, you'll be back in no time.

06.25

she is singing with a voice she doesn't recognize. she doesn't realize this voice is inside of her. they are not connected. she tries to climb back into her body with the song. her stomach is kneading, baking, a loaf of bread comes out, freshly baked strength with a coating of salt all over her body.

no midsummer night's dream, just luminous dough that sticks to her hands. she reads to her future. she sees parts of a road in the palm of her hand. perhaps a highway. she is sitting behind the wheel. it's clear and sunny. then she sees a path, sand or dry clay. it leads to a small house, a wooden structure. she goes outside at midnight and freezes in front of the *tambo*. the sky is so low that she has to bend over. the stars are saying good bye to her.

santuario. she will miss this place. mama reina, the steamy river, the unbearable lightness of vomiting. the pantomime she's mastered. after a quarter of a year, she's become a master of the gag—a shame she can't see herself. enrique has been a good university. he has certainly given her a lot to take home. he understands herbs, the spirits of plants and animals talk to him, and now they talk to her as well. ama now sees that cleansing the body is helpful, but it is not a cure. it won't destroy the defective programming. it won't ignite a flame that is not already burning. something has to happen from the inside, rise from the ground up, short-circuit the mainframe. just like the absolutist god, the shaman's ten commandments do not represent a true authority for her. his rules sometimes seem comical. they bring tension and an atmosphere of battle. and the raven— the raven does not fight it.

but who is this raven? perhaps another dictator.

the raven comes from within. it's the voice that appears when she is lingering between two worlds; a guide into her own underworld. it is here that she has realized this. it's better to listen to an inner authority than to the wisest of birds on the outside. even if her life is at stake.

she's awake after her midsummer night. good morning saint ivan, the battle with demons has ended. there is no battle with demons. you travel with demons to the underworld, and with any luck, you might just come back.

enrique packs up quickly, he's leaving for santa rosa. a messenger from honoria has told him that his child is sick.
what? a girl? how old?
chiquita. hegner gesticulates, indicating the size of an infant. about a month-and-a-half.
aha. so, the inappropriate and narrow-minded thoughts that have been circling around her, that enrique has another woman, might be inappropriate and narrow-minded, but they are also true. that he has been dieting and practicing celibacy because he didn't want to fuck reina was clear from the start. and from there, it's just one more step to another woman and another lie. hallelujah. señor milagros. she loves this about life. she wants to roll around laughing. is this the play that we've all been in?

dear enrique. you showed me so much.

how are you doing?
doing well. i hear you're leaving. my daughter is sick.
hegner is laughing. she didn't know.
no? enrique seems surprised. he is truly and genuinely surprised that she

didn't know it. it's a huge compromise, he says, and his eyes tear up. several lives at once. all going in different directions. it hurts, it tears you apart.
the little one is in the hospital, you know.
ama studies that face she knows so well and suddenly feels that she is seeing it for the first time in her life. she hears the river behind his back. the steam rises through the planks in the floor. they stand facing each other in the cafeteria above the water, and something is pulsating inside of her. she sees the beginning and the end and the beginning again, a newborn, enrique's daughter, who is pulling him into another story.

what's her name?
a soft light falls onto enrique's face, changing his features. the corners of his mouth begin to quiver. he lets out a mild cough. the hands of a child clench his voice.
ama harmonia.

ama's eyes are wide, suddenly flooded with tears. and the little one reaches out to her all of a sudden. she smiles and nods. she'll pray for her.
i prepared a remedy for you. don't tighten the top too much, or it will explode.
she is oddly touched. dear god, that enrique. so many memories are coming back. they're circling around her like a whirlpool in the river, while hot drops of water leave red dots on her skin. how many times did you hold my head in your hands, how many times did you give me strength, how many times did we fly above the crowns of the trees, hunting through the landscape, where people are tigers, and tigers are planets?

the jungle has grown quiet. it's a strange silence. enrique says goodbye.

i'll return before you leave.
ama nods. she sees another one of the shaman's faces, but she doesn't really care. she watches him in the distance, leaping from one stone to another. he does it so lightly, quickly and with confidence. she feels his

steps in her bones, his song in the crowns of the trees. when she first arrived, she saw a shaman in all his glory. now she sees a man facing everyday hardships.
what can i give you for the road? i'm standing here, and you are bouncing away from my riverbank, from my *santuario*.
bien viaje, enrique.

06.26

at night, i'm dreaming about the days that are getting closer. the indian in the desert, an old face and a quiet voice calling me in the morning. i hear his breathing, and the neighing of horses. i'm on my way.

the magic is interrupted by a flock of birds. thirty hatchlings shrieking over each other. go scream somewhere else you little shits. can't you see i'm meditating? the flock takes off and continues to shriek a few feet over.
it's time to be on the move.

she has traveled a lot, but this was her first time living with natives, with their mornings, their dreams and nightmares, bringing in the sky with them, cooking their soup.
at first, they were amazing because they were so different. but after a while, they were appalling because they're the same as we are. and then, finally, it's all good, because it could have been anticipated.

reina has returned from pucallpa. they miss each other, she and enrique, as if someone is arranging it that way. ama is putting together the pieces of the puzzle: it seems enrique has a child with nai, reina's daughter-in-law, who he took under his wing when reina's son drowned. franco's step-grandfather is also his little sister's father. an exquisite equation. you can't make this stuff up.
the conductor whistles out the evening departures. so, where will it be this time? ama screams a greeting to the jungle for the last time. from one gut to another. *hey ho*! when she goes back to the creek, hegner shows up with a flashlight and a machete. his eyes are bulging. he says he heard a scream, so he ran as fast as he could. apparently, he was

worried about her. jesus, that's so sweet, he was going to fight for her. a knight in shining armor, without fear, making a grand entrance. she would not have expected that from him. on the twelfth night, he had crept up on her, still hungover from the debauchery of the honoria. he wanted to talk to her. she kicked him out. with a brisk voice, she shut the imaginary door in his face. when he disappeared into the darkness, she had begun to speculate whether he'd dare do something to her. he was strong enough. these guys could carry an ox on their backs. but hegner was not made of vulgar matter, he just had a brittle side to him. and after all, he was the baby in his family. the youngest of ten siblings, so he knew how to whine. she thought he was chickenshit.

perhaps she has wronged him a bit. she takes back the chickenshit.

she lies down in her damp lair. the monkeys surround it and raid it in circles, over and over, as if they know that a snake is crawling out of her stomach, a rope that is pulling her further on. the jungle opens its veins and gracefully bleeds out. she's paying for her new life with her old one. *buenas noches, mi amor.*

06.27

lunch soaked in banana leaves and reina's tears. *triste mi, niña,* i will be completely alone from now on. *solita*. mama reina is crying. ama caresses her. she wants to say that reina is strong, that she will be able to carry her burden, but her voice makes no sound. she only gestures, a final embrace.
vamos? hegner carries her backpack to rio pachitea and then waits with her for a boat. they both wave down the boat, shouting. farewell. i will miss this place, hegner.
she watches the galloping roans in the sky. no one speaks inside of her. she can see how easy it is to lose her strength. she was supposed to see it. that's why she came here.

san pedro del casta • the donkey and jesus's father-in-law

06.28 pucallpa

for some reason, it isn't sinking in that she's finally done with the jungle. she staggers around pucallpa, through the bustle and the stench, and she's feeling out of it. the mud of the jungle was home, a hideaway from a different world. now she's walking through the city, wandering the streets, and she is trying to catch a glimpse of the tracks leading to the future. which one to choose?

the main avenues are dead ends.

when her sister asks her on the phone what her plans are, she almost falls off her chair. she replies with jokes in her emails. she has paved her inbox with them.

how's the tumor?

that sentence kicks off most of the emails she receives. no one asks how ama is , what ama is doing. they ask how her tumor is doing.
hey, how's your cancer doing?
the cancer is doing great. thanks for asking. we had a nice dinner together, now we're going downtown to buy the cancer a new pair of pants.
she is furious, a gathering storm when she realizes how they see her, like she's indistinguishable from the disease. she has become a canvas on which everyone paints the things they don't want to see in the mirror. illnesses, fears, death. she is looking forward to going to the desert, where no one knows her.

she's trying to chase her demons away, leave it all behind, but it's not working. after a horse's dose of emails, she's spitting fire. her skin is prickling. she can't go back yet. she would kill somebody, maim them.

go fuck yourselves, all of you! she storms into her hotel room, screaming and throwing things. a comb, a bottle, towels, demolishing everything she can get her hands on. a glass against the wall. two mangoes splatter on the mirror, she bangs a chair on the floor and tiles crack. she's stabbing pillows with her pen, a knife into human flesh. pieces of linen are flying all over the place. she doesn't know who they belong to, she doesn't care. perhaps they belong to you, or to me. she wants to call it a day. be six feet under already. she's lamenting her pitiful fate. grieving over a pile of trash, shattered glass, torn up notebooks, a broken chair; a character out of a tragedy, a child who wants something but can't reach it.
but despite the temper tantrum, despite the fury and the howling, there is a part of her that still maintains that peace. a witness with no voice, an eye that only watches.

she sorts through the ruins in the afternoon, sweeps the shattered glass, and takes a cab downtown to buy new pillows. she still doesn't know how she'll explain the broken chair. maybe she'll be able to find another one just like it.

it's hard, mom, i'm crying a river here. something is coming, but i can't see anything. i don't know where i'm going.
it's strange, ama dear, but i feel that you're at peace.

06.29 pucallpa

today, she sees her clearly: the woman she met on her journey. will she let her stay the night or will ama just leave her things with her? a grandmother wearing glasses who reads from the book of revelations.

suddenly, she's overcome by an awareness of distance, separation, everyone is so far away. only rei appears in her dreams from time to time, his black skin. she stretches it over her white flesh.
i dreamed about you yesterday. we talked, and you looked like you were happy, rei. and i was happy to see you.
ama, it looks like we visit each other's dreams. you have a place inside

me. i get that you have to go to nevada. you don't have to explain. i stand by you.

lake yarina ripples as the fish sizzles on the grill. *palomita* on a plate along with five plantains from the wide-hipped vendor behind the grill. *ya, mi amor.* but you have to wait a bit. i just put them on the grill. no problem. i have time. a whole lake of time. it always makes her smile, the way these matrons address a person as *mi amor*. like in the caribbean. huge markets filled with black venuses under the sun. they all call you *sweetheart, honey, love*, they are overflowing with terms of endearment. so how many bananas do you want, darling?

07.03 lima

hotel españa. living downtown for pennies. it's something between a hotel and a hostel. hallways, a courtyard, vistas, crystal chandeliers, unexpected nooks. replicas of antique statues and rembrandt paintings; generous mirrors multiplying the strange zest of the place. a terrace entwined with grapevines. an atmosphere like a sicilian villa. skulls at reception. the grandiose hallway reminds her of visconti's *gephard*.

ama, come. you'll like portland. you can live at my parents' house. they would love to meet you. nevada is just around the corner. you can rest a bit before you travel further, evan.

evan, you don't know it yet, but you're playing a key part in my story. i dreamed that the road to the indian who was calling me passed through you. so be careful. something might appear. look for signs in the trash bins, billboards, listen to what the homeless are saying, the paperboys, the birds. they might have a message for me. i'll fly up as soon as i manage to get on a plane. i'll take a few days off before i set out to follow jesus into the desert.

flights to the united states during the state holidays are sold out. tickets are overpriced but she was anticipating this and has decided to wait in lima until the travel wave blows over.

lima is cold, so she starts looking for a bank, so she can get money to buy a sweater made out of llama wool. instead of a bank, she finds a ship in heaven. the pomp of the spanish conquistadors, biblical images set in gold. the ship next to it is silent, intimate. an older man begins to cry. once in while, he blows his nose and wipes his eyes. here, no one is ashamed of kneeling. crawling on all fours, sobbing out loud. sing out of tune. what a relief. she's leaning. the wooden benches carry salt deposits of sin on their bodies, the sweat and tears of penitence, the touch of palms and the etch of fingernails. echoes hang from the ceiling. the past on a string. an island on which everyone is stranded. the loved and unloved, houses, places, where she will catch the wind, dreams that she has branded into matter. it's time to let it go. move on. she opens her hand. it's all in front of her like a faded postcard. she is distancing herself, rising higher, until it all ends up in a box of truffles. she'll tie a ribbon on it, set it on fire, and send it down the river like a chinese lantern.

07.05 lima

breakfast on a terrace, french in the air, youthful mops of hair lean over travel guides. the service is subtle, the sky is drooping. the ridges on the rooftops are sculpting the city that's loudly bustling in its streets. a huge, wooden turtle she noticed yesterday—and thought to be quite exquisite—is now moving across the cobblestones and picking at a head of lettuce. i guess it's not wooden after all.
jeff, somehow, i don't know what to do with myself. my mind tells me that i need to fly home, my legs would rather head straight back to the jungle. but that insistent face of a certain old indian is hammering a desert landscape into my heart. he's tying up my breath with his voice and so i'm just waiting until he lassoes me in. a vision. apparently, that's what they call it. a vision. can you make any sense of it? i can't. if i were to delve into it like an expert, i'm sure i'd find out that it originates from some sort of archetype of blah, blah etc. etc., but what the fuck is that scholarly bullshit for? definitions and categorizations are as useless as sneakers on a snake. in the meantime, i'm heading for the mountains

until there's an opening, and the universal computer processes through another part of my journey. does that make sense to you?

yes, it does. those fairytale-like petroglyphs in marcahuasi are well worth the extra trip. i read about them in a magazine. i would kill to be there. is there any public transportation going up to thirteen thousand feet? the cn tower here has its own elevator.

there's a bus that goes up to ten thousand feet, and there's a trail the rest of the way.

07.07

the alarm goes off at 5:00 a.m. you can't walk around by yourself in lima at this hour, the boy at the reception desk tells her. it's still dark, *señorita*, and it's dangerous. ok. she'll take the taxi in front of the hotel. the driver floors it, speeding through the empty streets, running several red lights, but he stops like a model citizen at the street lights on the three-lane avenue. he looks to the right and then to the left and then cracks his whip. ama tells him that she's not in a hurry, but here, words do not throw off the local coachman's rhythm.

here we are, *señorita. collectivos de chosica.*
the street is empty. just a group of men by a kiosk. an early morning snifter to get them on their feet. municipal workers with trash cans on wheels and brooms. along the street, a line of cars, their drivers snoozing in the back seats. the darkness is thinning. the car to chosica gets filled quickly. the driver starts his car, honks his horn to indicate he's going, and then he floors it through the city at a hundred miles an hour. chosica, she's finally on the bus with a sign that says marcahuasi. the passengers are filling the seats. a girl in an onion-like skirt walks down the aisle offering breakfast. *papa con huevo! papa con huevo!* an egg and potato on a paper tray. the sun works its way through the smog of the industrial suburban slums, and the bus doors close. in less than an hour, the grime of the city is long gone, just a faded memory. the bus huffs and puffs as it climbs. at times, the bus's tires are in the air.

the view down from the window is only for those who have a strong stomach or are blind. the radio plays moody blues, nights in white satin. the mountaineers sway in their seats with bags and baskets of food, live poultry. children with their noses pressed against the glass breathe in the landscape, leaving behind their steamy marks, tiny greasy imprints.

sleeping in the best hotel

that night, she sleeps at jesus's place. it would have sounded better to say she slept with jesus but that would be a lie. he is too young for her, and on top of that, he is happily married. jesus's father-in-law doesn't immediately introduce himself, but that doesn't matter. most important is that she meets jesus. he's the first jesus she's ever met in person. jesus greets her with a pack of dogs behind him. welcome, señorita. this is the best hotel in san pedro delcast, hotel marcahuasi. please come in. he tries to speak english, but he's not very successful. he mixes it up however it comes to him. a room with its own bathroom? yes, of course, follow me. you see, here is the bed, window, chair, and here is the bathroom, just no hot water. you know, there is no hot water in all of san pedro. and the shower, *señorita*, isn't working either. but the toilet flushes, and the sink works just fine. if you like, my wife will heat a pot of water for you, and i will bring it up to your room personally. what do you say? that won't be necessary. she waves her hand. she can survive a night with cold water. she doesn't realize that water doesn't even come out of the faucet, but rather an icy slush.

this is my father-in-law, said jesus. his name is oscar. she'd met that man, wearing a sombrero and chewing on a twig, when she arrived at the town square and asked for a place to stay the night. he immediately sent her to his son-in-law's grand hotel. and now he's asking her how she's planning to do tomorrow's climb. he offers her his donkey. it's young and strong. he points towards the animal, he's right over there. i will get him ready, if you wish. no thank you, i'd like to walk. how about a horse? i can get a horse for you, if you don't like my donkey. i like your donkey very much, and i would never exchange him for a horse, but i still want to go by foot. ama wonders, how many times will she have to repeat this conversation?

quiero caminar, claro! certainly, i understand, but allow me to guide you to the top, i will get you there safely. i will explain everything you see. not a chance! no, thank you. you're very nice, oscar, but i want to go alone. *sola*? you can't go alone, *señorita,* what if something happens to you? she is steaming, her heart is beating like a drum, she pulls in the reins, holds her tongue so as not complain to jesus about his father-in- law. oscar gives up after a while. the *gringa* is too pigheaded, he thinks to himself, but he just nods. very well, i understand. *señorita* will go alone. *sola*, and that's that.

in the afternoon, a walk to acclimate. the sky is painted blue. houses are built on an incline, donkeys are neighing. she takes the path uphill towards the summit, passing by the colorfully shabby local square. the view of the mountains is enticing and intoxicating. after walking a few feet, she starts breathing heavily. her pulse is racing at 200 beats per minute. she rests every 20 steps. there's a little field and a cabin in the distance. it all looks a bit blurry. she can hear a spring behind her, sounding like a strong wind. the rhythm of wood banging on rocks. an old man is banging on something in the field. his wife in a ragged skirt is filling a bag full of weeds. an older mountaineer passes by her. he's carrying a bundle of freshly cut oats. he says something to her, and with the childlike smile that is common among these locals, his barren gums show one or two teeth. where is the *señorita* from? is she here with her family? then he continues on at a quick pace. ama watches as he lightly climbs the hill. she drags herself slowly behind.

in the evening, she makes her way to the local square. two boys are playing soccer on the compacted clay, stirring up the dust. they're arguing over the score. instead of a soccer ball—a clump of wide duct tape. a few locals offer themselves as real fans. some dogs are running around. the dirt-poor mountaineers are kind to the dogs. none of the local mutts have been mutilated or show signs of a beating. there's no evidence that reminds her of the emaciated and aggressive outcasts from the streets of ucayali.

a donkey runs by, alone. behind him by a few hundred feet, there is a jangle. a woman with six kettles, three in each hand, her eyes on the ground, the rhythm of her steps both rapid and tired. the atmosphere is like once upon a time in the west. long shadows, a howling drunkard singing at the top of his lungs, zigzagging through the square, as a little girl in a pink apron chases a goat home.

the bed in jesus's grand hotel has a thick blanket in place of a mattress. she throws her sleeping bag on it and contemplates how to sleep so that there's no pressure on her bones. at eight o'clock, she's lying on the boards, shivering in the darkness. her upper back is like concrete, the chattering of her teeth doesn't warm her up. and the visions start coming—trains, wagons people, concentrations camps.

she's lying there, barely moving, a body without energy, gaunt, awaiting death. the sound of drums are coming from the outside. music at the village square, like a funeral march. someone inside of her speaks softly and kindly. it's time to let go. to abandon these islands of pain.

a dark morning. the fog in the valley is as thick as porridge. the peaks on the mountain range are changing colors when the sun glances off them. jesus's wife is cooking her breakfast, a sleeping baby hangs over her belly in a sling. she's humming a song for the infant and rocking it back and forth. will this be enough, *señorita*, an egg, potato, rice, and avocado, jesus is drawing her a map of the path to the summit, he explains to her how to get there, and where to be careful, he confirms one more time that she hasn't changed her mind about going alone, that she doesn't want the donkey or the father-in-law. do you have enough water? food? a hat and sunscreen?
yes, i have everything here. she points to her backpack.
jesus notices her sleeping bag.
do you want to spend the night there?
i don't know yet, but if i don't return tonight, don't worry about me. we will still worry until you come back. *señorita* is not too wise, but if she insists on refusing our advice, then we'll pray for her.
she tucks away jesus's drawing, and checks one more time to see if she has enough water. the road leads by a cemetery. *camino lago, camino corto*. she'll take the long way up. the cold morning air is numbing, sucking pins and needles into her lungs with every inhale. she stops

every 100 feet, looking around, catching her breath. she can still hear the bleating of donkeys like a morning liturgy. the bells in the village square ring seven o'clock. the sound becomes thinner, sinking into the valley through the mist. the sandy path starts to turn red. terracotta is everywhere. memories of mexico. the ascent gets her blood pumping. the veins in her throat are jumping. but her head is uninhabited. no more voices. no more commentary, just a mute witness, without a peep, sitting on her forehead. she's capturing pictures and then letting them go without sorting, labeling, or framing anything. she simply is.

she doesn't meet anyone, just a snake that quickly slithers across the path by her feet and disappears into the bushes. a condor soaring above her head cuts the sky into parts and sews them back together again. it's changing shape. *el condor pasa. i'd rather be a forest than a street.* there's a different world above. a bohemian paradise[19] at 13,000 feet, and cows, they graze even up here. she walks through a gate, an arc de triomphe among the cliffs. little pockets in the rocks. and then suddenly that head with a sharp beak, a silhouette of wing. it's flying directly at her, drawing closer, soaring thirty feet above her head. ama stops breathing. this is the year of the pilgrim. she sees the path she just hiked. she isn't leaving any tracks. her steps are resonating within her. footsteps in her flesh. she is alone, she is whole, she is missing nothing. the air billows, and words come falling out of it like a bookmark in a book that she just finished reading.

the qualities of the solitary bird are five:
the first, that it flies to the highest point;
the second, that it doesn't suffer company, not even of its own kind;
the third, that it holds its beak windward;
the fourth, that it has no specific color;
and the fifth, that it sings ever so gently.
— saint john of the cross

night on the cliff. the earth is covered in a thick mane, softer than the bed down below at jesus's place. she's lying in a fetal position, listening

[19] *Translator's note*: Český ráj or Bohemian Paradise is a nature reserve in Czechia known for its unique rock formations.

to the mountain. the stars are close by. a whole dream between a single inhale and exhale. in the morning, she shivers awake to a voice telling her it is time to get up. she stretches her back, collects herself, bids goodbye, and gives thanks for the lodgings. slowly, she descends the path that leads around the petroglyphs. she lets the path guide her, and she gets lost. she must have missed a turnoff on camino corto. but she lucks out and bumps into a couple with a herd of cows. the kindhearted mountaineers take her under their wing. the old woman nods in agreement, and salvador takes off with her and briskly ascends the path. he stops frequently and takes deep breaths, no need to rush. he becomes her guide, he points toward old graves, a pueblo and a cross. people once lived here, you know? they lived here all around. once in while, he picks a plant and offers it to her to smell. this herb is good for the kidneys, this one is for a headache. he's laughing at himself, a sound like when a child starts choking. a face sticks out of the bedrock, a giant turtle, a frog, and here you will see a path. that is your way back. this will take you down to the village. ama says goodbye. she knows that salvador is not expecting anything, regardless, she reaches into pockets to take out some change. it's no trouble for her, and for him it's a nice bonus. he thanks her shyly and wishes her plenty of luck and to go with god. ama looks back one more time, as the figure in the sun, with the sombrero and the confident step, slowly vanishes behind a cliff.

she runs down, rushing, collecting images in her head—the earth's curves and contours. she breathes in the dryness of plants. gravity gives her wings. once in a while she trips, learning a new skill: how to slide on her ass. she's becoming a pro. she's baptized her new pair of jeans here. perhaps she'll rip a few holes in them. finally, she sees the lagoon with a neck-breaking shortcut wrapping around it. her scraped hand hurts. perhaps she sprained her wrist. two mountain men are sitting by the lagoon. they say hello, and she asks which way is the fastest. *aquí.* they both point toward the edge of a cliff. aha. she might as well have asked a condor. she doesn't stop for anything anymore, not even to dust off her butt and knees. she just watches her step. she can't feel her toes. she had forgotten that the jungle ants chewed out the padding on the tip of her boot. those terrible thieves. it's going to feel great when she takes her shoes off.

running through the square, she only has 15 minutes left before departure. she quickly packs. jesus is close behind her, he helps her with everything, he opens the door. it helps.
hurry up! carlos is always on time, and he never waits for anyone. and the next bus doesn't come until tomorrow afternoon.
she runs. her legs are shaking. she doesn't want to spend another night at jesus's place. but carlos has taken off. he never waits. but he makes another stop down below by the turn. maybe you can make it with the help of god.
dear god, let's get going!
jesus grabs her backpack and rushes through a maze of alleys. someone is screaming from the hill, and the highlanders are passing it on. they're waving and calling from one door to another. ama is fluttering behind jesus, staggering over the cobblestones, blood soaking through the tip of her shoe. halfway down the hill, jesus's father-in-law, god's messenger, cups his ear and catches the words in the wind. when he hears the message, he turns his donkey and takes off, one hand holding the animal and the other his sombrero. the highlanders along the street are rooting for him. he's catching up to the bus, which is just closing its doors and starting to take off. carlos never waits. that punctual shit-for-brains. ama, all out of breath, gets on. jesus hands over her backpack.
bien viaje, señorita.
in lima, the *señorita* pops her blisters and pours alcohol over them. she has brought *sangre de grado* from the jungle and smears it all over her bloody toes.
mom, even though i hiked in tennis shoes plundered by ants, because i left my hiking boots in the hotel, san pedro del casta was the crown jewel of peru. i can still see the bedrock and dry grass, the rustling snakes and the flight of the condor.
i'm heading on, and i don't know where, but i'm done with those tons of desires and wishes, and those worn-out beacons showing how things ought to be.

3

“the intuitive mind is a sacred gift, and the rational mind is a faithful servant. we have created a society that honors the servant and has forgotten the gift.” – albert einstein

a sea in the desert • a pyramid in a lake • a mother made of stone

07.13.08 portland, oregon

evan in the crowd at the airport. he's thin and fit. visible shoulder muscles under a white t-shirt. a strong embrace. what's this? he points to a painted tube that she carries over her shoulder. that's my rain stick i got from the shipibo indians. she takes off the tube and turns it upside down. the seeds inside start to pour. it rattles. your very own rain. not bad. come on. i'll take you to my parents' place. they have dinner waiting for us. they're switching from one lane to the other on the road, just like her thoughts. it's hard to fit so much into such a small space.
remember how you pointed out to me once that i should always listen to what the garbagemen and the meter maids say? well, i bumped into a friend this morning in the parking lot in front of my building. i haven't seen her in a year. she knows a lot of indians. i immediately thought that this was not a coincidence. i'm going to introduce you to her. she's a bit crazy. you'll get along.

jeff, the change from the jungle to here is like falling from the third floor onto a concrete slab. it knocks you out a bit. if there's anything you don't miss in the jungle, it's the media. it's like mosquitos: it just sucks you dry. if you want a peaceful life, trade the news for cows.
i keep repeating to myself why i'm heading out to the desert. the thought is stuck in my head like a children's rhyme, like a summoning chant. a classified ad: searching for an indian, a needle in a haystack, fur on a rattlesnake, whatever you want to call it. maybe i'll even find the higgs boson. if i sum up the data, the odds look promising. i saw his face in the desert. he's old, and he has horses. maybe. i saw wooden structures and the silhouettes of hills. i heard his voice. and then there was that white granny i dreamed about. she'll help me on my journey.and a lake—the

shape of it and a spot on its bank came to me in a vivid dream. that should sum it up. who wouldn't set out on such a promising trip?
don't write to tell me what you think about it. i'm thinking the same. but what people think, including me, is irrelevant. it's better not to think about these things. then you don't have doubts. someone wrote to me not too long ago that it's good to nurture hope inside you. it sounds good, but at the same time, it's pure bullshit.

do you know why hope always dies last? it's because hope is basically a tease—it will never put out right here and right now. it's always next time, or sometime later. tongue-teasing in the ear about a fine future, with one finger poking toward the distant horizon and another poking into your eyeball. hope never dies, because death has no time for such baloney.

07.14 portland

the house reminds her of something. the smell of milk and dog bowls outside the doorway. the curves of trees in the windows. the shade of the colors on the walls. the room where she is staying now is a winter garden. boomer, with his grey snout and wobbly shuffle, his paws trembling when he has a dream. evan's family, georgia and gregory.

georgia and gregory

gregory came back from vietnam a changed man. his time in special forces carved him into a different person. he couldn't come back to his wife and children, he couldn't live on the farm that she kept afloat for all the years he was deployed. he packed his bags and headed for texas and planned never to return. and that's when he met georgia. their bodies and their stories locked together and blended into one. they took off along the west coast, all the way to canada, in an old volvo. they carried their home on its roof, greg's army tent. they would lie next to each other in the afternoon heat, sticking to each other with sweat and dirt, the earth beneath them throbbing. greg took one look at her and all of a sudden he proposed. georgia, your forehead lit up with a big yes, and that was that. at that moment, his entire life suddenly fit between her lips, flowed into the palms of his hands, disappearing in damp corners. AWOL. he left without permission in the summer of '72. after fourteen years in the united states army, after ten years of marriage, with no inhibitions, no regrets. he lay down with her, thrusting through her yes, nothing else mattered.

they tried it all, took in everything: parties, drugs, getting sober. they opened their first store with organic food on the west coast, and were fixing up a house. after they got married, georgia collapsed. in the hospital they told her it was multiple sclerosis, and her chances were not looking good. their story unraveled and got tangled up, but it kept on going. she knew what was at stake. she knew the way the wind was blowing all too well. her family history was infested with the disease. she remembered what it did to her brother. he had just turned twenty when it bloomed. she tried to go back to being a journalist, but she couldn't concentrate, she couldn't take the pressure. greg went back to the energy industry to support the two of them. the organic hippie venture went under. he liked to talk about it, about how they almost got divorced, but how god worked it out for them to stay together.

she wanted to leave me. she had made up her mind. she wasn't doing well and maybe she was burdened by guilt. everything was mixed up inside of her, she was fighting herself. i went back then to a church, i got on my knees and stayed there for hours, pleading for god to help me. when i came back home, she was waiting to tell me she was pregnant. and that's how evan was born. then came robin. god answered my prayers. my father used to force me to go to church, i would fight it like hell, and as soon as i could make my own decisions, no one would ever see me inside a church. when i came back from vietnam, i was a mess, disassembled into spare parts. i had no clue how to keep living. i was drinking, raising hell, taking drugs, which back then were all the rage, and suddenly i was standing in a church. it was as if they gave me a new set of batteries, i was rewound. it triggered something, and two weeks later, i met georgia.

georgia calls them to dinner. it's served on a terrace, pasta and salad of all colors. greg skillfully tackles the corkscrew, the wine gargles its pour, the glasses chime. bless us, oh lord, gregory prays, thank you for bringing us together today, in the spirit of your generosity and for thy gifts that we are about to receive. amen.
dinner is served: lasagna with god—greg's favorite subject is not so much a subject of conversation but rather a lengthy sermon. georgia gives ama a look that says she is used to her husband's preaching, but she, too, has her own opinions.
our lord has strange ways of insinuating, but what you're going through is a sign that you should give yourself to him. he is always with you when you utter his name. gregory talks on, the air pulsating with his odes to holy intentions, and after a while, ama switches to autopilot. she isn't listening to what he's saying. all she can see is vermillion-colored whirlwinds bursting out of him, swarming around, maybe she envies him a bit.
it's still hot outside. the horizon is dying down, gradually adding purple shades of color. darkness is taking its time.
after dinner, georgia clears the table, ama helps her fill up the dishwasher and scrubs the charred pan, during which they look at each other a few times and start to laugh.

ama feels how, suddenly, she is surrounded by christianity. greg reads to her from a book of commentaries on the scripture before bed. ama does not interrupt him, in respect for his grey hair, but it's getting on her nerves. especially the passage that's intruding, breathing down her neck. she can't shake it off. "i can't do it, god, i can't do it because i'm nothing. god, only you can do everything."
she can't stand it. she'd kick it to the curb like a dry piece of cow dung, but she knows that it is meant for her. as always, when something eludes her, it splits her up inside.

07.15

she has brought presents from the jungle, and greg asks about them the next morning.

noni juice is a universal remedy. if you drink it over the course of six months, it will renew all the cells in your body. there are serious studies about it, backed by science. you can find tons of references in just one click on the internet. the natives, however, have known this for thousands of years.
mom, evan introduced me to grace. we met in powell's bookstore on the corner of tenth and burnside, where grace worked when she was still in school. the bookstore has a story of its own. thirty years ago, some guy named walter powell decided he would find available editions of every book title, and he would stack them on shelves one spine next to another. both used and new. his recipe was simple: an independent bookstore, open every day of the year. the staff—exclusively book lovers. stacks filled with all the books you could imagine, including sold-out titles. it's not just a building, it's a city of books, four stories high—even in america, that's unparalleled. you can spend days in here. a green room, blue, orange, pearly white, a coffeehouse in between, and then more rooms, red, pink, gold. they give you a brochure with a map of the place at the entrance so you can find your way in the perfect labyrinth. it has a timeline that shows the history of books. in two thousand bc, they used scrolls made from animal hides in western asia. i didn't know that. the building has a european vibe, and i bought a few books, i simply couldn't resist.
then we went to a teahouse, but i don't remember where it was or what it was called. i don't even remember what i ordered. all i remember is that i was with grace.
grace does justice to her name, which also means mercy, beauty, and prayer. like georgia does for gregory, she shifts time within me. with people like them, a person lands somewhere in the middle, in a time when the relationship is no longer new, but it carries the trust from years of encounters, from chronicles of experiences, albums filled with photographs. you can know people for decades, share your life with them, but at the same time, have nothing in common and know nothing about them. with other people, it's like you get a key to a locked door, you unlock it, enter, and you're right at home. you light a fire in the fireplace, smoke a pipe, and a mutual story simply unfolds. grace talks

about her teacher, gilbert walking bull from the lakota tribe, who taught her everything. walking bull, she pronounces his name with a childlike pride, six years old again at that moment. she talks about spirit animals, about ravens and coyotes. the lakota call them *heyoka*. *heyoka* is a joker, a holy wisecracker, always turning everything upside down.

grace understands. my vision of the old indian from the desert is at home in her world, i've been picturing the shape of a lake, a place on the eastern bank, where i need to resurrect something. and that white-haired granny with a bible in her lap, who is going to help me on my journey.

after dinner, evan stops by. he wants to say goodbye. be careful, the indian reservation has an unbeatable crime rate. they sink into the armchairs on the terrace, the darkness is rustling in waves. they are each facing a different direction, far from one other.
ama, i'm glad that you came, but it is damn hard on me. i really wanted to show you everything here, but i had a different idea. our relationship was like a dream you never want to wake up from. you want it to last but you know that there's no chance of that. when you wrote about what's happening to you, i finally woke up. i saw you on the ship, the way the ocean was carrying you away, and it's still tearing me up.
ama breathes in the darkness, a gust of his body moving within her, revealing a shadow, a longing of some sort. all that she once had, all she could still have, his lips that once caressed her like algae caresses a fish in the sea, suddenly clawed at her.
if something happens to you, what do you want me to do?
it takes her a while before the words connect, and she links the sentence together and prints out the legend.
click. people around her sense something. they're trying to grasp what it is, trying to read her, she chokes on her spit, begins to cough out the nightmare within.
send me home.
in a casket or ashes?
i don't know. i couldn't care less.

ama, it's hard for me to hear you talk about dying.
i know, mom, i guess i haven't found what i'm looking for yet. it's hard to say, when i don't know exactly what that is.
georgia goes to bed early, greg pours himself a shot, loosens his suspenders and continues with his campaigning.
when you accept christ, you have it all, you don't need anything else. and when you read the bible, god lives within you.
ama is a bit tired of all of those saints, she has a slight headache and regrets that she didn't get up and leave when georgia did.
you know greg, jesus once told me that i don't have to read anything.
her words surprise him. he is certain that he knows more about jesus than she does.
what did he tell you?
he told me not to read the scriptures.
and was it truly jesus?
of course it was jesus. well, the raven, but that's the same thing, he's just wearing a different shirt.
her response doesn't settle well with him. he shakes his head and furrows his brows.
that raven of yours seems more like the devil to me.
in that case, jesus and the devil are saying the same thing.
ama is surprised at herself that she's not letting go. but something in greg's lobbying provokes her and entertains her at the same time. that faith of his. that belief that he is in that elite country club.
what does this jesus of yours look like?
something between popeye the sailor man and robert redford, she thinks to herself. dear god, people get hypnotized by an image from a book given to them by their grandmother, and they have a feeling that they know how things really are.
ama stops talking, and greg goes back to his broken record routine. for me, there is only one road. the road to jesus christ.
i don't want to take that away from you, greg, go with whomever you please. could you just let me do the same? gregory gets up. he fixes his suspenders and pours another glass of whiskey. she notices that his face is rather flushed when she disagrees with him. greg is one of those

people who needs leadership, and as a result, he feels the need to lead as well. when he left the military, he switched the morning roll call for church, but basically, nothing has changed. the same hierarchy, but this time he takes orders from god, who looks like a field marshal.
i'll tell you something. back in the day, when i was interested in buddhism, i read the *bhagavad gita*, and then i threw it all out the window. buddhists meditate to achieve emptiness. i don't want that. i don't want to be empty. when i meditate, jesus fills me up. god enters my soul.
ama lets in a respectful silence. she says to herself, keep quiet, remember your father. he wouldn't utter even a tenth of what you just blabbed out here. but she simply isn't capable of being the voice of edifying silence. when she pounds in a nail, she does it with a sledgehammer.
of course, they strive for emptiness in order to become buddha, which is one and the same, gregory. if a person is full of shit, she has no room for god.

07.16 pyramid lake

landing in reno. a desert airport. blinking lights. neon signs. the stench of fast food. the noise of slot machines and air-conditioned space.
she heads to the information booth where she asks an overweight man in a uniform how to get to pyramid lake.
only by car, ma'am. no buses go that way, absolutely nothing goes out there.

hertz has a car available, which is a miracle during this season. i just need a signature here, and we're done. here's a map. keys to the car. have a safe trip.
she finds a black chevy with a california license plate in a parking garage. it's quite a shock to find herself in a car whose windshield isn't taped together, straight from the jungle. she heads towards the lake. the radio plays on the way, *how does it feel, to be on your own . . .* bob dylan, by coincidence. his nasal whining, and lyrics that will hold up in a hundred years.

a pyramid in a lake. a calcium carbonite formation. pelicans above the water. the desert, millions of years below. types of fish that exist nowhere else. *cui-cui*. the bank is abandoned. fishing season is over.
the lake is rippled with sharp reflections of the sun's rays. ash and dust in the air. this is the place. ash and dust.
hunkered in the shade of the chevrolet, she can't help herself. she sees her reflection in the chrome. a strange creature curled into a ball on a roadside full of pebbles. each one of them carving a sign in her skin. she hugs her knees. her face is as salty as the lake.
in the early evening, she heads into sutcliff, where several houses are hunched together, showing signs of civilization. crosby's lodge, the only accommodations on the lake. just a bar and a little store where a person can buy anything she really needs. beans, ice cream, bait, and postcards. mobile homes instead of hotel rooms. number three is available for this evening, and it has a kitchen.

the mobile home has sweat dripping down its windows. the cupboard holds two beat-up old pots without handles. a chewed up old wooden spoon, and plastic bowls instead of plates. ama starts to cook. tonight, we're having beans. it just takes time, water, and salt. but the salt is missing—it probably fell out of the bag in the trunk, which is only a few steps away. the door of the camper slams shut. she has locked herself out. she runs to the store, to the cash counter, which is also the reception desk, and asks for a spare key. when she returns, the lake begins to howl, luring her towards its waters. she forgets the rice and beans burning on the stove and follows the voice of the lake. the moon rises slowly from behind the hills and onto the water. ama listens and the language of the lake surrounds her as if she were drugged, enchanted by the full moon, its sound engulfing the silence of the pebbles on the bank. she feels a light touching her shoulders, but she sees no one. someone whispers to her, pleading, warning her. dad, is that you? the beans. you left the beans on the stove.

she jumps up, pushing her body to go as fast as possible, one foot in front of the other. but her feet are not listening. they are tripping over each other. she runs back to the road where a white light writes the word RUN! she hears the echo of a starting gun, and so she runs as fast as she can. as if the sign appeared just at that moment. as if it was never there before she stopped at the lake. she speeds up for the last few feet. she was always able to squeeze out that last bit of juice when she ran the hundred-meter races, though in those days, she did a better job of catching her breath, and her calf muscles were not made out of phyllo pastry. the lock is resisting, of course. turn the key right or left? which way to unlock? she finally gets inside and finds all the water gone from both pots, which are lightly charred on the bottom and smell decently burned—but it's no catastrophe. she's seen worse. ok. everything's fine. but you should have your head examined. you almost burned the place down. you could have made headlines:

nevada desert: czech tourist on crusade for holy grail blows up mobile home with pot of great northern beans.

everything is fine. she just can't catch her breath. damn. she can't move. she falls onto the bed which is startled and tries to skitter out from under her. the window is smudged and fogged up. this isn't good. for another hour, she's overcome by coughing. there's a strange new sensation in the back of her spine. her chest feels like it's full of rocks. this is something she's never experienced before. shit. the voice inside of her is screaming, obnoxious, it has reached your lungs. it's clear that it will rip her to pieces soon enough. she slams her hand into the bed. silence! shut the fuck up!

the cough is gone in the morning.

in her sleep, she sees a snake. a large, silverish one. it rises from a geyser of water, grows from the lake. she is standing on the bank, her eyes wide open. the fanged creature doesn't do anything to her, it doesn't say anything. it just appears, turning her inward with its glance.

without a thought, she packs up her things and then sits in the car.

she doesn't know where she is going, but something is pulling her elsewhere. the desert is sizzling. the lake is gaining color, the salty mist is growing clearer. when she sees a signal on her screen, she listens to voice messages.

hey, this is grace, i have something to tell you. it's unbelievable, even if it's normal in that dimension of yours, so you'll most likely believe me. yesterday, just a a couple of hours after you left, i'm strolling around town, and i bump into this boy. when i come to, i realize that it is brad. i haven't known him that long. we met in nicaragua, when we were filming that documentary i told you about, but that's beside the point. he invites me for a drink, and we're chatting, and i tell him about you. about your trip and that you left for reno. now get this. apparently, his grandmother lives ten miles away from pyramid lake. she's a grey-haired, fiery old christian who wears glasses and is a bit crazy. just like you pictured her. isn't that fantastic? so here's her address. this can't be a coincidence. brad gave me the number of his cousin who lives about a mile away from his granny. you should call him.

ama hangs up. she is getting used to the fact that things will fall into place, even if she doesn't understand why. a wave of intention, jeff would say. *if you ride on a wave of intention, things happen. i know you'll find what you're looking for.*

she takes it in, then raises her sails and lets go of the helm.

besides a gas station, the town of nixon has a school and also a museum. when she comes through the door, gus takes care of her. he has long hair, a wide smile, and is soft-spoken. when he asks her why she has come here, she lays it out plainly. for some reason, she feels that these people won't think she is crazy. gus nods and calls harvey, who apparently understands these types of mysteries.

harvey is older, a little over sixty. he gives her a tour of the exhibition and shows her the art of basket-weaving. a little seat for a child, woven from wicker. women used it to carry their infant children on their backs. the paiute tribe calls its people the numu. his eyes smile but his voice drops lower when he talks about how they lived a long time ago. he offers her a cup of coffee and sits down with her at the table, putting his

hands in his lap. he begins to tell the legend about the stone mother, in the numu language. words flowing like water from inside him. the walk of wind on the water's surface. ama doesn't know what the words mean, but she hears the story nonetheless. it's growing inside her. the mother of mothers who turned to stone from grief.
harvey talks about ancient times, when the old indians were masters of their memories. when there were still stories to tell.
when i was a child, i witnessed remarkable things. over there, just a little distance from the lake, there lived an old man who was blind—but he could still see, he used to sit on a tree stump, and we would take turns using him as target practice with a rag ball. we were thoroughly enjoying ourselves. we would sneak up on him—no one would let out even a peep—but he saw us. he would call us by our names and threaten to tell our parents. we could never understand how he did that. one day, we decided to spy on him. he was heading to the lake, taking tiny steps. he knew the way by heart. he stopped right at the bank, and he spoke into the waves, as if he saw a creature beneath them. he stripped off his clothes and merged with the waves, disappearing under the water. he stayed there for hours. we were frightened. we ran home and looked for help. we thought that he had drowned. but my grandmother told us that he would do things like that. my grandmother understood. she knew the old rituals and the power of herbs. she herself would speak to ghosts. they would guide her hand when she cooked her potions. but after the christians stormed in, it was hard to maintain those traditions. everything disappeared. died out. we live in modern times, people will tell you. they'll say you're crazy if you don't live just like them.
he pauses for a bit. his eyesight fades, and he begins to move from side to side, as if he's watching a scene from a movie that's too painful for him.
my parents came from the generations of children that were kidnapped and sent to boarding schools. they were raised by priests and nuns who cut their hair and put them in uniforms. they were not allowed to speak their native language. the government banned our sundances and other rituals. everyone was supposed to become a good christian. when they were young, my parents danced the sundance ceremonies in

secret, filled with hatred towards the white government. harvey tells her about how he taught the old and the young on the reservation the paiute language, their mother tongue. he tells her about the medicine men who all died out. i saw them when i was still a child. i saw many things with my own eyes. nowadays, you won't find a single one of them. i didn't understand anything back then, but nowadays, when i'm already too old, i remember things, and everything falls into place. everything makes sense. i remember when my grandmother told me about the healer who abused his power. one day, when he walked with his wife to the lake, a gigantic snake emerged from the water, spat on the shaman, and disappeared back into the lake. the wife carried her husband home, put him to bed, and by nighttime, he had ballooned. in the morning, he was dead. grandmother said that the snake was his own power turned against him.
ama is silent. everything is bouncing inside of her. she knows about the snake in the lake. it came after her and slithered into her dream. she knows its power.

she gathers her things to leave. gus escorts her. she should certainly go in her car to see the stone mother. the best time is during the week, when no one is there. it is a powerful place. there's a good chance she will discover something there. the navajo, too, tell legends about her, and they say that the mother by the lake is also their eternal mother. they come here to pay tribute to her. they bring sacrificial gifts and chant prayers. they scolded us, saying that we should do a better job of taking care of her, that we let vandals go over there to get drunk. so, we banned camping and staying overnight. the best time to go there is early in the morning or just before dawn. but you can head out there anytime. maybe the place will whisper to you. maybe that is why one of the elders is beckoning you. maybe your journey does have a purpose, and you are bringing us a message. there could be a reason for this. maybe one of our ancestors is reaching out to us through this foreigner.

ama smiles. what kind of message could she possibly deliver? for whom? she herself is turned inside out. she can't tell right from left.

late that afternoon, she heads south, into fernley, to call the cousin, who apparently lives close to the fairytale grandmother. jason is a slow talker. he rolls out his words with an extra sigh. he is paving the way.
head out on pyramid highway and then turn right on the whiskey springs exit and then again on amy road. it's the first house on the left. i'll be waiting.

the sun is low. as she slows down, she stirs the dust on the road. jason stands at the door wearing a black shirt and jeans, and a light fragrance of cologne.

this is an unbelievable place, jason. this desert, the view. it's like another planet.
been here all my life. i grew up here.
his voice shakes a bit. he's about twenty-five or maybe older. she smells something on him, his hungry look. drugs or alcohol? but she can't see anything lying around. he may be clean after all, or maybe his stash is in the walls, in the corners. the house is on the prairie overlooking the foothills, the shadows sliding down the slope of the mountains, the nearest neighbor a couple of miles away. he points into the distance as it darkens. my grandmother lives over there with my uncle and my sister.

he invites her in, but there's no place to sit. he's just finished remodeling his house, the walls are soaked in the smell of paint. it feels fragile, uninhabited. the half-empty rooms give the impression of a divide, a pause between lives, phases. it's as if something has ended, but the thing that's yet to come hasn't developed any defining features. they sit down on a rug in the living room, with the white walls and a large window that's gradually turning dark. there is a fireplace made out of tufa stone. in the middle, a putting mat, a green runner. it lies there between them like a demarcation line.
every person that she meets is a story. every story opens a door to her own rooms with unexpected corners. then she creates new space, new lives out of them. she taps them into her keyboard.
jason has a voice with a wide wingspan. suddenly it becomes quieter. once in a while, he swings back, as if he's speaking with two voices.

maybe it's an echo that's bouncing sound back to a single pile.
i live here alone. my father died last year; he drank himself to death. he hadn't turned 50 yet. grandmother and kathy moved to my uncle's house, because when he drank, he was unbearable. i stayed with my dad until the end. i didn't take his abuse personally, when he shouted and started throwing furniture. when he woke up in the morning, he never remembered what he did the night before. it's a family tradition. his dad drank too. and his dad's dad did, too. i drank, too. i just finished my therapy, i'll get my driver's license back in a month. it was hard in the beginning, but it got easier as time went by. i think i learned a lot.
ama is getting used to the way people bend her ear, as if she has a key that fits right into them, and they just start spinning their stories and the years unwind, the experiences and situations. and so, she listens for hours at a time, she walks with him through his archive, his recent escapades. he crashed his car while drinking, so they took his driver's license. he was forced to stay home in the desert without a car. so, he became a hermit.
my drinking was social. i partied a lot, and i didn't know how to stop. even my father didn't really have a reason to drink. he had a good job, a house, healthy children. he didn't have a reason to drink.
he covers his burdens, addictions, family curses, and genetics. he talks about chains, treasures, and grief. a canvas with colorful dots looming in front of her. silhouettes of the drunks in his family, mixed with the belief in a christian god who keeps everything in place. everything leads to him. but it's still missing something. something keeps slipping away, falling through the cracks.
and what about your mother, jason?
he shrugs as if he's apologizing. as if he doesn't know what he's talking about.
don't know, i didn't know her. she left when i was nine months old. she was on drugs. heroine. apparently, she took off with another guy, and it was a relief. i got my last letter from her when i was twelve, and i never heard from her again. i tried to find her. for years, i played detective, and after some recon, i finally found her address. supposedly, she's living

somewhere in texas, unless there's someone else living there by that name, and it's really not her. sometimes i tell myself that i should write to her.
ama can see how it's eating him up inside, how he's digging out and cauterizing an empty cavity. those haunting eyes, sniffing her like a hungry dog. he'd like to fall in love with her just so that she can fill all those empty outlines, so he can get closer to this woman who'd dig a cavity inside him where she can constantly resonate.
our grandmother raised us, me and kathy, all by herself. not too far away from here, before this house was built. dad worked in construction. he would often be gone a whole month. she would homeschool us. we had textbooks, notebooks, and a rigid schedule. she would write out math problems for us on a folding blackboard that was very hard to erase. when i started high school. i didn't know too much. i was an outcast. my classmates would bully me, until they found out that i could play music. it's amazing how impressionable people are and how fast they can change their attitude. it's as if i became another person in a split second. then grandmother got sick. it's been ten years since. she had lymphoma but she pulled through. it will take a lot more to knock her down. you'll see for yourself. tomorrow, i'll take you to her, if you like.
it's almost midnight when he asks her what brought her here. ama tells him the plain truth in plain sentences. she doesn't need a lot of words. she listens to her own voice come back to her, so that she feels like she's talking about someone else. she sees herself staggering through this scene.
i have a spare room. there's nothing in it but a rug and a mattress. grandmother lived in it until she went to paul's. you can stay there if you need to. as you can see, the house is empty.
ama envisions the floor plan. a large kitchen. unfurnished rooms to the right, where jason's family once lived. father, sister, grandmother. jason's room is at the end of the hallway. it's the only place in the building that looks lived in, that has furniture. it's surrounded by music gear. speakers and instruments. guitars, keyboards, bongo drums.
i was in a band. i wrote songs with a friend of mine. we were pretty good. my dad and i built a studio in the garage with percussion. but my friend

wanted to be famous. he kept pushing us until we were burned out. it was as if he never realized that you can't play under so much pressure. all the guys joined other bands, and i spiraled all the way down to rehab.
he asks at the door if it's all right to light one up.
of course, why wouldn't you be allowed to light one up in front of your own house?
he laughs through the darkness.
i smoke one a day. that's all. it's my only vice left from the old days.

nevada 07.18.08

she has mountains in the fog for breakfast, the ashes from the forest fires in california. they head to mary's in a pickup truck on a dusty road surrounded by pasture with cattle. jason tells her how they used to raise horses, but now they just have dogs.
grandmother is in the doorway. surrounded by a pack. all of them are jumping up and down, barking for attention. this is trixie, and this is jiffy, angie, lorna, and that there is thorn. so come on in. i've been waiting for you. ama sees a familiar face, white hair, familiar eyes behind a pair of glasses. a familiar smile and voice. she still can't believe it. it stops her in her tracks, surprises her. it's as if there is a difference between meeting someone in the reality of dreaming and in the reality of wakefulness.
i made tea. have a seat. and what about you, jason? why don't you go watch tv. you won't be interested in what we have to say.
jason would rather stay, he doesn't want to leave, but grandmother is an admiral, and so he quietly disappears.
ama will recall the house long after she's left. inside there's a funny hodgepodge of antiques, cheap trinkets, and pictures of saints. outside, there's a garden with a fountain surrounded by birds and chipmunks.
i feed them all. each one of them that stops by, says mary. squirrels, chipmunks, birds. they come here day after day, and so i feed them.

the tale of the dog grandmother

my husband was a drunk. he never did anything right except for those four kids. i have to give him that. he made beautiful children. but each of the boys took after him when it came to drinking, as if it was their trade, their business, paul is the only one who avoids it. he won't touch alcohol, even on christmas. he's hard working. he does the work of six people and still keeps smiling. sometimes i ask myself, where did he come from? where did he learn this? it certainly wasn't from home. it's not that we were always down and out, we had fun once in a while, but most of the time, it was a struggle—breaking glass and aggravation. wondering whether that sorry excuse of a man would come back from being with god knows what woman, back home to us. he always came back. he'd clean up and sometimes bring flowers from somewhere and tell me how sorry he was. that he would change. he would never touch that shit again, but at the same time he still smelled like a brewery. my faith kept me going, nothing else. and love for my children. that goes without saying. but without faith, i don't know where i'd be, maybe they would have taken me to the loony bin, with those four kids in one trailer. yep girl, we lived in a trailer, it's amazing what a person can bear. but to leave him, divorce him? that i did not want to do. i was against it. i gave him my word, for better or worse. that's how i looked at it. i waited years for something to change. i grew up with the church, in a catholic family. i knew the lord's prayer before i knew my alphabet. eventually i started to see everything completely different. i didn't need a middle man. i wanted to deal directly with god. not to talk to him through a churchman, a priest, or a friar who didn't know any more than i did. maybe he read a little more than me. but how could he understand me? how could he advise me when he'd never touched a woman in his life? not to mention that they're all a bit off. sometimes you feel like you're in an insane asylum when you think about it. but i saw through it. one day, i saw the light. one big lantern. jesus didn't come here to give us religion. jesus came here to establish a relationship with each and every one of us, to offer himself directly. like there's no one between a mother and a child. a husband and a wife, between siblings. they don't need a

third party to be butting in. only when the two disagree, they need a lawyer. but i can always talk it through with jesus. i talk to him every day.
finally, i left my husband. i traveled to see him, then to alaska. i drove the whole way. the kids slept in the car. i found him again in the same state, and this time i got really mad. i would have beaten him with a baseball bat. i yelled at him for the first time in my life, because somewhere deep inside of me, i still loved him. i didn't want to give up my dreams.
the kids grew up in a blink of an eye. then i lived with james, my son, when his wife left him. she took off with a fella that did drugs. we were all relieved when that whore disappeared. and so, it was all on me. two grandkids and the trailer again. jason was not even a year old.
in today's world, there's a lot of atrocities, the devil feeds off of them. everyone is serving themselves to him on a silver platter. the doors are open everywhere. especially with greed and politics—his two favorite domains. all these casual relationships, men with men. you can't find spirituality and faith, even with a looking glass. paul is building a house on that hill, where we're organizing a sanctuary to help those who have strayed. i want to help people to hear the voice of god again. paul never married. he probably has never met the right one. but i don't know if he ever will, with his nature. he's a very nice man. he could make any girl happy. but i'm not one to interfere in his affairs. if he's happy by himself, then i'll be there for him as his mother. i moved in with him last year, a few months before james died. it's hard to bury a son. it's the saddest day for a mother. you bury a piece of your heart. but god knows what he's doing. and i say to myself that god took james in, and he is with him now.
i have faith. it's a rock behind your back. you can lean on it. it will always support you. i believe that god will grant me everything i need to live, everything i pray for.

ama is taken aback by how easily this woman has opened her home to her. come. you'll have lunch with me. i've prepared shrimp and salad and some fruit as well. here in the next room, kathy has a computer, if you want to write to your parents and let them know that you're safe here with us.
ama sits by the computer and looks over her piles of emails.

mom, i'm at grandmother mary's, just a short distance from the lake, so i have a place to sleep.

this is not our house, she says. this is a house of god. and you're on a journey and you need a place to stay and so the lord brought you to us, and now it's your house too. stay as long as you need and make yourself at home. jason has plenty of room, and you can visit me whenever you like. to talk, to eat. whatever you need. you're welcome.

the grey bushes hem the horizon. the raven and the dawning sun fill the sky with colors. ama returns to jason's house. she feels lightheaded and laden with books, and words that taste like bread. she opens a well in the desert—one of the books from mary—and skims a cluster of words: "in those days, people search for death but they do not find it. they will crave death, but death will run from them."
i can feel it, like it will strike me down to my bones. i thought i found my own strength in the jungle. but here, i've realized that the strength wasn't mine. now i'm learning how to get out of its way. something is guiding me when i allow myself to be guided. i don't know what god is. i only feel power, emotions. i'd rather call it a source.

nevada 07.19.08

"shall i not drink the cup that the father has given me?"

i'm looking for an indian. a needle in a haystack, a flame at the bottom of the sea. i'm searching for a holy grail.

the anatomy of the holy grail

at first glance, it looks like a normal house. an entrance and exit. chambers and atria, partitions, shoring. the walls of the left atrium are three times thicker than the walls of the right one. parietal and visceral layers, both with a lightly glazed surface. a mechanical system of tassel-like valves resembling ventilation. the interior upholstered with endocardia, walls vertically stripped under a roof with an arched aorta.

the quest for the grail is hard, because you never know where to search for it. on blind maps, in white places. somewhere down and to the left, under the ribs.

* * *

the pyramid splits in two on the water's surface. with one foot, it's standing on dry land and with the other, it's in a rain shower. a storm covers the sky and blends dark grey into the pale daylight and then swallows the lake. the desert opens its pores. the rain pounds the gravel and sand. the earth is bobbing up and down. the dust settles, turning into mud. the surface disappears in the fragrance of bushes and wind that cradles a stationary vehicle. ama is inside the car, pulling on the hand brake, and heaven unwinds within her. she loves a storm. she only hopes that its breath will not sweep her and the car into the water. it's jerking her back and forth, it's foaming, sprinkling the landscape with icy pearls. it doesn't stay long. within the blink of an eye, it's gone. when it passes, the desert smacks it lips. it pours the icy rosary down its cleavage and licks the last bits of water. the hills appear again and the ground starts smelling of fresh tobacco.

tea with jason in the evening. his long bones and tendons, black hair. she asks him about ravens. they are all around here. he begins to talk about birds, about the animals that live in the desert, about the canyon where, at dawn, a herd of wild mustangs comes to drink. he talks about california wild fires, about smoke that spreads through the landscape like rough clouds. a few weeks ago, it was impossible to go outdoors without a mask. every year, they have forest fires. but the smoke carries all the way here. i thought of the horses and what that annoying ash does to them.

and then he is silent, his eyes ripping into her like the claws of the jaguar. something moves inside her. she grasps for syllables, armoring herself with soft words.

she can't sleep that night. it must be the green tea. or maybe, those green eyes.

nevada 07.20.08

how to pray to god with your hand on your wallet

mary stops by to pick her up on sunday, wearing a light blue outfit, jade earrings and a locket, white sandals, a purse, and the sweet smell of violets all around her. ama is driving. they're headed to reno for morning mass. this interests her. when she was in new york, she dropped by for a few services in harlem, to take in the atmosphere, to taste the spirituals, the gospels and the black hair. the movement of bodies and the laughter, the solid arms of the matriarchs in colorful dresses—god bless you, honey—but she's never visited a traditional white church until now.

calvary chapel. the interior of the church is like a conference room with seats upholstered in red. about three hundred people, a setup like a rock concert in a convention center. on the stage is a guitar, bass, percussion, keyboards, and vocals. a rocking jesus. jeeesuuus! almighty god. the living bible, the crowds are standing, clapping in rhythm. the lyrics are popping up on two large tv screens. long live god! long live america, too! c'mon in! you'll see what you've never seen before! the final chapter of the first book of corinthians on the agenda. finally, the word of god. "i will very gladly spend and be spent for you."

the preacher sways behind the microphone. blue jeans, a white shirt, long sentences, and a wide smile. he talks so fast it makes her uneasy. as if he's being timed, or he has to go to the bathroom really bad.

he's out of breath and howling: dear sisters, dear brothers, i know what pains you. i understand you. i know how damn hard it is to look at the index every day and see how the stocks are plummeting. i don't like it either, that i'm losing money. i know exactly how you feel. you say to yourselves, dear lord, when will this end? when will it turn around? but don't be sad. don't give in to despair, because things are different than they seem at first glance. *god*, brothers and sisters, god is on your side. god is standing by you. that is good news! even if your earthly possessions are falling down head first. don't despair and know that your investments in heaven are growing every day, every hour, every minute. they are multiplying in a geometric progression. remember that each time you open the wall street journal—and realize that in that very instant, your wealth in the kingdom of heaven is multiplying and accumulating. what do you say? isn't it beautiful? isn't it a glorious feeling? so, let us sing!

ama is smiling all around. she has never seen anything like it. holy notes sneaking around her, accumulating and multiplying. it's beautiful. jeesuuus! almighty god! jeeesuuus, jeeesuus. jesus here and jesus there. jesus heads. jesus tails. it's even on the dollar: in god we trust. and then saint paul talks to the corinthians. "i'm making a fool out of myself here, but you all made me do it. you could have worshipped me alone, even though i'm not worth anything, compared to all those super apostles."

ama wants to get up on stage, grab the microphone, and piously announce to all those yanks in the room something that they have never heard before but that would amaze them for sure. so far, it's a secret, dear brothers and sisters, but scientists recently found proof of the existence of the almighty: god is brazilian. after the service, they pass the hat around. three novices walk through the aisles, reaching with their hats. the cash and checks are rustling against each other. the faithful can't drop them in fast enough. not even the wall street crisis could stop them from supporting the tabernacle and its shepherds, with whom they lucratively empathize. and this church looks like it unquestionably could provide for itself. even though the stocks of those poor believers are steadily falling, their god clearly loves them. greet each other with a blessed kiss. all the saints are greeting you.

on the way back, mary asks her about the indians on the reservation. she is mostly interested in whether they are christians. ama doesn't know how to talk to her about them. she doesn't know how much of it mary would listen too. and besides, she is still in a mild trance from that christian vaudeville show, and then suddenly she's supposed to talk about her encounter with indians, a people that believe in the healing powers of clean water, who talk to the sky. she is learning to walk between worlds, to quickly shift rails. she doesn't know where to start. each word about the paiute seems like an accusation. she says a few words about harvey, about how he is trying to resurrect his native language that devout christians buried in the ground. the chevrolet becomes divided in two. a thorny bush has risen between the driver and the passenger. ama could speak czech in this moment, and mary would hear the same scribbling.

nevada 07.21.08

jason lends her his laptop so she can write and surf the internet. the whole house has wifi. ama heads back into town, so she can purchase a set of earphones to skype and hear people from afar.

sometimes i feel that the ground below me is collapsing. i don't know what to do next. have i still not had enough of this? have i hit my lowest point yet? the breaking point is coming. maybe i'll reach it tomorrow. i'm close. i need someone who has gone through that.
jeff, i'm losing it. i can't dig myself out of this. i'm not finding any peace. that hysterical jaybird from the jungle keeps screaming in my head. something happened. something really happened, and you always have such a calming voice. a person can choose the knife or not, but the outcome can be the same. your gwen died exactly like that. they cut her open, and she was gone.
yeah, but gwen was always quick to jump into things, she never wasted time.

so, does it really matter which way i turn the wheel? you say that i might have found what i've been looking for, but i just can't see it yet. gus told me that exact thing yesterday. i don't understand it that well, but i'm open to any suggestions.

on the way to reno, she stops by the red lobster to get some food. the minute she sits down, bono comes blasting through the speakers. *sometimes you can't make it on your own.* her server's name is sven. hello, how are you? my name is sven and i'll be your server today. bono's voice is cutting her into little pieces. *sometimes you can't make*

it on your own. fuck. only god can do anything. she's anxious for god to show her something.
when she starts chowing on the fish, sven shows up again. how is everything? everything is great, sven. your shaved head, your clean white shirt, and your sculpted muscles, your professional smile, your modulated voice that spews out the daily specials, even that picture on the wall behind you of cape cod, a lighthouse and the sea, is perfect, sven. thank you.

mom, in the beginning, it seemed that none of the native americans here would even talk to me. they were afraid that they would be laughed at. that someone would write about them as superstitious lunatics who talk to ghosts. in the end, communism helped me. if i were a white american girl, most likely i would have failed. but my experience living in a totalitarian country was the ticket, because the indians understood that. being forbidden to speak what you think. going to school and singing a different song than is expected. the secret underground activities and culture. the brainwashing, the extra caution when meeting someone new. combined, those all create an interface on which we can build a relationship. the day before yesterday, harvey told me that he was training for the sundance. that was an act of great trust. yesterday, he took me to a sports field. we circled around the track in the noon sun, even though there was a warning issued because of the california fires. he didn't say much. but after i stopped asking him, he began to unfold. the air smelled like asphalt: golden, grey, trembling. he talked about healing, about the sundance, about sweat lodges, sitting in circles for hours. then he invited me to his home. a small bungalow. he introduced me to his wife and son. his wife was going to dance this year as well. her cousin was leading the sundance in south dakota. chief two dogs. it's a long way from here. they're leaving on monday.

harvey claimed that my indian wasn't necessarily from this world. he said it could be someone who had been among the dead for a long time. i admitted that it could be a possibility. regardless, i feel the need to find him. well, if we have a five-year plan, then it's our obligation to complete it. strange how we cling to the interpretation of visions rather than the visions themselves. even though these interpretations are often completely off the reservation.

nevada 07.22.08

the song of the stone mother

the difference between the jungle and the desert is that the desert doesn't say much. the wind here often holds its breath.
when she steps out of her car, the lizards show her the way. two little busybodies with their tails elevated. the lizard is a messenger, harvey explained. i once saw a shaman catch two little lizards. he put them on his temples and then sent them off into the world with a message. ama is walking through the dark grey sand and is sinking in. twilight begins around the lake. maybe she has it in her.

mother, i'm looking for a landscape that would give purpose to my walk. maybe i'm looking for you. i sensed your energy from afar. that blaze falling into the lake. the sky full of hollow spaces. something happened to me here, in my kidneys. the sound of the wind when it slides on the water, walking lightly. barefooted, skipping stones, radiating. the sand and fragments of pebbles sharply rustle, cutting each step. i don't feel any pain. in my branches, there is no room for pain, for it has no shape. i climb into your lap. the voices of your people sound within me. the wisdom of the rocks, light changes their faces, gradually they dwindle away. i am bringing no gifts, mother, forgive me. your breath here in the dust sticks to my fingers and seeps through my skin. leave it with me. you whisper through the mouths of fish. leave it all with me. the sorrow, the stone, the tears.

the boulder inside me has turned over and opened its fist.

petrified coral fans, an ocean puddle in the middle of to the desert, cliffs with drawings of the water levels. the water once reached high. the water is deep here. when i depart from you, i can only weigh anchor in the sand. a mother-of-pearl shell will flash at my feet. it takes on the shape of butterfly wings and flies into the palm of my hand. you offer gifts, but you accept none.

mother, show me the sorrow that turns you into stone.

nevada 07.23.08

"we lead a difficult life . . . we struggle and suffer to reconquer our solitude. but a day comes when the earth has its simple and primitive smile. then, it is as if the struggles and life within us were wiped away. millions of eyes have looked at this landscape, and for me it is like the first smile of the world. it takes me out of myself, in the deepest meaning of the expression. it assures me that nothing matters except my love, and that even this love has no value for me unless it remains innocent and free... the world is beautiful, and this is everything."

—albert camus

the desert always moves her. while she looks at the water, a different kind of downpour fills the lake. she feels the words. their rhythm, a voice. rei? someone is speaking to me like never before. maybe it's god.

i have a story for you. maybe it will grind something out of you as well. the paiute tribe tells the legend of the stone mother. the grandmother of all tribes. they call her the mother of mothers. once upon a time, when rocks were still people, she came here to the valley and sat down at the base of the mountains and began to cry for her lost children. she cried for days and nights, months and years, centuries. she covered the earth with her tears, and the desert couldn't soak it all in. the salt water began to collect into a sea. the natives say that the mother never set aside her sorrow. she never set her pain afloat. she just stayed at the bank of the lake. the pain thickened inside of her, imprisoned her and cursed her into stone. she sits here to this day with her gaze fixed upon the lake's surface.
i'm going to sleep. the darkness has replaced the storm. the scent of stone is in the air, water and dust, the fragrance of daisies.

nevada 07.24.08

baba yaga has a field day

it's good to do a review every morning, immediately, about why i'm here and what i'm doing. repetition is the mother of parrots. i'm looking for an indian. he's old, and he might have a horse. he might not be from this world. maybe he's broadcasting from the happy hunting grounds. it's good to remind myself about what's at stake here, just to have perspective.

jeff, i have a feeling that my indian is a test of whether i know how to listen or how to follow the signs. and so i'm waving my antennae here, and i'm trying to catch its signal and its static. desperation has dug a lair inside of me and is squatting in my entrails like a skunk. i can smell it. wherever i go, it pulls me to the ground, where i see nothing but darkness. and then, when i take a break and sit in the silence, fear and stress disappear, and so much light enters me that it's almost unbearable.

the shamans in the jungle blend thousand-year traditions with christian prayers and don't see a conflict of interest. the more saints and deities you mention, the better. over here, i meet people who believe in only one god. they cite passages from the bible, and so for the first time, i took the book of books in my hand and really started to read it. the book is a storyteller. it bakes stories like bread, its breasts are filled with milk. i have to admit, it did overwhelm me. but at the same time, preventive resistance grows inside me, when i sense that this new friendship is pushing me, demanding the exclusive passage. do you have any advice?

a daily dose of mary's scripture and greg's holy-babble via email. his chariots carrying the biblical mission. where does this obsession come from? the need to convert others to a true faith? greg even calls her in the afternoon and relentlessly keeps drilling into her the need to get baptized. ama tries not to hiss at him, but she isn't too successful. greg, i know you're preaching from your own experience, and i respect that, but for me, that would just be a pantomime.

when she hangs up, she goes to find an icepack and some baking soda. she needs to let out a healthy belch and a loud scream. she doesn't have the stomach to devour a gingerbread jesus dipped in chocolate three times a day. she demands compensation, a pinch of poison. she needs to enter a new fairy tale. baba yaga suddenly shows up and ama immediately pounces on her. her wheels start spinning. all the major literary hits are in the public domain. myths and fairy tales. every ancient myth, no matter how old it is, originates from an even older myth or legend, and baba yaga is everywhere.

baba yaga in the bible all references to baba yaga were wiped out in the second century after the birth of christ, and the name "baba yaga" was replaced with male names, most commonly, peter and paul. in the older, "purified" version, we often come across such errors as "her name was paul..." or "her name was peter ..." one version of the new testament noted paul's menstrual calendar. several pages in the bible b.y. wrote herself. no one can deny the alchemistic origin of corinthians 15, the resurrection of the dead: "so is it with the resurrection of the dead. what is sown is perishable, what is raised is imperishable."

baba yaga and jan hus. the basis for the old testament was an original text by baba yaga, written for king ptolemy ii, known in its latin form as the *vademecum of baba yaga.* this indisputable fact is refuted by the pharisees to this very day. jan hus brushed the dust off this *vademecum*, then imposed his famous diacritics[20] and tried to rehabilitate its original author. in this attempt, however, in the year of our lord 1415, he was publicly burnt alive. in comparison to the bohemian preacher, baba yaga remained, remains, and will always remain evasive. she operates below the surface, where she formed an underground movement [see baba yaga's activities in the resistance movement].

for decades, the holy see, known for its ability to react to historical progress, has been contemplating reforms of various stands and arguments, including bans on condoms.

---

[20] *Translator's note*: Jan Hus was also an accomplished linguist who developed a system of diacritics in the Czech language to eliminate confusing consonant clusters.

in ancient times, there were several reasons to discriminate against baba yaga: she was of the female sex, which in itself represented a handicap in christianity. during her youth, she fornicated more times than mary magdalen, and had seven abortions. to top that, she wasn't too presentable. she didn't shave her legs or brush her teeth. she never cared to keep up her appearances. what mattered to her was principles. nowadays, she dresses up in armani and uses chanel no. 5, but only because she likes disguises. another reason for bias against the individual named b.y. are her eccentric means of travel and her malicious comments about the pope's mobile terrarium. currently, the main reason to vilify b.y. is unequivocally her spells, her magic. on the other hand, the reason why access to jan hus's ashes is banned even after six centuries, remains covered in vatican fog.

baba yaga's family tree. ninchursaga was the mother of baba yaga and the virgin mary. the father was unknown.

baba yaga and jesus. jesus never denied the fact that he gained his healing abilities from baba yaga. he claimed that without her, he wouldn't have been able to cure even a bunion. when he was still a small boy, mary sent jesus to her sister's, so she could take a break from his philosophizing and so he would stop getting on joe's nerves. baba yaga took a liking to the boy because he was sharp and sensitive. she gradually taught him her tricks and magic, from cloning loaves of bread to walking on water [see jesus's miracles]. jesus didn't understand her at first, because baba yaga spoke in similes, but in the end, he got so used to it that later on in life, it was the only way he would express himself. with the measure you use, it will be measured to you—and he got that from baba yaga, too.
finally, baba yaga paid a visit to judas carrying a bottle of booze, waited until the useless wimp got decently drunk, and then easily convinced him to betray the messiah, because it was only then that everything would have a purpose. she knew that jesus's dream and destiny was to die a martyr, and more importantly, to rise from the dead, which was an escape artist's act that they had perfected years earlier. all that was

left was to pray to all the saints for him to be crucified, rather than that asshole, barabas. she realized the historical ramifications and the total quagmire that would follow if she didn't succeed. she was relieved when it all went according to plan. jeremiah lamented, pontius pilate washed his hands of everything, and then it went like clockwork. classics on the program. a duet for the whip and jesus's back in b-minor, a stroll up golgota with a cane. it wasn't so pleasant in that heat, but the view was worth it. and then that transformational trip for which he went through all that hassle. baba yaga knew very well that eden was an old sumerian word that, in translation, did not mean "paradise," but rather, "open steppe."

a knock. jason stands in the doorway.
i thought i might take you to the canyon. there's a chance you might see the wild mustangs before it gets dark, but it looks like you're writing.
no, i'm not writing at all. just crazy shit. the horses seem like a much better idea.
she turns off her computer and grabs a sweatshirt. then she stops in the doorway.
jason, has it ever occurred to you that historical contexts are created by those who write about them?
jason pauses for a second.
so you mean that no one will ever know what really happened?
he smiles a bit and then nods. you've been out in the sun for too long today, haven't you?
jason's profile is lit in colors of the west, the sky with clouds shaped like human faces and the curves of horses, their movement with the background of mountains are streaks drawn with a chinese paintbrush. unruly blood thickens the air.

nevada 07.26

tension is high in the morning. a greater desire to recover, to live. a greater inner pressure to pack it all in, to end it. is this not the definition of insanity? several blimps are floating around in my head with opposing slogans. if i can shoot some of them down, i'll feel better.

"small is the gate, and narrow is the way that leads to life, and only a few find it."

the sound of the vacuum cleaner makes her feel good. the strokes of the mop on the floor. thoughts about stephen hawking, a genius in an immobile body. we can't pity him, we can only be inspired by him. it makes her happy that she has the ability to clean. sometimes she feels pain through her arm, all the way to the armpit, and a cold sweat appears on her forehead.

sorry, jason, i can smell that broccoli through the whole house.
but that's a good thing. this place is finally smelling like a home and not a construction site.

ama, can you hear me?
grace is a gargoyle, a thermal hot spring. she fires up the coagulated blood inside of ama and sets atoms into motion.
i have something for you. i couldn't sleep after our discussion yesterday. i kept thinking about you, and this morning, i woke up ready to explode like a bomb, thinking i'd be damned if i couldn't do anything for you. i was feeling helpless. i couldn't come up with anything. this was eating me alive. it was torture. in that moment, naira calls me. her husband is one of the elders of the akimel o'odham tribe. she once taught me about dreams in the indian tradition. she asked me why she hadn't heard from me for so long and what was going on. i told her about you and she asked if you'd like to come over. she spends half of the year living in portland with gil and the other half in the desert on the nevada-oregon border where they have a farm. they're in the desert now, about five hundred miles from pyramid lake. they just returned from a sundance. they would make a sweat lodge for you. what would you say to that? if you'd like, i'll come with you, and so would brad.

grace. i don't know what to say to that. you are really turning me inside out.

sleep on it and decide. when i first heard about that indian that calls in your dreams, i immediately thought of gil. but i cast that thought aside, because it seemed like you were supposed to find him at the lake. it occurred to me that it was just an interpretation that was standing on water. literally. he doesn't have to be at a lake. i don't know, we'll see. maybe gil is the one.

ama packs her things. she looks for princeton on the map. gil has said that monday would be good, so they'll take off tomorrow, with four hundred miles along dried-up desert lake as a stage.
could i come back here, jason? i would only stay for a few days then. you can always come back here. come back here for sure.

the north is on the white side and the world in a grain of sand

homestead 07.27

"i will turn all my mountains into roads."

she prints out her map and directions from google. it will take about seven-and-a-half hours. she scans the email from grace. when you enter a sweat lodge, you have to say *mitakuye oyasin*. that means "we are all related." the lakotas start all their prayers with those words. it means the trees, birds, animals, all the continents and oceans, stars and planets. when you arrive, you have to officially ask gil for a ceremony. in that moment, you address him as grandfather. bring some good tobacco with you, and some dark chocolate.

she turns off her computer and throws her things into her suitcase. so, first she'll take i-80 east and stay on the course for a few hours.

a smoky curtain on the way and just the anticipation of mountains to come. visibility is at about half a kilometer. the landscape is silent. it's keeping everything to itself. at the gas station in winnemucca, she accidentally grabs the green handle at the pump and almost pours diesel into the gas tank. the nevada natives have it the other way around. luckily, the nozzle is wider so it doesn't fit into the filler pipe.
after sixty miles of driving, finally there's a change. she exits off the ramp to i-95, which will stretch out for another three hours. the fog gradually disappears. she sees one mountain after another. one climbs over the next. the rockies, vistas, camel-colored plateaus. something tells her that she will find that needle in this desert haystack. "if you have faith as small as a mustard seed, you can say to this mountain, 'move from here to there,' and it will move. nothing will be impossible for you." after seven hours, she feels a crick in her neck. a massage would really do the trick. it has to be here somewhere.

a car is parked by the homestead's gate. grace and brad are standing next to it. is this possible?
hi, did you just arrive? yeah, and you?
about a minute ago.
brad is charming. mary said that her grandson was a lady's man, and she's right. naira is in the doorway, waving, welcoming. others come out to greet them: this is michael, he's an experienced fireman, the one who watches over the fire. this is thierry, our cowboy from france. a tall, blond, young man with a smile that stretches out across the sky. he reaches out his large hand to shake. macay the dog and two puppies. and then finally, gil. he comes out from the stable, an old indian in a white t-shirt with a bald eagle on it. he's wearing a bandanna as a headband. come on in.

ama looks him in the eye, but it is when he begins to speak that she recognizes his voice.

i was preparing for your arrival and praying since naira told me you would come.
he's a slow talker with that ancient native american demeanor, speaking with long pauses, well-rounded fluid sentences, which curdle into clumps and turn sour in the language of the white man. welcome. it's time to rest. you're flying with a blindfold, and you're questioning the meaning of existence. you're chasing a storm, always searching for something, and you don't realize that you already have everything you need.
nature does not ask what breath is for. stop for a moment and just look around. observe the way a shadow stretches, the way it cools the sand at your feet, how it gracefully disappears. follow the moon as it approaches and recedes. watch the way a tree grows, how it sheds leaves and blossoms.
when a person is lost, he should reach out to the earth to find roots. they will bring him back home.
ama is sitting and listening, she observes the map of his capillaries on his sclera and the tear that lingers in the corner of his eye. it slowly begins to bulge, waiting to break and spill down his face. it looks as

if someone inside him is doing the talking, as if he isn't even the one sitting there with her.
tomorrow, we'll summon the ancestors in the sweat lodge. the people of stone will be there, our most ancient relatives. and water, which is the best medicine. then the four-legged and two-legged creatures, the nations of the eagles and wolves. all of them will be present. it will not be me who will be speaking and deciding. they will be the ones speaking through my voice.
grey hair with streaks of black are flowing down his shoulders. his voice sounds like it carries the footprints of the centuries, imprints of a world behind a curtain. is he the one who was speaking to her through the fragrance of rain and resin?
it's time to unload old formulas of thinking, old paths, objects that are long gone. you're feeding that thing growing inside of you. you have remarkable strength, but you use it to destroy yourself. it's you who is killing yourself. in order to heal, first you must give your thoughts a new wind. tomorrow you'll leave behind your old self in the sweat lodge and be reborn.

ama sleeps in a teepee. she shares it with the french cowboy, who talks in his sleep. around midnight, she hears coyotes. they're close by, and they're hungry. brad has lent her a thermal mattress. regardless, around four in the morning, she starts shivering. she unpacks the alpaca sweater she bought in lima. thierry wakes up at first light to ride the horses.
my apologies, i didn't mean to wake you.
no problem. you were talking in your sleep.
really? what was i saying?
i don't know. i don't speak french.

the art of the coyote

a long time ago, various monsters and giants roamed the earth, that loved to snack on young animals and children. everyone was afraid of the monsters except the coyote, heyoka, a prankster among pranksters, who decided that enough was enough, and it was time to teach the

monsters a lesson. so, he headed out to the stone city in the desert, where after a few steps, he stumbled upon one of the giants. and as was common with these creatures, this one, too, was rough and gluttonous, but he was also slow—stupidity reeked out of him like his body odor. the coyote got to talking with him, and with sly words, he convinced the giant to help build a sweat lodge.
if you sit next to me around the sacred stones, i will show you a few tricks, and you will become as smart as me.
the monster agreed. when the darkness of the sweat lodge was filled with steam, the coyote told the giant that he would show him how to break his leg and fix it again. he took a rock and bashed it over the leg of a deer he had secretly smuggled into the lodge, until it snapped. the giant blindly started feeling for the broken leg and listened in awe to the coyote spit on it while singing "oh leg you can grow now." the coyote then let the giant feel his own leg to show him that he was completely healed. after that, the coyote offered to break the giant's leg and then mend it. the giant stuck out his leg, and the coyote bashed it with a sharp rock and immediately broke it. the giant screamed in pain and begged the coyote to heal him. don't you worry. your leg will heal if you spit on it. the giant spat on his leg until his mouth dried up, but the pain didn't go away, and the leg did not mend. so, he continued to beg the coyote for help. keep spitting on it, the coyote soothingly urged the giant. then he slipped out of the sweat lodge and went to look for another fool who wanted to snack on little children.

great story. so, which one of you plans to be the coyote?

the medicine circle is divided into the four directions of the world; four elements, four colors. north is white. each point of the circle is the beginning and the end at the same time. building a sweat lodge is easy for anyone who knows how to do it. just like anything else. the structure, a round woven basket, is made from sticks and leaves in the shape of a dome. parallel lines are covered by blankets and mats. maybe over a hundred of them. the entrance faces east. it is hot and windless out. perfect weather for a sweat lodge. grace straightens the

blankets inside, so no light can come in, she must be boiling in that heat. thierry digs a hole for the fire. michael prepares the stones. gil oversees everything. in the morning, ama hears him by the horses, his voice soft and calm, as if he were casually chanting in his own language. an indian horse is prancing about in the corral. he's spotted, just like the horses in western movies. a newborn colt tripping over its own legs is close by.
gil sits by the fire in the afternoon sun, dressed only in jeans, without a shirt or a hat. ama wonders how he can stand it. he's pushing eighty. is it even humanly possible? when she brings him some cakes, he smiles at her like a little boy. thank you.
should i bring you some water? you must be baking out here.
he shakes his head and smiles once more. i do this on purpose, so you have pity on me.
hmm. i don't pity you. i'm impressed.
she notices that he has scars on his chest just above his nipples. it's as if he has cut out pieces of his skin in a regular pattern. during the construction of the lodge, grace chants a prayer that she learned from chief jake swamp from the mohawk tribe. she's calling out to everything living in the universe. she begins with water, the oceans, mother earth, the nation of stones, everything that lives on the planet, and then she reaches out to the stars. she calls upon the nations of storms and thunders, then turns to the sun, a forefather, whose eyes are the bees that cry honey into our hearts. we send all of our greetings to you. we remember and stand by you. remember and stand by us.
when everything is done, gil invites everyone for lunch at a diner in the town of crane. it's about ten miles to the east. ama and grace exchange glances.
but we'll be happy to cook, grandfather.
gil smiles from ear to ear.
you didn't listen to me. that was not a question.
the preparations culminate in the afternoon. cutting up squares from blue fabric is a quiet job. they're used to wrapping tobacco into a line of pouches meant for those inside the lodge. little baggies tied to a red string: each one of them represents a year in ama's life.

the *inýpí* is a darkened hemisphere that symbolizes the womb; a return to it offers rebirth. a narrow path leads from the fire to the entrance of the sweat lodge. it's called the heart trail. ama dresses in cotton clothes that she bought in reno. michael carries a container in his hand that looks like a censer. everyone is cleansed in lavender and cedar smoke. just before entering, everyone greets the cardinal directions, and then they crawl in on four legs to get into the *inýpí. mitakuye oyasin*, we are all related. gil is waiting inside. ama has a seat on the north end. the fire guards stay outside and heat up the stones. it's pitch-black inside. only the hot stones gradually placed in the circular pit in the middle of the lodge give out a dim light. these stones represent the ancestors, and gil calls upon them step by step, speaks to them, respecting their wisdom. he sprinkles them with sage, and during the ceremony, he pours water on the stones. the temperature in the lodge increases.
naira, grace, and brad, the stones and singing. the rhythm of drums a slow start three-quarter beat. the stress is on the first beat. a call to the north, then a brief exhale and a transition to four-four time. the stress remains on the first beat, the tempo increases, moving faster, the heat and the vibration of darkness mix with prayer. each in his own language, each one blending with the other. the smoke and steam carry them all to the great spirit. it lasts for hours. wakan tanka hears the screams and laments. naira's song is in the language of the lakotas. *remember*. someone constantly repeats that word. the drums stir up her blood. remember. remember. naira's song tears walls apart, it forges new wheels to turn in her head: what are we willing to die for? what are we willing to live for? a monotonous sound like moving trains. it pulls me out of my body and carries me to the planets.
the frequency of the beats, the stretched-out leather resonating. the sound of rattles joins in, a snake-like sound. gil speaks to her, calling her back, returning her to the ground. *relax. let go. go beyond.* remember. she submits to the heat. the feeling i can't go on anymore slowly melts away. she is finally home.

after a ceremonial dinner, she stumbles back into the teepee. she sees the sky out of the corner of her eye. a comet cuts open the belly of the night.

homestead 07.29

to see the world in a grain of sand
and heaven in a wildflower
hold infinity in the palm of your hand
and eternity in an hour

—william blake

awaking before sunrise. naira's voice. drums and a lakota song. the homestead, a wooden house with a chimney that she saw in her dreams.

grace and brad say goodbye before lunch. they're going back to portland. michael is also leaving. ama stays.
don't leave just yet, gil says to her. you're still tired after yesterday. it would be better for you to rest a few days.

i don't know how to write to you about this. i found the needle. it was spinning like a bullet pointing to the north. all you need to do is thread it and start sewing. the thread sews on its own. you just hold the course.
i'm sitting with gil on the porch. colors are feeding themselves. the heat is receding. the wind blows from time to time. he wants to tell me something, so i'm waiting. i'm pushing aside mountains of thoughts just to have space. when i look at him, he gives me a slight nod. he shifts his headband on his forehead. he speaks slowly, waiting till the words and their melodies come to him.
a person who lives in fear and chaos, in depression, is a being that has forgotten about its heritage, strength comes from the roots, from the wisdom of the ancestors who painted the sky with their dreams, who prayed to it. they looked to the sky and found themselves in it. humans are nature, and nature is human. a culture that cuts its roots loses its soul. the never- ending growth that a person strives for is not possible. we can't always just inhale. we must also exhale and rest.
i'm saving everything on a disc drive. sometimes my stubbornness gets the best of me and eggs me on to ask questions. the fervor of a first grader.

use your mind, but don't let it control you. your mind can play tricks on you. if you know how to define something with words, that doesn't mean you know exactly what it is. many intelligent people do not know this difference, because they are slaves to their minds.

the door to the porch opens. naira walks carefully in with a tray in her hands. the pot clinks against the glasses. she settles the tray on a wicker table, unloading the cups and a plate of cookies. she pours tea and disappears into the house.

i'm afraid of death, grandfather.

gil leans forward and reaches out for a cup of tea. he doesn't drink it, he just holds it in his hand and stares at its contents as if he were looking for something in the cup.

there is no death. there is only a new beginning. and somewhere deep inside of you, you know it. we were just raised to believe, they told us that death is something terrible, but it's not true,when you reach the horizon, a new one opens up for you.

but what do i do when doubt is eating me up inside, when i don't understand anything?

a gust of wind carries the smell of a mane. the whinnying of a horse sounds nearby. hooves prancing on the surface of the desert sound soft and murky. thierry has let the horses out of the stable. he puts on his hat and his gloves, and swings into the saddle. tohono begins a light gallop.

you're on a path from which you can't go back to your old ways of being. doubts will appear if you place yourself in the role of the creator. then you lack humility. when you work as one with the creator, your doubt will disappear. right now, you know that something is guiding you. you've been traveling for some time, learning about the strength of visions. how they work. you're realizing that visions mean you see people, animals, and landscapes through your heart, not through your eyes. but you have to accept the fact that you're only human. if you do so, you'll stop being afraid.

he sips his tea and returns the cup back to the tray. thierry disappears with the horse in a cloud of dust. gil watches him disappear. he squints his eyes and smacks his lips as if he were in a saddle. tohono is the desert.

but for me, visions are a field in which i am a stranger. i don't know how to move within them. i wander aimlessly around in them and end up going in circles.
gil nods. he rubs his right eye and moves his jaw in a strange way, as if he is fixing a denture. she hears a slight cracking of his teeth. your visions guide you, but at the same time, they tend to confuse you, because you cleave to them. you hold them hostage, instead of letting them flow you start to analyze them, turning them upside down, but then you have to stand on your head to understand them.
he reaches for a wooden box of tobacco, placing it on his lap and taking out a pack of rolling papers. he snorts as if he's laughing.
visions are accurate, but you are staggering through a bunch of interpretations because your mind is a trickster and likes to play games that you get pulled into. visions guide you when you don't try to saddle them. once you turn your vision into an obsession, then it's lost. if you dress it in riding gear, it's your mind that guides you and not your vision. your mind is in the saddle.
he pinches a little tobacco lightly with his fingers and gives it a smell.
a vision is like the wind, which is the breath of the earth. it needs space. it needs to keep flowing. a wind that is closed in a room dies out, and you're only left with the smell of your own wind.
i spit out and start coughing. i've just taken a sip of naira's herbal tea, and now it's on my shirt. don't make me laugh like that, gil!
gil is chuckling, and he's messed up his tobacco that he just arranged artfully in his rolling paper. he fixes it and rolls up his cigarette, his skillful movements speaking of decades of experience. he takes out a lighter from the back pocket of his jeans, then holds the cigarette in his hand and observes it carefully, with affection, as if he's never seen anything like it before. the whole world lies in a cup of tea, in a single cigarette. be grateful for everything you have, because you have all you need. i can't tell you what you have to do. i can only tell you what the voices of the ancestors tell me. but it's up to you to decide your path. i don't know anything myself. i just reiterate what i hear.
the landscape begins to show sharper contrasts; visibility is greater in the dimming light. we sit in silence. shadows are stretching out, gil

is smoking, squinting and looking towards the spot where a cowboy disappeared with his horse. i hear my own thoughts rushing forward, swarms of questions that are having a fiesta. i'm trying to stop them. in the presence of this man, everything is suddenly simple. at the moment, when i think about what is happening, i am grateful that he is so normal. he doesn't act like a know-it-all, a mystic, or a teacher. what a relief. when he says that he's just an ordinary man, it's not for show, it's a fact. you need time. when you return home, it'll be possible that you might feel strange, because it's difficult to live in two worlds at once. maybe you'll want to share what you learned with people around you, with your family and friends. but they might not understand you. you paid tuition for where you are now. a person who hasn't paid will not know what you are talking about. it's possible that you'll feel alone.
it sounds to me like a far-off future, and on top of that, i don't really know what he is talking about. hmm. that doesn't bother me much. at the moment, i'm just contemplating what to do next. i don't know what choice to make.
a bundle of fur and noises jumps into my words. the puppies and macay are rolling around, one body over the other. they're wresting, growling. a moment later, they're at it a little farther away. it doesn't matter what you decide. no road is bad or good. a road is just a road. when you don't know which one to choose. relax, set yourself free. turn off your mind and wait. then you'll feel that golden thread that guides you.

thierry returns from his ride. he unsaddles the horse, washes up, and changes his clothes. naira calls everyone to supper, and we slowly get up from the wicker chairs. one more thing, gil says, when we enter the door. i'm hanging on every one of his words, waiting for another piece of wisdom that i won't understand. don't forget to tell a dirty joke once in a while.

08.31

she's woodcarving, totems in her memory, masks and naked faces. she wants to remember the gusts of wind, the voiceless gestures of the sand.

naira's song and the drumming that, in the morning, strikes out in every direction. her calm walk. gil. his long eyelashes, the movement of his lips when he's looking for words. his taste for dark, bitter chocolate. come, i'll take you to the springs. it's not far from here.
crystal crane hot springs. a geothermal vibration deep under the earth. the springs are gargling, pushing minerals up to the light. there are no voices under the water, just the clatter of their own churning. water out in the open and deep within. the indians of his tribe were famous for their generosity. when the white man came to them, the indians told them to take whatever they wanted. but when the whites were emboldened. nothing much was left of the indians.
gil brushes his long hair, wrings off the water from the hot springs like a coattail. he can shift a cloud across the sky with his stare. the wisdom of the stones speak through him. when you lean against stone, that stone speaks to you. it puts your thoughts on solid ground, gives them strong legs. just like a river feels the bodies of fish that live within it. living stones are all around us. they continue to remain silent, but when they speak, they will reveal their secrets, and nothing will be as it was before.

stories are like us, they have their lives. if no one reads them or tells them, they will go on vacation, land on desert islands. but after a while, they can't help themselves, and they'll fly back. a story will find its human, whom it will embrace like smoke. it will seep through her skin and travel into the bloodstream. then that human will carry this story within herself. it will grow along with her, and then one day, the human will start drawing the story or singing it or playing it. the story will come to life in her voice, her eyes, her fingers, it will change her through and through, and it will return to the circle, dancing again, changed, resurrected. like when a gardener grafts the trees. our stories have magical powers. the storyteller prints her story into the scenery, she gives it a new look, the scenery changes, and the story changes with it. and so does the storyteller.

it's late, the men have gone to sleep, the women are staying up. as naira undoes her braids, she whispers about resurrecting traditions, about

weaving baskets, about the sundance, about how she met gil. and how they were a fit for each other. how they grew into one. in a week, we will return to portland, and you can visit us there. you can stay at our place, if you'd like. good night, naira. thank you for all your gifts.
the stars are overflowing the night. do you remember how we would watch the meteor showers? i wanted to dance the noon heat into dusk, but you got tangled up in my strings and dressed me in another story. past the gates of your walls no one wore silk, only diamonds and gold. they weighed me down to the ground. my steps grew heavy. i was weeping salt, so you would rust away.

08.01.08 solar eclipse

she takes one more, packing in all the images she can. a strange feeling. it's hard to explain how she has ended up here. how it's all linked to her life. could this all be a dream? the old indian, the neighing of horses, the homestead.
maybe she feels gratitude.

ama doesn't know how to say good bye. naira and thierry, the dogs frolicking around them, the sun trampling over the last bits of dew.
gil asks her whether she has enough water, and whether she knows the way, and to please drive carefully.

in my native tongue, there is no word for farewell. we believe that we will always meet again, someday, somewhere. we're happy that you came.
and i'm happy that i found you.
his eyes twinkle, and he smiles for a moment.
careful what you say, you know that i'm happily married.
ama walks with a lightness, as if someone is holding her, as if gravity has been silenced.
and stay sober! he calls from behind her when she is already at the car.
i'm sober all the time, that's my problem.

the path she saw in her dreams is bending under her feet. the sand is scratching the bottom of her shoes. the scenery is whipping the air. she takes a handful of dust with her, and fragments of his smile.
death dines on holy wishes, the bones point north. what hurts most? when an illusion dies. prepare a funeral for fantasy, invite death in for a pint. you won't find a better merchant. only the old grim reaper labels the price tags accurately.
she has three hundred miles behind her, no music, no air conditioning. the desert is steaming, burning. ama drives on the three-lane i-80. her speedometer is at eighty. her foot is far from the pedal, far from everything. you'll fall asleep at the wheel if you keep this up. she hears someone's voice. and then nothing at all. when she comes to, she doesn't know what is real. perhaps this is all a dream. the car, with her in it, is flying off the highway. she's driving on gravel. everything is flickering. the speedometer maintains its velocity, eighty miles per hour. she sees her hands on the wheel, she tries to move them. the car flings back, she's back on the asphalt, on the three-lane highway. the rubber is slippery, she skids and turns. she's spinning in large circles across all three lanes. she's trying get a handle on things, she doesn't understand. she can't even count how many times she spins. suddenly, someone steps on the brakes. a long honk, and then a stop. the smell of tires. smoke and tremors. the car is stationery, the heart takes off. she comes to earth very slowly.
an eighteen-wheeler stops just a few meters behind her. the grey- haired driver runs towards her, opens the door, and pulls her out.
are you ok? ama nods.
i've never seen anything like it. it looked like you were flying. i thought for sure you would land on your hood.
i'm so sorry.
no worries, you must have fallen asleep, unfortunately. i'm glad that nothing happened to you.
yep, i must have dozed off.
the main thing is that you're okay. your car is also drivable. i don't understand how your tires are intact. you're lucky, young lady. god is on your side. the next rest area is twenty miles ahead in lovelock. you

should stop there and take a nap. you just have to get there. can you handle it? turn your radio on full blast, open all your windows and sing, howl. and most of all—keep that car on the road.

damn. where do you go when you're a danger in your own company?

she starts the car, turns the wheel and takes off back on the highway. she turns on the radio with a shaky hand. the doors. *riders in the storm la-la-la-la-la (ta-da-da-da-da) there's a killer on the road*. dear lord— that was her. she could have killed someone. she was so close to doing it. how far do you want to go? she's split, torn, that soul inside of her that wants to free itself, break through that thick glass. she doesn't know where there is more of her, on this side or the other.

mary welcomes her and pulls her to the table. you have to eat something. here. have some fish. i'll make you some tea. then you need to lie down. a journey that long can tire a person out. and we'll pray and thank god that you came back to us. you're alive, and that's what matters. don't think about anything else. jason, go turn on the ac in the room so she can sleep better.

nevada 08.02

while she was spinning on the highway, her mother was writing that she couldn't stop worrying about her.

i keep comforting myself that everything is alright, but i can't wait to hear from you again. i think about how you are coping with such a long journey, and i pray to god you make it home safely.

jeff, it's unbelievable. my mother and three of my friends, including you, had the same fears at the exact same time. all three of you were men. rei called me to tell me that for some reason, he suddenly began to feel really scared for me. don't tell me that men don't have a sixth sense. you're a superstar in the super-universe, and your intuition is like a laser. you should open up an oracle.

i'm afraid that i'm just a superstar. i'm glad that you're still here. damn, you're giving me too much to swallow. can you just feed me smaller portions?
i have to admit, i feel sad. maybe it's because i'm still here, as i'm writing these words. i don't know who i represent. i feel like i've been knocked to the ground. i can see how it's all mixed up inside of me. i'm completely overstretched. who do i bet on, when everything is neck-and-neck?

i see it all in front of me. the highway. you, ama, behind the wheel. the wave that's pulling you away from this life of yours. the force of it. but another wave comes too. the part of you that slams the brakes. that wave is stronger. otherwise, you wouldn't have been here. just think of a tennis ball that is heading for a wall. this is the point of return.

nevada 08.07.08

jeff, gil strikes me as a completely normal person. he doesn't have the need to tell you where you stand, even though he knows it. he doesn't have the need to show off how he can summon a storm or walk into your dreams, he just exists, and with his presence, he creates space where things that are usually out of your reach suddenly happen. you can experience something in this space. understand things. he doesn't force you, push you. it's up to you to enter this space or not.
he showed me the power of a vision and what humility looks like. he helped me understand the difference between life and death. that is, that there is no difference, life is just as good as death.

in the afternoon, she drives over to the reservation to say goodbye. harvey has the day off. he hasn't returned from the sundance. she finds gus in the museum. she's grateful she can at least thank someone. they sit together at a round table. gus offers her coffee.
i'm glad that you stopped by, and that you found what you were looking for. even i figured out why you came here.
ama looks at the pictures of the fish from the lake that are hanging behind gus's back. gus nods. our ancestors were fishermen, but the

younger generation is not interested. they don't want to sit by the bank and wait. they prefer sitting at a computer. we used to have an influx of fishermen from all over the states, and we had to limit the number who came. there's a difference between the reasons why a person hunts for fish and what he does with that fish after it's caught.
ama raises her eyebrows, confused. she can sense a scolding in gus's tone. he has his reservations about something she does not understand.
what else can you do with a fish other than eat it?
gus starts to laugh. you see? it never occurred to you that a lot of people put their fish on display to show off. come and see what i caught.
oh. that never crossed my mind. but i'm not a hunter.
they are both silent for a moment, drinking coffee. ama contemplates whether she should ask another question.
how did you figure out what i came here for, gus?
he gets up, goes to the kitchen, and brings back a plastic bottle along with two small glasses. the cap starts to sizzle. he pours the seltzer and mumbles as he sits back down on a plastic chair.
when you left for the north, i thought about you. i remembered a photo that i saw on the cover of a magazine. it might have been time or something like that, but that's not important. there was a girl in that photo, she was beautiful, she could have been about six years old. she had light skin, red hair, green eyes, and wide lips. she looked almost as if she had african features and possibly slanted eyes. she was very graceful. the caption said that she was a quarter irish, a quarter chinese, one-eighth african and jewish, and one-eighth indian and swedish. so what was she?
gus smiles and gets up again. he comes back with a leather bracelet with tassels and lays it in front of her on table.
your presence reminded us that it's good to honor the legacy of our ancestors, to keep alive our traditions and customs, but it's also good to remember that we are part of a greater whole. we're all connected. it's not heathy to cut yourself off.

ama sits at the wheel and keeps thinking about what gus said. she admires his ability to get under the surface and read the character of things from an open palm, to find a connection between a picture in time magazine and a crazy white girl passing by, and to take pleasure from who she is.

warrior's point exhales at dawn. the same place as yesterday, but a different sky. the mountains have fallen into the lake like burning coals, hesitating to cool down and darken. the sky is dry and blurry, half of the lake is in darkness, the other still lives in the light. the california smoke is gone.
she sits for a long time, looking at the surface of the lake, the night ruffles the dust and the bushes. then suddenly, she freezes. a coyote, standing close by. they're staring eye to eye. ama breathes silently, inhaling the creature's smell, waiting to see if it dares to come closer. she smacks her lips at him, and he approaches, closer and even closer. he speaks with wisdom about the smell of fish and all the pearls at the bottom of the lake, then he turns around and runs to the water. he looks back once and then blends into the darkness.
late that evening, she brings a present to mary, the grandmother who helped her along the road. what will she bring home with her? mary's generosity, her simple gesture of offering her home to a pilgrim. one day she would like to live like that. ama likes her, for her kindness and for the peace that she fed her. even though she knows she is a homophobe and a bit of a racist. even though she has built a christian center in a canyon that belonged to the paiute.
at dawn, a herd of wild mustangs comes to drink by this center.

ama returns to jason's house, where music is blasting most of the time. sometimes it's even bach or vivaldi. tonight, it's only darkness and silence. she finds jason on the terrace, leaning against the house. she almost doesn't see him. the air becomes colder, but when she bends over and touches the ground, she can feel the remnants of heat.
will you have tea with me?
the sound of rustling, maybe a bird or a squirrel in the bushes. she's a bit startled.
gladly, if you don't mind that i'll be packing at the same time. i have to be at the airport at eight in the morning.

she opens lara's backpack as she hears jason in the kitchen. the clinking of the kettle, the sound of water pouring, then the clinking of teacups, his steps on the wooden floor resonating through the empty house. he enters her room. he puts the teacups on the floor and then sits down on the rug by the wall. he watches her as she stuffs her backpack. and during the commotion, they bounce sentences off the walls. sentences about inspiration, how to stay in touch, about direction, music, the future, the taste of new beginnings. around midnight, ama leans against the opposite wall and carries on the thread. during pauses, question marks billow through a fog of words. he unharnesses the silence with a single sentence, spoken quietly.
it looks like we're at the end of our words. what happens next? ama gets up and bounces that look off her wall.
you'll be in my book, jason, if you don't mind. when he smiles, he's hard to resist.
i give you free range—write whatever you like. and don't forget that you're making history.
they both start laughing, and he gets up slowly, as if his muscles are stiff. he's hunting for signs. he doesn't want to give up.

the night spills the taste of your name on a white pillow.
the dawn harvests the shadows of stars from burned-out bones.

08.08.08

the morning offers her tears and that smile she likes so much. i hope you'll stop by here again someday.

i forgive this lunar landscape its nakedness the fire in its bosom, the last shadow of a coyote. i spin these stories out of the waves and fragments of mother-of-pearl, out of the silk of a spider's silence.

all these people will live with her inside her book. just open it, and they will come back to life.

portland

she returns here as if it were home. there are no more blueberries in the garden. georgia leans over the bushes, pruning, she snips some lavender. ama takes the full basket from her hand. what are you going to do with that?
we'll sew up some scented sachets and then put them in our laundry. are you hungry?
in the evening, greg asks her about the indians, but he's listening like mary. he has them clearly defined: a gang of drunkards that don't follow jesus christ and have no chance of salvation. ama is glad that he isn't taking about god, but once he starts ranting about the tax breaks that american laws give to those lazy asses on the reservations, she feels like she is in a land of puppets.
of course, greg, taking their land and giving them casinos and kickbacks on taxes is very noble, as long as nobody looks at what is swept under the rug. a person could be driven down a trail of tears by all that generosity. but the money made in the casinos stays on the reservation for the natives. they can use it.
yeah, right. the casino owners pump every spare penny to the orphans, the drunks, and all the cultural events at the reservation. give me a break.
greg's face turns red. the dog, sleeping until now, gets up and runs towards his master. he begins sniffing around. in his eyes are variations of greg's familiar features. he's thinking about the kindness of the grey-haired master when he takes him for a walk on the meadow in the morning, the smell of the palms that pour his food into a bowl or pet his fur, the voice that will pull him back, hold him on a leash when the neighbor's cat promenades through the garden.
unlike you, i have indian blood in me! my great grandfather was a choctaw indian, and the only thing i know about him is that he spent most of his life behind bars, because he was a murderer.
we're all murderers, greg, it's in our genes. each one of us has someone in their genealogy who we murdered. it's just not written on our birth certificates.

ama sees two trains heading on a collision course. greg is shifting into high gear, back on morning roll call.
that's bullshit! what do you mean by that?!
this land belonged to the indians, and you smoked them out pretty well in the name of captain jesus christ and his posse. it's called genocide. it's a lot easier to sow democracy around the world, run off to vietnam, chase osama bin laden, the werewolf, and other ghosts, than to clean up your own pile of shit.
greg jumps out of his chair, his voice bouncing off the pale walls. you have no idea what's at stake here.
ama knows very well what's at stake here. vietnam hit a nerve, greg is livid. she should stop while there is still time. suddenly, she feels sick. she waves her hand.
i'm a bit tired, greg, i'm going to go lie down.
gregory releases his grip and gulps. he bends over, and the dog sticks his nose into his palm.
i'm sorry i yelled.

08.12.08

an indian wedding. will you argue? without doubt.
the early morning is covered in fog. a piercing humidity is in the air, a chill that reaches to the bone. soon it'll change—as soon as the sun wakes up and goes to do the laundry. ama rings the doorbell. gil opens the door. come in, come on in and sit. naira went out to do some errands, but she'll be back soon. would you like tea? no, thank you, i brought you something.
ama gives him a bottle of noni juice and tells him that it's booze, just so she can hear that boyish laugh of his. and here is a fossilized shell from the amazon forest. a greeting from the tribal nations of peru.
gil turns the fossil over in his hand. unlike the noni juice, the shell sparks his interest. he studies it for a long time, touching it, feeling it. he is strangely moved.
when she tells him how she spun out on the highway, she notices his tears. i'm grateful that i could be there for you, that i could support you on that road.

those are supposed to be her words. she is the one who came to thank him. but instead, she starts harassing him with her questions, like some aggressive reporter. she tells him that she doesn't know how to write about such things.
you can only tell a story when you understand it yourself. when you realize what actually happened to you. but not when you're still searching for the meaning, when you're still confused. all you have to do is wait.
i guess i'm waiting, then, because since the sweat lodge, i haven't written a word. so much has happened, but there's still nothing to write about.

naira enters the door. are you ready? we have to go now, or we'll be late.

the wedding takes place in a park, on a lawn, in a space between trees. a folding tent is stretched over a long table covered with food. a winding path leads from the tent to a *tipi*. hermione and mike greet everyone. their six-year-old daughter is running around them in circles. they call her lady bug.
the ceremony is conducted in the lakota language, the sacred ritual accompanied by the sound of drums and singing. please don't record this, no pictures. it begins with a prayer, sporadic drumming and a long flute, a plea for a hearing: great grandfather, guardian of the great secret, hear our plea. mike is standing with his back towards the lakota elder who will perform the ceremony. everyone is looking towards the teepee, from which, after lengthy drumming and chanting, a bride appears, walking along the path toward the groom, slowly coming closer, her long hair slightly swaying. her gown is simple and graceful, reflecting the light of the afternoon sun. it looks like a costume from vinnetou, out of soft and light leather, with colorful braiding and tassels. moccasins on her feet. the sun is blazing on the heads of all the guests. there is nowhere to hide. the bride and groom are both wrapped up in a quilt. ama doesn't understand the parts in lakota, she just follows behind the men with drums and watches the movements of the elder, his chanting and the strange tone in which he speaks. when they take the quilt off the bride and groom, they tie their hands together and shower them with questions.

will you love each other? yes.
the drums pick up speed and a few hands begin to applaud. the women sing *heya-ho-hey*.
will you help each other? yes.
more hands start clapping, more drumming, and above that, there are rattles and a flute as soft as snow.
will you argue? without doubt.
the drums are suddenly at full volume, laughter is all around. the women chant *heya-ho-hey.*
will you get on each other's nerves? for sure! *heya-ho-heya* will it be on purpose? no.
the drumming is at the finish line, it comes to a climax, *heya-ho-heya, heya-ho-heya*. the rhythm slows down. the voices begin to dwindle.
will you use the fire of anger to seek reconciliation, to rekindle your love? yes.
mike smiles. hermione nods and looks down at her daughter. at that moment, the little lady bug becomes part of the ceremony, and mike vows to take care of her. to accept her as his own child.
after the ceremony, the bride circles around and gives thanks to all the cardinal directions, to the elder performing the ceremony, and to all the participants. i hope that all of you will bring home from this wedding the healing touch of our love.
her voice begins to waver, her eyes glisten with tears. then her lips move with no sound, as if she were praying. and mike looks like the happiest man in the world.
there's a potluck in the big tent. a feast. each of the guests has brought something to eat. everything is spread out as a buffet. the wedding guests go around and fill their plates. all you can eat.
ama sits in the shade, looking around, observing the guests. gil sits in a chair next to her, smoking and smiling. she is interested in his journey. she wants to know how he got to where he is now. grace has told her that gil was an orphan. he grew up on an arizona reservation. he says that the desert raised him. he worked for decades with alcoholics and drug addicts, and even with inmates, most of them natives. he knows all the prisons in the northwest. to this day, he performs ceremonies

in oregon and washington. ama thinks she might know how a person can get involved with that scene, but she asks him anyway. i was never sober until i was fifty, he answers softly, just confirming a fact. and then something pulled me away from it, and at the same time, a path opened up for me. i stopped drinking cold turkey. i got hooked on chocolate instead—you know, it's better for the skin.

he asks about her father. ama smiles even as she talks about drinking and depression, about how her father also managed to escape from all of it. he died just a few days before his wedding anniversary, so he wouldn't have to buy any rubies. that was just like him. gil laughs. men are beasts.

hi, uncle gil. that is what they call him. uncle or grandfather. they come to shake his hand, say a few words. how are you doing, uncle gil? doing good, he says, i'm sober today.

that laugh of his will always get to her. she meets his people. john quickwater and his wife, willow, dozens of faces, dozens of names that she won't remember.

gil chit-chats with them, calmly nodding, listening, and then he leans over to ama and rolls his eyes. most of the time, i don't know who these people are. naira could tell me. she remembers them all, i'm just arm candy.

naira emerges from time to time and asks if everything is all right, and then runs off. before the ceremony, she helped the bride, now she's sitting among a group of women and deliberating over something with them.

the bride and groom summon the guests to a giveaway. the newlyweds do not receive gifts, they give them out. now that they have each other, they don't need much in the way of possessions. a sea of objects is laid out on the grass, and the guests surround it. only gil remains seated in the shade. everyone looks at what is available. the eyes of children and adults alike light up at the quilts, handkerchiefs, a chainsaw, a dozen jars of honey, toys, skis, jeans, candlesticks, a sleeping bag, colorful scarfs, tennis rackets, baseball bats, baskets, placemats.

nothing can be left behind—divide it all amongst yourselves. the groom commences the auction. anyone who is older than a hundred can chose one object. no one answers. anyone over ninety. no one. any one over—mike looks inquiringly at naira, who represents her husband—seventy-nine? when mike calls out the number seventy-nine, naira crouches like a cat, pounces, and grabs the chainsaw on behalf of uncle gil. it will be useful at the ranch, you know, she winks. ama will never forget her smile. the guests pause for a bit. hey, you look great for seventy-nine. yeah, it's botox. naira grins, and the auction continues. anyone over sixty? fifty? until it comes to the children, who have been worried that someone before them would pick their toy.

naira shows her prize to her husband. gil almost falls off his chair when he sees her prancing across the lawn with that serrated monstrosity.

i guess i didn't pray long enough today, he laughs. the heavenly father outsmarted me again.

ama looks at the old indian and his wife carrying a chainsaw, the hodgepodge of people in the park, who are dancing and rejoice at their trivial gifts, the jars of honey and the woven baskets, by the newlyweds who promised that they would argue, and she has a feeling that she has found what she was looking for. when she ponders over it, she can't understand the source of this feeling, because she still can't grasp what exactly it is she is seeking.

at that moment, she remembers what the old man told her by the hot springs in crystal crane.

you don't need to look for anything. you just have to see what's in front of you. when you can see that you have everything you need, you'll realize that there is nothing else to search for.

08.13.08

ad: looking for god

rabindranath thakur wrote in one of his poems about how he was searching for the house of god.

he set out into the world and began searching, crisscrossing, plowing through the land, and from time to time he managed to catch a glimpse of god. it was flickering out there, far away on the horizon. just a speck on the edge between heaven and earth, like a newly hatched star. he headed in that direction, but just when he was about to reach that star,

god moved over the next mountain. the poet did not give up, he continued to ask around, persisting with his trek, until one day he actually found a house with a sign above the door in large letters: GOD LIVES HERE.
the poet becomes joyful, his heart skips a beat, and with a wide grin, he runs up the stairs and, at the moment when he is about to knock on the door, he pauses. suddenly, a thought blocks his path: what if god actually does live here? then it's all over, including my search. everything will end. all these years i've been searching, i've known nothing else, i have no other skill. and if this door opens and god appears before me, the search is over. what will i do next?
the poet tiptoes back down the staircase, sneaking away, so that no one will see him or hear him, and then he takes to his heels and runs away as fast as he can.
in the end, the poet explains: to this day, i am still searching for god. i know where he lives and so i avoid that place and search for him in other parts. it's a great adventure. the task is not easy, but as long as i am searching, i exist. god means danger: if i were to meet him, nothing would be the same as before. but i'm not afraid anymore, because i know where he lives, and so i search for him everywhere else, in the entire universe besides there. and sometimes, deep inside, i know that the goal of my search is not to find god, but to maintain my minuscule existence.

4

i was born to my mother. that's the way it goes here. we are born to mothers. even though mothers often think that they give birth to us. they are mistaken, we birth ourselves. the planets are born out of silence, they flesh out with the awareness of a beginning and an end with an awareness of eternity.

theory of probability • you find yourself at rock-bottom

prague 08.22.08

landing at ruzyně airport, mother prague at last. the luggage stays behind in amsterdam, but relatively speaking, that's a secondary distraction.

i'm hanging around your neck. mom.
just how long was i holding back that weary rain, ready to drop.

prague 09.01.08

"you know enough of the warrior's way to act accordingly, but your old habits and routines stand in your way."

my voice is in a cage. each word is scraping my mucous membrane like sandpaper. i can't talk. there's nothing to talk about. an avalanche of everyone. questions like a line and sinker, waiting to catch a big fish. hordes of sentences and stories. friends. it's endearing how much they care, how much they want to help.

it's like walking into a ring, jeff. this disease is my boxing match against the old world that i'm trying to abandon.
thank you for the books. they were waiting here for me when i got back from my trip. i read them both in a single breath. those books gave me a beating. they messed up what little i recalled of descriptive geometry, but that goswami thoroughly got me. once in a while, i had to slow down. that feeling when you have a galaxy circling around each one of your fingers. the post-quantum charade is just as inspiring as bach or hafiz. that quantum physics of yours often dives deeper into the basic questions of existence than that religious bullshit of the new ageists. it seems as if true scientists could relate to the mystics, because they both question the meaning of existence. some of their texts are like poems.
ama, just a little.

p.s. about those platonic solids. you probably already know that those five shapes have the same external and internal angles. all volumes of regular polygons derive from them. in *timaios*, plato links them to four elements. the fifth element, plato links to the ether. and i just read that archaeologists dug up these five objects in scotland where neolithic tribes lived thousands of years before plato. i thought to myself, you'd be interested.

will we ever become enlightened? plato claimed that ancient greek doctors made the most mistakes in treating people because their diagnosis and therapy separated the body from the spirit, which forcefully divides the indivisible.

09.03.08

so, how are you settling in at home?

it's hard, grace. it's ripping into my skin like a pair of jeans three sizes too small. everyone around me is trying. they're great, really. but i feel like i just landed on mars, as if i just arrived at the santuario, but this time i feel like i'm even more of a lunatic than before. i'm like a deer in the headlights, not understanding what is going on. people around me are babbling strangely, they're talking gibberish, and once in a while, you recognize a familiar sound, and nod, but flies are a lot easier to understand. way out there, it was much easier. in those foreign regions, your rails are not worn out. you don't have to dress in the rusted armor of tradition. when a pilgrim returns home, he's not what he used to be. they don't recognize you; they want that foot-soldier to whom they were waving goodbye six months ago, but she's out the window. dead. decaying in the rainforest, the ants are tearing her into tiny pieces, cooking a pot roast. but here, they have the contract you signed with them, silent agreements, well, not with you but with that corpse rotting in the jungle. and so, nothing matches up, because you are not producing. you are not who you once were, and it's really pissing you off. this new wind that is inside of you can no longer push and break the walls of those old buildings, which you no longer wish to enter anyway.

09.09.08

when she was on the road, she never had the feeling that she was missing something. she turns to gould, and it occurs to her how much she has been missing him. she looks through her books and finds hafiz. she needs him like she needs air.

now
that it is obvious
all of your fears
are profitless tradecraft
wouldn't it be time
to find
a better trade?

09.11.08

meditation is ayahuasca andante

she watches the night sky. she turns the hemispheres a bit and sees the southern cross, her santuario. the darkness and humidity that drills deep into the bone. the jaguar walks in the sky, wearing flashy stars on his fur.

are you there? i've wanted to ask you for some time now: do you miss the ayahuasca?

no, jeff, i don't miss it, really. it's actually a disgusting drink. i cringe even now when i think of how it tasted. but it's inside of me, whether i drink it or not. those plants live inside of you once you let them enter your body.

and become friends with them. errari said that really powerful herbs live inside of you forever. back then, i didn't have the steam to realize what he was talking about. it occurred to me just now. i don't need to drink ayahuasca. i am completely fine with meditation or breathing.

meditation?

the difference between meditation and ayahuasca isn't as big as it might seem. during meditation, you usually don't throw up, true. colors

are more vibrant and your wheels turn more at andante. but you're flying in the same universes. the only real difference, even though quite a significant one, is that you can stop meditation at any time. if it's too much, you can just turn it off. take a break, have a kit kat. in czech we call that a *tajmout* or "time out." with ayahuasca, you take a seat and take off into lala land. and even if you learn how to hold the steering wheel and maintain orbit, you simply can't exit a errari at full speed. and since this particular model has no brakes, then you have to ride with your pedal to the metal until you have an empty tank. you know me. i'm a lightweight. i drink half a liter of green tea, and i wind up tighter than an eight-day clock.
oh, how lucky the woman, božena would say. (you don't know her.)

09.12.08

happy birthday!
i'm coming to visit you, granny, and at the same time, i'm already with you. your hands in your lap, your swollen joints, your pale skin with wrinkles, the platinum wedding ring carved into your finger like a handcuff. i notice every vein, your warmth, soft touch.
granny, tell me everything that has happened to you, everything that you lived. stories of sorrow that we heard so many times, that so many times we did not want to hear, and so many times we didn't hear. how you survived the wars, how they nationalized everything, how your husband died. but you hung in and held on. suddenly i've become speechless in awe of your life. i never realized how wonderful you were. i'm coming home to finally listen. i look upon the hundred years you've lived through, and i am driven to tears by my own blindness.

here's to you, granny. you're one of a kind. personally, i don't know anyone besides you who has reached the age of one hundred.
granny raises a glass of port, takes a sip, and then waves her hand for me to stop.

my grandmother lived to a hundred and five.

well then, we have something to look forward to. i heard that someone from the city council and a tv crew wanted to come, but you refused.
granny makes a face that floors me.
let the comrades at the council go to the zoo instead of visiting me. why would they show my hundred-year-old mug on tv? they should have come by earlier with the camera. fifty years ago, when i was still good-looking. i was a cleaning lady back then. i wore a scarf, and those bitches on the street would look down on me, the communists, they called me *milady*. they felt good about seeing me like that, after they took everything from us.
granny, i'm so glad you held on. i was worried that i would never see you again. you look great.
i'm doing well—why wouldn't i be? i dug myself out of it again. what can i tell you? the kids got older, you know, the grandkids, too. i've looked at them so many times and asked myself, what's happening to them? those actors on tv are getting older quickly too. it's always a surprise. i'm the only one here who still feels like she's young, like i'm still twenty. or maybe sixty. who cares? i can't do too much work. i'm always on a break. i have all kinds of ways of doing that, and i can still choose how i do it. either i lie down, you know, like a corpse. or i sit like a stick-in-the-mud. i know how to do that well. a hundred years. go figure. i was so sick when i was eight years old. all i did was lie in bed. my father built a dollhouse for me. he did it at night, when i couldn't sleep, i would watch him carve out the furniture sets. i had it for a long time, until we moved, you know, and there, in that house on dělostřelecká ulice, lived a meek little girl. she was sickly, she had green-sickness. do you know what green-sickness is? and so, my parents decided to give her the dollhouse. she was very happy. the eyes lit up in that pale little face of hers. well, life ran by. it didn't walk, it ran. two wars, we went to school by the army barracks where this one officer would slap the soldiers, shouting orders in german, but the soldiers were from the hills and villages, and they didn't understand a word he said. so, they would copy the ones who understood at least something. and that officer would still beat them. we watched them as children, and we almost had tears in our eyes. that was long ago, during the empire, you know. and look, before you even

turn around, all of a sudden, you have zeros leaning on the side of your fence.

09.14.08

i came back with the notion that i would start treatment. but it's not happening. i'm running around here at full speed while holding onto the emergency brake. it seems like i need it to be hopeless from the start in order to see the writing on the wall. i have to fall lower, further down, completely run myself into the ground. consume the meat of our ancestors to the bone. i feel like it's only after i cross the border of what is humanly possible that i'll wake up with the drive i need.

09.17.08

ama waits at the airport. she feels at home in this crowd. she loves airports. they are places of meetings, embraces, and goodbyes, where destinies blend together. she listens to the echo of the massive hall. millions of stories buzzing, melodies from their travels. a gust of memories from her, times when she was homeless in first class, then a homeless v.i.p., then just *homeless go home*. she finally sees her. paula. the soul closest to her in new york. they would sit on the floor across from each other, and paula would imitate accents and read out parts of her new play. they would laugh together until their sides split. they haven't seen each other in a year. paula looks different. everything around her seems curvy and inflated. at dinner, it finally clicks. paula is going to have a child. she is pregnant, for sure. ama, i'm so glad to see you. howard says hello, and so does everyone else. we were just thinking about that summer when we all lived together in that house in santa fe.
the waiter hovers over them and asks them something, but neither one pays attention. they turn on a switch and suddenly both of them are in a different story, a chapter they shared together. they're not sitting across from each other in a prague restaurant, but rather next to each other in an amphitheater.

an evening with a younger crowd, the best performance after the production of *turandot*, one scene after another of buoyant hodgepodge—novices showing off their talent, it is still ringing in her ears, a brisk number about a hat with peacock feathers, a brilliant musical story by samuel barber with a touch of jazz. *a hand of bridge*. a ten-minute skit where two married couples play cards while they fling their thoughts into the ether in over-saturated monologues. paula laughs out loud. at times, ama is more amused by her laughter than by what is happening on stage. the distressed geraldine, mezzo, shaking off fear for her sickly mother, while her husband, baritone david, has erotic fantasies of girls and boys. bill, the tenor, nearly has an orgasm with his new lover, while his wife, sally the soprano, sings about the hat with the peacock feathers. something like havel's *private view* in an opera. especially sally's aria. her singing in eight tones, *i want to buy that hat of peacock feathers* is painfully piercing. her emotional outpouring is in a different key from the musical accompaniment, so it is straining everyone's nerves. there is no escaping from her remedy for a rickety marriage in the form of a hat with peacock feathers. in the car on the way back, ama cannot stop singing, *i want to buy that hat of peacock feathers!*

all her fellow travelers are undone by her singing. honey, you really have a great soprano, rich says, it's too bad you don't sing more often.

ama, i still remember. when i'm sad, i always think about how brazen that energy was when it came out of you. i always end up laughing.

ama looks at her and her glazed eyes. she's silent. paula, you came because you're afraid that we'll never see each other again.

10.02

in the morning, she has to go to šárka.[21] she's missing the jungle, the desert, temples where you could pray. a man waters his plants in the window with a watering can. he's still in his pajamas, his duvets are hanging from his balcony like white whales.

jeff, i'm begging to be able to postpone the sobbing. i'm all sobbed out.

[21] *Translator's note*: Šárka is a nature preserve located on the outskirts of Prague.

i'm in a vise grip, getting pressure from all sides. i have people around me who want me to get treatment, which is quite understandable. that's just one clamp. but then there are others who are showing their disappointment, like soccer fans whose team has lost, they were expecting me to return cured, they were expecting a miracle. and they cling to their expectations so much that they consider classic treatment a failure. of course, they don't want me to die, they just want me to recover through self-help. they want the spectacle that they feel i owe them. they'll take antibiotics when they have a sore throat, but they expect me to recover from cancer with yoga and hot tea. some of them are my closest friends. these expectations are pretty cruel, but i also see myself in them. the desire for perfection is always blind and heartless.

fuck 'em, ama! fuck anyone who tells you what you're supposed to do while they load you with their infantile notions of what makes the world go round, they need a smack in the head. even if it's your best friends, cut them off before it goes any further, because they will drain you. they're completely out of touch, and you can't be bothered with minions. surround yourself with people who give you support. and those who offer their enlightened bullshit but go to the doctor at the first sign of a corn on their toes — tell them to go to hell. - jeff

11.06

the trees discard their memories so they can sleep better. a blaze from the yellow tamaracks on the hillside and the fire in the stove. the logs are crackling. burning slowly—everything she has. everything she's thrown away. gifts that she couldn't accept. she sees clearly the part that she tortures, at the end, a person always has to atone.

grace,

when i talk to you, it's like talking to myself.

it's like autumn has settled in my body. the fog and molding leaves. i try to wake up. is there a door i have to go through? i need to wake up,

grace. i hear a voice repeating this to me. wake up, wake up, for god's sake, wake up at last! and i know that i'm sleeping, and i want to wake up, i want to get treatment, but i'm in a bubble, hovering about half a meter over the earth. i want out. i want to burst it, but i don't know how. sometimes i feel like it will only burst if i kill myself.
ama, i thought about what you wrote to me, and i have an idea. that friend of yours who quit architecture to pursue hypnosis, i forget her name, couldn't she help you? could she hypnotize you so that you can wake up? maybe it's just rubbish, but i had to write to you about it. i just keep thinking about it, i can't help it. i feel like you'll get out of this. that fucked-up cocoon of yours has to pop at some point.

11.07.08

ama, i figured something out. superposition, i mean, how waves layer over one another. it's a unique characteristic that occurs whenever waves collide. this layering leads to the fact that waves either multiply or break. superposition can happen in a situation where one part of yourself says yes, and the other part says no. it seems that these two parts behave like waves that hinder each other, so you don't move forward or backwards. everything just becomes condensed. superposition is a universal law. you have to split it in two.

she understands. it's necessary to be clear on things. why am i here? who am i? where am i going? those are questions she posed when she was fourteen or perhaps even younger. and now she's standing here after all these years, decades, centuries, facing the same swarm of question marks. has she become any wiser? she's constantly grinding at it, confusing herself. she's confused by hamlet's t*o be or not to be*.

so, wake up and decide where you want be.

suddenly, she stops listening to bach or to any of her other fixed stars. she only hears jim morrison over and over, *this is the end, my only friend, this is the end,* she never noticed before that he sings about a snake and a lake. an ancient lake, an ancient snake, his skin is cold, father, i want to kill you, mother, the screams spread inside of her. you can kill them both at once. two birds with one stone that you will throw at yourself. you have to decide. so split it in two!

11.10

grace, you are the best! your idea of hypnosis was genius. i broke through. i'm back, standing on the ground. i'm opening the door of my stuffy pad, and i'm breathing in the rocks, the moss is tickling my throat. i see an open door. dáša was here, that's the name of my friend who does neurolinguistic programming according to milton erickson. she chose a method they call framing, first, the therapist guides you into a trance, and then she encourages you to remember a situation where your body automatically cured itself. it could be anything. a finger cut, a flu, basically an instance where you know that you don't need to do anything and the body will heal itself. in the meantime, you study how that situation reveals itself, how you perceive it, if you see it in black-and-white or in color. if the situation is static or is moving like a film, from what angle you're looking at it, and so on. and then you do the same with the situation you're in at the moment. then you record the difference. at the end, you reframe your current illness in a way that has the same parameters as the one with the automatic healing.
i imagined that i was lying in bed with a virus, dáša was writing down all the details, and when the picture was complete, she told me to give a summary of my emotions. the answer: a release, a resignation. after a quick pause, we track the cancer and all the differences. when we have a picture of the disease, dáša wants another summary.
how do you feel?
i am . . . i feel . . . i feel like i'm spellbound . . . bewitched.
i was completely dumbfounded. we finished the reframing, and i came out of my trance. and i couldn't believe it. i don't know how it happened, maybe just being able to describe it all, but the bubble burst.
do you know that feeling when you wake up from a dream, and right away you realize that you were sleeping? you even know exactly when you fell asleep, what you dreamed about. you see the entire dream,

its context, in a way you've never seen before. i was asleep for six years, grace. it's exactly six years since i fell asleep. since the death of my father, i've been just sailing by, finishing nothing, writing nothing, feeling nothing, and i didn't see it.

i don't know if you have something similar over there, but here, we have a fairy tale about an evil warlock who guards a spellbound princess in a tower. the warlock has three bands, symbols of his power. a prince appears who has to fulfill three tasks to free the princess. each time he fulfills a task, one of the warlock's bands breaks, but it's only after the third one that the princess can be freed.

i looked back and saw my entire journey. the exact moments when those bands broke. in the jungle, when i screamed for the first time. the next one was when i was spinning on that desert highway and someone stepped on the brakes. and this is the last time.

11.12.08

ivona? i think it's time.

ivona had carried out three cognitive health assessments, but she still supported ama's decision to travel to the rainforest. she believed that ama would get better. and now she is happy that she has changed her mind.

so finally you've gotten rolling, the girls have been calling me, one after another. they were afraid that you had given up. i'll take you to the hospital, i'll call to let them know that you need a sonogram, ct scan, and biopsies. if you'd like, i can give you a ride. then we'll see what to do next.

a boy in red overalls stands in the hallway in front of radiology. his phone rings to the tune of *pat & mat*. the walls are painted white everywhere. an echo bounces off the tiled floor. disinfectant is in the air, and a slightly chilling shadow.

ivona is pale.

do you get it? metastases in the ganglia and throughout the lungs. it's totally fucked up. if you don't do something about it now, you won't have much time.

a paramedic rolls by, pushing an old man on a stretcher. make room, please.

ivona, calm down. what happened? your colleagues really let you have it, didn't they? they sure did! they think i must have lost my mind, they ganged up on me, throwing stones. *take a look*. this is your friend? you weren't able to get her in here sooner? to persuade her? aren't you a doctor? you must have known what would happen. how could you let this happen? they were looking at me as if i were a total moron.
ama is still fascinated when someone behaves as if her cancer is someone else's responsibility. as if her life is being directed by other people. as if a doctor, a mother, or jesus carries the burden of her decisions.
ivona, you don't need to feel guilty just because it didn't turn out the way you imagined.

11.26

at homolka hospital. waiting doesn't bother her, she is in no hurry. the hallway is crowded. a yellowish man in a wheelchair, women on the bench waiting for ultrasounds. nervous glances. everyone needs something. and you're sitting next to me. once in a while, i'll look at you from the corner of my eye. i'm sorry for you. i'm sorry for every mother who has a sick child. those eyes of yours when you ask me how i'm doing. do i feel any pain? no, don't worry, i don't. i feel no pain. i'll say it over and over again, even though you most likely don't believe me.
a young man is sitting next to me with a car seat on his lap. in it is a baby with a pink hat and little shoes. the baby is sleeping, and the father can't take his eyes off of her. he's studying a part of himself. the young man with an earring adjusts the tiny shoes with his giant hands. i will store away this portrait of quiet happiness like an ace up my sleeve.
come on in.
doctor aptová nods understandingly. i had a friend who did exactly what you did. in the end, she decided to seek medical treatment. each day was well worth it. i will send you to the department chief.

11.28.08 friday

chief šafanda is a man of action. no nonsense. at first, he looks at her like she's a moron, but she's used to that. you could say that she likes

to dwell on it. so you have decided to get treatment? then roll call is on monday morning for your first chemotherapy. you shouldn't waste a single day if you want to be here a little while longer. one more thing. tell me what you expect from the treatment.
hmm. she doesn't want to tell him because she knows how he's going to respond. it's a lost cause, if you had come here about nine months ago, we could have done much more. now, all we can do is slow the process down.
i know. monday it is.
she's overwhelmed by all the help around her. chief vymazal, chief skovajsová. doctor tesařová. i'm at your disposal, she says, what can we do for you?
ama leaves, and something is happening inside her. maybe, in her own way, she is looking forward to it, even though she is scared shitless. it will be another adventure. and she loves adventures so much. after all she's been through, why not take a shot of chemo. how this will end is not up to the doctor or up to statistics.

ama,

take the leap. you'll manage. everything you now know will be of use to you. all the years of yoga, meditation, years of crazy seminars and trainings, breathing exercises, systemic constellations, hypnosis, and god knows what else. you have all of this at your disposal. it's time to cash in your spiritual dividends. use everything you have, everything you believe in. i'm watching you, and i have a feeling that i am seeing all my experiments in practice. that journey of yours is like a pilot wave with a thousand waves in it.
as long as you're here, it's not too late. you need time for the changes in your consciousness to manifest themselves in tangible matter; for you to build new neuronal networks, to create a new order, a new universe, it will take time.
and avoid any prophets of doom. run the word incurable through a shredder. remember that, according to the theory of probability, nothing can be ruled out. matter has certain tendencies, but your consciousness will choose which direction to go.

a taste of hard reality

12.01

chemo. a crow's winter outside, but she doesn't notice too much. she's kind of on fire. oncology is spinning in a mild haze. the infusion area is kind of pleasant, the nurses are angelic. do you have anything to drink? did you eat? you don't want to get sick from hunger.
before they hook her up to the hardcore, they give her some compazine that will stop the nausea and vomiting for the first 24 hours, because this chemo is also a pretty decent poison. regardless, her body realizes that it's poisoned just a few hours after the last round of iv.
lara takes her home. the car is shaking. it's filled with shopping bags and concerned questions. she feels every pothole. if you need anything, just call. hopefully it won't be too bad. thank you. i'll call.
the living room gets dark. the armchair saves face—hers and its own. it's easy to get lost in hafez. but soon, the drum starts to trill inside her, a cement mixer replaces her stomach. she'll never forget the look on her mother's face when she first crouches in front of that porcelain devil. it feels like it will never end.

12.02

the marathon continues, between bouts of vomiting, feeling like i have to throw up, and the sleep that won't come. it's like seasickness—until you get off the boat, it won't go away.
that time when we went scuba diving, somewhere in the caribbean, the boat putted through the waves and that french girl who was with us said in that sweet mumbling accent that only the french can produce, that the best remedy for the sea monster is to chew ginger and to put a plug in your right ear. for some people, it works if you plug your left ear. so, i'm trying it. i'm plugging my right ear canal and the dizziness has eased. the vomiting still continues to buoyantly shift the tiller.

12.03

at three in the morning, i try to vomit quietly so that i don't wake you up. but quiet vomiting is not my forte. the bucket is baaing like an injured

sheep. one sheep, two sheep. in the morning, i'm vanishing from this world. break on through! when i come to, your eyes are spinning over me, a bit smudged. you're holding my wrist with your cold hand, hunting for a pulse.
you can't keep this up, ama. call the doctor.
you're making a big deal out of a little nausea. and what am i supposed to tell him?
that you haven't had any fluids for at least forty-eight hours. that you're vomiting every hour even though there's nothing to vomit. and that shit they poured into you can grind your kidneys.
could you please not call my medicine shit?

the doctor, when she calls, is unfazed. today, you should break through, i think that the worst is behind you. if this continues, we'll have to take you in and hook you up to an iv.
and just as the doctor said, there's a breaking point at noon. her first gulps of water that stay down.
the aftertaste is the worst. it's like going to the gas station and filling up your stomach.
she saw her life, standing over her, pondering whether to revive her or whether it isn't worth the effort. it was sick of the waiting, tired of wandering without her, empty, uninhabited, idle. come on, get up! she only realized that when it moved far enough away for her to stop noticing. and when she came to and realized that her life was nowhere to be found, that it might have completely vanished beyond the hills, she sensed the closeness in the air, she knew it well. a closeness that exuded its scent only when someone split off and moved away. when someone was out of reach. at that moment, she started running.

treatment by feynman

12.07.08

it's hard to tell where i am. i would call it a place of wonder. sometimes i have a feeling that everything happening to me does not concern me at all. i'm standing here like the london eye and just gaping. i don't

know what to believe. it seems like there's nothing to believe in, since everything is equally believable and unbelievable anyway. what is reality and what is an illusion? and is there even a difference between the two? and do i even need to know? i'd rather say that it's all the same to me.
then there are moments like today, here and now, when i appreciate the most ordinary things, such as the simple fact that i can sit here and write, hallelujah, the sight of birds on the barren branches of the tamaracks, the sound of an eggshell, two suns in a glass for breakfast. the five fragrances of green tea. finger-play on the keys of a piano, your sentences in the morning mail.
so, i'm sailing between this foolishly happy gratitude and the other dimension, the distant one, an impersonal place where everything makes sense but nothing really matters, in a place of infinite light and darkness (they are so similar that you can't tell them apart) and then beyond, in that space where nothing exists and everything is possible.
does that make sense? i'm trying to describe this place for you, but i might be writing it just for myself to determine where exactly i am. as if it matters.

i feel an echo coming from my gut. it's clawing under my breastbone, something like a memory, ancient motions, windings, and the language of trilobites, telling me that i am older than this planet and at the same time, i have not yet been born.

it's raining outside my window. the roofs are slippery, and they are dripping into my writing. i went outside in the morning, and the rain, so cold on my face, felt real.

12.08

ama,

while i was reading your letter, i remembered what feynman said at a conference for the society of physicists in '59. he said that the principles of physics do not oppose the possibility of controlling everything through atoms. in practice this does not occur because we are simply too big . . .

without sugarcoating it, he already asked the question whether, in the future, there will be a time when we will be able to arrange atoms any way we like.

i think this might interest you.

that's great, jeff. i love feynman. that means all i need is to shrink myself to a point where i can move among *nano* branches, so, hurray! another trip.

12.19.08 zlín

ama negotiates a christmas dose in the zlin hospital. she's grateful to the head physician that they are willing to take her in, because this way, at least she can celebrate christmas eve by vomiting in her childhood home, right under the decorated christmas tree in the circle of her closest family.
the results of the tests before chemotherapy are not great. white blood cell count is a big fat zero. the infusion is postponed. she gets a shot to stimulate her bone marrow. the side effects are pain all over her body, joints, and muscles like with a fever. so, once again, she gets to spends two days under the covers.
the house where she grew up has changed. but it could be because she, herself, moves in a different way. she sees things differently—everything has come to life. things that were grey are in shocking color, people around her look so overly beautiful that she wonders whether she's in another dream.
a quarter century ago, her mother was experiencing the same thing. but in those days, everything was different. or was it, really?
mom rolls her eyes, yet she is also amused. it's as if she wants to say that nothing is ever like it seems on the surface.
it was quite different, ami. no one talked to you, actually, most of the time, no one would even tell you what was wrong with you. nowadays, you have the right to read your file, and you give informed consent, you have control. in the eighties, they treated you like a child. hilda was

the head oncology nurse, and so i went to cry on her shoulder. i was angry that no one would tell me what was going on. i knew nothing. the doctor didn't answer my questions. she slapped her forehead and told me that i was needlessly getting all worked up, why are you cackling in my office like that, and why are you getting so angry? your whining is utterly useless, and if you have questions, write to dear abby. you're in a hospital, what do you want to talk about? you have to understand that you're like laundry that needs to be washed. we stick you in a washing machine, add a little detergent. we press the right button, and the program runs on automatic. it fills with water, the drum turns, and you don't have to do anything or worry about a thing. all you have to do is get cleaned. there is no need for you to ask questions or think about anything. don't engage in anything, don't try to solve anything, just keep getting yourself cleaned up. when the program ends, it will spit you out. do you understand?
oh, that's great, mom. so, i'm just getting myself laundered.
they're sitting together at the dining table, ama is in her mother's robe. she's finishing up a pancake with some marmalade she dreamed about in the jungle. i was terrified that you would make me an orphan. i'd dream about coffins and funerals, about black veils and high heels; and now i see you, with that strange anxiety you try to wash off your face whenever you look at me. i guess you know how i felt.
mom shakes her head and straightens her back. she rubs the handle of her tea mug with her thumb. a wisp of steam blurs half her face.
ami, i'm not afraid that you'll die on me, because i raised you well.
so, what are you thinking?
mom picks up the mug and takes a sip.
i'm betting on the fact that you'll be decent enough not go before me.

12.23

the morning forest is a drug. she observes her steps on the pine needles, the air filled with blue spruce, the squirming inchworms, the movement of things in phases. the shapes of trees, the trees that have been cut down, chopped into pieces, into carousels of growth rings. she picks up

a cut piece of oak and places it on a stump like a slice of watermelon.
instead of lunch, she goes for a joyride to zlín oncology.
the blood has improved for us with the neupogen, so we can proceed with the infusion, the doctor rejoices.
she likes the way the doctors speak to her in first person plural, like sovereign rulers. our blood has improved, not just hers. of course, the us in the first sentence could indicate that the doctor is identifying with the patient and that he is empathetically implying that a doctor and a patient are two cheeks on one ass. that possibility exists, but the we in the second sentence is clearly emperor-like. we. we will insert, apply, take, we is sort of a cipher, a secret language, a covert form of exorcism that offers strength. ama understands this. a doctor dressed in a coat of we is no longer an ordinary mortal, he becomes a shaman. with his we he clearly shows: look who stands by me: collegium musicum, consilium, chamber and cellar, all the king's horses and all the king's men, and in the fog of this all-important we, a shack is hiding, a shed, the ringling bros. circus, attestation, erudition, six bears in a ring.
so we can proceed with the infusion.
great, an early santa, she can begin unwrapping presents, because she was especially good all year long. she can sense that, this year, it's going to be a bountiful christmas eve, even though santa, who brings the presents, sounds like bullshit. this year, he decides to make an example out of her and rub her face in all of it so that she starts believing again.
the long-legged nurse leads her to an empty bed, carrying all the gadgets and ingredients. have you ever dripped with us before?
that's a pretty sentence. have you ever dripped out on us? the hospital slang has a knack for neologisms its prime directive is to entertain. she is here to the last drip.
during dripping, she plays music, so she can put herself in a trance and program her cellular structure, coagulate her blood cells. she talks to her connective tissue, howls at her brain membranes. in the meantime, the nurses interrupt her quite a bit; they are pleasant and overly accommodating and are constantly asking if she needs anything.
is the dripping going too fast, does it burn? do you mind the open window? the lady over there got sick, so we need to air the room out.

no, i don't mind anything, except maybe the fact that i'm here.
but on the other hand, somewhere deep down in her pigeon hole, she's grateful for the fact that she can actually be here.
for the remainder of the day, she is turning inside out. one act after another; from one fairytale to another. closer to the evening, it's just foam. i've never vomited foam before. mom, i know how doggy felt when he ate kitty's soap.[22] her stomach is a laboratory. tubes and vials. around midnight—fainting spells. a neon-colored stain at the bottom of the bucket, death beckons whitely, it feels close. it would be a pleasant change.

12.24

christmas eve. presents in the morning. hair on the pillow is coming out in clusters. i cut my hair to a buzz cut, and i call you: can you run the clipper for me and shave my head?

i can feel your hands shaking. merry christmas, mom.

in the evening, she admires her new head. a person can vomit a lot more easily when her hair is not in the way.

12.26.08

"i'll give them my heart, to know me."

you'll find youself at ground zero
a stone around the neck, a well that is deep, today she does not resist. she falls, flies, and knows that at ground zero lies heaven. there, she will find what she is looking for.

i like space. i'm heading for low ground because there's a lot of space there. no one is rushing over.

---

[22] *Translator's note*: Doggy and Kitty are characters from a children's book titled, "I Had a Dog and a Cat" by Czech writer, Karel Čapek.

* * *

therapist: i'll start a sentence, and you'll finish it without thinking, ok?
client: yes. therapist: i am... client: a dolt.
therapist: what does dolt mean?
client: dolt... stupid, an imbecile, an idiot.

during the holiday, ama tests this phone call on several subjects. elsa laughs, i came up with beast and then cow after that, lara reacts immediately. i'm a cow, why? because i keep trying, and it's futile, what do you keep trying to do? i don't know. trying to make things great, are you trying to be perfect? yes, perfect. a perfect cow.
dáša says old cow. markéta says she's an artistic cow.
a cow is, above all, a favorite animal. usually, it wants to be useful.

12.27

the shaved head inspires her to read buddhist texts, somehow it seems appropriate. it's necessary to maintain a style. she could take advantage of her bald head to enter other worlds, she could fit in with the hare krishnas, or among the skinheads. or both. krishna in the morning, skinheads at night. she could find out the difference between them and then write a comparative study about it.

the topic of cattle keeps emerging. today, reading a book by a zen monk she got information that turned her into an enlightened specimen of beef cattle. she reads and reads, and the words are impenetrable, like clay. she's royally bored, and then bam! a blow with a blunt object in the back of the head. the left-turning villi in the brain suddenly begin turning to the right, and a geyser erupts in the middle. transform into another being, advises the monk, or change into an object, an animal. don't imagine anything, you have to actually become it. it doesn't matter what it is. become a waterlily, become water in a lake, become a cow that is just taking a shit.
a cow that is taking a shit. great advice. so today she's a cow, and she feels great. she'll start by being a cow that's just standing around, so that it won't be too hard on her.

ciao, elsa. i'm writing to share my current escapades, in which i become a cow. i know that you will be interested in this. well actually, there is nothing much to share, because when i'm a cow, nothing really happens. but that's what it's all about. to have nothing happen to you, because that is the core of enlightenment. to understand that nothing is happening. people have a hard time with that, but cows are the ones that truly live it.

ama shares her new discovery with other friends, she thinks it will fundamentally change their lives.

who am i?
you name yourself by the things you do, says the wise horse to prince bajaja[23]—the inner voice, character, that guides him and then disappears at the end, because it's no longer needed. maybe her raven and wolf and all the saints will disappear as well but she has gotten used to them and she'd be sorry if they no longer stopped by for a visit.

---

[23] *Translator's note*: Prince Bajaja was a character from a fairytale by Czech writer Božena Němcová about a brave knight who had a wise and cunning horse that helped him slay dragon and save a princess.

quantum cow, the equation of laughter, and a parallel wolf pack

january 2009

dear ama, it's calm in jerusalem, no new year's celebrations, just a few people playing soldiers nearby. missiles can't reach out here, so we spend our winter days in relative peace. i'm up to my neck in work, but that's the way it should be. at worst i think, i'm an ass that's taking a shit... - leo

the psychedelic trip that carried number 008 has ended. it was enough. the tumors are packing up. little janis is dancing a jig, i can feel him energizing me. how does he do that? such a little man and he has 150 horsepower, although i'm beat after a few hours with janis. i return to prague for another dose of chemicals, and in the meantime, i'm roaming through my body, sitting on the banks of my river of blood, and i'm talking to each cell, like fidel castro, i'm howling my mission at them so they can chew through it, take what they need and spit out the rest. i should try everything. now, i know how it feels to be without hair. i was scared at first, but now i'm grateful. i feel sexy with a bald head—i've attached photos for you. if only i weren't so cold all the time. you don't realize that the mop on your head is a natural insulator until it's shaved off. a set of chic hats, berets, and caps will have to do the job. a stylish wig is sticking out of my drawer, where it's been ever since i bought it, somehow i like the bald head a lot more. i feel like a hare krishna. i even managed to dig up a salmon-colored toga that i wear at home. it's a shame that it's too cold to wear the outfit outdoors. i've internalized the role so much that i find myself singing hare rama, hare rama, rama rama, hare hare. of course, not everyone is so unhinged by my bald head. during dinner at lara's, little adele sat on my lap and said that she didn't like my bald head at all.

you looked better when you had hair.

then i'll grow it back, okay?

okay, and don't do stupid things like that again.

grace sent me a book by carl simonton for christmas, which i'm using like a manual. the author is a veteran doctor, he has been working with terminally ill patients for thirty years. he claims that no two people are the same or have the same path to recovery. something that can cure one person can kill another. how to proceed? don't listen to advice from others. do what makes you happy, whatever it may be.
at a time when you're all mixed up, when a pack of your own demons are baring their teeth at you, when so many of your loved ones gift you their fear and dread, that you won't recover, that you won't choose the right treatment—it's as if there was only one way to get better and that path was the right one. cancer forces you to change your filters. with a barrel pointed at your head, you start throwing people and things that bother you overboard. you say no to things you don't want and you invite over pieces of yourself that were locked up in a cage. cancer is, in fact, a liberator of sorts.
i've learned not to listen to the advice of people who have not experienced cancer and yet have plenty to say. it's like a flea telling a dog how to wag its tail.

a lot of things are happening that she did not anticipate. the beer diet has surprised her the most. and meat. after twenty years of not even touching red meat, she craves game. and liver.
mom, could you please find a boar's leg? i really would like to have one.
how do you know that you're craving boar when you've never eaten it?
i don't know. i just need to eat boar. or venison, if they don't carry it. but boar is first on my list.
elsa found the boar's leg, mom roasted it, and ama scarfed it down.
beer is another novelty, the aftertaste of chemo gets thoroughly entrenched in the pores of your tongue, so you have to drink it out. but water and tea turn her stomach and so she drinks four to six bottles of beer a day, just to get some liquid into her. after a few days of this drinking routine, she had to change her beverage menu, because she was constantly wasted: since the chemistry of medicine and the chemistry of hops add up, she was cheerfully whistling and singing until the neighbors complained. and so instead of a pilsen, she drinks that pathetic non-alcoholic beer.

she has heard from several sources that chemotherapy will make her foggy and fatigued, but she feels the tides rushing in, she has a craving for life. her mother comes to visit every three weeks and hovers over her. otherwise, she would have to spend several days in the hospital after each infusion. she takes home glucose and physiological saline to ensure that during hurling nights, she will manage to get some liquid into her veins. after four days of pure concentrated hell, she slowly gets back on her feet, and begins to live every moment like she never has before—now that they've told her that the outcome is definitive, damn, but the classic tune is that you never know, quantum physics confirms that. you can only ever talk about higher or lower probabilities. period. every once in a while someone stops by. lara and elsa bring groceries, fruits and vegetables, a home-baked cake. dana brings a basket with goodies. here's soup, here's marmalade. do you have enough food? are you sure you don't need anything else? books, movies, money?
others continue with their questioning. hiding behind a stage whisper, avoiding eye contact.
what do the doctors say? what's the prognosis?
it's like what they were saying about the bolsheviks. one year. two max.
damn it!
and you know how long the bolsheviks lasted.

01.20

the equation of laughter

jeff, i've become the visible source of pain for my whole family that no one can miss, everyone circles around me in this strange way, stammering. maybe it's the bald head that's making them uneasy, even though it looks so good on me.
i have a feeling that this close to death, i am more alive. don juan was right. death is the best ally. when nothing else makes sense, the touch of death gives you direction. i've been observing a peace within me for the past several weeks that i never had before. i even laugh more. i don't understand where it's coming from. where is laughter born? in the cells, in the veins, in the platelets? please, write me the equation

for laughter. the movement of atoms through the crevices of pleasure. i'm filling up a hologram of myself, weaving spiderwebs, the neurons are hissing like golden eels.

there are a few minor details she has to tune up, to define the difference between support and pressure, pressure arouses counterpressure and that takes away energy. everyone means well, but a person who is surrounded by too large a crowd of do-gooders can get smothered in a thick mash of good intentions.
it's fine to ask me how i am or how i am feeling, , but you don't have to ask me every time about my medical status. i don't want keep jabbering about it twenty-four hours a day. if i want to talk about it, i'll mention it myself, okay?

01.22.09

how do you reach your inner self? by plane, train, car? which means of transport do you take to get home?

life is simple, like leaves growing on branches, like the sun rising in the morning. once again, she wonders, and asks the trees, doesn't it hurt? what's it like to lose all your leaves? to become a bald head in the cold, when your hands get numb under the snow?
i know nothing about pain. i just know how things are.

01.25.09

quantumists vs. spiritualists
you're right, jeff, the spiritual world is great, as long as it has roots in the ground. many spiritualists don't do anything spiritual. they're just full of shit. spirituality that turns its nose up at the body and at matter is bullshit, but tell me why scientists mostly fear the word spirituality? sometimes, it seems that they see it as a perversion of some sort.

because it's assumed that a scientific and rational opinion is incongruous with mystical experience. rationality fears these alleys of love and searches for more tangible, settled roads. it wants a respectable family. and you have to admit that most spiritual people don't stand with their feet on the ground. they don't think logically, and they ignore science because they don't understand complex equations.

i agree, and i don't understand why it cannot come together. standing on one foot is quite strenuous. we could use a bit of balance. especially when quantum physics basically states that consciousness affects reality.

it certainly can come together, but you have to understand that walking on both sides of the fence at the same time is hard to do, for most people it is unimaginable, at least for now, it requires courage, a certain bravado, and a willingness to get your face smashed in once in a while. but from a quantum perspective, walking on both sides of the fence is the same thing as moving within two parallel realities. In other words, it's normal. (see my last essay about superpositions, which you apparently haven't read.)

understood. but if a single electron can be in two places at the same time, then why can't a normal person walk on both sides of the fence? can you give me a formula for that? ☺

i keep reading that quantum physics is the physics of possibility, what exactly does that mean?

sorry, creating a formula for people who have not read bohr and heisenberg is a waste of time.

quantum physics describes something that doesn't exist but could exist, something that is a mere possibility, and uses very sensible formulas for that, it doesn't describe physical matter, but the possibilities of that matter. what is it that you are reading? goswami?

no, i'm reading wolf. i like him. his quantum leaps. he's like a tornado. he says that thought—or more like consciousness—is everywhere. it's not in or outside the brain, it's just everywhere around us.

and what do you make of that?

that he's basically talking about jung's collective unconscious. taddah! and at this historical moment, a quantum physicist shakes the hand of an amazon shaman.

don't make me take a trip to the tropical jungle in my old age.

wow! thanks to this conversation of ours, i've just had another epiphany.

i'm dying to hear about it . . .

it's clear, a native shaman with his pagan tradition can worship jesus, because at the level of consciousness where all is everything, jesus is everything, and everything is jesus—or an anaconda, a jaguar, the universe. the shaman knows that it's all the same.

that's brilliant. i'm buying my ticket now. but seriously, i'm glad that you're bringing me into this. the principles on which classical physics are based, the notion of time, space, and matter, all fall apart. they crumble like rotten rubber. we inch our way through a field where it's hard to objectively prove anything, because we're working with ideas that fundamentally break down the well-oiled mechanical approach. we discover that we're creating a reality through our interpretation of effects.

damn it, professor. don't do this to me! who am i going to argue with, if we're both singing the same tune? this is exactly the same thing castaneda's don juan says. what are we going to do about that? i liked it when we screamed at each other until our voices were hoarse.

you were the one doing the screaming. i would just silently fume. when gwen brought you to us, you were just a rebellious brat and an ignoramus who had no equal, near or far. i couldn't believe your audacity to question my grandeur.

i learned so much from you.

that last statement of yours is a testament to your greatness, jeff. i would never admit that i learned anything from you.

i'm too old to mind a bit of sentimentality. i'm feeling kind of unhinged—it's been snowing for two days straight.

toronto is quite an unappealing city, half a year of winter, sterile architecture, canadians everywhere ☺. but still, i love toronto, if only because of you and glenn.

02.03.09

chemo, my bro, we'll roll up our sleeves and sit in the lazyboy that looks like a dentist's chair, although, it's true that dental procedures are somewhat more pleasant. the nurse scolds her with a finger. don't you dare run off on us back into the jungle.
ama smiles, but says nothing.
this time around, she has to change the music, because the music she played during her last three infusions made her sick. reflexes are good—you can always count on pavlov. the young beauty that's poking her veins and hanging the infusion is going to get married in a month. she lights up when she talks about her fiancé.

at home, hunger. she has to eat something that's easy to throw up. maybe porridge. it has to be something she doesn't mind wasting. so far, bananas have taken the brunt of it. standard procedure. mom has that worried look on her face. ama tries to lighten up the mood with some comedy. as long as she has enough energy. in the evenings, she falls into bed. she starts editing scenes of what she's shedding, sci-fi, a drip-feed in her arm, it's hard to vomit with a cannula stuck in her vein. after a few hours of vomiting, even the muscles in her back are hurting.

mom, get me the glucose so i can get rid of this feeding tube. i've had it with this thing.
a cliche, but it's appropriate. mom is balancing on the bed and hanging half-liter iv bags on the pelmets.
done. is everything alright?
no, slow it down a bit. i feel like it's going to freeze my veins. you can feel it?

yes, i can! it's coming in too fast. slow it down! okay. hold on! is this better?
after the glucose, another liter of the saline solution. by midnight, half of the bag is empty. in the meantime, a few sessions of vomiting. mom, get this off of me. please.
don't you want it to drip till it's empty?
no, i can't take it anymore. it's really bothering me while i'm throwing up.
that's a shame.
just take it away, or i'm going to fucking lose it.
ama can't control herself. she's hissing through her teeth, she's not begging, but barking commands, yelling, almost screaming. and she's sorry for it.
the things that mothers endure.

the night is a roller coaster riding her brain, the same thing over and over. it's february. the fourth infusion. relaxation is impossible, so she tries something different. another loophole. another obsession is needed, something pleasant. what'll it be? screenplays. a song for abdul, rhymes for scheherazade, that's simple—and it works perfectly. anytime she comes across a topic that pisses her off, she sets scheherazade on it, and problem solved! no one could fight scheherazade. she has to laugh.
what's going on?
nothing mom, forgive me, i'm just cracking up. mom squints in the doorway.
are you feeling any better?
not really, but i'm keeping myself entertained. what time is it? two-thirty. go lie down, mom. try to get some sleep.
it's hard for ama to get any sleep with this sea monster, and so she goes over scheherazade several times. it's going to be quite the rhyme. lada[24] would be amazed. ring around the rosy, a pocket full of posies, all the way till morning.

---

[24] *Translator's note*: Josef Lada was a Czech painter and illustrator born in the late nineteenth century, know for writing and illustrating a book of traditional Czech rhymes and considered a pioneer of the Czech comic book tradition.

02.05.09

she recognizes the faces of the sun. its daily costumes and nightly transformations. at night, she walks in the skin of the jaguar through the underworld. jaguars can be invisible because they know it's possible.
in the morning, she looks for points of reference. if i walk from the bed to the door, i will hold onto the door knob. four steps, lean on the door frame, then i can reach the light switch. if i press it, light shoots out. the layout of the parquet floor beneath my feet. steady breathing. the surface where i shuffle each foot onto the next square. the geometry of certainty. the door, the doorknob, the door frame, the threshold into the study. the corner of the table on the horizon. if i can get to that, it will hold me. six steps. thank you, table, birch tree trunk, for your generosity. my laptop on a pile of paper, from those blank pages i dare to venture towards the window. I grasp onto the windowsill. the arrowroot plant airs out its tricolored face in the sun. two more steps. an old tamarack beyond the glass. it stretches out its stiff arms, trying to pull me outside. a mirror behind me, a sobering ellipse. no one was in it yesterday, but today i noticed a body that didn't have a face.
if i make it to tomorrow, maybe my face will come back.

when she is so weak that she can't even move, she listens to her evergreens. bach's d-minor. gould spices it up like pepper in a sauce. it's as if the master himself was sitting right here, in his white wig. eloquent fingers and ink stains. it's almost unbearable. a person can suffer cramps in her hand just from listening. gould does not play bach. gould lives bach.

gould's bach is perfect but his mozart doesn't hold up. - jeff

i agree. he plays him like he's making fun of amadeus. but mozart isn't the only one. he wipes out on his appassionato. he cuts out a caricature with exemplary percussion, as if he were saying, okay, okay, you pompous ass, if you want pomp—let's make it real! and then he sprays the keys with coca cola.

you surprise me. i thought gould was untouchable.☺

it doesn't change the fact that he is a genius. i just discovered a superb video on youtube. just search "glenn gould plays bach," it will show a part of the film, the art of the piano. it's three minutes long. just a chunk of bach's second partita. the recording is terrible quality but it's worth it to watch his passion each time he hits the keys. in the middle of it, he stands up and just does a dee da, da, da, da, da, da, dee. and then he sits down and continues as if nothing happened. it's as if he weren't from this world.

02.09.09
full moon—eclipse
if you know you have weaknesses, then you are at the core of your strength. the issue is not to find a cure, but to live to the fullest. a full life often leads to a cure.

jerusalem is calling.
ciao, leo, i have been thinking about you a lot, about the war over there. well, i had my first free weekend since christmas. what about you? where are you now?
i'm standing next to a madonna in šárka, and i'm watching how her long shadow sinks down into the valley. i'm talking to the universe, and it's answering me.
and what is the universe saying?
it's talking to me like aladdin's genie. your wish is my command.

in the evening, she reads the conclusion of her latest email from jeff. she tries to think it over, even though she has a feeling that the chemotherapy didn't just wipe off the hair on her skull but also the cortex in her brain. certainly, high toxicity doesn't just clean out your hair follicles.

in quantum physics, we observe activity that renders fluctuation. those quantum leaps that no one can control or predict. it's like watching a slow-moving drop of water on a window and trying to guess where it's going. newton's physics set a goal to define such effects precisely and, by doing so, control them. quantum physics proves that on the level of atoms, classical postulates don't count. for a physicist, the thrill of such a discovery turns into a nightmare, because as a result of this, we discover that we have no control over matter. perhaps you can imagine how heisenberg must've freaked out when he discovered the principle of uncertainty.

ciao, jeff, thank you for yesterday's ration of quantum cuisine. i have to admit that, besides bach and his flawless counterpoint, it's my communication with you that keeps my head above water.
i value the fact that you think about what i'm doing for all these days between my doses of chemotherapy. from the outside, it might seem that i'm doing nothing. i have a talent for that, and i would be able to write well-turned essays about the benefits of doing nothing. on the other hand, so much is going on that i can't write fast enough. i could also give you a feynmanish answer. you know his famous verse in which he described introspection during his studies at mit? i research why. i research why, i research why i research."
my version would be:
i don't know why i don't know why.
i don't know why i don't know.
i don't know why i don't know why.
i don't know why i don't know!
there is no i want to live or i want to die, it's only i'm living or i'm dying. and i'm living even though i don't know why. i'm writing, and i don't know why. i'm learning to write just for the heck of it. it's the same as getting up or walking. just for the heck of it. like a cat that wanders around and doesn't care where it is, because la-dee-daaa.
it's strange, jeff, the silence. no voices, no one inside talks to me, no one is babbling or has comments. and when i want to break the silence, i just turn the knob and change the channel. i see a wolf, i see jesus, i have a chat with the light switch, the drawer, or a pile of paper that lies on my table. they all talk to me, and then i just shut them off. most of the time, i choose the silence without the comments. i do a lot of work during the night, you wouldn't believe all the places i travel too. i return to the place where the river boils, where the natives salt their food with ash. i

dream about my double, and i have funny dreams. i am often woken by my own laughter.
i start the day with a walk, i mean, after i get back on my feet following a dose of chemo. in those early days, i sort of shuffle like someone with polio. it helps me to sing my horse is being saddled, that's one of our traditional songs about a kind of a czech mustang. not too long ago, two teenagers were staring at me so much that they almost slid on the snow. did you see that?
wow. wasted like that at eight-thirty in the morning. that's what you call an early bird .
in my morning outfit and with my horse...i crawl to the nearest park so i can make the frozen trees laugh. their bark flows downward like gray rapids. i observe the ravens. there are so many of them, all my relatives. i love those birds. although my raven doesn't come by so often. perhaps you don't know that the raven in native american mythology is the creator. in some of the legends, the raven finds light. one legend tells the story of how it used to be a beautiful bird with colorful feathers and a singing voice. once, it set out for a risky expedition to bring the sun to the earth. it cleverly stole the sun from an evil spirit and carried it in his beak the whole way back home, burning itself a bit. that is how it lost its fancy facade and its voice. that is why it has feathers like ash and cackles to this day. but the raven is the only bird that can fly to the eternal hunting ground and return.
my personal guardians, the wolf and the raven, were accompanied by a bear. apparently, i picked him up in the desert. i'm not surprised because the stone mother's husband was a bear. in those days, the land was ruled by the wise wolf and his brother, the coyote, would make a mess of things. the natives consider the bear half human, because they lived on the same continent and hunted salmon in the same rivers. bears are like people. they dance and frolic, and sleep through the whole winter. my bear is an entertainer. he skis on one foot wearing a straw hat, does somersaults, and plays the banjo.
besides my animals, people come and visit me. dáša stops by once a week to do a hypnosis session. every two weeks, i take a breather with elsa.

as you know, there are several techniques. from good old groff to reich to satori. you made quite an impression on me that you know reich and the experiments he conducted with einstein. what really makes me laugh is that, in the fifties, the american government was burning his books like the inquisition, and reich ended up in prison because he defended himself in court with an embarrassingly naïve argument that government officials have no right to decide about scientific findings. it's strange that eugene mall, who wrote about reich as well as cold fusion was murdered randomly five years ago. in february of this year, they reportedly announced a huge reward for anyone who captures his killer. someone is taking their sweet time. i'm curious how this investigation will end and what will happen to cold fusion. the japanese and the indians have apparently revamped the research. i don't quite understand what is so controversial about all this. will you enlighten me, professor?

ok, back to the breathing. as you can see, i can't hold a steady line of thought for even two paragraphs. well, we practice the mildest version of this activity. they call it satori, or quantum breath. i'm not kidding. the basis for it is deep breathing that leads to a release and the calming of one's consciousness. because i feel that this would certainly interest you, i expect to see a solid study on quantum breath. what are our atoms doing there? write me what you think about it. and then i will become a lung quark, and i'll tell you if you're right.

just so you know, beside spiritualists, i'm visited by ordinary people. lech stopped by not too long ago—the builder of the unfinished bridge in the santuario. well, i'm not sure if he is completely normal, . we reminisced about the mosquitos, our skin covered with insect bites and ayahuasca. i honestly felt nostalgic for the monkeys and the jungle folk as well. i would fly there in a heartbeat.

from time to time, between chemo rounds, i go to zlín, to enjoy little janis. he's at that adorable age where he jumps into everything head-on, and i need to take advantage of that. on top of that, i'm not limited by parental responsibility. last saturday, i took him to the playground. and because it was slushy outside, i brought him back all covered in mud. why would i stop him from doing log rolls in the sandbox when he was so happy doing it? my sis, who does not allow him to indulge in

such activities, acted mad and asked me if i would let him swim in the river, if he wanted to. can you believe that? she must think that i'm a complete moron.
i also have a lot of work to do for the club of enlightened cows, which i founded. you'd be surprised how fast our organization has grown. how so many new members have unexpectedly emerged—there are more of us every day. i know you were interested in this, and i am sorry that i can't offer you membership. if you were of the right sex, then you would undoubtedly qualify. a quantum cow would be to our advantage. perhaps you can stir things up in due time. since i don't usually do a lot of thinking, i made an exception today and spent almost the whole day mulling over quantum leaps in practice. i found some great examples among my friends.
at the top of the list, unrivaled, is loreen, who after fifteen years of roaming the world with a camera for cbs, gave a day's notice, packed her things, sold her apartment in central london, and moved to a farm in tasmania, where she now plants trees and even shears sheep. after a few years, she met the local version of brad pitt and started a family with him. from the sidelines, this story can't be explained. it was so unexpected, illogical, she had no reason to act the way she did. similarly, the industrial chemist eda embraced his quantum leap in the form of the smashed head he experienced while engaged in acrobatic skiing. evidently, it ignited something in him, because when he came out of the hospital standing on his own two feet, he hung up his chemistry and became an herbalist. and then there is dáša, who leaped from architecture to hypnosis, and rich, from a top business firm, who sang his way to the top tiers of the opera. libuška left her job as the head of a credit department to build family constellations. these changes can't be reasonably explained to an outsider. and so, not just particles, but people can quantum leap as well, or am i mistaken?

02.11.09

ama, i'll take a look into quantum breath. just give me a little time. i wrote that on purpose, because i know you, you'll get a kick out of the phrase, "give me a little time."

in the case of cold fusion, and the ridicule fleischmann received along with ponse twenty years ago, the basis here is the classical problem of discovery and evidence. it is important to understand that discovery and evidence are two different things.

there are, for instance, equations that are so beautiful that when you look at them, you think they have to be correct. it's like when a man looks at a beautiful woman and says to himself that she's the one. but even if the equation is beautiful, it can resist evidence in an ugly way. the main difference between discovery and evidence lies in time, when you discover something, it takes time to prove it. that doesn't mean that the discovery is nonsense. in the context of discoveries, everything is possible. but almost always, an orthodox gang instantly emerges with a pile of criteria, old ragged standards, and measures them against the new thing. and therein lies the entire controversy. today, cold fusion has many different names in order to avoid the aphorism of skeptical ridicule. and the research continues not only in india and pakistan, but also with the us army.

as you know, the probability theory states that nothing is impossible, you can only discuss higher or lower probability. the conservatives like to forget this.

your examples of quantum leaps in practice were entertaining, but basically you are correct. the occurrences among particles happen to people as well. your darling feynman added to this that natural occurrences are driven by their future statuses. he claimed that nature will investigate all paths and choose the one that relates to the least amount of action.

in quantum aerodynamics, he described this by giving the example of a lifeguard who acts like a beam of light. when someone in the water starts shouting for help, the lifeguard (photon) observes all the possible routes he can take to get to the victim. because life is at stake, he will choose the shortest route. light works in the same fashion.

a similar observation was made by planck, who often referenced psychology. he noted that photons act like intelligent human beings: from all imaginable curves, they find the one that will bring them to the finish line the fastest.

when i think about your pilgrimage, i see that you did the same. what an outsider would consider quite the detour was rather a shortcut. you did not search for a cure. you wanted to investigate how things are. and you chose the shortest route possible. sometimes the biggest shitshows ultimately prove to be the greatest blessings.

many thanks for your kind words, jeffosimo, in terms of how things are, i still don't know much. the only difference is that it's not tearing me to pieces. it doesn't bother me anymore that i don't have a clue about how the world works. on the contrary, i've started to enjoy living without a purpose, just living. for the heck of it, just to try out as many things as possible, and there's so much i can try out. also, a minor comment about discoveries, proof, and blessings. thanks to you, i now understand the difference between science and scientific materialism. it's a shame that the term scientific is used over and over like a nursery rhyme, just as once the term blessing was used. when the pope gave a blessing over something, it became holy. nowadays, the word *scientific* is the blessing. if you label it that way, most people will buy it without thinking about it. it's similar to the way we throw ourselves at produce that claims to be organic. if we say that there is no scientific evidence about an item, it sounds educated and skeptical, but it translates to the fact that we haven't found proof yet. saying that it is impossible is like declaring that tones we can't hear don't exist. but a dog can hear them.

02.24.09

another round of chemo.
she can't wear the clothes she wore last time—that would make her throw up immediately. she has to bring something comfortable. something that she can later do without. she has a need to constantly shine, to hold the neuron networks and fill them with gold. the glass elevator in her brain sends her headfirst into the clouds. she can see in all directions, as if everything is in the palm of her hand.
the nurses in the oncology department are nice and compassionate, they ask her if they are making her nauseous. some people start getting sick just by looking at the nurses. the infusion maintains a standard

course. at home, she blows out her iv vein, so glucose is out of the question. in the evening, she is so exhausted that she can't imagine holding a cannula in her hand. sleep is out of the question, the waves are terrible. the schooner is swimming. the rescuers are in life jackets. she's shivering and waiting for the sea to exhaust itself.

02.28.09

old habits are like chewed-up pieces of gum. they might not have any flavor left but they are a whole lot stickier. ama chews once in a while, and when she realizes, she bitches at herself and tries to get unstuck. and then she tries not to try. she battles so that she will not have to battle.

just before she moved from new york, a friend took her to aikido. the master, an old japanese man, chatted with her for a while in broken english.
i don't know if you really want to learn, but i will tell you everything needed to master the martial arts.
he turned the palms of his hands against hers and stood still. she felt waves of warm air, and her knees buckled a bit.
whatever you give will come back at you, he said. if you wish to gain a result through battle, the battle will come back at you. you cannot defeat evil from without.
he saw inside her. she had a feeling that he was raking through the wheels in her brain.
he moved even closer to her. her head was spinning a bit. she could feel his breath on her face. he lightly touched her breastbone.
here. the core of everything you don't want, of everything you fight for, is inside of you. the heart does not know the battle between good and evil. it absorbs everything that is. the heart is the best master of the art of battle. remember that.
she remembered it, even though she forgot. all of a sudden it floated out. it dug itself out like a coin in the back pocket of her pants.

radio waves and a parallel gang

03.01.09

jeff, since you were interested in my animals and spirits that live here with me, today i experienced an incident that you might appreciate. once a week, a therapist, zuzana, visits me, who conducts craniosacral therapy. basically, it's work with energy that follows the movement of cerebrospinal fluid, and it treats so-called formulas of tension. it can all be compared to ocean waves. the deepest waves equal dynamic peace, in which you are somewhere at the bottom, and nothing happens. then there are other layers, from mild waves to waves breaking on the surface, which is called craniosacral movement. nowadays, craniosacral movement is measured by instruments, it has an average pulse of six per minute, and it is even taught at medical schools.

now, about the incident.

after today's treatment, i got up and paused to look at zuzana's face. we haven't known each other that long, and we don't know much about one another. so, i couldn't understand what exactly was happening. personally, i was enjoying myself, i felt great.

did something happen?

she rubbed her eyes for a while as if she was trying to wring out a burning fingerprint lodged in the retina. when she spoke, she suddenly started stuttering and twitching her head, which helped her words come out.

well, this has never happened to me before, but i saw a bear. first he was lying on the ground, and then he was walking around, pacing from one side of the room to the other with a bear-like walk.

her face lost all color, it looked like she needed some oxygen. i thought it was great, and so i asked if by any chance a wolf had run by.

she put her hand on her forehead and answered in a pitch an octave higher than usual. yes, a wolf was over there, and above you, perched right above your head, was a raven. calm down, zuzana, they live with me here. and congratulations, you are the first other person to see them.

she was terrified, jeff. but can you imagine how happy i was?

now, i have to work out a conclusion for you. do you remember when you explained the principles of radio waves to me? it occurred to me

that the same principle applies to my animals. i sit here in my apartment in prague, and i can tune into radio moscow or bbc london or czech vysočina, depending on what mood i'm in and if my antenna will reach it. and even though i'm not listening to any radio station, all those radio waves are still there in my room everywhere. they're real, even though i don't see them. even though they're intangible. it's the same with my wolf, or my bear. they're from a different reality, even though i can't see them all the time i know that they're with me, i just need to receive them at certain wavelengths. it seems that my therapist managed to tune into these waves. it strikes me as a great example of parallel worlds.
that means that parallel realities are always around us, here and now. they are not somewhere beyond the mountains, and the nanoworlds that some people see and maybe call an elf paradise are just a form of consciousness. some people see angels, others see ufos. all of these are parallel worlds present in the room where a person sits. it all depends on your receiver. we all move in parallel realities, we just don't notice it most of the time.

03.03.09

"a woman should always wear make-up. in her natural state she is boring, plain, and ugly . . . i believe that plastic surgery is practically necessary for today's woman."

french fashion designer sonia ryliel

suffering and guilty feelings are out of fashion. it's time to replenish the wardrobe. cleaning out a wardrobe in and of itself is a pain because your whole apartment is full of rags, and among them, janáček, stacks of notebooks, snippets of unfinished plays, stories, books. it's no wonder that you sort of wanted to die. it's a lot of work to finish it all.
a night in the arms of lovers. bach, that overplayed rain summoner, first prelude in d major. the first few beats and something happens in my head behind my left eye. a white flicker. the wind picks up in my rib cage, and i can feel the typhoon coming. gould bends the notes to the breaking point. in a few strokes, he turns the steinway into a flying carpet.

is this gratitude? this intoxicating feeling that such music is possible. people like shütz, bach, gould. that life jacket that carries a person onward, and it doesn't matter where.

falling asleep at three in the morning has several rules that are set in stone. first, she can't fall asleep because she's hungry. when she eats, she can't fall asleep because her stomach is full, and it's hard to fall asleep with a full stomach. then the birds start to chatter, and then it's impossible to go to sleep, and in the end, the most ironclad rule, when she goes to bed so late, there will always be a moron who will wake her up before eight in the morning.
the doorbell rings at 7:30, and a boy with overalls stands in the doorway. she has to park her car elsewhere. did she see the notice? today we're trimming the poplar trees in front of the building. please can you do it now? we're ready to start.
she sees two of him, and she is about to tell both of them to fuck off, but it really is not his fault. trimming the poplar trees is necessary. she notices how shabby they are. there is always something to gnaw off. the head physician would like to do that to her as well. but then they would have to take out her whole lungs, and you can't live without them, they say. but maybe those doctors are right in some cases.

03.09.09

i'm riding on light. first, it looks like a horse but it isn't, light is light and not a horse. it's white and bronze calico. it carries me to a place where i don't have a name or a shape. it's strange, jeff, ordinary effects play with colors, those that are predictable in daily reality become mysterious and magical. the things that i would consider unreal seem more real today than anything that i ever considered real before. does that make sense? i can see a clear outline of the difference between literature of fact and magic realism. magic realism is much closer to reality.
most of the time, i'm in such a great mood that i don't feel good. reading seems inappropriate. before, i would devour books three times a day. can a person be surprised that she is sickly? but seriously, i don't really

read anything. only kabir, and hafiz, and sometimes that quantum of yours. if i happen to be feeling a little low, hafiz always picks me up.

and what about you? what are your quarks looking like these days, professor?
yesterday my neighbors invited me for dinner. it was quite an interesting evening. it started with mildly spicy lentil soup. and then it all went downhill. two law professors argued for hours about the international situation. conclusion: never invite more than one lawyer to your table. and how about you? are you on your last dose?

no, just one more left. in a week. this fascinates me about life, jeff. i was always such a healthy biogal and alternativist, and now i've become the poster child for the harshest form of chemotherapy. who would have thought it? chemo, you have to experience the things that you fear the most to find out that you no longer need to fear anything. i convinced myself that it is the best medicine i can offer my body. and there's the rub: a person asks a fairly useless question, to which treatment you say yes, and to which treatment you say no.
the answer: any treatment, as long as that person believes in it and doesn't doubt it. then, it doesn't matter. if she doubts it, it doesn't matter either. the only liberation is the knowledge that you can't make a wrong choice.

today, i wouldn't stop anyone from touching the ground.

something happened to me. i'm walking through the city, and people are smiling at me. and i found out that, for most of the day, i've been grinning like a court jester. i completely lost that highly intelligent, morose, pissed-off look on my face. i must look like a complete clown, and i'm feeling good. i stand in the park with the expression of a person who just achieved universal consciousness (to an outsider, it might look like i just had a lobotomy), i'm laughing at the trees that are shaking their asses and lifting up their skirts. i remember ginder and the always-grinning people of the jungle, and i would fly there in a heartbeat. and then i realize that i don't have to go anywhere, i have everything i need here. all i need to do is dream the right way, i tip my shipibo rain stick, and in those seeds, i hear their voices, the jaguar's breath.

03.17

a vertical ride at night. the bedroom has no ceiling. above, looms the vast laughter of heaven and body cramps that come and stay from time to time. the raven is nowhere to be found, but he resonates in her, pulling her downward. go back to that original matrix. find the dna imprint. go back there. you know the way.
well, aren't you sad that it's ending? this is the last chemo. you are laughing.
not really, ami.
you have to admit, we've never had so much fun together before. that's true.
who would have thought? who would believe that this would be the best year of our lives, that happiness would come at this point in time?

mom, i wanted to do this for you, but it didn't work out. at the end, i did it for myself.

i've stopped asking whether i fulfill the criteria for sanity. as usual with rules and regulations, the criteria for sanity are defined by those who are the least sane.

tomorrow is the anniversary of the start of my trip. the detour that became a shortcut. how did you describe it, old man? you fear the unknown. go take a look at what's behind it. you told me that the natives had a great goddess who was called the one who will push you off the riverbank, i have a feeling that i'm not afraid anymore. i don't know when it happened, but i just stopped being an obstacle on my own path. and you gave me that push.

03.20.09

i'm reading letters that you're tapping out with the soles of your shoes

on the streets of foreign cities. my life, which you are not a part of. you just observe it from a distance like an airplane in the sky, and you search for places where time doesn't rush, where everything is played andante. and you do it to get a taste of every leaf, tree, shabby wind. you could come with me to the pinnacle, to rock bottom, all the way to the end.
why am i telling you this? my story might give you the courage to ignite your own.

jeff, my jeffrey, i'm standing on a meadow, and i'm drawing a circle of light in the sky in which future days appear. the land of poets is the land that belongs to no one. a landscape between a word and an image, and my laughter is more and more insane.

i wrote a fairytale for you, professor.

about hemispheres

a new fairytale about two sisters.
through the forest, over the field, past baykal lake, lived an old widow who had two daughters, dextra and sinistra.
sinistra was beautiful, but vain, demanding, assertive, and extremely competitive. she was also prodigiously jealous. when she set her mind on something, she would cross mountains, step over dead bodies—in the name of logic and scientific progress, she achieved everything she wanted to. rational through and through, she was bursting with monotonous objectivity and a registry of scavenged truths. she carried a spindle that would unspool like her thoughts. linear, dependent on the laws of cause and effect, bound by the weight of gravity.
dextra was like a radio. she knew how to tune in, catch various frequencies, latch on to people, animals, landscapes. she was lovable, light as a breeze on her feet. she could taste sounds, images, and fragrances. she understood the speed of lightning. she could see sound waves, the shapes of the molecules that would flow through her nose when she inhaled. she loved to play and dream, day and night.

sinistra would behave condescendingly to her sister and look down on her. everything that dextra did or said would make sinistra smirk at her. because sinistra did not understand her sister, secretly she was afraid of her, and every time dextra would spin something with her own spindle, her sister was there to undo it immediately. when sinistra had had enough of her childish sister, she ripped the spindle out of dextra's hand and threw it into an old well. when the widow found out about it, she ordered dextra to jump into the well to get the spool. and because dextra had no difficulty doing things, she jumped into the well, and immediately she found herself on a green meadow. she walked and walked, passing sheep whose wool she combed, cows that she milked, horses whose manes she brushed, until she finally reached a cottage that belonged to baba yaga. baba yaga greeted her and hired her as a servant. dextra weaved, cooked, cleaned, oiled the chicken leg her cottage rested on, she dusted off all the human skulls on the fence, and she always sang while she worked. after a year, dextra returned with a rich bounty. she got a golden spindle from baba yaga, the sheep gave her a lamb, the cows a calf, and the horse a colt. she completely changed. she was more beautiful than before, and when she laughed, rubies would fall from her lips. she would cry pearls and talk diamonds. sinistra greeted her sister apathetically, but she watched her from the corner of her eye. she herself never laughed or cried. when she spoke, she spat out roaches, flies, and other logical relations.

when the widow saw all the gifts dextra had brought, she pulled sinistra to the side and forced her to jump into the old well so that she, too, would return with a pile of useful souvenirs.

but because this is a modern fairytale, sinistra did not make the sequence of embarrassing mistakes that is commonly prescribed in the old version. she decided not to listen to her mother: she would not jump into the well and return home covered in grease. why would i jump into the well, mother? dextra will gladly share her gifts. all you need to do is reach out your hand, and my childish sister will throw herself around my neck. i can avoid the long journey and the hard work, and my sister's diamonds, rubies, and pearls will be mine anyway. all i have to do is not trip her up. and she did what she said. but when she gave her sister a lukewarm and awkward hug, because she didn't know any other way to do it, something happened to her. it was as if she were no longer the same person. as if, in that moment, she died and was reborn. she began to laugh, and at the same time, to cry. rubies and pearls. she laughed and cried rubies and pearls, and laughter and tears. rubies and pearls. and once in a while, a diamond, because there was no need for words.

03.29.09

ama,

you're allowed to die
when you've painted all the beauty that you see around you.
when you've sung all the notes that sound within you.
when you've written all the stories that you've lived.
how far along are you?

grace

i'm writing, grace, writing, though i don't know why.
writing is like building bridges, weaving spiderwebs, finding relationships, parallels, conjunctions to write in order to show off is foolish. it takes the weight and lightness away from words, it makes a fool out of every sentence, a tiny cripple that stands on the tip of her toes. the only writing that makes any real sense is the kind i want to give away. it has to come from within me—linens of the soul, not just a few old rags for the salvation army. writing that i want to share opens a space— it binds foot bridges, suspension bridges. at that moment a hand reaches out from the page that you are reading and touches a furrow on your forehead. thoughts that occurred to you yesterday for the first time, you suddenly read about today, in this book. and maybe you'll realize that everything you ever thought of has already been thought of by thousands of other people. and that hand that reaches out to you from that page might just be yours.

04.03.09

the department of clinical oncology at homolka hospital.

i have unexpectedly good news for you. we found nothing on your lungs.
the ganglia are also clear. we'll do only radiation for now.
that sounds good. so, what's next?
what's next? that's up to the almighty.
ama starts laughing.
surely you don't mean god, doctor?

04.09.09

majid nili, the iranian charge d'affaires, answering a question in *today* magazine: what's his marriage like?

"we've been together for seventeen years, and we've had a lot of luck. we have no problems, and we do not differ in anything, everything is great, and we're happy together."

that's called nirvana.

grace, i'm so happy that you have an interest in joining the club of enlightened cows. we are now an international club. since we have no cows abroad, you will at least be the first in something.
the only condition is that you have to be an enlightened cow. we don't accept normal cows. the difference between an ec and an nc is simple.
the enlightened cow differs from the normal cow by the fact that she knows who she is. in other words, she is a cow who knows that she's a cow and is at peace with it. that way, she is at peace with the whole universe. such a cow has the koan of "moo" and the koan of "who am i" all figured out.
that's about it. if you have any questions, feel free to contact me or any other cow in our club. there is no hierarchy, because we know that we are all the same cows.

04.11.09 zlín

a sakura in bloom in the garden. pollen in the air carries the fragrance of the cetico leaves. the dust from cetico ash is what the shipibo use to salt their plantains. it's still in her. she's waiting for the sun, when it will take her into its arms like a flute, and she will start frying up some of her stories.

she reads her notes and ponders over how simple and intimately familiar is irony, a cynical sneer, skeptical prying. how awkward is kindness. to her surroundings and to herself, when she observes herself with a tolerant smile in the same way she observes a little child that missteps once in a while, because it is just learning about gravity and other curiosities in the earthly world, because they never had anything like it in their universe.

in the afternoon, she is standing on a meadow in the forest, in a place of pure wonder at the amount of things that surround her.
you are surrounded by eternity, don juan tells castaneda. what do you think about that?
she passes by a clearing and about half a dozen older women bending over, planting trees. tiny spruces, one by one. they wave at her, and she comes closer.
i'd like to join you.
the women laugh, sun on their faces, wiping off sweat. we would love it. here, if you really mean it, grab a hoe.
it's good to start the spring by planting trees. it seemed fitting to her, and so she's bent over along with the rest of them, putting new life into the earth.

04.22

radiology at motol hospital. a pale man with a greek profile, blood vessels spread out between the wrinkles on his skin. he leans on a cane, hunched over, his voice raspy. once in a while, he starts to cough, and in the meantime, something is tearing up his insides. an explosive charge in a quarry, the breaking of walls. next to him, his wife watches him nervously. she moves closer to him, and when it shakes his whole body, she scolds him in a quiet voice. she's out of her element and doesn't know what to do. while her husband is annoying everyone with his loud dying, he's poisoning the air. some dying people just don't care about their surroundings.

a lesson for patients treated with radiation. we have three linear accelerators that offer radiation of several types (photons and electrons) using different energy. after radiation, the patient isn't dangerous to others in his surroundings since radioactivity does not radiate from the patient.

she signs these sheets of paper with her eyes closed, but the sentence about the photons sparks her interest.
jeff, i'm getting energy. i'm testing the practical side of things again, and i've been amazed that these linear particle accelerators look like spaceships.
i'm amazed by the mothers of small children who i see here. they sit quietly, hugging their bald-headed angels. some of them cry silently. they sound like butterflies breathing.
radiation takes seven weeks. every day, except on weekends. it doesn't take long most of the time, but sometimes, the waiting room gets packed. there's a glitch somewhere, and you have to wait for hours. then, someone always shows up who begins to raise havoc, and it spreads around, and others suddenly go wild. no judgment, because many of these people are in pain and sitting for a long time is hard to endure. at that moment, i always imagine that i'm sitting on the bank of rio pachitea, waiting for a boat. when it comes, it comes. patience is a pleasant change. there is nowhere to fly to, no hurry. i just turn on glenn in my headphones, and i'm far down the river.

05.12.09

clear tones outside the window, graceless and rigid colors and blanched sheets on a clothes line. in the tiny garden behind the house, an old lady, a withered flower, ravaging with a hoe, ripping the weeds from the flowerbeds near the fence. pressing new bulbs into the pores of the earth.

during her sunday walk, they approach her and surround her in a small circle. young lady, we have something very pleasant for you in this world where everyone complains and laments. look, we have something that will improve your mood, give you encouragement.
but i'm not complaining. i'm not missing anything.
the jehovah's witnesses are waving their pamphlets, grinning divinely, getting by with a quote from psalms. "the righteous will inherit the land and live in it forever."
yes, my dear sisters, the end will come, the book of revelations says. god will wipe away every tear from our eyes, and death will no longer be. but you should know that you no longer have to wait, because you have found who you were looking for. come home with me. we can talk about it.
a significant pause slips through the gesture of invitation; the heralds of faith step back, they are in no hurry.
come, sisters, don't be afraid, i am the savior, perhaps you imagined him differently, but believe me when i tell you, i am jesus, i am god.
she doffs her hat and illuminates them with her bald head. she wants to make an impression. she shouts so the entire street can hear her. the jehovah's witnesses quickly say goodbye and begin hurrying somewhere, they couldn't even say where they were going.
you don't believe me? is your faith smaller than a single mustard seed? too bad. they didn't even give her a chance to lean into it. unfortunately, the sisters were not ready to meet a messiah. people are always looking for something, and when they finally find it, they're scared shitless.

06.06.09

i'm looking at the sky. the birds stop in flight. they just got stuck in one place. they're fluttering their wings, but they're not moving forward one bit. when i try to push them with the thought of moving forward, they begin to retreat. and so, i leave them alone. i give up the effort, and then as if nothing had happened, they begin flying forward.

i'm carving out the inside of my body, making room for my soul, so it can finally settle down.

i'm scribbling casual notes, lists, so as not to forget all my tasks.

1. steal geryon's cows
2. clean out augias's stables
3. acquire hyppolyte's belt
4. catch cerberus

and so on, and so on. don't forget hesperides's golden apples. and of course, learn how to turn things into gold, then you won't have to worry that you will lose your riches. if you know how to turn things into gold, the fear of losing your wealth doesn't drive you. just beware of the story of king midas. whatever he touched turned to gold, so the fear of dying of starvation loomed over him.

06.14.09

today, i'm firmly holding everything you won't touch in the palms of my hands. i'm getting used to the state of revered emptiness. can you write silence? i'd like to get to that, to write without words. certainly, there are universes where it's possible. they just have to be found. i have to take another journey. slowly, i distance myself from the cities of greed, where most people have paper cups where their hearts used to be.
i'm trying to describe
what it's like
when gold rains
into your heart.

06.19

i said goodbye at radiology, and i almost felt sorry. they were all so nice to me and those huge machines that looked like rocket-planes, so luxurious and flawless. a person can only be amazed about today's possibilities. perhaps there is a touch of gratitude in that feeling of amazement. the therapy has ended, and if i am not enlightened yet, then at least i can claim, without a doubt, that i am irradiated. well, tell me, who can say that about themselves? maybe all that radiation will illuminate many things. yesterday, i noted the different stages of my progress:

1. the first stage is everydayness, the existence that we were used to, in this stage, i don't know what is going in, and i'm not interested in it. i'm chasing after what is shown on billboards, in the headlines, by mom and dad, teachers, and wiseasses.
2. the second stage features the flooding of emotions. the accompanying symptoms are hiccups, ticks, and tremors. i'm beginning to anticipate an imminent drop of emotions on the assembly line.
3. in the next phase, not only do i understand what is happening, but also the way it relates to me. in other words, i play a role in it.
4. in the fourth stage, there is a breakthrough moment, where i completely understand what is going on and how i participate in it. in this stage, i still don't know how to control it.
5. in stage five, i slowly begin to learn how to control it. actually, it comes to me on its own. i can see better with the eyes of my palms.

07.11

sleeping beauty and a group trance

the city streets, trains filled with sleeping people. the sufi poets say that our eyes see only a vague and superficial picture, one that occupies our senses so much that we don't see the wider reality. sleeping beauty, just like many other fairy tales, is a perfect picture of the world that we are used to living in. the whole kingdom is snoring away, all the decent people walk by eagle-eyed, wearing a blindfold in order to see "normally," so that they don't turn into lasers, a collective trance has even merged into our language. when we talk about reality, we mean matter.

don juan calls us creatures of light. a person with clear eyes is filled with light and, at the same time, sees light in everyone around her.

the eye is the lamp of the body. if your eyes are good, your whole body will be full of light (matthew 6:22).

ama, i'm no longer surprised by anything. when i was reading your thoughts about enlightened entities, i came across an article about the new japanese research, with supersensitive cameras. they've discovered that the human body emanates light. this light is tied to our metabolism and is different from infrared radiation that we produce with our body heat. hitoshi okamura claims that in the future, sensitive cameras could help diagnose the dysfunctions of human organs.

07.12.09

i'm lying down with my feet in the clouds, and the sun has just risen out of my chest. i'm a sound wave, the color of wind. now it's all beginning to be interesting.
solitude in the cells, bones. kind and healing. for some people, it is much easier to love from a distance.
evan, thank you for your news from the west bank. now i only go to prague for quick visits, just to water my flowers and empty the mailbox. i'm spending most of the time in the country at the cottage of lara and her husband, by the beroun river. the grass is fresh, the birds are chatty, the trees are joyous. a table under the birches, a glass and a bottle of red wine on the table. house martins in their tuxedos pour the drinks. i taste the earth with my bare feet. the earthworms are weaving between my toes. i'm gradually recovering. it was quite a long run. i'm lying down on the lazy meadow; the ants are breathing in my ear. i'm listening to my hair grow back. it's a fight over what color to choose. umber, ash, or motley. something is always going on. yesterday, i realized that when i listen to dead can dance, all my cells dance. isn't that amazing?
your letter reminded me that i know something about walls. they fall apart very gradually. it's in the character of a wall to last. they don't like to give up. in addition to that, we were taught that we can't live without barriers, without things being compartmentalized. that even the heart has walls. now, i'm not so sure about that anymore. i can see that even

you started to take apart some of the brick, and you're a bit out of your element. while you're at it, feel free to curse a little. it's allowed.

in september, i'm heading for jerusalem. i haven't been anywhere in a year. i don't understand how i survived that.

inside is outside and above is below, and everywhere is heaven. it's fluttering above my head, splashing under my feet. wherever i look, i see it—a heaven that has no ground.
they should really start setting up clinics for lunatics that shout absurdities such as: i have nothing in common with all of you, and: my dreams are not real.

i'm sitting and shivering, uninhibited, like beethoven's fourth in g major. the final round. vivace. and in the meantime, i'm sifting through my amazing life. it's strange, jeff, i wouldn't change anything, wouldn't strike out a single note.
it seems that the cancer put me back on my feet.

a story is a river, and on it a boat, and the boatman is a storyteller. the current carries it through the landscape, with the boat landing on the bank from time to time. someone gets off, and another gets on. the river turns the boat, heads for a port, where it possibly drops its anchor. the river rushes on.

this is a new book. or at least it can be one. there can be a pause here, where the bard gathers wind for his sail. where does one story end and another begin, when behind the horizon, a new horizon opens, and everything becomes one story?

5

as for me, i know nothing else but miracles.

—walt whitman

the holy land and the freedom of lunatics

holy, holy, holy, four is a holy number just as five is, or any other number on which we hang this price tag. and when someone buys it, it becomes reality. holy, holy, holy. four is a holy number. the more people say it, the more it becomes true.

jerusalem

leo picks her up at ben gurion airport. it's hot in the car, but leo has a cold, so he asks if she would mind if he doesn't turn on the ac. let there be heat. she's here for it, after all. the desert landscape gradually curves, climbing into the hills. after 40 minutes, they enter the city via east jerusalem to shuafat. halka and little sandra are waiting with a late lunch.

the house is pleasantly shaded; an apartment with a generous terrace and a view into the garden. cats everywhere. by the huge garbage dumpsters, the cats from all over shuafat are having a party. some are gorgeous. a person would assume that they would be lying on a pillow at someone's house, not rummaging through the trash.

sandra immediately announces through the door that she's going to school. and her eyes significantly light up. when she opens her present, she says "thanky thanky." she takes ama by the hand and leads her to the guest room.

09.22.09

old jerusalem, apparently the navel of the world. i feel its fire, its rhythm in my ribcage. walking through the zion gate, the jafa gate, blindly i let myself be lead. i have no map. and when i think about the basilica of the holy sepulcher, i suddenly stand before it. when i am hungry, the street baker hands me bread and offers me his seat.

in the courtyard of the basilica, a man with a badge heads toward me.

maybe a tour guide, and asks if i know where i am, i know exactly where i am, i tell him,i know it well here. it's true, even though it is my first time in jerusalem. and he wants to know where i am from. the sun is hitting us hard. the rocks around us are radiating. finally, he asks me, what are you? christian, jew, muslim? and i laugh and say nothing. i am nothing, and everything at the same time.

the man nods as if he understands, and he pushes his cap downward.

aha! so you don't believe in god?

all around—walls that beckon me, stones that are dying to tell a story, and i want to be by myself, which is quite a challenge in such a crowded place. i choose a well-tested tactic on this faith-hunter. when i answer, i gesticulate excessively, my voice that of a lunatic.

i believe that god is the universe and that is much greater than all religions put together

i'm smiling while i'm saying these words, and instead of a period after my sentence, i clasp my hands.

if the man looks hard, he must see my halo. he bids me good luck and leaves me alone.

i'm standing inside, and i can't move. it's all gathering within me, piling up. i'm waiting for it to blow up on the surface. my roots, past lives, the cries of the missing, the pages of future centuries. i'm leafing through epochs, reading about my loves in the hot wax. the candles are stretched out along the wall, flickering, burning. people with their foreheads on the ground, they're breaking off blessings from the granite. people with papers in their hands stick their folded laments into the cracks. people with the look of hunters, hanging the burden of their wishes on the shoulders of the walls.

tears are at home here, simple as breathing.

i want to pray but my words have been burned out. only mute eyes of ash and salty lashes remain. all i want is to be able to share this. it's almost unbearable to carry. that is why i need to share it with you.

i'm sitting in a corner, propping up a stone. it must be falling over from exhaustion after all those centuries. a priest comes by, gomidass sherbetdzhiyan. he sits next to me and says he's armenian, which must be an important fact, because he mentions it several times. he studied theology in montreal and speaks english fluently. he wants me to dictate the names of my loved ones. he will pray for them. and so, he puts you all on a list in his orthodox handwriting in that part of the world. you can sleep peacefully. god knows about you now.

* * *

crooked streets, with a continuous flow of shops and merchandise of all kinds. and when i think about the wailing wall, a square opens up before me. the generous space is divided for men and women by a wall. in the noon heat, each person laments separately,. the women get less than one third of the wall. they are crowding over one another, breathing down each other's necks. they wait until one finishes her lamenting and makes room for the other. behind the wall, the men sway back and forth. they have plenty of room around them. they don't have to wait for a spot by the stone. the image of the square is drawn up in a strange way. the asymmetry of space for men and women hits you in the face and seems comical, pathetic from a human perspective, and a little sad.

from the western wall, i walk to the dung gate, but i don't want to exit, i haven't had my fill. i turn around and crisscross through the streets, through the noise and clamor of the arab quarter. i pass the stream of crowds, faces, faces, faces. each one of them is a mirror. i meet hundreds of my faces, hustling and bustling all the way to the damascus gate. and under it, small clusters of people, the smell of falafel and baked bread, pita, and the quick fingers of the merchants clinking and rustling. an arab baker sells me kaek, a sesame bread twisted into a circle. five shekels. it's still hot and melts on the tongue.

late in the evening, i'm sitting in a hyper-modern coffee house next to a museum, with a view to a windmill, and i'm waiting for halka. the city walls are behind me, as well as the zion gate. carrot juice and a sandwich in front of me. and a little boy with a yarmulka on his head and his arms stretched out. he's flying in circles. by the sound of his overly loud humming, he is just landing his airplane.

* * *

the next day i'm standing on mount of olives. in the basilica of the ascension. no one is in it, just an old arab custodian selling tickets and postcards. we talk a little until a group of polish tourists with a tour guide comes in. the tour guide's voice is commanding and overwhelms the entire space. the believers fall to the ground. one by one, they press their lips to the stone from where jesus rose to heaven. i gather myself and slowly descend down the hill to get to the gardens of gethsemane. the hundred-year-old olive trees are graciously fragrant among the chattering birds and the crowds of people. their curvy branches braid the sun into their hair. the streets are filled with souvenirs. hands and merchant slogans cut through the air, pulling one by the shirt. buy a branch here. help support our church's spiritual brotherhood. they will pray for you. buy a rosary of olive wood. only two dollars. you can pray on your own.

a few yards from the garden lies the grave of virgin mary. an old monk sits by the entrance on a trunk made of dark wood in the shade of the wall. quietly breathing out clusters of words, he looks as if he just stepped out a painting by rembrandt. with his hand on the scriptures, he guards a wide staircase leading underground. the stone steps are silent about the never- ending contact they endure from the footsteps of the pilgrims.
i find a bench, put in bach's hymns, and transcend time. when i return into my own skin, the wall cools my back. empty space around the masses. only sound slithers along the walls. a young nun lies in the crypt, curled up in a corner. she doesn't see anyone or notice anyone. a closed bundle of black cloth. the stone passionately laments below her. she prays, begs, using her bones as leverage, she urges the virgin mary to have mercy, shakes her god to listen.

09.24

masada

the trip by car from jerusalem to masada is about two hours, so it's good to get up a bit early, before the sun rises and before crowds of tourists start swarming in. leo drives, and ama watches the landscape flicker outside the window. the desert is like a stage, images from fables. leo finds a spot in the shade. he orders a coffee and starts answering his phone calls. ama heads out for the clouds.

open masada, your gates, and i, the refugee, will enter!
behold, at your feet i will place my crumbling spirit place it
on the anvil of your rocks and hammer it. hammer and form
anew!

—yitzhak lamdan

a serpentine path and a cable car lead to the fortress of herod the great. the royal rooms, water cisterns, synagogues, store rooms for food. the spectacular residence on a cliff in the middle of the desert defies rational thinking. the northern palace on the edge of the cliff, architectural wonder, just like the innovative waterworks system. the rocks carry signs of ancient fires, and to this day, they breathe out the laments of hundreds of jews, who committed mass suicide so they would not become slaves to the romans conquerors.

i stand on these walls that originated in the first century before christ, and i'm thinking about you. ravens and the sun are around me, a view of the dead sea, which is slowly dying. it is strange, strong and mysterious. the afternoon heat blows images into the air. ranks of warriors approach and then disappear into the dust. and that thought inside me, claiming that the more souls i carry on my shoulders, the lighter my step will be.

here, you notice that if you're walking in the desert, you're walking on water. the trees walk on water and splash each other like kids in puddles. the mountains and the sea are philosophers, wisemen. they become street merchants, weaving maidens, they become ravens, rattlesnakes, and flies. all beings are expressed by water.

we're going to the sea that is so salty that you can't drown in it. balls of salt form on the bottom. they look like jewels, wasp's nests made out of gems cut the soles of your feet. the water is warm, oily, like heated grease, stretching your skin with its tongue. if you drink it, it burns.

* * *

the sand is spilling, the water is rising. a fisherman on the bank catches words in a net. his pots are grumbling from emptiness. the mind is a monkey that turns upside-down what it doesn't see, what it doesn't reach. on these maps, i see stories, a landscape that tells its history.

09.24.

ramallah

it's half an hour to the palestinian capital, even though it's only ten kilometers away from jerusalem. you must go through the checkpoints. border crossings with bars, metal plates, barriers, and soldiers with machine guns who wish to see your papers. walls and fortifications are everywhere. it's very confusing and asking the locals doesn't shed much light on things. the palestinians have their truth, and the jews have their own. it seems petty and laughable, like when children pound shovels over each other's heads in a sandbox. but instead of buckets and toys, they have guns and live rounds. leo drops me off on a circular plaza with statues of lions and drives off to his office. i walk through the heat. all the women are covered from head to toe. they must be baking inside. i head toward the old town. streets filled with people, a market of tastes and shouting, blaring whistles, men's stares, welcome! they laugh, beckon, hackle with gestures, voices, and glances. unveiled, walking against the current of people, the heat stuck on the bowl of a scale, with my white hand, i sift through the hills, the mountains. weighing my options. a mango cut in half for people to admire. a dark glance. look miss, this one is as sweet as your smile and the size of your heart. i buy one heart for five shekels.

the men sit in front of the stores and the coffee shops, smoking shishas, the women shop in stores selling cheap clothes. once in a while, i enter one of them and sift through the piles of dresses and scarves. a superb arab hangout. in the afternoon, i sit in the eiffel sweets cafe. in the street below is a demonstration, waves of signs, emotional gesticulation, shouting at the cameras, police with fingers on triggers.

a missed call on my phone. i guess they're looking for me. i send a quick sms. *ciao* leo, i'm standing at the roundabout with the lions in front of the arab bank, i hope you can find me in the crowd.

09.25

jeff,
i'm in the holy land. i am losing and finding myself in a place where, apparently, a person isn't who she is at birth, but rather who she becomes. a place where everything is blowing up and cutting itself to pieces. where you can fit the whole world into a bag of explosives, packed into several square kilometers, the sum of love and hate, conflicts and cravings for redemption. human greatness and pettiness on the plates of a scale. everyone wants the same, searches for the same. thou shalt have no other gods before me, everyone here believes in one god, and at the same time, they act as if it isn't one and the same god. where is the logic in that? if two believe in one, then the one must be the same god. the feud of the monotheistic religions is the eighth wonder of the world, hatred that springs out of a glance in the mirror. all these centuries, and they never noticed how similar they are to each other. why do you notice the splinter in your brother's eye, but do not perceive the wooden beam in your own?

it's like living with pieces on a chessboard, you yourself, all of humanity, each of us. thousand-year walls fringe around the bones of those who believe that only one piece of land will ensure a place in heaven.
the holy land. i'm having strange dreams here. i'm hunting light in the darkness.
i'm falling into a well. the walls are pouring downward through a shaft. i keep falling faster and faster. suddenly, the tube makes a turn, and i'm flying upward, faster, and then another turn, and i don't know if i'm flying downward, horizontally, or upward. it all seems the same. there is no difference, and i never reach the ground.

ama, i just got connected, are you still there? i sent you some more books yesterday.

yes. thank you. i look forward to reading them.
jeff, something just occurred to me. all these years, you've been sending me all kinds of quantum books and essays, and you've engaged in exhausting debates on various topics that i had no knowledge about, and here i've been hit by a wave. in such heat, a person can't think too straight, but it occurred to me that you never gave up on me. dear lord. it really threw me off balance. i was very touched by this thought. perhaps i will later accuse you of being the reason why my laptop is ruined because i cried a river over my keyboard.

it's true ama, but unlike you, i realized that if you get past all your psycho-spiritual rambling, you're a quantum physicist at the core, even though you will never admit to it. even if it were only three quarks, i discovered them.

damn it, i have a feeling i know how you're going to answer me on this one.

your feeling is not in vain. because unlike you, i realized that when you get past all your quantum mumbo jumbo, deep down in your soul, you are a pythoness, even though you won't admit to it.:-))))) that's what you call mirror imagery. i'm happy about that, jeffrey. and i admit that thanks to quantum-ers, the world is a more colorful place. there is more fun in it and more poetry.

* * *

the eye is a black hole that swallows what it sees and stores away pictures from journeys. it will never let them go. bethlehem, jericho, herodion, tel aviv. dinner in shuafat, a generous table set up by leo and halka, the driver rajeda's smile, and sandra's giggling. she loves to fly by plane but she can't stand when it gets caught up in turbulence. when she refuses to go to bed, we go on the terrace and collect the stars from the sky and throw them in the laundry basket. and after we wash them, we'll hang them up in the trees. in the morning, we try to chase away the knots in our hair. we're chasing them past the mountains and into the valleys with a jagged comb.

after breakfast, we head out into the desert to the monastery of saint george in the cliff. sandra in the backseat sings in a language from a different galaxy. she's holding a baedeker travel guide through the holy land that she will not let go of, not even if the devil is chasing her with a big potato sack, tongue sticking out, with a horse's hoof for a foot. she calmly lets it flutter in the back of car. the soldier at the check point gives her a friendly smile and opens up the gate, and we continue driving.
the path to the monastery abruptly scales down, and then it rises upward on a counter slope, all the way to the monastery door. the dry river stirs up the dust that zigzags between the cliffs. the sun is sharpening its blade. halfway up the road, two young bedouins in traditional outfits offer their animals for a ride. they beckon sandra and the women to saddle up. sandra contemplates the ride on a donkey so that her legs won't hurt tomorrow. the men are surprised that ama has no hat. the sun rays here are like hungry vultures—they will peck holes in your skin. one of them immediately jumps to her aid and with skillful movements, he wraps her head with a white handkerchief like a loaf of bread. much better, he winks. now you are like a bedouin.

and that is how ama meets fadhi.

10.01.09 wadi al-murar

dear jára,

before i left for the holy land, you ensured me that you would be able to keep at least two camels in your backyard, if i happened to meet a bedouin in the desert who would like to come visit me in the czech republic. your vision has come true, so i'm still counting on your offer.
fadhi, my husband (photo attached), has only one camel (photo of fadhi's camel) but he also has two horses, two donkeys, and a herd of goats. i now live with fadhi. his bayt (photo of fadhi's tent) is woven from goatskin and, at the moment, it is pitched in wadi al-murar near the river jordan. not too far from fadhi's goum: his two mothers, seven brothers, six sisters, his brothers' partners and their children. his father unfortunately, did not live to see our happiness. the valley of wadi al-

murar is not too far from jericho, a few kilometers from the dead sea, and just a stone's throw from jordan. the bedouins travel freely across the border. they are able to go to egypt, which can take as long as two days, depending on the weather and the camel's mood. our camel's name is said, and if you give him a banana peel, he gives you a smile (photo: said's smile). you can start collecting banana peels. his smile is totally worth it.
and i'm always smiling too, because fadhi says that a frowning woman is worse than a lazy camel. everyone here calls me "amina," which means faithful in their language. the mother of the prophet mohamed was called amina as well. my fadhi is fifteen years younger than i am, and it was love at first sight. we understand each other completely, and we are both happy. when we first met, fadhi told me: lucky the man who touches your heart. so, you see, my husband is not only a shepherd but also a poet. in addition to that, he plays the rebab and sings. usually, it's improvised texts and melodies—he's kind of a bedouin jiří stivín.25 he sings mainly to the camels so that they will remain happy and strong. when we come, he'll teach you how to do it. it's good to get on their good side with banana peels and singing, so they don't spit all over you. their spit is pretty thick and is hard to wash off. if you can't sing for shit, just let said listen to dan bárta. that will drive him into ecstasy, make him bang his lower lips against his teeth rhythmically. and mimic bárṭa's[26] scatting (photo: said sings bárta). i play it for him through the headphones when fadhi and i want a moment alone. i will let you know when we arrive.

مكيلع مالسلا

asalamu 'aleykum
ama

10.02.09 prague

i have absolutely nothing to add to that. :o)). you simply have to have talent to be able to experience something like that. i half envy that

---

[25] *Translator's note*: Jiří Stivín is a popular Czech singer.

[26] *Translator's note*: Dan Bárta is a well-known Czech rock musician.

talent, and i half fear it. so, i'm escaping you at the dacha where it's safe . . . but the pictures of said and how you describe him put me in a state of ecstasy. the lot in my backyard is, of course, at your disposal, even if i'm doubtful that they will allow you onto the airplane with that entire menagerie. let me know. my offer still stands. jára.

10.02.09 prague

ama, i got an email addressed dear jára. i'm not sure if this was meant for me, but its contents are keeping me up at night. that man in the picture by your side with his tent and his animals interests me. at least i have a new topic of conversation with radek while drinking wine. unlike me, radek is doubtful that you actually married fadhi and that you live with him in the desert among donkeys and camels.

it's raining here, it's a cold autumn day after a sunny weekend. nothing out of the ordinary. the kids are the same, my husband is patient. and i'm like the weather. i watered the flowers at your house. they look good. sending greetings from far way. - larina

10.03.09 wadi al-murar

lara, everything is as it should be. that email was addressed to jára, but because i'm worse than a lazy camel, rather than writing to everyone separately, i chose the easier path and forwarded it to everyone who needed to know. all the good news in one push of a button. happiness spreads with an increase in the number of beings who share it, fadhi says, and is bringing in another donkey and two goats.

i'm hugging you all in my heart. fadhi says hello and is looking forward to meeting you. i'm going to clean off said. - amina

10.04.09 prague

ama - today, i opened your email after a looong delay. and a camel popped out at me, and some girl named amina dressed in white, and a man in white as well. ama! you have a husband, love, and a camel!!! and you're writing that you will both be coming!!! that's quite the story! are you really both coming back? i guess everything is still fresh?????? i'm thinking about you a lot. - dana.

10.05.09 wadi al-murar

my dear friends. i guess this will disappoint you, but in the end, i will be coming back alone, because fadhi has not yet got his visa, due to the fact that he's a bedouin. apparently, it's harder for them. anyway, red tape at work. not even true love can move it. never mind! i will come back here soon. it's important that we have each other, where we live doesn't matter. - ama

10.06.09 toronto

ama, i'm sitting at fran's on the corner of college and yonge streets, and i'm grinning into my plate at my regular turkey sandwich with a double portion of onions. i have to admit that, while i was reading your latest emails, for a nanosecond i wasn't sure, a great mystification! those photos really look like they were taken at a wedding. that strapping fadhi, his craving look, your clothes, your canny smile, the tent made of goatskin, said's smiling lips. that animal is really cute. anyway, it was interesting to see that most of your friends believed the story. i was quite delighted by that fact. is this another one of your quantum leaps? to be honest, it's not important whether the story is true or not. what's interesting is that you can act as crazy as you wish, and no one will consider it too crazy when it comes to you. people around you will accept it as something quite normal. i'm proud of you. you've managed to go so far out that you can act like a complete lunatic, and no one will stop to make sense of it. i think there is no greater freedom than that.

Printed in the USA
CPSIA information can be obtained
at www.ICGtesting.com
LVHW040613031123
762649LV00031B/974/J

9 781951 508371